Forever, DUNCAN

FOREVER, DUNCAN

THE MISSISSIPPI QUEEN TRILOGY

TRACY BROEMMER

CHAPTER 1

YEP. SHE WAS PROBABLY GONNA KILL HIM. GUYS HIS AGE AND younger dropped dead from sudden cardiac arrest, right? Jesus. No way was Duncan Marks gonna live through much more of this. If she leaned over one more time, anywhere near him, and treated him to a glimpse of the smooth, tan skin in the deep v of her blouse and the pale pink lace of her bra, he was down. For the count. Knock out. He had tried—Scout's honor times a trillion—not to look. But damn, even keeping his eyes on the long, slender column of her neck and her strong cheekbones, the curve of her full lips when she smiled—her full pink lips and thoughts of what they might taste like, *feel* like, could kill him, too—made his heart race and his dick kick to life in his jeans.

Tried and failed. Given up. Looked as often as he could. Working the bar—hell, *breathing in* the same room—with Stevi Hague was lethal. His blood pressure was in stroke zone; he felt it skyrocket whenever she was around.

And to make matters worse? Didn't help to look away. So save the *save yourself, Marks* thing, thanks anyway. He could give the woman his back—oh, he'd fantasized about that, too, wondered what her skin would feel like pressed up against him, her breasts against his bare back—all night long, but he was still skating on the edge. Just her whiskey thick voice and deep, throaty laugh turned his dick to steel. No getting around it.

If he didn't get his hands on her soon, done. Over. Heart attack.

If he did get his hands on her anytime soon, still done. Dead by shotgun, maybe. Stevi's dad's finger on the trigger. Or even her sister Leah's.

Stevi Hague was Off-Limits. Hands. Off. Do not pass go. Do not collect kisses and definitely no touching. Do not engage.

The strappy shoes she wore tonight were enough to drive a man fucking crazy. Never mind the skin in the v of her blouse—she had six freckles and a faint puckery scar near the hollow of her throat—and her hands—he loved the sight of her long, elegant fingers wrapped around a pint glass or a wine bottle when she poured, the red straps around her ankles and her bare feet brought to mind those same red straps and ankles wrapped around his waist and similar red straps around her wrists—

"I need you."

Back to her in a useless attempt at self-preservation, Duncan clamped his jaws shut and clacked his teeth together hard enough to make them hurt. He ran through a mental list of the spirits he used to mix drinks, called to mind the many times he'd overdone it on said spirits and spent the next day cozied up to the porcelain god, and breathed deeply through his nose. Might've worked, but then there she was, soft curves pressed up against his side. Instead of calming him, the deep breath filled him with the scent of Stevi's shampoo and perfume and a whole damned lot of longing.

"Wondered when you'd come to your senses." He bumped her hip and dropped a wink, even though technically, that should be off-limits, too. She had started flirting back a while ago, and holy hell, if that didn't just make his life more complicated.

Stevi rolled her eyes and shook her head, which only gave him another strong whiff of her shampoo.

"I need Blue Balls," she told him with a sweet grin.

"Yeah? How about that? I got some," he muttered as he looked away from her big green eyes.

"What?"

Duncan wasn't sure what was more painful: her hearty laugh (because he sure as hell wasn't joking) or that she rested her hand on the back of his wrist. Because hello? There were times when skin-on-skin contact with her was like a lit match on a stream of gasoline.

"That all?" He cleared his throat and set the bottle of Merlot he had been pouring down on the back bar.

"Um."

He heard the little giggle and braced himself for whatever she was about to ask for next.

"An Angel's Tit." She offered him a little grin and wriggled her eyebrows at him.

He snorted. "Yeah, not going there," he answered. "Thought I taught you how to make that one."

"You did…"

He turned with the two glasses of Merlot in his hands and set them on the bar. Stevi hovered beside him as he pushed the glasses gently over the polished wood to the guy waiting on them.

"But?" Duncan spared her a quick glance—she was leaning just so again, and this time not only did he get a peek of the skin in the v of her blouse, but also the curve of her right breast twisted just so in the pink lace.

"Um. I was gonna go hit that table in the back. They've been waiting a while."

Already fixing the Blue Balls, the first drink she'd asked for, Duncan shot a look toward the table Stevi mentioned. Four guys, all of them probably in Stevi's wheelhouse, stood around a tall table. One of them was talking with his hands, and from where he stood at the bar, Duncan saw a tattoo peeking out from under the t-shirt straining over his bicep. Definitely something Stevi would go for, no doubt.

Stevi still waited at his side. Duncan swallowed down a snide comment—it was one thing to tease her about her serial dating habits, but he would never take a serious shot at her for it—and gave her a curt nod.

"Go."

"Yeah?"

"Yep. I got this."

He watched her go, mesmerized by the sway of her hips, but he caught himself. Turned his attention back to the Blue Curacao in his hand and let his anger—okay, jealousy—kill the damned raging hard-on. It did kind of frustrate the hell out of him. He'd known Stevi since she was sixteen or seventeen and he was twenty, and suddenly, ten years later, he noticed she was pretty and sexy as hell, and he didn't remember inviting his dick to the party, but here it was, and it had to notice and approve of every damned thing she did.

Determined not to look at her again, because who the hell wanted to watch the woman he wanted flirt with a whole table full of guys, Duncan finished the Blue Balls and started mixing the Angel's Tit.

"Is Leah okay?"

He nodded without looking at Tania. He liked the new girl they had hired to waitress okay—was she still new, he wondered, after a month of working here?— and sure, she was cute to look at, too. But he wasn't going to discuss Stevi's sister or any of her particulars with her just yet. Leah had been fine a half hour ago, but she was tired, and Trace—her boyfriend or fiancé or whatever the hell they were calling it these days—had insisted she sit down for a bit. Duncan had to give the guy credit. If Leah were his girlfriend and carrying his baby—complications or not—he would insist a lot harder and a lot more often that she take it easy.

Of course, Leah would get in his face if he did so. One thing about the Hague women—and even though his stepsister Margo's name wasn't Hague, she was a first cousin, so Margo, too—they were damned stubborn and independent and a man better be damned sure of himself if he thought he was going to step in front of one of them to catch a bullet for her. He wouldn't put it past any of them to shove that man aside and catch the bullet barehanded. And then mosey home to put dinner on the table or to the Queen to serve up a round of drinks.

Aaannddd, there he went again. Looking over at Stevi. The girls owned the bar; Duncan worked for them. They had talked a time or two about Duncan buying in. He wanted a piece of the place. First of all, it was prime real estate. Second, the bar had wobbled a bit in the beginning and recently baby-stepped to the top five bars in Adam's Bay, Illinois. Having Trace Dixon—country music songwriter and brother of Tanner Dixon country music sensation—here didn't hurt business, either. Tanner Dixon and the Lightnin' Congregation had topped billboard charts on and off for a few years, mostly with hit songs Trace wrote, and Duncan was man enough to admit both Dixon brothers were good-looking guys.

Might not say that if Trace had fallen so stupidly in love with Stevi Hague rather than Leah.

Duncan had tended bar here and there through the years. That he had a degree in business management surprised a lot of people. He hoped it was because he tended to dress in a style best described as 90s grunge and not because people assumed he was dumb or not ambitious. When he started working with the girls, he upgraded from bartender to mixologist, but he helped with everything at the Queen.

Including security.

Not that they ever needed much in the way of muscle.

Still, he sized the guys up at the table where Stevi was just walking away. Two of them were head to head, eyes directed toward a girl at the end of the bar, so Duncan all but dismissed them. As a threat to himself or Stevi, not general safety, because at the moment he was more in tune with Stevi than the safety of anyone in the place. One of them was looking at his phone, but the fourth one—the guy with the bulging biceps and the tattoo—was watching her. Eyes on her ass, actually. Duncan squeezed his hands into fists.

"Easy."

His stepsister's voice at his left shoulder was cool and calm. She eased by him, patted his back as if he were a toddler gearing up to throw a tantrum—Margo would know, as she was the mother of a thirteen-month-old tyrant slash princess —and settled in to stand at his right side.

"She won't go out with any of them." Margo spoke quietly as she reached over the bar to gather empty glasses. Three girls slid up to the bar even as Margo cleared the spot.

He knew that. Stevi was a flirt, with a capital F, and a serial dater who just loved to be on the go. She rarely dated the same guy twice, and she often told them—Duncan and Leah and Margo—that the goodnight kisses were about all she could bear. Duncan got it; listening to her talk about goodnight kisses or good morning kisses or any other kinds of kisses made him see red. The thought of anything else happening on her dates drove him to the gym more often than not. Not like he could go anywhere else and throw punches and not end up arrested for assault or property damage.

"Tania asked about Leah," he ignored Margo's comment. With a room full of people, Green Day on the sound system, and Stevi making her way back over to him to tell him again what she needed, now wasn't the time to talk about Stevi and how he felt about her.

Duncan nudged the dirty sounding cocktails at Stevi as she approached, heard her ask for four drafts—a Blue Moon and three Buds—and glanced at Margo.

"I was just up there. Trace is rubbing her feet," she told him. "How anyone can make you feel like you're interrupting something wildly intimate when it's a foot rub is beyond me, but they did it."

"Because she moans the same way when they're having sex," Stevi announced as she picked up the drinks and slipped behind them down the bar to deliver them.

"She knows this how?" Duncan narrowed his eyes at Margo.

"She lives there," Margo reminded him with a shrug.

"She's never home!" He tossed his hands up and laughed. Tried to anyway. His brain was still hung up on the guy with the tattooed gun who had kept his eyes on Stevi's ass until she reached the bar to deliver his order.

"You think I should ask her to move in with me?"

"What?"

"To give Leah and Trace some room?"

"Their bedroom is upstairs." He reached for a pint glass, stuck it under the Blue Moon tap, and stared at Margo with wide eyes this time.

"Yeah, well, me and Berkley don't need privacy like they do."

"They'll have a live-in babysitter." He set the first glass on the bar and reached for another, eyes still on Margo.

"I could use a live-in babysitter." Margo tipped her head and arched her eyebrows. Duncan opened his mouth, ready to deliver the line she most likely knew was coming. Trace and Leah might need private time and a babysitter, eventually. Margo didn't. He didn't say it, though, because Margo's ex had been poking around a bit lately, and Margo looked exhausted and sad about it. And Jess suddenly appearing in Margo and Berkley's life again made Duncan angry.

No need to argue about that here.

"Really?" Margo eyed him suspiciously. "You're goin' easy on me? God, it's time to do something a little crazy if you're goin' easy on me."

"No need for crazy," he answered as he draped an arm around her shoulders and gave her a squeeze.

"Remind me," Stevi clutched at Margo's arm as she appeared behind her again. "When Leah and Trace do get engaged, we are not having an asinine drink-fest bachelorette party. 'Kay?"

"Sure we are." Margo shrugged. "Duncan just told me I need to do something crazy. You can babysit Berkley that night if you're not looking for a good time."

Stevi watched Margo duck away from Duncan's arm and slip out the other end of the bar. She blinked and looked up at Duncan.

"Really, it might be a good thing for Margo to do something crazy," she mumbled as she reached for two of the beers he'd just pulled. "I, for one, am done with it. Crazy is so overrated."

"Right." Duncan nodded. For the hell of it—who didn't want to follow Stevi across a room and watch her ass work her sexy little jeans—and also just to get a feel for the guys at the table she was serving, he picked up the remaining two beers and followed her over.

CHAPTER 2

STEVI WATCHED TRACE USHER LEAH OUT THE BACK DOOR. Swoon worthy. The man was truly perfect for her sister. True, they had already ridden out a storm of sorts in the beginning of their relationship, but they were so sweet together, it gave Stevi a toothache to be around them these days. Trace's right hand on Leah's lower back—all the time, not just since the pregnancy and the complications—he reached with his left to push the door open. Waited while Leah stepped through, looked back at Stevi and waved, and then they were gone. Stevi looked at Margo.

"Why are you still here?"

"Mom's got Berkley tonight," Margo answered around a yawn. In a heap on the end barstool, Margo looked a little pale. Stevi took a drink of her wine and watched Margo poke at the big cut healing on the palm of her hand.

"So go home and get some rest." Stevi scooted down the bar and covered Margo's hand with hers. "Stop picking at that."

"It's fine."

"Yeah, well, you're gonna make me barf." When Margo looked at her with only her eyes, Stevi stared her down.

"Good thing it wasn't you here with me the day I did it," Margo mumbled.

"Right. Because from what I hear Leah was almost on the floor because of all the blood."

Margo laughed.

"Okay, good thing it was Trace here with me."

"Good thing what was Trace?" Duncan appeared behind them from the kitchen. Stevi, leaning over the bar, twisted around to watch him gather more glasses from the bar top.

"The day I cut my hand." Margo yawned again.

"Go home." Duncan fixed a stern gaze on her. "I'll walk you out."

Margo shrugged and looked from him to Stevi. "Sure you don't mind?"

"No." Stevi shook her head. "We're good."

"Okay." Margo slid off the barstool. Duncan slipped back to the kitchen again to load the glasses in the industrial dishwasher, and Stevi stepped around the end of the bar to hug Margo.

"Get some rest."

Margo nodded.

"I mean it. Rest. Not phone sex."

Margo snorted. "Right."

Stevi grinned. She peeked at Duncan when she saw him standing in the kitchen doorway waiting for Margo.

"Be right back," he told her. She nodded and watched the two of them walk out the back. When they were out of sight, she stirred. Crossed the floor to start stacking glasses from the tables. Matchbox Twenty played now on the sound system, and she sang along as she carried glasses back to the kitchen.

She loaded them in the dishwasher, went back for another load, and had them in the dishwasher when Duncan came back inside. He hovered in the door of the kitchen for a second.

"What?"

"I don't do this often, but I'm gonna ask."

Stevi swallowed hard. She wondered if he could see her pulse beating wildly in her throat or if her hair covered it. Crazy the way her step cousin—was that a thing?—could launch her blood pressure into the next galaxy these days. She usually tried to breathe through it. Deflected. Teased back and hoped Leah or Margo would rescue her once she swam out too far to touch. There was no rescue when she and Duncan were alone, though, so she tended toward big tales and whopper lies about all of her crazy dating escapades. Not that she worried that Duncan would make a move. But because she worried that *her* body would do something crazy. Like maybe her hands would just move—against her better judgment—and slide up over his button-down shirt to cup his shoulders. She bumped up against his body a million times a day, and sure, it was hard as a rock. But only recently, those innocent touches were anything but innocent for Stevi, and if she touched his shoulders on purpose now? Who knew what the hell she might do next?

They had been doing this flirty thing for a while now, but since their overnight trip to St. Louis last month, Stevi couldn't control the way her heart charged out of control around him. Her palms got sweaty, and she would never admit this to anyone else, not even Leah, but sometimes when Duncan looked at her, her whole body quivered, and the southern part of her body actually clenched with…desire. Or need. Or both.

"Ask what?" she asked quietly. She tilted her chin up and held their eye contact, half hoping, half fearing that his question would be something…personal. Would she tell him? If he asked her something personal, would she answer him truthfully?

Maybe. Maybe some night. Not tonight. She was only sipping her first glass of wine; she had full control over her tongue. Her tongue wasn't going to give up any secrets, and it damned sure wasn't going to trace the cords of Duncan's neck or lick the black stubble on his chin.

"Phone sex?"

Her sigh of frustration sounded more like a hiss. Rather than answer him, she looked away and busied herself rinsing the sink out again. She snagged the scouring pad by the faucet and scrubbed at a spot that was nothing more than a scratch that they had each attacked more than once through the years. Was she frustrated because she had really hoped Duncan would flirt with her? That he would ask her something personal? Because if he did, she would take it like a dare, just as he would want her to. Or was she frustrated because she didn't want to talk about Margo when she wasn't here to defend herself? The four of them were pretty open— although Leah had tried to keep her pregnancy a secret, and Stevi, Margo, and Duncan had all been a little bit hurt by that

—and probably, Margo talked to Duncan about Jess. But that didn't make Stevi any more comfortable with the idea of ratting her out.

"Stevi?"

"Hmm?"

"With Jess?"

"Duncan, don't." She hunched her shoulders and dropped her chin to her chest.

"The guy's a dickhead—"

"I know." Stevi groaned. "I know. But Duncan…"

"Look at how he hurt her."

Duncan joined her at the sink, and even now, both of them thinking about Margo and all the other women Jess had been into then, Stevi was keenly aware of the charge in the air between them. She drew her hands back and bumped his elbow with hers. Only the fact that Duncan watched her so closely kept her from looking back to see if sparks flew.

"Haven't you ever been in love?" she whispered. Margo had pretended to be okay when she asked Jess to leave. She had stubbornly refused to give in to the hurt when he did leave. But months later, she had finally confessed that she missed him, that she loved him, and that it had broken her when she'd gone into labor with Berkley and Jess hadn't been there. Because he was with another woman.

Side by side, Stevi turned to look up at Duncan.

"She's in love with him?"

Stevi shrugged, ashamed to have said that much. "I dunno.

And I was teasing her about phone sex. But women say a lot of things to cover up how much they hurt sometimes."

"Fucker." Duncan rested his fisted hands on the sink and hung his head.

"Maybe he'll get…" She was going to say get bored. That maybe Jess would get bored and leave Margo alone again. But that sounded harsh, and Stevi loved Margo too much to wish something so harsh for her. She loved Jess, too, even though she had to agree with Duncan sometimes. Dickhead. Fucker. Whatever. He'd done a number on someone they cared about. Left without so much as an *I'm sorry*. Pretty hard to swallow that when they'd been left to see how badly it hurt Margo. Not to mention that Berkley was growing up without a father.

Duncan cleared his throat. "Are there still glasses out there?"

"Oh, yeah." She nodded and followed him back out to the main room of the Queen.

"We need a new game."

"What?"

Duncan went to the front of the room to bus the tables by the big plate glass window. Stevi stuck around the back of the room to work those tables. The two of them had gotten good at the closing routine since Leah had started seeing Trace. When he had first come up from Nashville to visit Leah, they had all insisted that Leah leave early and enjoy as much time with him as she could. And they usually tried to get Margo home early so she could be with Berkley.

But they used to close together—the four of them. And they often had more fun closing the place down than they did during business hours.

"No more karaoke." Duncan shrugged as he carried two stacks of glasses back to the kitchen. Stevi laughed softly. True. Their karaoke game had crashed and burned when Trace became a permanent fixture at the Queen. Not that he wasn't game to stick around and pitch in. Even in the beginning of his and Leah's relationship, when Leah had held him at arm's length and insisted they were just friends, Trace was always willing and eager to jump in and do whatever needed to be done.

"Okay." She nodded when he glanced at her as she joined him in the kitchen. "What do you wanna play?"

"How about strip poker?"

Stevi gasped out loud and then laughed. "I don't know how to play poker."

"Better yet." He nodded and winked.

"Duncan." She huffed a quick breath and turned away from him when her face flooded with heat. Carefully now, because his words had sent a rumble of desire through her and her hands were a little shaky, she set the glasses down to load them in the dishwasher.

"I'll teach you," he offered.

She shot a glance at him over her shoulder and watched when he hefted himself up to sit on the counter and stared at her with a grin.

"I don't think I trust you."

"You got a piece of paper?"

"What?" She turned around now to face him. "Why?"

"Stevi Hague backs down from a challenge. Gotta write that down."

She rolled her eyes.

"No date tonight, huh?"

"Um." Stevi looked around the kitchen and shook her head. "Nope."

"How come?"

"Had to work."

"You can get off when you want to. You know that."

Stevi shrugged her eyebrows. Honestly, she was tired of dating. Tired of the men. Some were old friends that she just liked to hang out with. Some were old friends who needed a date for a wedding or a work function. At least the old friends never expected kissing or sex. She was tired of meeting new guys, too, though. And most of them did expect some action; some of them even got downright handsy from time to time. Stevi was just plain tired of expending so much energy just to appear normal. She wasn't cut out for love, never felt an inkling of it. So she might end up the spinster aunt to Leah and Trace's kids. There were worse things.

Besides. It was kind of more fun to be at work these days.

Duncan's gaze was so heavy, so intense, she squirmed a bit and then nodded her head to the door.

"My wine's out there."

He hopped off the counter, ready to follow her back to the bar.

X-ray vision. Sometimes Duncan looked at her like he could see right through her. Sometimes he looked at her like he could see right through her clothes. Stevi wasn't sure which made her more…fidgety.

"Score with the table full of guys?" he asked her. She picked up her glass and took a drink before fixing her gaze on him again.

"No."

"Why not?"

"I wasn't interested." She leaned her elbows on the bar and propped her chin in her hand. "How about you?"

"They really weren't my type," he answered. He settled on the end barstool and reached for her glass. Stevi watched silently as he took a drink, but his lips on her glass sent a tingle down through her center. She was grateful she was behind the bar, just in case her legs shook. Good grief. They'd shared glasses and forks a million times, and now, suddenly, she had to go school girl crazy when he did it?

She laughed and nodded her head toward the front of the room.

"The girls at the front table. That ordered the Blue Balls and—"

"The Angel's Tit," he interrupted her with a grin.

"Yeah. They were part of a bachelorette party. There were several of them talking about you."

"Really?"

"Yeah. I heard one of them say she wanted to lick your bald head like a lollipop."

Duncan roared with laughter. Stevi reached for her wine and gulped down a mouthful. She didn't think it was that funny.

Maybe she shouldn't have told him, but he had ribbed her about the guys, so she'd thrown the bachelorette party at him. Apparently, it was more of a lob than a sharp pass. She would have to get better with the teasing if she was going to play games with him. Otherwise, she might end up getting hurt.

"Why didn't you tell me that sooner?"

"You had to stay and lock up with me anyway."

"I could've met them later for a drink."

"Do you do that a lot?" Stevi cleared her throat.

"Meet girls who are probably barely legal to drink?"

She meant hook up with girls probably barely legal, but she decided maybe it was better not to clarify. Rather than answer him, she lifted a shoulder in a tiny shrug.

"Nope. Not really."

"Not really?" Glass in hand again, she cut Duncan a look of disbelief over the top of it. "Either you do or you don't, Duncan."

"I haven't for a while." He stretched his arms up over his head and slid off the stool. Was he ready to call it a night already? Stevi dragged her teeth over her lower lip and stared into her glass to hide her disappointment.

"Slinking out of here at the mention of young girls?" she asked before she realized he was moving toward her and not away from her. He gave her the side eye as he moved up close to her and reached around her to grab a glass.

"Why? Are you scared of my stories?"

She watched him pluck a bottle of bourbon from the bar and twist the cap off. He poured a dash in the glass and replaced the cap and then the bottle to the bar before he looked at her again.

"Maybe," she hedged, because as curious as she was about… Duncan…and the mysteries of his body…and his moves, she wasn't sure she wanted to hear about any sexcapades. Especially not if they involved young girls. Cute, young, sexy girls.

"I thought Stevi Hague was fearless." He lifted the glass and sipped the liquor. Lowered it slowly. Kept his gray eyes on hers, daring her to run.

"Okay." She lifted her chin a notch and folded her arms over her chest. "Tell me one."

"What do you wanna know?"

Her heart crashed so hard in her chest, she almost winced. Her palms were sweaty again, and afraid she would drop her glass, she sipped from it and then set it down.

"I have to ask?"

He angled his head and shrugged. "Seems like a good way to do this."

"What are we doing?"

"Truth or dare."

Stevi laughed, though nerves lit up her insides like a Christmas tree. She lowered her eyes over his face and down over his shoulders. A hundred and one things she'd like to know about Duncan Marks, but she damned sure couldn't ask a one. For instance, what did the skin on his collarbone taste like? If she pressed her tongue to that spot—hidden now under his button up, of course—would she taste soap? Something woodsy, or did he use a soap that ran more toward a male hair product? Rich and tangy? Or maybe after a decent night of business at the Queen, would she taste a hint of salt from sweat?

"So?"

Stevi jumped when he nudged her. She watched him slide his foot back in place and played his action back in her head. The touch of his Sperry loafer on her leg. She scrunched her toes up in her sandal and wondered if he liked her new shoes. Had he even noticed them? She wouldn't admit this to Leah or Margo, either, but she gave Duncan way too damned much thought now when she dressed to be at the Queen. Which was pretty much all the time.

"Youngest girl you've met for drinks."

"I've met for drinks or hooked up with?"

"Same thing?"

"Um."

Stevi lifted her gaze from their feet to his face in time to see him arch an eyebrow in apology.

"No?"

"You choose."

He nodded and settled his back against the bar under the mirror. Stevi didn't want to watch him admit this, because she suspected it was going to make her jealous. But the alternative—watching her own face in the mirror at his back—wasn't appealing, either.

"I've been drinking with barely legal girls before." He swallowed more bourbon. "And I hooked up with a nineteen-year-old once."

From the corner of her eye, she saw that her face remained impassive. If she decided to sell out her share of the bar, she could always pack it in and head for Broadway with that kind of acting.

"Nineteen?" she repeated.

"It was a few years ago."

She nodded. Still kind of bugged her. Like okay, nineteen was legally an adult. But that didn't mean she liked the idea of nineteen-year-old girls hitting on older guys. Like Duncan. And also, if girls that young turned him on, she had nothing he would be interested in.

"Well." She nibbled on her lip and raised her eyebrows. "I guess if that's what turns you on—"

"Stevi, I was like, twenty-five at the time."

Okay. Not quite like thirty—ish. Like now. Because that would definitely freak her out. But still. If Duncan liked them young, Stevi was out of the game.

"Hey." She lifted her hands in surrender. "No judgment."

"You're so judging me."

Again with the toe of his shoe. Only this time he slid it up her leg a bit. For the lick of flame it sent up her inner thigh, could just as well have been his fingers.

"Okay, kind of." She sighed. "I mean. At nineteen, I didn't have a clue what I was doing. Then again, I guess guys might like that."

"What does that mean?"

Stevi blinked at him and shook her head. "Never mind. I should get going."

"Nope."

When she turned to grab her glass, he sank his fingers into her upper arm and spun her around to look at him again.

"Tell me." He dropped his hand to his side.

"Well." She sighed. "I guess if a girl doesn't…know how to get off…and doesn't know better that you're not trying to get her off, it's more fun for you. Right?"

She wondered if her cheeks were as red as they felt.

"There are so many things wrong with what you just said."

"Yeah? Like what?"

Duncan pursed his lips as he studied her face. Stevi wondered if he regretted pushing her to say what she was thinking. Because she regretted opening her mouth, that was for damned sure.

"You got somewhere you need to be?"

"At one o'clock on a Wednesday morning?" She tipped her head in disbelief.

"Does Leah wait up for you?"

This time, she could only blink at him.

"Eh. Yeah. That was a stupid question."

"Wait." She frowned, rested her hand on his chest when he leaned into her. "What does that mean?"

"Hang on." He snagged the stem of her glass. Stevi watched him uncork the Dykstra cab and splash more in her glass. When he handed it to her, she watched him pour more bourbon in his own glass. "Okay. Let's go."

"Go?" She stood firm in her spot behind the bar as he took a step away from her.

He reached back for her hand and led her out from behind the bar.

"What're we doing?" she asked when he flipped the lights off. Kitchen light still spilled through the doorway, but most of the bar was hidden now in shades of gray. Duncan, still holding her hand, led her to the bottom of the staircase. Stevi —thoughts on the long leather couch in the office upstairs— tried to swallow, but her mouth was bone dry.

"I think you insulted me," he announced as he lowered himself to sit on the fourth step. Stevi stared at him silently, looked back over her shoulder at the street out the front window, and finally turned back to him.

"I didn't mean it as a personal shot against you," she told him. Duncan patted a spot on the step beside him. Once she sat down there with him, he handed her the glass of wine. "Just…men…in general."

Duncan, elbows resting on his bent knees, sipped his drink.

"Makes me wonder what kind of men you sleep with."

CHAPTER 3

Duncan sat still as stone and waited for Stevi to say something. Part of his brain was still shocked that he had just tossed that out there, questioning the men Stevi slept with. Hell, part of his brain was still trying to process that they were having this conversation at all. Sure, they'd upped the flirty glances and smiles lately, and Duncan took what little fun he could in giving her grief about her dates. But they hadn't talked like this, not just the two of them.

He kept his eyes trained on the silvery street out the front window, even when he felt her eyes on him. The city was intriguing through the filter of moonlight and streetlight. Duncan had sat in this very spot on more than one occasion after seeing the girls off. Sometimes, he sipped a tumbler of bourbon; sometimes he knocked back a beer or two. Considered world issues like peace and social equality. Worried about the girls and worried about their friends, Kenzi and Joe, who had moved to the East Coast earlier in the year. He'd never come up with answers for anyone—not the big world questions and not how to comfort a man whose wife had a stroke during labor—but he would never tire of the view, either.

"I don't think you need to worry about the men I sleep with." Stevi's thick voice raised the hair on the back of his neck.

"Yeah? How's that fair? You're giving me shit for who I hook up with."

"I'm not," she answered. "And also, I can honestly say I've never been with a guy with fresh ink on his high school diploma."

"Nineteen-year-old girls have changed since you were a kid, Stevi." He swallowed more liquor and closed his eyes as the warmth numbed his throat and spread through his chest.

"Ouch." She laughed. Smacked his side playfully and then leaned into him. "Damn. Not enough that you sit here and tell me you like 'em young. You have to remind me that I'm old?"

Duncan hesitated before drawing his eyes from the window, the empty street out front.

"First of all, I did not tell you I like young girls. I told you it happened once."

In the shadows, their eyes met, hers bright with amusement, maybe?

"It's okay, Duncan." She shrugged. "I'm really not judging you."

"Girls are a lot…"

"Savvier?" she suggested.

"Well, I was gonna say…more in tune with…themselves than when we were kids." He sighed. "But sure. Savvier works."

"I really need to go home." She stretched her legs out in front of her. "I won't make it if I drink anymore."

"You hardly touched the wine."

"I didn't eat much today," she mumbled.

"And anyway?" He didn't want her to leave. No, he wouldn't hold her down and force her to stay, or force her to drink the wine, but he didn't want the night to end. He let the words hang until she tipped her head, anxious for him to continue.

"Anyway, what?"

"I tried," he glanced at her and quickly turned his attention back to the street. "With her. I mean…I don't…just take. Maybe when I was a kid. But—"

Stevi blinked at him in the shadows. Finally, she gave him a slow nod. "Okay. Fair enough."

"That's the biggest turn on," he added when she looked at her feet, her legs still stretched out in front of her. Duncan let his eyes slide over her face—in profile, in shadows, she looked soft and sweet—down over her shoulders and finally to her legs and her feet. Her toes were painted. In the darkness, they were just a darker shade, but he knew they were some kind of hot pink.

"What's the biggest turn on?" she whispered without looking at him.

"Making a woman come."

He saw her eyes pop wide with surprise. Wondered if she was blushing.

"Yeah?" She turned to look at him and arched her eyebrows. "You like screamers?"

He didn't. And he didn't like that she was pushing back, joking with him to back him off. He liked honest women. Pretty women. Sexy women. Sure, there had to be some sort of physical attraction, though Duncan found most women some sort of combination of pretty and sexy. Unfortunately for every other woman in the world, there was only one Stevi Hague, and so he wasn't interested.

Wondering now if Stevi was a screamer, he grinned at her. Recognized that it was time to put an end to this conversation, because he was making her uncomfortable.

"I'll walk you out," he told her.

She laughed, but it sounded a little forced. He climbed to his feet and then offered her a hand.

"You okay?"

"Yeah." They walked together through the bar. Duncan took her glass and set it and his on the end of the bar.

"Is your purse upstairs?"

"Damn." She nodded. For a brief moment, Duncan let his mind go. Imagined Stevi going up to get her purse. Following her. Catching her for a kiss. The two of them lying together on the couch in the office.

"I'll get it," he offered.

"Really?"

"Sure. Is it in the desk?"

"Yeah."

He nodded and turned to lope back across the room in a few long strides. The distance from Stevi, from her perfume, was probably a good thing. His dick was caught up in that visual of the two of them wrapped up in each other's arms on the couch. He forced himself to breathe deeply, recited all the different brands and types of spirits and other alcohols they served as he grabbed her purse from the desk drawer and then hurried back downstairs with it. Stevi stood near the back door, hip hitched against the wall and her arms folded over her chest.

"Thank you." She offered him a smile as she took her purse. He watched her dig through it for her keys. Wondered what the hell the woman kept in her purse, because it looked like she lived out of it. Duncan wouldn't be surprised if she pulled out a carjack or a basketball hoop one day.

"You okay to drive?"

"Yeah." She nodded. "Just tired."

"I can take you."

The shadows back here were deeper and darker, so he couldn't read the expression on her face. She lifted her hand, though, and patted his chest. It was a practiced move that she'd done a hundred times, but tonight, Duncan wondered if she felt his heart racing under her hand.

"I'm fine."

"Okay." He nodded. She let her hand slide and turned away, but he stopped her. Linked his fingers through hers and held on until she looked back at him.

"What?"

"We're okay?"

Rather than blow him off and promise they were fine, Stevi hesitated. Duncan's blood felt like ice now, and he figured if anyone knew this sprite of a woman had this kind of power over him, they would seize his man card. Probably shred it. Burn it. Never return it; that was for damned sure.

"Of course we're okay." She spoke softly, and Duncan thought, without conviction. But she did squeeze his fingers. That was something, right?

"I shouldn't have told you—"

"Oh my god." She laughed. He couldn't swear to it, but it looked like she rolled her eyes. "Relax. You know, when I was nineteen, you were twenty-two. Not that much of a difference, right?"

"Did you—?" He rubbed his thumb over the back of her hand.

"Duncan." He heard the uncertainty in her whisper, but he didn't know what to make of it.

They stood close, though only their hands touched. Duncan was drawn to her, but he forced himself to stand still.

"Is that why you said what you did?"

"I should go." She squeezed his hand again.

"Right." He nodded. "You need to get home. I'll lock up."

She stood a moment longer, and Duncan considered tasting her. Just a flick of his tongue over her upper lip. In the shadows, she watched him, and Duncan thought she looked hungry. For that same kind of touch. Then again, Duncan knew his dick was doing a whole lot of talking, and this was Stevi. Stevi, for God's sake. As much as he liked making his dick happy, he couldn't hurt Stevi.

"Goodnight." She stepped back from him and her heels— God, wouldn't she be dynamite in those heels and his sheets —clicked on the floor as she took the last few steps to the back door. The glance she directed at him when she was at the door stirred him into action, and he moved quickly to step outside with her.

"Be careful."

"Yep." She nodded. "Wish me luck."

"What kind of luck am I wishing for?"

"That the lovebirds will be sleeping when I get home."

"It's after one in the morning," he reminded her.

"Trace writes in the basement at all hours. Woke up once to some couch percussion going on."

"Hey. It's nice that someone's having some fun."

Stevi laughed softly as she turned away and headed to her car. Duncan watched her climb in and then in the streetlight in the parking lot, he saw her pull her seatbelt on and then she backed out of her spot and drove away without looking back.

With Stevi gone, he had two options. More bourbon. Appealing, but for the jack hammer headache that thought invited. Or a cold shower.

He huffed out a sigh as he went back inside the Queen. The music was still playing when he scooped their glasses up and carried them back to the kitchen. Fall Out Boy raged on while he rinsed the glasses and considered the way Stevi had reacted when he suggested strip poker. The way she had shut down when he mentioned the young girl he had hooked up with.

What she had said about how he preferred young girls and that he had taken a shot at her age.

Okay, so she had sworn she wasn't judging him. He didn't think she would. Hell, the four of them—six when Joe and Kenzi had still been around—had been ridiculously open, and Stevi wasn't one to flinch about anything personal. She had sounded normal when she promised she wasn't judging him.

But *something* was off. Even when she left, and she said they were okay—burn the man card and toss the ashes in the Mississippi—something was off.

Duncan scrubbed his hands over his bald head and then hooked his fingers behind his neck.

Was it possible she was jealous?

CHAPTER 4

BEING AT THE QUEEN AFTER HOURS MADE FOR LATER mornings. Tossing and turning through the rest of the night with a brain—and okay, other body parts, too—that wouldn't shut down made for really crappy later mornings. Stevi smelled the coffee long before she wanted to get up, though she had been awake for hours. In fact, she wasn't sure she had slept much past four. The thought of finding her sister in the kitchen almost made her drag herself out of bed by eight-thirty, but then she remembered that most likely, she would find Leah and Trace in the kitchen, and she didn't want to get up.

She loved the guy. Loved. Him. Loved her sister. Couldn't be happier for the two of them. Didn't mean she wanted to watch the Leah and Nashville show every day. Not that the two of them had their hands on each other all the time. It wasn't even like they had to say syrupy, sweet things and hold hands over the tabletop. Just the fact that Leah knew when Trace—she had called him Nashville for so long, it was sometimes hard for Stevi to remember that was her pet name for him and maybe not everyone needed to call him that—needed more coffee. Or that Trace nudged the butter closer to Leah just as she picked up her knife and her toast. It was the country music almost always playing in the kitchen now, and no, not the actual music, but the look of contentment on her sister's face when she listened to it.

It was time for Stevi to move out. Add that to the list of things to worry about. She had some money. She made some money, though the girls didn't take much of a salary at this point. Together, she and Leah had been okay with home ownership. Add in Trace's share, and they were golden. But a young, happy couple like Leah and Trace deserved some privacy. Not to mention that as happy as Stevi was for Leah, it did make her heart hurt a bit for herself.

She had enough on her mind. Leah appeared to be settled down now, but it wasn't that long ago that her sister had called her in the middle of the night and asked for her help. Stevi still shook when she thought of rushing upstairs to the attic bedroom and finding Leah in a puddle of blood. Leah had denied the pregnancy, and then she had kept it from Trace, always claiming she needed to find the right time to tell him, and then before she could do that, he had joined his brother's tour and what it boiled down to was Leah miscarrying one of her babies—Leah still promised she hadn't known then that she was carrying twins—and Stevi being front and center support.

Stevi, who didn't handle paper cuts well. Stevi, who loved her cousin Margo's baby dearly and who was thrilled at the idea of being an aunt to Leah's baby. Okay, so Leah had just fallen in love and was just now looking at marriage and having a baby, and she was thirty. So technically, Stevi wasn't too old for any of it. But Stevi had always been different than Leah, a little colder, more aloof. Happy to play the field and have a good time, rather than looking for love. It had taken Leah a while to find her happily-ever-after, but Leah had been looking. Stevi wasn't sure she wanted anything to do with any of it, she wasn't sure how to figure out if she did or didn't—especially when she'd probably dated every single guy in Adam's Bay and had no desire to get to know any of them better, or biblically, in the case of her good friends.

And then there was Duncan.

Holy hot bed of coals. Duncan Marks.

Stevi had driven a block from the Queen last night, and then she had had to pull over for a second just to simmer down.

She pushed her bedspread back now and swung her legs over the edge of the bed. Her door was closed, as always, but now and then she could still hear Leah or Trace up and moving around. She sat for a moment and waited to see if there was life outside the door. Maybe not. Maybe the coffee fairy had delivered her magic elixir and flown away already.

She thought he was going to kiss her. Last night. At the door. When he took her hand, she had swallowed down a little gasp of surprise, and she nodded and said sure they were okay, and she had offered up a silent prayer that he would kiss her. A sweet, soft brush of his lips over hers. A deep, wet tongue-against-tongue lip lock. She wasn't picky; the thought of Duncan's lips on hers had ripped through her with the force of a volcano and left her shaking with desire.

Disappointment had flooded her when he didn't. When he only looked at her. Disappointment and then a tidal wave of raw, harsh embarrassment. If he had just confessed to being with a girl almost ten years her junior, she would have to be stupid to think he was interested in her. Her prayer changed from asking for kisses to getting to her car on her own two feet. She'd been so wrapped up in that thought that she hadn't waved goodbye when she left. Instead, she had driven a block with lightning shooting down her arms, her stomach clenched with desire and shame, and her face on fire with embarrassment.

Car in park, she had counted to ten. Breathed in and out slowly, deeply, as if she knew what the hell she was doing with cleansing breaths. And then when her damned eyes had filled, she poked her fingers in them and rubbed them hard, pissed off that they would betray her like that.

And then, after she was home and in bed, then came the dreams.

Stevi wasn't one to wallow, so she slipped out of bed and out of her room. The music in the kitchen was not country, so maybe she would be lucky enough to not have to see her soon to be brother-in-law first thing today. She slipped into the bathroom to take care of business. Splashed cold water on her face and combed her hair, and then gave in and went in search of coffee.

Leah sat at the table, eyes on the iPad in front of her. She looked up, flashed Stevi a warm smile, and glanced back at the iPad. Stevi took in the rest of the kitchen—no sign of Trace, although there were dishes in the sink, so the two of them had breakfast not long ago. She slipped into the kitchen and reached for the mug they had left on the counter for her. Silly, really, because Stevi was capable of reaching up to open a cabinet to get her own mug. Because she knew she was feeling surly after not sleeping much, after the scene with Duncan, she bit her tongue, poured her coffee and splashed in a lot of creamer, and mixed it. The song on the radio was Karen Carpenter, she thought, and though it was neither raining nor Monday, she was already down and didn't want to listen to it.

"Hey!" Leah caught her as she tiptoed out of the kitchen, hoping to sneak back to her room without having to talk. "Where're you going?"

Stevi stood with her back to Leah for a moment.

"Where's Trace?" she asked as she turned slowly to look at her sister.

"Why?" Leah shook her head. "You don't wanna sit out here if he's around?"

Stevi stared at Leah from the safety of the living room.

"What happened?" Leah pushed her chair back. Her sister wasn't big yet; in fact, if you didn't know she was pregnant, you wouldn't think she was showing. Still. Stevi didn't want her to get up and follow her into her bedroom. Especially not if Stevi intended to be moody and quiet, and she did.

"Nothing." She sipped from her mug as she made her way back to the table. Leah watched her with eyes that saw more than she ever commented on. Stevi lowered herself into her chair at the table and set her mug down. She rubbed her eyes and then finally met her sister's eyes.

"Why are you avoiding Trace?"

Stevi shook her head and shrugged one shoulder. "I'm not, Leah. I'm just tired."

"What time did you get home?"

Leah closed the cover on her iPad and fixed Stevi with a concerned stare.

"I got home just after one." She yawned. "But I didn't sleep well."

"Sometimes I get the feeling you're not happy about Trace. And the baby."

Guilt punched her in the stomach and sucked her breath away. She reached over the table and skimmed her fingers over the back of Leah's hand.

"He makes my big sister happy," she said softly. "How can I not like that?"

"But?"

Stevi sat back in her chair and thought about Duncan.

"Can I ask you something?"

"Yeah." Leah waved her fingers and shrugged. "Ask away."

"Who made the first move?"

As if the curve of her hand resting over her belly wasn't enough, Leah's eyes grew distant, and Stevi's teeth hurt watching that beatific smile cross her face.

"Well. He approached me at the bar. I told him no."

Stevi nodded. She had heard the story several times, and though she loved it—she really did—she didn't want to hear it today. Not with every nerve ending in her body on overdrive, still waiting for the touch, the kiss that wasn't going to happen.

"He pursued me. With the texts. The phone calls. And he came here."

"So he did?"

Leah shrugged. "I kissed him. That night we were dancing at the Queen. I kissed him. That was that."

Stevi drew in a deep breath.

"I've never known you to hesitate." Leah tipped her head and arched her eyebrows. The scrutiny, even if it was born of concern, made Stevi squirm.

She couldn't answer that. For a number of reasons—not the least of which was that they were talking about Duncan, *Duncan* for God's sake—she wouldn't respond.

"Have you talked to Joe lately?" She cleared her throat and stared at Leah boldly.

"Yeah. He's good. He was really happy. I guess Addelyn spent some time with Kenzi the other day."

Stevi nodded. Yep. Good news. Kenzi was recovering from a stroke during labor with her third child, and all of them gobbled up the positive reports Joe relayed. She looked away, though, because she was stuck in a blue spot and everyone else's happiness grated on her nerves right now. It was a daily toss up on whether other people's happiness would make her sad or piss her off.

Stevi figured it was best for everyone around her to steer clear until she got over the ridiculous infatuation with Duncan.

"You could just kiss him," Leah suggested.

Stevi shook her head.

"I know you're mooning over a guy—"

"I don't do that," Stevi argued. "I've never done that."

"First time for everything." Leah shrugged. "And you are, and I even know who it is. And you could just kiss him. And see—"

"You don't know who it is, and I can't just kiss him." Stevi pushed her chair back and stood. She picked up her mug and stepped away from the table.

"Why not? You have plenty of alone time with him these days."

Leah's words stopped her on the spot, and she cradled her mug so she wouldn't spill her coffee.

"You know what? Never mind. It doesn't matter."

Her stomach quivered at the thought that Leah knew whom she was thinking about. Had she been that obvious? Not so sly with the way she watched him at the Queen? Did her whole face light up when he walked in a room? Because her body tended to kick into high gear whenever she knew he was around, but she thought she had kept it hidden.

"Why doesn't it matter? Of course, it matters."

Stevi looked back over her shoulder when she heard Leah's chair squeak. Her sister climbed to her feet and carried her mug to the sink.

"He's not interested anyway."

"Really?" Leah gave her a look that said she was being ridiculous. "We are talking about Dun—"

"Don't." Stevi shook her head quickly. "Please. Don't. I shouldn't have said anything."

"Why not? Stevi, you guys care about—"

"Once you say it out loud," Stevi whispered, only because her throat was thick and tight with a rush of emotion. "We can't make it go away. So please, do not say anything. I'm being ridiculous. It'll pass. Maybe it's just PMS."

Leah stared at her silently for a moment. Finally she shrugged her eyebrows and nodded.

"Okay. Whatever you say." She reached for Stevi, cupped her upper arm in her hand and rubbed her thumb over her cool skin. "But Stevi, it's not just gonna go away. If you feel it, and you do, you can't just ignore it and make it go away."

Torn, Stevi lowered her eyes to the floor between them. What if she sat down and talked to Leah? Confessed her feelings? That she was attracted to Duncan, but afraid that if things didn't work out, they would ruin their friendship? Okay, that was a common worry. Hello to every romance novel or movie ever written. But this was different. She and Duncan were friends, sure, but Duncan was practically family. He was their cousin's stepbrother. And they ran a business together. Talk about a disaster waiting to happen.

"And there's the pot." Stevi nodded. As much as she wanted to admit it to Leah, just gush the words out in a rushed whisper that she was stupidly attracted to Duncan Marks, she couldn't do it. Plan B. Push her away. Even if it meant pissing her off. "Calling the kettle."

Leah rolled her eyes.

"What happened last night?"

A little bit surprised that Leah hadn't let it go, that she hadn't walked away, Stevi met her eyes briefly and then looked away.

"What?"

"What happened? When you guys were alone?"

"Nothing." Stevi shrugged. Thank God, she could shoot straight and honest here. "We cleaned up and left."

She turned on her heel to head to the bedroom. Time to fold up the pissy feelings and tuck them away and find Fun Stevi. Happy Stevi.

"Stevi."

"Hmm?"

"What about St. Louis?"

"What?" White hot energy surged from her heart through her fingers, and Stevi thought if she aimed them at the wall, she could start a fire. Cautiously, she curled her fingers into fists, mindful of the mug in her hand.

"Did you sleep with him?"

Completely shocked by Leah's question, Stevi gaped at her silently. A hundred different words and images, too, rushed through Stevi's mind, including memories from the recent overnight trip she and Duncan had taken. Stomach in her throat, she couldn't have said a word if she wanted to, and she didn't—because what the hell could she say to that—she backed a step away from Leah and turned again to escape to her bedroom.

"Stevi?"

Leah followed her right into her room. She watched her set her mug on the dresser and rummage around in her drawers for something to wear.

"No, Leah, I didn't sleep with him!" She finally snapped, hurt over her sister's assumption trumping the rest of the ugly emotions at war inside her. "Is that what you really think of me?"

When Stevi spun around to look at her sister, she found her perched on the side of her bed.

"What does that mean?" Leah's voice was gruff.

"First of all." Stevi huffed out a sigh and blew her bangs from her eyes. "I didn't go to that tasting event just to get away with him. And I hate myself for being gone. I hate that I wasn't here for Margo—"

"Stevi, you would have passed out and banged your head and made more work for everyone."

Stevi looked away when her eyes filled. Of course, Leah was right, and yes, they had all teased her for being woozy at the sight of blood since she was a little kid. But at the moment, Leah's gentle reminder only made her feel worse.

"Well." She shrugged. Flicked her eyes back over her sister and hoped Leah didn't notice how close to tears she was. "I didn't sleep with him. We shared a bed, yes, but nothing happened."

"Ste—"

"And to be honest, Leah, it hurts that you think something did."

CHAPTER 5

WHEN STEVI STORMED IN THROUGH THE BACK DOOR EARLIER, Duncan could tell just from the rapid clacking of her heels over the floor that she was in a *fuck you* sort of mood. Behind the bar, playing with a new tequila idea, he had lifted his eyes to watch her strut across the room to the staircase. Worried that she had changed her mind and decided she was upset about last night, relief zapped through him when she shot him a smile from half way up the steps.

But then, when she stayed upstairs, locked away in the office for hours before they opened, he wondered if maybe he'd read her smile wrong. Wasn't sure how to do that, really, because in all the years he had known Stevi, the two of them had never really been sideways. She had a few different smiles up her sleeves, and Duncan had to admit there was one—that sexy little smirk—that seemed to be reserved for him these days, at least when she was here, but he didn't think she had ever sneered at him before.

Deciding it was best to give her some time, he stayed parked at the bar and played with some drink ideas. Usually, when he did come up with anything that was a little bit new, he had Stevi taste test it. Probably not a good plan today. Instead, he tasted a bit here and there and then called Trace over once he and Leah came in.

"Nope." Trace grimaced when he put the tequila drink down. Pushed it over the bar toward Duncan. "But then, I'm not much into hard liquor, so probably not your best critique."

Duncan nodded. He'd just have to wait and hit Stevi with it later to see what she thought.

"Why don't you ask Stevi? Isn't she here?" Trace looked over his shoulder and then back at Duncan.

"She's upstairs," Duncan answered. "Came in a few hours ago, looking like an angry cat, so I haven't even ventured up there."

"Really." Trace drummed his fingertips on the bar and stared at Duncan with a frown.

"Yeah. Why?" Duncan tipped his wrist to peek at his watch. Opening in T-twenty. He was ready to jump into the night and get things rolling. After a cold shower and a night of tossing and turning and thoughts of Stevi—of that last few moments at the back door, when he had wanted to kiss her— he had come in late this morning ready to pick up where they'd left off. Some fun flirting or some simple conversation. Stocking the condiments behind the bar. Making sure the kitchen was ready for the happy hour specials and dinner prep. Anything to be with her. Instead, he had spent the better part of his day alone, with Stevi up in the office and Margo breezing in and out as she fluttered around, crossing things off her to do list.

Trace sighed and offered Duncan a shrug. "Leah's upset about something. Maybe they got into it."

"They don't do that very often, though," Duncan argued.

"No, they don't. But Leah and I had breakfast this morning. And I left to get a new doorbell kit because—"

Duncan nodded to hurry him along. Leah and Stevi's doorbell had been broken since the day after they moved in.

"When I came home, Stevi was in the bathroom, and Leah was upset. Like mopey upset."

"Yeah, well, judging from the way Stevi stalked through the bar intent on killing every wooden plank in the floor with her heels, I'll say pissed with a side of fuck you."

Trace flinched. "Okay. I'm gonna see what I can find out."

"Yeah, well, we're out of full body armor, so I'd stay away from the office."

Leah wandered into the bar area from the kitchen, one hand smoothing her belly—Duncan still had a hard time believing she was pregnant, because she sure wasn't showing—and the other covering a big yawn.

"Need anything?" Trace asked her. With a sheepish grin because he caught her yawning, she laughed softly and shook her head.

"I'm good, Nashville."

"Did you talk to Stevi this morning?" Trace asked. Duncan kept his eyes on the bar, the towel in his hand as he wiped up any spills from his mixology session.

"Yeah." Leah eased onto a barstool and rubbed her hands over her face. "Why?"

To hell with pretending he wasn't listening. Duncan moseyed down her way and leaned on the bar, the towel still trapped under his hand.

"She okay?"

Leah opened her mouth to answer him, but she hesitated. He resisted the urge to look at Trace; if Leah was covering something up, it was something to do with Stevi, not herself.

"Yeah. She's fine." She shrugged, but she frowned first at Duncan and then at Trace. "Why do you ask?"

"Well, she charged in here like her hair was on fire a while ago and went straight upstairs. Haven't seen her since."

Leah cleared her throat. "Can I have a glass of water, Duncan?"

"Of course."

"She's fine. She's probably trying to come up with a plan for the Octoberfest."

"What's the Octoberfest?" Trace asked her.

Duncan turned in time to see Leah's lazy grin. "Another big festival during which the citizens of Adam's Bay gather to imbibe and eat tons of food."

When Trace glanced at Duncan, he nodded.

"Yeah. We thought we would really bring money in last year, but we actually went in the red a few times last fall."

"So who plans the festival?"

"The community economic foundation." Leah sipped her water. "Stevi was on the board for a couple of years. She's still involved, but she took it personally last year when our business leveled off during what should have been another peak time."

"You think that's what she's doing?" Duncan narrowed his eyes at Leah. Again, he thought she was going to say something, but they all heard the office door click open, and Leah clapped her mouth closed and nodded.

"What playlist do we want tonight?" Stevi called from the mezzanine level. "Why is there a table up here with glasses?"

"We must've missed that one last night," Duncan answered.

"You choose the music," Leah told her.

"Great. Because our guests are into death metal."

"I'm thinking maybe not the Octoberfest," Duncan mumbled. Leah stared at him with wide, innocent eyes and finally slipped off the barstool and headed back to the kitchen.

"Do you have…death metal…playlists?" Trace asked hesitantly. "I mean, if that's what she—"

"No." Duncan shook his head. He tossed the bar towel down and looked around when Steely Dan was suddenly on the sound system.

"Well, that doesn't seem so scary," Trace mumbled as he walked away. Duncan watched him disappear out the back door, knowing he would make sure the patio was set up and ready for patrons.

Not so scary compared to death metal, but then again, the Steely Dan song playing was "Hey Nineteen." Duncan couldn't help but assume she was sending him a message. And if he asked for help again to decipher that message— judgment or jealousy—she might slip one of her spiky pink heels off and stab him in the brains with it.

CHAPTER 6

DUNCAN WORE A T-SHIRT TONIGHT, AND SO STEVI HAD worked most of the night without looking at him. It ought to be illegal, that a guy could look that damned good in a gray t-shirt and jeans. It didn't matter, though, if she worked most of the night with her eyes averted or spent more time schmoozing the patrons than talking to him, because the sight of him behind the bar when she had come in earlier was burned into her eyes and her brain. He wasn't particularly tall, but she was short, so okay, he was definitely taller than her. He wasn't necessarily body-builder big, either, but he was wiry and wicked strong. Didn't he sweep her off her feet and throw her over his shoulder now and then in a fireman's hold? Nine times out of ten, he did it for the sole purpose of pissing her off. Sort of worked, but secretly, she didn't mind so much.

She steered clear of Leah, too, though any heat Stevi felt when she thought about Leah had nothing to do with a physical attraction and everything to do with anger and hurt feelings. She hadn't bothered to explain herself to Leah; in fact, she hadn't bothered to talk to her sister since she'd suggested that maybe Stevi had tangled with Duncan at the liquor trade show.

Leah worked the bar with Duncan, and to her credit, she treated Stevi as if nothing had happened earlier at home. Whether she was trying to offer an olive branch or protecting Stevi from Duncan reading too much into anything said between them, Stevi appreciated her efforts at being normal. Duncan sent Margo home before ten. As much as Stevi had enjoyed the buffer between herself and the bartenders, she agreed with Duncan that Margo should head home and bunk down. Her cousin looked exhausted, and Stevi suspected it really had nothing to do with phone sex and maybe more to do with just wishing Jess would come back.

Stevi had the back tables bussed when Duncan locked the front door. She hummed along to the current tune—thanks to Trace, they were all a lot more knowledgeable about music —and carried two big stacks of pint glasses to the kitchen.

"Hey."

"Hey, Duncan." She offered him a smile when he joined her at the sink. He loaded the dishwasher, nudged her foot with his.

"I feel like I haven't talked to you all night."

Eyes on the glasses as he set them in the rack, she swallowed a mouthful of guilt.

"I know." She darted her eyes up to meet his, but with what Leah had asked her earlier, she couldn't hold the eye contact. She lowered her gaze to her own fisted hands, resting on the sink. "We were slammed there for a while."

"Did you get anything figured out for the Octoberfest?"

Stevi blinked and lifted a curious frown to him. It was late July. The Octoberfest was mid-October. The big planning was done; well, the big planning was taken care of by the community economic foundation, but—

"Leah said you were working on it earlier today."

Stevi answered with a slow nod. "Right. Yeah."

Actually, she'd spent quite a bit of time upstairs looking at real estate websites, but she wasn't going to share that with Duncan.

"I know we were all disappointed with last year's business that weekend—"

Stevi pressed her lips together, but when Duncan just stopped talking midsentence, she arched her eyebrows curiously. Interesting that apparently everyone in the bar was hanging that albatross around her shoulders. The Queen dipped into the red now and then—they were an up-and-coming bar, for God's sake. Comforting to know her partners were blaming her lame marketing efforts for some of those losses.

"Are there more tables?" she asked quietly. She rubbed the bridge of her nose, not in the mood to argue. Or happy lie and pretend she'd spent the day coming up with something brilliant that would strike up some big business come fall. She wasn't really in the mood for flirting, either, not after Leah had made it clear she assumed Stevi had climbed into bed with Duncan the first time that particular opportunity had knocked.

"Yeah." He nodded. She half expected him to follow her back to the main room of the bar, and yes, she was more than half disappointed when he didn't. No, she didn't want to flirt.

Obviously, that had gotten out of hand, if her own sister was seeing more than there was between them. But she liked Duncan. He was one of her best friends, and she missed him. Working with Duncan, Leah, and Margo was what she loved most about being at the Queen.

The Eagles had segued into Abba, and she laughed softly when she heard "Dancing Queen" on the sound system. Interesting. She liked Abba, but she wasn't sure Duncan or Trace were fans. She wondered which of them had created this playlist and if this song got dropped in accidentally.

"So, did Margo get her phone sex last night?" Duncan asked when she carried a second load of glasses back to the kitchen. She shot him a look of surprise and chuckled as she set the glasses on the counter.

"How would I know?"

"She didn't tell you?"

"I was busy," she reminded him. She started to step around him to go back for a final walk through to make sure they had all the tables, but Duncan turned and caught her arm.

"Upstairs."

She looked at his fingers on her arm and then lifted her eyes to his. He let go when she nodded. The air around them was charged with awareness, but Stevi refused to acknowledge it. Nothing had even happened, and she was consumed with guilt over Leah's assumption. Imagine how she would feel if she allowed her body to act on the attraction she felt for Duncan Marks.

When clearing her throat did little to clear the tension in the air, she looked away and slipped out of the room. She took her time, swept the main room with her gaze, slipped out back to check the patio, and then moved quickly up the steps to make sure the few tables on the mezzanine level were cleared. Duncan was waiting for her at the bar when she came back down.

She reached for the rag to wipe the tables down, but Duncan waved her away to do it himself.

"Aren't you having a drink with me tonight?" he called from the front of the room. The bar lights were still on, so the street behind him was dark. No silvery image like the memory in her mind from last night.

"Um." She perched on the edge of a stool and shook her head. "No."

"So." He drew the word out like it had seven syllables as he moved methodically from table to table and wiped each one down. Stevi rested her elbows on the bar and propped her chin in her hand, eyes on him.

"What?" she asked when he stood neck and neck with her. He finished the table to her left and then stood, arms wide, hands resting on the chairs there.

"You lied to me."

"I've never lied to you," she answered quietly.

"Says you." He shrugged. She waited as he worked his way to the back of the room. "Tables upstairs?"

"All good," she answered. "Leah must have taken care of them before she left."

He nodded. Stevi rubbed carefully at her eyes and then pushed her hair back from her face when he retreated to the kitchen. She should go up and get her purse. Hit the road. Trouble with that was, she had nowhere to go but home. And no desire to go there, whether she was speaking to Leah or not.

"So." Duncan reappeared a few minutes later. Stevi, forehead resting on her fists now, gave him a long, silent look. "I thought of a new game we can play."

"Yeah? Does it involve pencils and x's and o's? Because I'm not up for much more than that."

Duncan reached into his hip pocket and then pulled his hand out, and with a flourish and a grin, he tossed a pair of dice down on the bar.

"Bar dice?" She eyed the dice for a second and then lifted only her eyes to look at him. "Really?"

"Not just any bar dice." He raised his eyebrows. "You roll a one, you tell a truth. Two, you extract a truth—"

"I'd rather extract a tooth, Duncan," she mumbled.

"Three, you get to dare me something. Four, I dare you. Five, you ask me for something."

"Like what?" She dropped her hands to her lap and sat back.

"Anything."

"So, if I roll a five, I can ask you to track down a big-ass cup of coffee?"

"If that's what you want."

She licked her lips and looked at the dice again. "Six?"

"I ask you for anything."

"Such as?"

"I could ask you to bring me cookies tomorrow."

Stevi considered the game. Her head still hurt, and her heart hurt more, because she hated being at odds with her sister. But even more than that, she hated that her sister apparently believed she slept with every guy she went out with. No wonder Duncan was in full throttle flirt mode these days. Maybe he was hard up, and he figured she was a sure tap.

She wasn't that girl, and that the people she loved the most thought that of her was a sinking feeling inside her. Add to that the way Duncan lit a room on fire just by walking in, that Duncan's fire burned right damned through the oxygen around her, and Stevi couldn't breathe. Hard to reconcile feeling shamed for the very thing she did want, though wanting someone as much as she did Duncan was entirely new to her.

"And a seven?"

He shrugged. "Haven't gotten that far."

"You're making this up as you go?" She laughed in spite of herself.

"Maybe."

His grin was a direct hit on her resolve. And her heart—she actually gasped out loud in a struggle to catch a breath—and her girl parts.

"Oh, Duncan." She groaned and leaned forward to rest her arms on the bar again.

"I think we could come up with something…fun…for snake eyes."

"We could just play for money," she suggested.

"What did I do?" he asked quietly. Stevi lifted her eyes to his again, startled that the grin was gone and a look of deep concern had replaced it.

"What?"

"You avoided me all day—"

"I was working—"

"And all night."

Stevi licked her lips and lowered her head to rest on her arms.

"Leah and I got into it this morning," she mumbled. "Just not in a very good mood."

"What about?" he asked. She shook her head without lifting it. No way she would tell him what Leah had asked her. "That's not like you guys."

"Yeah." She closed her eyes. "I know."

"What I find interesting, though…" His voice grew distant and then suddenly, she felt him standing so close she could have lifted a finger and touched his arm. Would his skin be warm? The A/C tended to chill her, especially after hours when she stopped moving. But she suspected Duncan would be warm. In fact, she could almost feel heat emanating from his body. "Stevi."

"Hmm?" She blinked her eyes open and realized he had turned the big, overhead lights down, and now, like last night, the big room was lit only by the long, rectangle of light that fell through the door from the kitchen and the silvery glow of the street out front.

"What I find interesting is that you say you got into it with Leah, but it was me you avoided all night."

"Duncan." She sighed and straightened in the stool again.

"At one point tonight, you went to Leah seven straight times in a row for an order."

"You counted?" she asked in disbelief.

"So, you lied to me. Last night and just now."

"No. Leah and I got into it this morning," she said softly.

"Tell me." He leaned in, rested his arms on the bar as she had done just moments before, and swallowed her whole with his eyes.

"I can't."

"So, it's something to do with Leah."

"I promise you I don't lie to you." She nudged his elbow and grinned. "Figure out the dice game. And write the rules down, because you'll cheat and change them every time I roll."

"So, you'll play if we figure out the rest?"

"Maybe."

"Then, let's play with one die right now."

She drew in a sharp breath, careful to hide it under his intense gaze.

"What do you want to drink?"

"I have to drink to play?"

"Yep, bartender's rules."

"I have a headache, Duncan."

He studied her face for a second and finally nodded. "Okay. We'll pass on the drinks." She nodded. Might be easier to play a game like this if she had a drink, but the thought of drinking so much as a swallow of beer was too much. Her neck and shoulders were tight, and the back of her head pounded with painful awareness that she was getting in too deep to back away safely. She didn't appreciate that Leah assumed she had slept with Duncan, and all the while, she was crashing head first into something exciting and dangerous with him. Sleeping with Duncan had infinite possibilities, including what she believed would be scorching hot sex and also maybe tearing down the business they had all worked so hard to create and maybe hurting everyone in her family, including herself and Duncan.

"You go first." He nudged the dice at her.

"I thought we were just using one."

"Let's do two. Just for the sake of snake eyes."

Stevi nibbled on her lip as she plucked the dice up and shook them in her hand. "And what happens with snake eyes?"

"How about a double dare?"

"So, are we talking racing down Maine Street naked dares? Or prank phone calls? Or…what?"

"Roll."

Stevi tossed the dice and held her breath. The first one stopped on one, and when the other bounced a bit before stopping on a three, Stevi felt a ripple of disappointment under the immediate relief. Good grief. She wasn't going to make out with him, unless it came down to a dare? Really? How old was she? Because this felt like playing spin the bottle when she was twelve or thirteen, wanting to kiss boys but afraid to do it. Only the game and the fact that her friends were playing, too, made it okay.

"So is that a three or four?" she lifted only her eyes to his.

"Which do you want it to be?"

She stared at him for a long time, wishing she could do this. Wishing this morning hadn't happened. Wishing she didn't need the alcohol to boost her confidence. Wishing she were anywhere but here right now.

"Well, my brain hurts right now, so my heart isn't in this, and I can't come up with a good dare for you."

"So you're calling it a four? And passing me the dare?"

She wondered what he would dare her to do. If she would do it or just get up and walk out.

"Yeah. I guess I am."

"Okay." He nodded.

"Don't make it illegal, Duncan," she warned him. "We're adults now. Business owners."

He answered with a dramatic groan. "Well, shoot. I was gonna dare you to steal a car and drive it down Broadway at eighty miles an hour."

"Didn't you do that when you were—? What? Seventeen?"

"I didn't steal it," he argued. "I borrowed it."

"Semantics."

"Okay, are you ready?"

"Yeah. I guess so."

"I dare you to tell me what you were thinking when you walked out of here last night."

Stevi squeezed her eyes closed and shook her head. "And what if I was thinking about going home to do laundry? Or if I was thinking about watching porn—"

Duncan shrugged when she blinked her eyes open. "What were you thinking?"

"Why do I have to go first?" she whined.

"You passed, remember?"

"I was thinking…" she swallowed hard, "about you."

"What about me?" Duncan leaned in closer still.

"How specific do I have to be? You asked, and I answered."

"Pretty sure the rules say you have to be very specific in your answers." His low, tight voice was a soft caress over the back of her neck. "Or you could be penalized."

Unable to stop herself, Stevi lifted her head to look at him and laughed.

"I thought…" She hesitated and watched with wide eyes and her heart in her throat when he reached for her hand. His skin was warm on hers—as she figured it would be—and his hold firm, but gentle. "You're really gonna make me say this, aren't you?"

"Do you wanna be penalized?"

"Stop it." She dipped her chin to her chest and laughed to herself. "I thought you were going to kiss me. Before you walked me out…and…"

"And?" He arched his eyebrows impatiently as he waited for her to say more.

"I was shaking so much, I had to pull over a block away and sit for a minute."

"Because you wished I would have?"

"Maybe."

"Stevi." He hooked a finger under her chin when she tried to look away.

"I don't think this is a good idea, Duncan." Her whisper hung between them in the shadows. Even the whisper seemed clandestine and dangerous.

"I wanted to kiss you," he admitted. She felt her heart, her lungs, everything inside melt at his words.

"Then why didn't you?"

"Still do."

His eyes dropped to her parted lips, but Stevi pressed them together when she felt the heat in his gaze.

"What if someone's watching us?" This time, her words were ragged with nerves and need.

Duncan shrugged. "We're not doing anything wrong."

Her arms still resting on the bar, Stevi tipped her head as he leaned closer to her. His fingers moved slightly on her hand; the friction of his skin on hers sending shivers up her arm and her neck. From the corner of her eye—because her gaze was locked with his, and she couldn't, wouldn't look away— she saw his other hand drop to rest on the back of her barstool.

His gray eyes held hers as he leaned in, closer still. Stevi parted her lips as he touched them with his. The soft, simple touch took her breath away, and embarrassed to be so hungry for him, she tried to shy away. Duncan, hands still where they had been just a moment ago, drew back just enough to kiss her again. Still the same soft touch of skin. Stevi's heart pounded up her throat and in her mouth and her lips, and this time, Duncan moved his mouth slowly over hers. Just a whisper of a kiss, his warm lips on the corner of hers.

Stevi's toes tingled, and her heart still beat in her throat and her ears. She wondered if Duncan could feel her ragged breathing, wished she could catch a deep breath because she wanted to draw his scent inside herself. She balled the fingers of her free hand into a fist, because she ached to touch him. To smooth her hand up over the bulge of muscle that disappeared under his shirtsleeve, to test the feel of his skin on her fingertips.

Duncan teased her again with his lips, warm over hers. He seemed happy to linger there, to press chaste kisses over her parted lips, but Stevi wanted to grab him and sink into him.

"Stevi." He said her name against her lips, and she heard his desire in the jagged edges of his voice. She wanted to scoot off the barstool and press herself against his heat. Rest her head on his chest and hear his heartbeat. The thought of his nimble fingers unbuttoning and parting her blouse, of his rough skin sliding over hers made her moan softly, and the sound of her own moaning in the empty bar was so sensual, she wanted to twist around on the stool and wrap her legs around his waist.

And yet, there was something so sweet and still so sexy in the way they were standing. Close enough to touch, but with enough space between them to make her desperate for him to move. The air around them crackled with electric awareness, but only their hands and their lips touched.

She mewled in protest when he started to pull away, but he only came back to her lips again to graze. Stevi gritted her teeth to hold herself together when he nibbled on her lower lip.

"Duncan."

He nipped at her, closing his teeth on her lip and then Stevi gasped with delight when he rubbed his tongue over the same spot to soothe her skin. The warm, velvety softness pressed against her sensitive skin made her want the same sort of kiss on other sensitive skin. Her eyes slid closed as he stroked her lip with the flat of his tongue; Stevi shivered with pleasure. Pulse hammering in her fingertips, she wondered what it would feel like for his lips to hover over her inner wrists and her neck and her breasts.

She sucked in another quick breath when he flicked the center of her top lip with the tip of his tongue. Playful now, rather than healing, she simmered at his touch. Desperate for the intimacy, she finally kissed him back. She licked his tongue; his low, guttural growl kindled the simmer deep in her belly to full throttle flames.

Still, though, he held her hand; his other rested on the back of her chair. Stevi's chest was tight with pressure and excitement and the need to breathe. Their tongues danced and slid and stroked. Stevi was vaguely aware of Howie Day's song "Collide" playing around them, and she thought it was kind of fitting, and then Duncan's lips were on hers again, and he swept his tongue inside her mouth. The fire inside her roared to life. The taste of bourbon and Duncan filled her, and she clenched her fist again.

"Why didn't I kiss you last night?" he whispered. He drew away from her, but rather than let go of her hand or walk away, he pressed his lips to her cheek and then rubbed his face against hers.

She breathed deeply, this time just to settle the nerves that burned inside her. Sure, she wondered why he hadn't kissed her last night after the way he had looked at her. She wondered why he had stopped now. She wondered what was next, and the hell of it was she didn't know what she *wanted* to happen next.

Her chest rose and fell with each desperate breath; her nipples were hard, ready for his lips, his tongue. Her stomach clenched with each breath, and other parts clenched with desire for him.

But her heart was afraid to say yes. Because Duncan Marks was a five-alarm fire, and playing with him would burn her before it was over. The scars he left her with would certainly be an issue. For the Queen. The family.

"Why didn't I kiss you that night in St. Louis?" His ragged whisper drew a shiver up from the base of her spine.

Reminded of that night, of what Leah had asked her this morning, Stevi ducked her head.

"Are you okay?" He squeezed her hand, and then loosened his grip to trace his fingers up over her arm and to cup the back of her neck. Somehow that touch felt more intimate than the French kissing they'd just done moments ago.

"Yeah." She nodded. Swallowed hard. And lifted her head to look him in the eye. Protecting her heart had to start right here. If he wanted to play, she had to be worthy of the game. Getting wrapped up in what she might feel for him or what it might do to their family if things went wrong would automatically disqualify her. "Yeah. I'm good."

He tipped his head and arched his eyebrows. "Is there more?'

Stevi's mouth suddenly dry, she cleared her throat.

"More?"

Did he mean tonight? Did he want to go up to the couch in the office and make out like kids? Have sex? Now?

Duncan lifted a shoulder and offered her a lazy smile.

"If I walk you out now, is this it?"

She licked her lips and lowered her gaze. "No."

"Because if tonight is all you want with me, I'm going to need to kiss you again before you go."

CHAPTER 7

STEVI HADN'T SLEPT MUCH, AND THE FACT THAT SHE TOSSED and turned more because Duncan had left her shortchanged and not because she was still upset with Leah hit her square in the face the next morning when she walked into the office and found Leah at the desk. Guilt added to the unrequited desire-hangover was so unpleasant that she turned on her heel to walk out before Leah could say anything.

"Stevi." Leah's whine followed her out to the hall. Stevi stopped walking, but she hesitated before she turned to go back into the office. She sipped from the iced coffee she had picked up on the way here, kept her eyes on the floor as she tiptoed into the room. Even on her tiptoes, the wooden floor squeaked, and the sound was loud and awkward in the otherwise quiet room.

From the corner of her eye, she saw Leah pick up her mug and take a sip. A high-risk pregnancy had made Leah switch from the strong, black brew she preferred to some kind of decaffeinated tea. Stevi saw her sister shudder at the taste; if she weren't angry with Leah, she would laugh at her, *with her* about it. For Leah, giving up her take-no-prisoners coffee had been a sad side effect of being pregnant.

"Are you ever going to talk to me again?" Leah finally broke the silence. Stevi stood at the window that overlooked the Mississippi. July in the Midwest was unforgiving; the humidity alone was unbearable. Today was no different. The morning had started out at 93 glorious degrees. Stevi's cotton blouse was stuck to the skin between her shoulder blades before she got settled in her car to hit the drive-thru for coffee and get to work.

Now, she focused on the dying grass in the riverfront park. Lifted her gaze to the river beyond, the bridge that spanned the Mississippi. Wondered if Duncan had slept last night.

"I dunno," she mumbled finally when Leah sighed impatiently.

"Stevi—"

"Just don't." Stevi shook her head. "Please?"

"But—"

Leah stopped talking when Stevi shot her a look over her shoulder.

"Where's Trace?"

"He went to Pake's Market for fresh produce." Leah rolled the chair closer to the desk and plunked her elbows down. "You didn't even clear your browser history."

"What?" Stevi turned and lowered herself to sit in the window seat. She curled her leg under her, aware that Leah was sweating bullets watching her. They were three stories up, and it made Leah queasy when she sat here, as if Stevi was going to throw herself through the glass and take a nosedive to the pavement.

"You wanna move out?"

Stevi chewed on her straw. Considered how to answer the question.

"I dunno."

"Because of what I said yesterday?" Leah's voice jumped an octave in surprise. "Really?"

Stevi leaned back on the wall, saw the color leach out of her sister's face.

"Don't you guys need privacy?"

Leah opened her mouth to answer her, but she hesitated.

"Why would you ask me that? Does it bother you that Trace and I are sleeping together upstairs?"

Stevi shrugged. It didn't. Not even on the occasions when she heard them making love—which didn't happen that often, considering the hours she kept with the bar and her nights out—or when she found them whispering and hugging and kissing in the kitchen over coffee or in the hallway between the bathroom and the spare room that led to the staircase to their attic room.

Still. If Leah and Trace were having a baby, Stevi assumed there would be a wedding on the calendar soon. If they were getting married, then their little family certainly deserved its own space. Honestly, she hated the thought of leaving. She loved the house; she loved her sister, and she loved Trace. But she felt kind of pathetic, a little too student-like to be living there with them now. They were starting a family; she was twenty-eight years old. Definitely time to stand on her own two feet.

"It's just time, Leah." She shrugged. Sighed, too tired to have this argument. Too tied up in thoughts of what had happened last night with Duncan. What *hadn't* happened and what she wanted to happen. Never mind that those sorts of desires were what her sister judged her for.

"Look, I'm sorry, Stevi." Leah pushed her hair off her face and then plopped her chin in her hand and stared at Stevi with big eyes. "I didn't mean anything by what I asked. I like the idea of you and—"

"Don't." Stevi shook her head as Margo appeared in the doorway.

"What? I mean, I see you guys—"

"Leah." Stevi bit her lip. Margo blinked at Stevi and then turned to look at Leah as she traipsed across the room.

"What's going on?" She arched her eyebrows as she lowered herself to perch on the edge of the couch. "Big powwow?"

"Nothing," Stevi answered. She jumped on the question before Leah could answer Margo, but she was proud of herself for not sounding wheedling and desperate.

"Stevi, if you're attracted—"

"I'm not." Stevi cleared her throat, frustrated that Leah wouldn't let it go, especially now that Margo had joined them. Yes, they were all close; if Stevi were attracted to someone else, she would tell them both in a heartbeat. But this was different. Duncan was Margo's stepbrother, and the possibility of anything happening between herself and

Duncan had possible side effects that could hurt all of them. Including the Queen.

"Wow." Margo sighed. "You guys are keeping secrets from me again."

"Again?" Stevi frowned and tipped her head to study Margo.

"Well, I was the last to know about the babies," Margo reminded them.

"Nope, that was Trace," Stevi corrected her.

"Stevi wants to move out," Leah mumbled.

"Why?" Margo flopped backwards and closed her eyes.

"Because I pissed her off." Leah scooted her chair back as Margo opened her eyes and eyeballed Stevi.

"It's not because you pissed me off." Stevi sighed and rolled her eyes. "I just feel like it's time for me to get out. I'm too old to be mooching off you, and you have a new family. Trace probably—"

"First?" Leah climbed to her feet and slipped around to the front of the desk. "We're roommates. We're in it together. I've never put a dime more into that house than you have. We've done everything equally from the beginning, so don't give me that line. Second, you're part of my family. And Trace loves you—"

"Yep, okay." Stevi shook her head. Her heart slammed in her chest when she noticed Duncan peek his head in the doorway. He glanced from Leah to Margo, and then Stevi held her breath when their eyes met. "Kumbaya. We're all good. I still think it's time."

"Move in with me," Margo suggested.

"Trace back yet?" Duncan asked. His voice trailed over Stevi's skin like a warm whisper. As hot as it was outside—her blouse was still a little damp with sweat—Stevi was chilled now, and the warmth in Duncan's voice chased a shiver down her spine.

"No." Leah shook her head. Stevi turned away from the conversation and studied the view out the window again. Had he thought about it? The kiss? Had it kept him awake last night? Thinking about what her lips and her tongue tasted like? Stevi had closed her eyes a hundred times and opened them a hundred more. She'd relived the kiss, thankful that he had taken it slow. Not because she was afraid—of course, there were first kiss butterflies in her belly when Duncan leaned in and touched her mouth with his— but because it had given her time to really sink into him and feel the kiss. To feel the texture of his lips, the pressure he applied when he pressed them to hers. She had reveled in the slide of his tongue over hers, and even then, even when he cupped the back of her neck in his hand, she had felt her body awaken.

Stevi was a serial dater, but after several disastrous experiences when she was younger, she wasn't terribly interested in sex. It wasn't that she couldn't enjoy it, but it had always been too much trouble. Now, after the past few months of flirting with Duncan, after the kiss last night, she wondered if maybe she had been sleeping with the wrong guys, as Duncan mentioned the other night.

Then again, maybe sex with Duncan wouldn't be any more exciting than any other experience for her, and if that was the case, if they slept together and then decided it was a mistake, where would that leave them? She loved Duncan as a friend, as family. And the last thing she wanted to do was tear down this business she and her sister and cousin had put their hearts, souls, and bank accounts into.

"Was he going to Pake's?"

"Yeah."

Stevi glanced over her shoulder at Leah, half expecting to catch her trying to use the force to propel Duncan into the room to stand by her. She sagged in relief when she saw him nod and then disappear.

"So." Margo's deep breath drew Stevi's attention. She twisted around to face them now that Duncan was gone. "That's how this is gonna go, huh?"

"How what's gonna go?" Stevi asked quietly.

"Suddenly, now that we're adults, you're going to keep secrets from me."

"Oh my God," Stevi groaned. "There are no secrets. Leah is delusional. Maybe it's because she's happy now with Mr. Right, so she thinks we all need to feel the same way. But there's—"

"I just asked her if she and Duncan slept together when they went to the tradeshow."

Stevi ducked her head, certain her cheeks were on fire.

"And?" Margo sounded unimpressed. "Duncan said you shared a bed, because you hadn't planned to go, and he only had one bed."

Slowly, Stevi lifted her chin. Eyes on Margo, she gave in with a small, tight nod.

"He also said nothing happened."

"Nothing happened," Stevi repeated.

"Then why are you so mad at me?" Leah tossed her hands up in defeat. A drop of tea splashed over the rim of her cup. She sighed with irritation and rubbed the wet spot on her blouse.

"I don't sleep with every guy I go out with, Leah," Stevi said quietly. "I guess it just sucks that you would think that of me."

"What—? That—? I didn't say that. I didn't say anything remotely—"

"Stevi!" Margo called as Stevi stalked back across the office. She hurried down the hall to the break room, tossed the remnants of her iced coffee in the garbage, and then headed down to the main floor, aware that she was running from Leah and Margo and probably most likely running right to Duncan.

CHAPTER 8

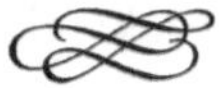

DUNCAN WONDERED WHAT WAS GOING ON IN THE OFFICE, BUT he sure as hell had no intention of sticking around to find out. As badly as he wondered what the girls were talking about, he didn't even linger in the hall or the break room, hoping to overhear something. Didn't plan to nose around and ask Margo, either.

He was too old for games. Well, he didn't mind playing games with Stevi, at least not the kind that involved stepping outside their comfort zone and taking a chance. Kissing her. He'd play any damned game in the world—even Chutes and Ladders—if it meant kissing Stevi Hague again.

But he was too old for the whole what did she say about me game. Hell yes, he was dying to know what Stevi was thinking. If she had told Leah and Margo about the kiss last night—he didn't care if she did, but he doubted that she would have—and if she had, what words she might have used to describe it.

He had gone to bed with a hard-on for Stevi, done his best to ignore it, to wish it away—spent some time thinking about scrubbing the kitchen at the Queen and cleaning up the men's bathroom last weekend—but when that had proved to be impossible, he had given in. He hadn't needed porn. Hadn't needed to think about Stevi, nude and waiting for him in bed. Just the memory of her tongue rubbing against his and a few tugs on his dick and he had come hard and fast.

In the shower this morning before he returned to the Queen, rather than go for round two, he hung his head and hurried through the motions, soaping first his hair and then his body. Guilt trumped the desire—for God's sake, Stevi was his friend, he loved her like a little sister—and combined with the cold shower, managed to keep his dick under control.

Except he didn't. Love her like a little sister. Maybe he was supposed to. Maybe that's how she thought of him—like a big brother—but somewhere along the way, Duncan's feelings for Stevi had grown a lot more complicated and a lot more X-rated.

He wondered if she had given him a second thought. Had she relived their kiss about a hundred times? Like he had? Or had she passed it off as a challenge, just a dare that was part of the new bar dice game he had suggested? Surely, she knew he had brought the dice and shared his game just as way to get closer to her. Stevi was too smart not to see that.

With Trace gone and the girls holed up in the office talking about who knows what, Duncan headed down to the cellar. He needed to restock the more popular bottled beer behind the bar. Tonight would be busy, and while Trace would be around, and Tania worked also, Duncan always liked to have the bar stocked and ready to go before every shift started.

The cellar was cool and damp. Duncan stood at the bottom of the wooden steps for a moment. He drew in a deep breath and thought again about Stevi. Would she stick around tonight? After close? Would she want to talk? Play dice? Or would she make an excuse to leave?

Or worse. What if she had a date? Duncan hated it when she didn't come in to work. She was entitled to time off, just the same as the rest of them. But he hated knowing she was out with other guys. Just the thought of her laughing, talking to someone else the way she did with him made him see red. Hated watching her leave the Queen for a date, too. Somehow that was even worse. Seeing her all dolled up, heading out for a night of fun—whether that meant going bowling or some stud like Grant Deavers touching her in all the right places and making her scream in ecstasy after hanging with him all evening—made Duncan want to punch something.

Check that. He didn't think Stevi was a screamer. The memory of that soft moan last night when he had kissed her made him groan out loud. His dick kicked to life again, too, which was not a good thing here at work. In broad daylight. When all hands were on deck, and it wasn't just him and Stevi.

Time to get to work. He eyed the wine racks behind him for a moment. Just recently, he and Trace had started working to organize the stock down here. Duncan had shared his idea for building new shelving, racks for the wine and shelving for the beer and other liquor. Country music sensation that he was, Trace had jumped in to help, no questions asked. Duncan had to admit he couldn't have handpicked anyone better for Leah.

He had worried at first. Not about Leah. There had never been a question that Trace was in love with her; no, Duncan worried about how Leah being in love would affect the dynamics of their group. How it would change the bar scene. He never once thought Leah would walk away from the Queen or shy away from the work to be done. But if he were being honest, he would admit, he had worried that having Trace around would change the dynamics of the friendship the four of them shared.

Sure, Margo had been involved before. Involved enough to get pregnant. But not involved enough to be in love and let an outsider into their circle. Then again, apparently he was wrong about that. Stevi had said something about Margo being in love with Jess, so maybe Margo didn't tell him everything.

Which kind of sucked ass, since Duncan had mulled over telling Margo that he was having really inappropriate feelings for Stevi. In fact, he had mentioned once or twice—in passing—that he thought Stevi was pretty, that he hated the way she flounced her ass around the guys in the bar…she didn't, but every damned guy in this bar except Trace Dixon eyed her ass anytime she walked by.

Kind of made him feel like a chump if he was considering talking about this *thing* he felt for Stevi with Margo, but she wasn't being honest with him.

He moseyed deeper into the cellar, toward the bottled beer. Reached to grab a case of longnecks and hesitated when he heard footsteps on the old wooden stairs. He pulled the case off the shoulder-high shelf and lowered it to the ground. Wondered who had come downstairs. The footfalls had been too soft for it to be Trace, had to be one of the girls. He would rather not see Leah climbing up and down the cellar stairs, but that didn't mean Leah wouldn't do it.

He hefted another case from the shelf to the floor and waited, but no one hollered or joined him. They had joked when they first moved in and opened the doors that the cellar was prime territory for ghosts. Duncan didn't believe in ghosts, but he *was* still kind of curious about what Stevi was thinking.

What if Margo had come down here? Forgetting that he didn't want to play games, because hell yes, he was dying to know what the tension had been about earlier in the office, Duncan stepped around the boxes stacked now on the floor and looked toward the steps. When he didn't see anyone, he headed over to the other side of the cellar, where they kept dry goods for the kitchen, decorative items they rotated upstairs, and anything needed for special events. Convinced for some reason that it was Margo, he searched for her, assuming he would know what he wanted to say or ask when he saw her.

"Margo?"

He heard movement back under the steps, so he followed the sounds. His lips were already moving around the words—*what's going on*—when he saw Stevi squatted down in front of the cabinet where they stored table centerpieces.

"What's—?"

"Hey." Stevi looked up at him and flashed him the same ornery grin she always did. A wave of relief rolled over him, but it was gone just as quickly as the grin on Stevi's face. Graceful and lithe, she straightened to stand in front of him, a glass jar in hand.

"Hi."

"Were you down here? When I came down?"

"Yeah. Stocking the bar."

She nodded. "Margo has the Wiegand baby shower tomorrow. I was thinking about using these mason jars—" She stopped talking.

Duncan stood where he was, but he watched her closely. Saw the color creep into her cheeks. Noticed the cords of her neck flair when she swallowed. Damned near flinched in pain when she darted her tongue out and flicked it over her lips. She was nervous; he knew her well enough to read her. But damned if her tongue on her lips didn't grab him by the balls.

He had been fully prepared to march over and say something to his stepsister. Now that he was on this side of the cellar only to find Stevi and not Margo, he had no idea what he had planned to say. But this was the first moment he and Stevi had alone today, and he wanted to ask if she was okay. He wanted to know if she had slept. If kissing him set her on fire.

If she regretted it.

God help him if she regretted that kiss.

Because he wanted to do it again. He wanted to slide his fingers into her hair and settle his lips over hers and plunge his tongue inside her mouth. He wanted to taste every inch of her lips and her tongue, and he wanted to do something to make her feel so good she would cut loose with that soft, little moan again.

"Are you okay?" His voice was gruff, and his dick decided to wake up, and Duncan prayed she wouldn't lower her gaze and notice his erection. He wasn't sure what she was thinking about any of this. For all he knew, she was simply playing Bar Dice, and his dick wasn't welcome in the game. He didn't want to overstep the boundaries, and he sure as hell didn't want to offend her.

"Yeah." She nodded. But the color in her cheeks deepened to a brighter red.

"Things seemed pretty tense upstairs." He arched his eyebrows, determined to proceed cautiously. As much as he wanted this woman, as badly as he wanted to bury himself between her thighs and feel her fingernails scrape over his back as he pumped his hips over hers, he cared about her. And if she wasn't interested, he was going to have to figure out what to do with all of these feelings. Because he sure as hell had no intention of hurting her or losing her friendship.

Stevi's shoulders tensed when he stepped closer to her. She swallowed again and parted her lips to say something, but she apparently changed her mind. With a shrug, she lowered her gaze to his shoulders.

"It's fine."

"You're still mad at Leah."

"It's fine, Duncan," she repeated.

"What did she say?"

Stevi looked down at the jar in her hands. Duncan let his eyes roam over the top of her head. He noticed the frown, looked at her fingers on the jar.

"I was thinking of filling these with pastel candies." She cleared her throat. "The girl said something about doing a gender reveal, so I was thinking—"

"Stevi."

Gently, he pried the jar from her hands and set it on a shelf back inside the cabinet. Stevi huffed out a quick, shaky breath when he reached for her. Duncan wondered again if he was pushing something she simply wasn't interested in. Obviously, this was new for the two of them, but didn't he know just a little something about women? Didn't it mean she was attracted to him? If she flirted with ease and then got nervous when it was just the two of them alone?

"It's not after hours," she reminded him in a hoarse whisper.

"They're all upstairs."

Careful to keep a small space between them, still unsure Stevi wanted to be yanked up against his hard-on, Duncan framed her face in his hands.

"Kiss me." As if to prove her point, to show him that she did want him to kiss her, she pushed up on her tiptoes and leaned into him. Duncan had a moment to think about her breasts pushed up against his chest, to remember the v of skin she showed when she leaned over at the bar, the curve of her breast under the lace, and then her lips touched his, and he was a goner.

It was the same soft kiss from last night, as if they had never stopped. The only difference now was that she was standing, which meant her small curves were touching him, and heat radiated from her body, and her lips tasted sweet and exotic with a touch of coffee and coconut.

When Stevi parted her lips, Duncan wasted no time. He swept his tongue inside her mouth, stroking, taking everything she offered. She kissed him back, as hungry for the intimacy as he was, and when she broke the contact—to breathe—he plunged his fingers back through her hair and angled her face so he could kiss her cheek and her jaw, and finally, he nipped at the delicate skin under her ear.

"Duncan." Her breaths were soft and uneven as he dragged his teeth gently over her skin. Desperate to press against her —head to toe—desperate for a hell of a lot more than he could do right here, right now, Duncan backed her up a couple of steps until he eased her against the wall. Mindful of the old, cement blocks, he was careful not to jar her as he sought a new angle and pressed his open mouth to the hollow at the base of her neck.

"Ohhhh." She dragged out the soft moan and closed her fingers around his shirt. She was quick to let go and smooth her hands over his shoulders. Duncan wanted to hear it again, the soft, throaty moan that meant he'd found a good spot to play. He flicked her neck there with the tip of his tongue and then sucked her skin into his mouth.

"No, no, no." She laughed. "You can't mark me."

He smiled, his lips still pressed against her. He lowered one hand to her hip, the other still cradling the back of her head.

"I want to mark you, Stevi—"

Her soft chuckle turned him on just as sure as the rapid beat of her pulse on his tongue had a moment ago when he'd kissed her neck.

"I can't come down to the cellar and go back up with a hickey on my skin."

He pulled away to look at her. When their eyes met, they shared a small smile. Duncan stole another kiss before she could move.

"Duncan?"

He jumped when Leah's voice carried down the stairs. Stevi let her hand slide back over his shoulder, but she let it rest on his chest. He widened his eyes at her and tilted his head back so he wouldn't yell in her face.

"Yeah?"

"Is Stevi down there?"

He saw Stevi shake her head, but he reassured her with the stroke of his fingers over her lips.

"She's getting stuff for that baby shower tomorrow."

"Oh. Okay."

"What if she comes down here?" Stevi smacked at him, tried to push him away.

"Do you need her?" he called loudly so Leah would hear him.

"No. It can wait."

He turned his attention back to Stevi. "What happened with you guys? What did she say?"

"She asked me if you and I slept together that night we were at the trade show."

Shocked that something so simple had obviously made Stevi so angry, Duncan stared at her silently.

"Duncan?"

This time when they heard Leah's voice, Duncan leaned in to drop a quick peck on Stevi's lips, and then because the kisses —backing her up against the wall and licking the smooth, creamy skin of her neck—weren't enough, he brushed a kiss over her cheek and backed away.

Apparently, Stevi didn't want anyone to know they were playing around.

Frustrated—with Stevi for wanting something simple and fun and with himself for wanting more—Duncan buttoned his lips and moved quietly back to the other side of the cellar. He prayed he wouldn't run into Leah on the way over there, because he wasn't sure what might come out of his mouth.

CHAPTER 9

STEVI SET TWO PINT GLASSES ON THE TALL TABLE, FLASHED THE guys there a big smile, and then slipped on to the next table to check on the rowdy crowd there. From the corner of her eye, she could see Duncan pulling a beer, in conversation with a couple at the bar. They had stayed busy earlier, after the kissing in the cellar, and since the Queen had opened and patrons had started filling the tables, she and Duncan had danced a few steps around each other behind the bar. No time for anything else—like heart-to-heart talks or true confessions—which Stevi decided might be a good thing.

He was friendly and flirty as ever, and relieved, Stevi was ready to throw herself back into the regular routine, too. She had eased back into bumping into him on purpose, offering the snarky smile she knew he liked, and looking to him to make eye contact so they could communicate without a word. Sort of the way Leah and Trace did, Stevi realized now.

Still, try as she did, something seemed just a bit off between them. She wanted to ask him if they were okay, but then she figured the more she lingered over it, the more childish it was and the more immature she appeared. Bottom line, they were adults. Unattached, consenting adults, so technically, there was nothing to worry about.

Maybe they could talk later, if nothing else. Or play with the dice again. Stevi's knees went weak at the thought. Sure, it was more than a little pathetic that they were adults, and she was open to making out with him if it was part of a game. But the idea of having the bar to themselves tonight, the thought of Duncan's tongue dipping into her mouth again and stroking and curling around hers left her a little warm and breathless.

"You okay?" Margo asked as she slipped up to stand at the bar.

"Yeah. I'm good." She nodded. She leaned around Margo and caught Duncan's eye. "Can I have a beer?"

Duncan nodded and moved to grab it, all the while swinging his eyes down the bar to make sure everyone was happy. Stevi felt Margo's eyes on her as she watched Duncan plunge a hand into the cooler to snag a cold bottle for her. Her eyes ate up the hard knot of muscle beneath his shirtsleeve, the determined set of his jaw, the curve of his lips when he finally pulled a cold beer from the depths of the cooler. Those lips had devoured hers earlier, and they had nuzzled her neck and her ear and the hollow at the base of her neck, and Stevi wondered what would have happened if Leah hadn't hollered down the steps. Would Duncan have pushed her shirt away and nipped at her collarbone?

She shivered now at the thought. A wave of heat fanned over her at the thought of the firm pressure of his lips on her skin. The scrape of his teeth and the warmth of his tongue. Her knees still weak, now her thighs felt shaky, and the skin on her inner thighs tingled with awareness.

"Stevi?" Margo nudged her. Stevi averted her gaze when the rush of sexual heat turned to embarrassment. She huffed out a quick breath and flashed Margo a smile.

"Hmm?"

"Why are you fighting this?"

"Margo."

"Okay, why are you *denying* it?" Margo shrugged. "God, I told you I've been dreaming about Jess. I told you he's calling me."

"I'm not denying anything," Stevi argued. "There's nothing to deny."

"Right." Margo nodded.

"I'm gonna…." Stevi sighed. "Take a few minutes? That okay? I'll be outside."

"Sure." Margo nodded her head in the direction of the back door. "But Leah's out there."

Stevi almost turned around. She could go upstairs for a few minutes and sit down on the couch. Put her feet up. But Margo would obviously see her, and she would tell Leah, and this whole ridiculous situation would just get even worse. Time to put an end to the speculation for once and for all. Sure that someone was watching her as she headed out the back of the bar, she pulled in a deep breath for courage. Took a long drink of the cold beer and wondered what the hell she was doing.

If she wanted sex that badly, she could call Grant Deavers. He was the only guy she went out with that she ever slept with, and even then, it didn't happen that often. She and Grant were friends. Somewhere along the way, they had started adding benefits. Grant was fun. He was good-looking. Had a nice body. Nice to look at, anyway. But he didn't do much with it, not as far as Stevi was concerned.

Pretty sad state of affairs if she had taken to faking orgasm with a friend just to get their nights over with.

The music out here on the patio seemed a bit louder and softer at the same time. Louder maybe because there wasn't a big buzz of conversation drowning it out, and softer because there were no walls holding it inside an enclosed area. Stevi carried her beer across the patio to the table where Leah sat. She had a glass of water at her right hand, her left rested on her belly.

Fleetwood Mac crooned as Stevi lowered herself into the chair across from Leah's. Her sister didn't even look at her. Stevi studied her face silently; it wasn't that long ago, Leah was terrified of the idea of being pregnant, of giving birth. Leah had been in the birthing room with their friends Kenzi and Joe when Kenzi was delivering their third baby. Kenzi had suffered a stroke that left her with aphasia and partially paralyzed. Kenzi's recovery had been a long, sometimes painful process, but Stevi reminded herself daily that she *was* recovering.

Stevi hadn't asked Leah lately how she was doing, how she felt about all of it. For all she knew, her big sister lived in constant terror of something like that happening to her.

"Do you still think about it?" Stevi finally asked. There were only two occupied tables out here, besides the one she now shared with Leah. Stevi spoke softly, though, and the other patrons were laughing loudly and carrying on conversations, so she doubted they could hear her.

Because she was watching her so closely, Stevi saw Leah's tiny flinch. She chewed on her lip for a moment and finally she shrugged and nodded at the same time.

"Do I still think about Kenzi?" Leah didn't look at Stevi. "Yes I don't think I'm ever gonna forget it, Stevi. Even if she eventually makes a full recovery, I don't know how I'll be able to look at her and not see that second of her life."

Stevi nodded. She smoothed her thumb over her bottle, watched the condensation disappear and come back immediately.

"But I don't know...that I'm as scared as I was."

"Really?" Stevi flicked her eyes up to meet Leah's, but they both looked away quickly.

"I'm scared. I know all kinds of things can go wrong," Leah continued. "Things have already gone really wrong."

"Leah—"

"But." Leah rubbed her hand over her belly and leaned her head back on the iron patio chair. She closed her eyes. "It feels different now. Since he knows. And we're doing it together."

A rare whip of jealousy got Stevi, shocking and painful like a bee sting. Her throat was tight with unwanted emotion, so when Leah did finally turn to really look at her, she could only nod. When she was a kid, she had assumed—probably as most young girls do—that she would eventually get married and have a kid or two, but since she'd grown up and found herself unimpressed with any of the guys she dated, any of the men she'd slept with, she had mostly given up the idea. She loved hanging out with her guy friends, but there wasn't one of them she felt anything beyond friendship for. And certainly none of them she would want to father a child.

Except maybe Duncan.

What the hell?

The thought had come from out of nowhere, and following so closely on the wild green envy she had felt moments ago for her sister and Trace, it was ridiculous and unwelcome, and Stevi squeezed her eyes closed and groaned out loud.

First of all, Duncan didn't want kids. He didn't want a family. He had never hinted to any of them that he wanted to settle down and get married. Duncan with a wife was as foreign to her as wine with a beer chaser. You didn't need both. One was enough. Duncan was enough.

"I'm sorry that you think…" Leah started, but her voice trailed off. "I'm sorry. I don't think that, and it's not why I asked."

Stevi swallowed hard and turned her head the other way. She took a drink of her beer and watched a newer model Camaro prowl down the street. Fleetwood Mac segued into Foreigner.

"Stevi."

"Can we just let it go?" she whispered.

"Does that mean you accept my apology?"

"Yes, but can we let it go?"

"You don't want to talk about Duncan."

"No. I don't."

"Do you remember what you said to me? When Trace and I first started spending time together?"

"No."

"You reminded me that you're my best friend. That I talk to you."

"Did you tell me? When you were pregnant?"

"We talked about it."

"But you didn't tell me."

"But we talked about it. We talked, Stevi. And I would've told you. You knew…"

"What? How could I not know? You looked seasick after the car drive that morning! I thought you were—"

"When I was ready…" Leah cleared her throat. "To be with him. You knew."

"Again. How could I not know? After all that time when you were saying you were just friends, I saw you kiss him here that night."

"And you don't think I know you that well?"

"You haven't seen me…" Stevi's anger lost some steam. She shrugged and fixed her gaze on the bottle in her hand. "It's not the same. Because it's not…the same."

"I think he's sexy."

"He's family, Leah."

"He might be family, Stevi, but he's not relation. There's nothing wrong—"

"I asked you if we could just drop it."

Stevi's eyes burned when she lifted her chin to look at Leah. Her sister wore an expression of shock, as if she was hurt to be shut down again, but she finally stirred to life and nodded.

"Sure."

"Thank you." Stevi stood, but before she could get away from the table, Leah reached for her hand.

"Stevi."

"What?"

"C'mere." Leah stood up. Stevi drew away from her when she reached for her hair.

"What are you doing?"

"You have…something in your hair."

"What?"

"Dust. Gravel?" Leah shrugged and shook her head.

Stevi sighed and decided she wasn't going to explain, even if Leah asked. When she didn't, Stevi wasn't sure if she should be relieved or suspicious.

"Why didn't you say something?"

"Just noticed it," Leah said quietly. "Look."

Stevi rolled her eyes and arched her eyebrows.

"If you…had feelings…for him." Leah pursed her lips. "I would be happy…for you."

"Great." Stevi nodded, deadpan. "If I decide I want to screw around with the hired help slash family member, I have your blessing."

She tugged at her hand to walk away from Leah, but Leah didn't let go.

"That's not what I said," Leah argued. "Stop twisting what I'm saying to make me out to be the bad guy."

"Maybe this will help you out." Stevi finally pulled away from Leah. "I have a date tomorrow night. With Grant."

Rather than appease Leah, Stevi thought she looked disappointed.

CHAPTER 10

DUNCAN FLIPPED THE LOCK ON THE DOOR JUST PAST MIDNIGHT. When he turned back to the bar, he found Leah and Trace pressed close together, slow dancing to some 70s song. Margo and Stevi were deep in conversation as they cleaned; Stevi bussed the tables at the front of the room and Margo worked from the back. He didn't know if he should be happy for the help, because yes, they had been slammed, and the clean-up and shut down would take a while tonight. Besides, they were a rowdy bunch, and it had been awhile since they had all hung out together after hours.

On the other hand, he was disappointed that he and Stevi weren't going to have any time alone tonight. He wasn't sure after the kiss in the cellar where any alone time might lead them, but he damned sure wanted to find out. He snuck a glance at her as he shuffled away from the door to head back over to the bar. She met his eyes and held the look for a moment. Again, Duncan wasn't sure what might have happened tonight, couldn't read any more in Stevi's face now than he had earlier, but he could tell from the pink in her cheeks and the soft sigh that escaped her lips that she was thinking about the kiss.

"I'm hungry," Leah announced. "Let's order pizza."

"You sure about that, darlin'?"

Duncan arched his eyebrows at Stevi before turning away from her. She lowered her gaze to the table between them, but her lips turned up in a tiny grin.

"Last time we had pizza, you had heartburn really bad."

"Nashville, the last time I ate I had heartburn really bad," Leah answered.

Duncan slipped back behind the bar and started stacking glasses.

"She's right," Margo agreed. "Plus, she's pregnant and hungry. Let's order pizza."

Duncan swung his gaze down the bar to Stevi. Her wide eyes staring back at him punched him in the gut and took his breath away. She wanted to be alone with him, too.

"Guys? What do you say?" Leah hollered. "Stevi, you want pizza?"

Stevi cleared her throat and dragged her eyes from his.

"Sure."

"Duncan?"

"Sounds good." He nodded. Turned his back to Stevi to carry the glasses to the kitchen.

"Okay, but nothing crazy," Trace suggested as Duncan left the big room. Once in the kitchen, he leaned over and gently set the glasses on the counter.

"So…"

He looked up as Stevi entered, several dirty glasses in her hands. She eased up beside him at the counter and set them down.

"Not how I hoped we were going to spend our time tonight," she said quietly.

"Really?"

She nodded. Duncan turned sideways at the counter and reached to stroke his fingers over the back of her hand. Stevi curled her own fingers into a fist and raised only her eyes to look at him.

"Could be fun," she said softly.

His tipped his head, curious if she meant hanging out with the whole group could be fun or if it could be fun if just the two of them were here again. Rather than ask, he stepped closer to her and leaned over to brush her lips with his.

"Duncan, we can't do this now." Her whisper slid over his lips, and he tasted it on his tongue: a little bit haunting and familiar, a lot of intrigue, and the beer she drank earlier. As a mixologist, Duncan was interested in new flavors. Stevi was his new favorite. Couldn't bottle that and sell it, and he wouldn't do it if he could. He wanted her to himself.

She didn't move, though, when he kissed her again. With this pass over her lips, he stroked the delicate skin with his tongue and was rewarded with that soft moan that made his heart thrum to life in every damned part of his body.

"I love it when you make that sound."

"I love the way you kiss me," she answered.

His heart already pounding—he wondered again if desire for this woman might drive him to an early grave—his dick throbbed to life in his jeans. Thankfully, he had a button up shirt on, tail untucked. Still. He wanted her to know what she did to him.

Before he could move, though, even just to rub his lips over hers again, they heard the clack of Margo's heeled sandals on the floor. Stevi moved quickly, turned back to the glasses on the counter, but she opened her hand and touched his fingers as she did so. Duncan stepped away from her, moved to the safety of the sink, and mentally recited the preamble to the constitution. Wasn't working. Stevi's breathy little moan and the fact that she loved the way he kissed her had his heart rate jacked up to the heart-attack-is-imminent zone, and his dick had popped a tent in his jeans.

"Hey. What do you guys want on the pizza?" Margo leaned her head in the open doorway, braced her arms on the frame.

"Don't care," Duncan answered through teeth clenched tightly together.

"You sure? You okay with green peppers?" Margo sounded doubtful.

"No, but I can pick 'em off," he reminded her. Hands clenched around the edge of the sink, Duncan glanced at Margo and smiled, even though at the moment, he wanted her to go home.

"Stevi?"

"Sure." Stevi shrugged and nodded, but she kept her eyes on the glasses she loaded into the dishwasher.

"Sure? On green peppers?"

"Yeah. Whatever, Margo, doesn't matter."

Margo hovered there in the doorway for a second. She finally moved her gaze from Stevi to Duncan. He stared back calmly, hoping he didn't look like a man desperate to get his hands on the woman at his sides. Margo arched an eyebrow in question, but Duncan kept his face impassive, and finally, she nodded and turned to walk away.

Stevi looked up when Margo was gone. He waited for her to look at him, but when she did, she skated her eyes over his face so quickly, he couldn't read her expression.

"Maybe it's a good thing," she said quietly, her eyes back on her task.

"Not being alone tonight?"

She nodded but said nothing.

"Why is that a good thing?"

Curious about what she would say—she wanted to explore whatever was going on between them just as much as he did, Duncan knew desire when he saw it, tasted it—he turned sideways again and propped his hip on the cabinet under the sink. The look Margo had given him had been enough to kill the wood, but even if it hadn't, he decided he wouldn't hide it from Stevi. She was interested; she knew he was interested. The question was why didn't she want anyone to know?

What if she was ashamed of what they were doing?

"Gives you more time to figure out the game plan for that second die." She tossed him a wink and the sassy grin he had come to love, and then she sashayed out of the kitchen and left him alone again with his dick. And this time he couldn't do a damned thing about the party in his pants.

STEVI BLINKED AT TRACE OVER THE TABLE. HOW IN THE HELL had she gotten herself into this? He put his left elbow on the table and held out his hand. Gave her a look that said *bring it,* topped it off with that damned grin. Stevi got why Leah loved him; the guy was so easy on the eyes, it actually hurt to look at him, and he had proved to have a heart made for loving Stevi's sister.

Didn't mean she wanted to arm wrestle him, though. Margo hooted at Stevi to get moving, to represent. Stevi rolled her eyes at Margo as she put her right elbow on the table.

"I'll make lasagna for you Sunday if you beat him," Leah offered.

Stevi flicked her eyes at Leah and laughed softly.

"I'll give you fifty bucks if you beat him." Margo continued cleaning up the paper plates and napkins from their late-night pizza party.

"What'll you give her if she beats him, Duncan?" Leah asked him. Stevi hesitated before looking at him, a bit afraid of what he might say. Duncan, elbows resting on the bar at his back, eyed her silently. When he finally arched his eyebrows and smiled, Stevi's stomach clenched in fear.

"I'll give her anything she wants," he said simply.

Stevi coughed and ducked her head to cover her mouth, all to hide the furious heat that flooded her face.

"But I might be too much for her," Duncan continued. That sounded like the usual comment he would make to her, so

Stevi grabbed on to the words and laughed the way she would have before he had kissed her the first time.

"You wish." She shook her head and looked around again at Leah and Margo. "Why? Are we doing this again? Why doesn't Leah just wrestle with you, Trace? Why me?"

"Leah already did," Margo reminded Stevi. "That's how she got pregnant. Remember?"

Stevi snorted and snatched her fingers back from Trace's open hand. "Yeah, I'm not crazy about the idea of getting pregnant."

"I don't know." Leah chuckled and stretched on the loveseat in the back corner of the bar. "I loved the getting there part."

Stevi met Trace's eyes, unable to look away. The blush only deepened when his lips tipped up in his trademark grin.

"You must be an animal." Margo bumped Trace as she walked by him, the pizza boxes in her hands.

Stevi glanced at Duncan as she slipped her hand inside Trace's. She felt a jolt of awareness, but not from the touch of Trace's skin. Duncan's stare was heated and intense. Stevi closed her fingers around Trace's hand, but her mind was on the feel of Duncan's fingers on the back of her neck last night.

"Can I use two hands?" She dragged her eyes back to Trace.

"That's the same thing Leah said."

Stevi snorted and dipped her head to cover her face again. Trace took advantage of the moment and pushed her hand easily to the table.

"That's cheating!" Margo yelped.

"Babe?" Leah yawned.

"Hmm?"

"That was cheating, but I'm exhausted. Are you ready?"

"Sorry, Stevi." Trace pushed his chair back and stood. He leaned over the table to drop a kiss on the top of Stevi's head. "My queen's ready."

Stevi grinned. "I'm exhausted, too. How about a rematch? When I haven't been drinking? And you have. And we'll tie you to a chair, and Leah can hold her hand over your mouth. Then maybe I can beat you."

"You're on." He moved to Leah's side and offered her a hand.

"I'm gonna follow you guys," Stevi decided. She glanced at her phone, not surprised to find that it was after three. "I'm ready for bed."

"Hey." Margo gave her a quick hug as she dug through her purse for her keys. "See you Monday. Have fun tomorrow night."

Stevi shrugged her eyebrows as she hugged Margo back. She wasn't excited about the date with Grant. She wouldn't be excited even if she hadn't been testing the waters with Duncan; she wasn't attracted to Grant. The night off sounded good, though.

Too bad she couldn't spend it with Duncan. Away from the bar. From the dice. She glanced at him. Wondered what he would be like if they went out somewhere together. If they didn't have the rules of their game to lean on and they didn't have work to do, how would they interact?

He had moved away from the bar, so he watched them from the door to the kitchen. Gave her a small, impersonal nod and turned away without a word. His dismissal made Stevi's heart hurt, and her belly plummeted, but she swallowed the emotions and managed a quick smile when she looked back at Margo.

"Hear from Jess lately?"

Margo folded her arms over her chest and shook her head sadly. "No. He wanted me to call him last weekend. When I did, he…sounded…distracted."

"Guys suck," Stevi mumbled.

"No, they don't." Margo shook her head. She pinned Stevi in place with a harsh look. "Not all of them. Sometimes there's a perfect guy right in front of us, and we trip over him trying to get to all the ones that do."

Stevi swallowed hard and pursed her lips.

"Are you talking about Jess?" She decided to play stupid and prayed Margo would play along with her.

"You know I'm not talking about Jess."

CHAPTER 11

Duncan tapped the hammer twice more over the shelf, though the nail head was good and buried in the lumber. He straightened, pulled the tail of his shirt up to wipe the sweat from his face, and then leaned to the side to set the hammer on the floor at his feet. He would like to swing it a bit harder. Maybe put the head of it on a piece of glass and watch it shatter. And kick something while he was at it.

He hadn't slept a wink last night. The events of the last two days and nights played out in his memory over and over, whether he tried to sleep or stared in the darkness at the ceiling above his bed. This was hell. Probably why love guru people counseled against messing around with good friends. Falling in love with friends.

His heartbeat stuttered a bit at the words. Nope. No, no, and hell no. He wasn't falling in love with Stevi Hague. He absolutely cared about her, loved her like a friend, and wanted to get his hands on her. He wanted to feel her thighs wrapped around his waist, around his head. He wanted to do every damned thing to every part of her hot little body, but no way did that mean he was in love with her.

Made things pretty damned complicated. Pretty hard to tell her he wanted to fuck her, but he wasn't interested in more. If things were already this messy, how the hell would he look her in the eye behind the bar the morning after if she let him in her pants? How the hell could he watch her walk out the door on anyone else's arm if he took her to bed?

He didn't want anything long term, nothing more than the friendship they'd always had, but he sure as hell didn't want to think about her with other men, either.

Frustration and denial still warring inside him, Duncan kicked the hammer and then cut loose with a string of curse words that might have blistered the girls' ears. He didn't love her, did he? Hell, he didn't know love from bourbon, but he did know this thing with Stevi was new. Not the wanting to get her alone and touch her in all of her secret spots to make her moan with pleasure. He'd wanted women before; maybe none with this blinding hot intensity, but he was no stranger to lust. But this primal possessive thing? Wanting to hunt down Stevi's friend Grant Deavers and sink his fist in his teeth? That was kind of new.

He wondered what their plans were for the night. After Stevi left last night, Duncan had managed to worm out of Margo who Stevi was seeing tonight. He had hoped he had played it cool and Margo wouldn't see right through him. She had eyed him closely when she answered, but she hadn't said anything about his clenched fists or the fact that he was sullen and hardly spoke a word the rest of the time they finished up in the kitchen and walked outside together.

Couldn't even consider Stevi putting her mouth on another guy. Damned sure that would kill him, he had come down to the cellar first thing this afternoon to work on the shelving units. The hell of it was it made him just as damned restless and on edge to think of her sitting at a dinner table, sharing a glass of wine and conversation with someone else.

"You're fucked, dude," he muttered, because even though he refused to believe he was in love, something in his gut told him he was falling too hard and too fast for a woman who didn't appear to want the same thing from him.

"What?"

He looked up when he heard Margo's voice. Their eyes met, and Duncan held his breath wondering how many of his thoughts he might have actually rambled on about out loud. And if he had mumbled something out loud, had Margo heard him?

"What's up?" He shook his head, hoping to deflect the question.

"Why are you fucked?" Margo stood in front of him. She folded her arms over her chest and tipped her head, waiting for him to answer her.

"Because I just jammed my toe on the stupid hammer," he said simply.

"Mmm." She nodded, but Duncan knew the mmmm meant she didn't believe him. He turned back to the shelving and thought about asking her if Trace was here yet. He could use a hand to raise the shelving unit to standing. Then again, he obviously needed the work out. An hour down here, give or take, hadn't worked Stevi out of his head. He would push harder and see if he could stop obsessing over her. Over what she and Grant Deavers were going to do tonight.

"Need something?"

"Just checking on you," she said quickly.

Duncan eyed her silently as he moved around to the other side of the shelf he'd just put together.

"I'm fine."

"Need help?" She moved to squat beside him and reached out to put her hands on the lumber.

"She didn't even—" He cut himself off before he could finish his sentence.

"What?" Margo looked at him with a small frown. "Is this gonna be heavy? Why don't you wait for Trace?"

He had been about to say that Stevi hadn't even bothered to tell him to his face that she had a date tonight. But apropos of nothing, it would certainly sound off the wall to Margo, and it would require an explanation.

"It's not that heavy," he mumbled.

"Okay, I'll help—"

"It's fine, Margo. I got it." He shook his head not only to dismiss her offer of help, but also just to let her know he wasn't in the mood for conversation.

"Remember when Berkley was born?"

Her voice had shrunk to barely more than a whisper, but the words themselves were so big. Duncan had started to lift the shelf, but he hesitated now and cut a sharp look at her.

"Of course I do," he answered. He was crazy about his niece, tyrant that she was.

"Push." Margo, half standing, half crouched there beside him, nodded at the shelf. The weight of the wood strained the muscles in his forearms. He looked away from Margo and back at the shelf, and then with her help, he pushed and leveraged it to stand on its own.

"Everybody wanted to hold Berkley. Everyone was in love with my baby."

Duncan, breathing heavy from the strain of that last push to stand the shelf upright, turned his head to look at her. Where the hell was she going with this? He gave her a cautious nod.

"Not you."

"What? Berk's my—"

"You came to see me," she interrupted him. "Because you were worried about me. And when I cried, you climbed in bed with me and held me."

Duncan sighed and nodded, but the memory made him uncomfortable. Crying females made him uncomfortable; didn't matter how much time he spent with Margo and Stevi and Leah. Tears made him want to fix everything, and damned if he could run around breaking noses or knees now. He was an adult, a businessman, as Stevi had pointed out the other night, and assault was frowned upon in the business world.

He broke the eye contact and looked back at the shelf. Only about seven or eight more to go, and they might get half of the room organized. With a deep, tired sigh—didn't bode well for the night, since they had most likely just opened the doors upstairs—he laid his hands on the shelf at shoulder height and looked around to figure out where to drag the unit.

"Are you trying to break it to me gently that you still have feelings for him?" He gave a tug on the wood in his hands, but the cement floor was uneven in spots and the shelf didn't budge. Duncan groaned and then dropped his hands to rub them over his jeans.

"No." Margo stared at him until the quiet dragged out long enough to be awkward. Duncan sighed and met her gaze.

"She didn't even tell me," he said quietly.

"Tell you what?"

"That she had a date tonight."

Margo stared at him silently, waiting for more of an explanation.

"I mean..." He shrugged. "Just. We've gotten...closer lately. And she didn't tell me she had a date."

"Define closer."

"No."

"Are you sleeping with her?"

"Margo." He groaned.

"Is that a yes?"

"No." He turned his back to his stepsister and paced away from her. "No, we aren't sleeping together."

"But you want to? You want to sleep with her?"

"This is Stevi we're talking about here," he reminded her.

"I know." Her voice was louder, as if she had moved to follow him, but Duncan refused to turn and acknowledge her.

"I just…" He shrugged and lifted his hands to scrub them over the top of his head. Hooked his fingers behind his neck. "I hate the thought of her out…with him."

"Duncan, if there's something going on between you, Stevi's not gonna…do anything…"

He pivoted on the ball of his foot and rolled his eyes at her.

"There's not."

"Coulda fooled me." Margo shrugged. "Something happened in the kitchen last night. Before I asked about the pizza."

"There's not enough between us to make her feel…loyal to me. She likes that guy. That Grant guy."

Margo pursed her lips, but she didn't answer him.

"I know she does. She's told me they're good friends, and I know they hook up."

This time, Margo flinched and looked away. The gesture hurt more than anything she could have said to deny it.

"That's great," he muttered. "I get to sit here all fucking night thinking about some dick with his hands on her."

"Maybe you should talk to her about how you feel."

Duncan dropped his hands. He stepped around Margo, anxious to move again. To swing the hammer and smash something. Pull the whole damned shelf across the room by himself and put it next to the last one he and Trace had put together.

"Duncan."

"It's too new, Margo," he said quietly as he put his hands on the shelf at shoulder height again. "It's too fucking new to go saying anything about anything. For all I know, she's playing me."

"Stevi's not like that."

"You don't know that part of Stevi," he reminded her.

"Look."

From the corner of his eye, he saw Margo wince when he gripped the wood and pulled again. The unit scooted about an inch; the bark of the wood sliding and catching on the cement echoed off the stone walls.

"What?" Arms still raised, hands on the shelf, Duncan ducked his head to wipe the sweat from his face on his shirtsleeve.

"Whatever is or isn't going on with you guys has her tied in knots." Margo took a step backwards. "So, no, I don't think she's playing you."

"Yep. So tied in knots, she's at home right now getting dolled up to go out with someone else. Maybe they'll hang out at a bar and watch a few innings of a ballgame on a big screen. And maybe she'll have her clothes off to ride him before the night's over. Whatever. I'm not doing this."

"Duncan."

He straightened and sucked in a long, sharp breath. "Shouldn't you be upstairs?"

It was an asshole thing to say, to push her away, and his voice was cool, and he regretted it the second the words left his mouth. But the look of shock on Margo's face, the way her mouth dropped open, like she was dumbfounded that he'd pushed her away drove it home. He was a dick. He and Stevi weren't even involved, and already, he was allowing the situation to make him treat the people he loved carelessly.

"Margs—"

"I'm sorry." She turned to walk away, mumbling something else that he didn't hear. Rather than call out to her, Duncan watched her go, the guilt over what he'd said to her and what he had said about Stevi making him clench his fists in anger.

CHAPTER 12

"ARE YOU KIDDING ME RIGHT NOW?" STEVI LAUGHED AND pushed Grant's hand away from her basket of fries.

"What?" Grant brushed her hand with his and then snagged a handful of fries. "You're not gonna eat them all anyway."

Stevi grinned and shrugged. He was right. This was their thing. Stevi wasn't one of those girly girls who ordered salads, ate two bites, and decided she was full. But no matter what she ordered, she could never eat everything, and Grant finished off what she couldn't.

It had also become their thing to end their dates at his place in his bed. Stevi hadn't been particularly thrilled with the habit for a few months now, but she had no interest tonight. While she and Grant had been friends for years, and she genuinely enjoyed his company, tonight she couldn't keep her mind off the Queen. More specifically, Duncan.

Like the feel of his fingers on the back of her neck. The brush of his lips over hers. The way her knees had gone weak and her heart had crashed painfully hard in her chest when he'd backed her up against the wall and tangled his fingers in her hair. Stevi couldn't remember the last time her body had reacted that way to a kiss.

Grant was pointing at the big screen on the wall across the bar and rattling about something, but Stevi wasn't listening. Her whole body was warm, and she figured her face was flushed just from thinking about Duncan's lips traveling down her neck to suck on the skin at the hollow of her throat. The way they'd laughed together when she stopped him.

She swallowed hard now, aware that Grant was watching her expectantly. Busted, she could only arch her eyebrows and roll her lips inward.

"Stevi Hague." Grant tipped his head and offered her a knowing smile. "That's the fourth time you've zoned out on me tonight."

Embarrassed to be caught, Stevi fought off a stick of guilt. She shouldn't be on a date with Grant and thinking about someone else. They had both agreed last summer when they added benefits to their friendship that either of them could put things on hold indefinitely for any reason, no questions asked. And Grant had pressed pause once around Christmas because an ex-girlfriend had been in town for the holidays. Stevi shouldn't feel guilty for invoking the hold clause, but she did.

How many times had she wondered if there was something wrong with her that she wasn't seriously attracted to Grant? Or anyone for that matter? She hadn't met anyone who made her mouth water and her body clench with desire or need.

Until suddenly, Duncan Marks—practically her cousin, close enough to be a brother—had the power to turn her on and leave her desperate for more. She had thought about him—inappropriately, she thought—for a long time now, and Duncan seemed to sense it, and he had decided he was up for some fun. He started flirting back. Now after a few stolen kisses, he had her craving his touch. A night in his bed.

"I'm sorry," she whispered. She avoided Grant's eyes as she picked up her draft beer and drained the glass.

"It's okay." He nudged her arm with his elbow. He grinned and shrugged. "You know that."

"I know." She nodded. Even though they had been honest about their expectations up front, she still felt a little guilty for sitting here with Grant and thinking about someone else.

"Who is it?"

She shook her head. No way she was ready to share anything, especially Duncan's name.

"Too soon?"

She huffed out a deep breath, rested her elbow on the table, and propped her chin in her hand.

"Maybe." She stared at Grant for a moment. Considered telling him about Duncan. Grant and Duncan weren't friends, by any shape of the imagination. But Grant knew who Duncan was. And Grant was a guy. Might be helpful to get a guy's thoughts on the situation.

"The wheels are turning." Grant nudged her again with his elbow.

She laughed softly and shook her head. "I just…don't know… what I'm doing. With him. I'm kind of scared."

"Stevi Hague," Grant leaned closer to her and kissed her cheek, "you do know what you're doing. You're good in bed, and you know it."

Honestly amused, Stevi threw her head back and laughed out loud.

"No, I don't," she mumbled. "And that's not what I mean, anyway."

"You think I don't know that you fake it with me?" Grant arched his eyebrows. "I hate that. I come undone with one touch, and I can't get the job done for you anymore."

Stevi started to answer him, but instead she shook her head. Reached for her beer, only to remember she had finished it already.

"I'm sorry." She lowered her gaze to the table, embarrassed to be called out. Ready to be back at home. Alone. Maybe with a pint of ice cream and Netflix. Maybe with another beer.

"You like this guy?"

"I do."

"So what's the hold up? Does he not know what you feel for him?"

"We've..." She licked her lips and shrugged. "He's a good friend. And if things don't work out between us, we could hurt a lot of people."

"Holy fuck." Grant sighed. "You're talking about Duncan Marks."

Stevi blinked at him.

"You finally figured it out, huh?"

"Figured what out?"

Desperate for a drink, Stevi reached for Grant's beer. He gave her the evil eye when she took a healthy drink, but his smile took the edge off.

"That guy's been hot for you for a long damned time."

"Whatever."

"Stevi, anytime I'm in the bar, I worry about him coming after me. I think he'd like to cut my dick off, so I can't get it inside you."

"I don't know what he wants," she whispered. "I don't know what I want. I just know we have the potential to hurt our families. And to hurt the business."

Grant nodded his head as if to confirm what she said. Stevi watched him look around the bar and then swing his gaze back to her. He picked up his glass, held it for a moment, and then finally took a drink.

"And what if you have the potential to be really happy with him?"

Surprised by his words, Stevi drew in a deep breath and considered it. Something intimate and possibly long lasting with Duncan.

"I don't know if I have the guts to do it."

"So you haven't slept with him?"

"No."

"Stevi, you owe it to yourself to see if there's something there. The guy is crazy about you."

"What if he's hard up? And he thinks I'm easy? God knows, I've probably been out with every single guy in Adam's Bay. What if he thinks I end every date on my back, and he wants a piece of the action?"

"If that's the case, I think I'd knock his teeth down his throat," Grant said simply. "But I don't think that's what he thinks, Stevi. No one thinks that about you. You're like everyone's best friend. Or sister or something."

"Well, I'm not like your sister," she reminded him.

Grant laughed softly. "Do you think I feel that way? That I heard rumors about you and wanted in on the action?"

Stevi turned her head away from Grant's heavy stare. She shook her head, but she didn't say anything.

"Stevi?"

She was tempted not to answer him, but the silence between them felt awkward. She didn't particularly want to sleep with him anymore, but she did like Grant, and she didn't want to lose their friendship.

"Not in the beginning, Grant," she mumbled.

"So, you're telling me you don't like what we're doing?" He covered her hand with his. Rather than look him in the eyes, Stevi stared at their hands.

"I did. But." She swallowed hard. "I think I want more. My sister's madly in love with the best guy in the world. And they're having a baby. And Trace acts like Leah walks on water, and she acts like he's the only man who exists, and oh my god. I'm saying this. I'm saying this to you. What the hell is wrong with me?"

Stevi dropped her chin to her chest and buried her face in her hands.

"I'm sorry."

"So. What? You tell me you don't want to sleep with me anymore, and now you can't talk to me, either?"

"I don't know what's wrong with me, Grant." Her words were muffled behind her hands. "I don't get this, but it's not your problem. You're a great guy. I shouldn't be wasting your time—"

"Hey."

With gentle fingers, Grant pried Stevi's hands from her face.

"You're not wasting my time. Talk to me. Let's figure this out."

"I can't figure anything out. I don't know if I'm fixated on… on love and babies because of Leah. I don't know if my biological clock is ticking suddenly. I don't know if I'm just jealous. I don't know if I'm in love with—" She stopped talking. Lightheaded now, she closed her eyes and shook her head.

"You're in love with him?"

"No." She rubbed the skin under her eyes and then tucked her hair behind her ears. "No. I just…feel…a connection to him. That I'm not sure I've ever felt. And with all this other stuff…"

"You're attracted to him."

She flicked her gaze to Grant's and answered with a slow nod.

"And you're in love with him, and you're scared that he doesn't feel the same way."

"I don't know if I'm in love with him—"

"Well, I think you owe it to yourself to find out."

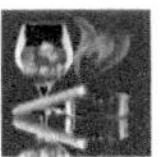

THE DISASTROUS DATE OVER, STEVI CURLED UP ON THE COUCH before nine. She could have gone to the Queen. Slipped inside and worked the bar. Hung out with the people she loved most in the world. But the thought made her chest hurt and her palms sweaty. Instead, Grant had brought her home. He had hugged her long and hard, and then he'd kissed her forehead and told her to call him if she needed to talk.

Pajamas on, she decided to forego the ice cream. Didn't want another beer. In fact, she didn't want anything except Duncan. The danger factor was sometimes alluring, but tonight, it was too much to think about it. Instead, she found a chick flick on TV and tried to lose herself in it.

She considered grabbing her laptop. Duncan and Leah weren't wrong. The Octoberfest was coming up, and they had an opportunity to really draw folks into the bar. She should be breaking her neck to make that work. The community economic foundation did the planning for the main event. Stevi had no desire to be in charge; been there, done that, designed the damned t-shirt. But she could add some fun stuff to the Queen's schedule in hopes of drumming up more business. The festival might draw people in, but she needed to make sure those people loved the Queen so much, they had to come back.

Not tonight. Her head hurt almost as much as her heart. She had thrown her thoughts out there for Grant tonight, and though he talked her through them, she was still ashamed that she had given voice to most of what she had said. Jealous? Good God, she loved Leah so much, and she was crazy about Trace. But the love highs in the house were sort of like salt in an open flesh wound. True, she had blown off the whole love question all through the years. But not because she didn't want her own great love affair. She just wasn't sure there was anything that remarkable about her, when Leah Hague was her sister.

Some days, Nashville drove that point home with a Ferrari. Other days, he made her feel special, reminded her that Leah was a wonderful woman, and made her feel that love might be waiting for her out there.

Her phone buzzed. Assuming it was Grant, Stevi reached up over her head to find it on the end table by the arm of the couch. She pressed the home button, surprised to find a text from Margo.

Tell me you're having wild, passionate sex. Let me live vicariously.

Stevi laughed softly.

Not even close. Home alone. PJs on. Watching tv.

Why aren't you with Grant?

Wasn't up for it.

He wasn't?

Rather than text her back, Stevi tapped the phone icon and waited while it rang for Margo to pick up.

"What's that supposed to mean?"

The music at the bar nearly drowned out Margo's laugh Suddenly overcome with homesickness, Stevi opened her mouth to take a deep, silent breath. She wanted to be there. With her cousin and her sister. She wanted to be hip to hip with Duncan behind the bar.

She wanted him to want her there. But it was Margo who had texted her. Not Duncan.

"Just thought maybe he couldn't get it up."

"He told me I'm good in bed." Stevi squeezed her eyes closed. "So, there's that."

"So, why aren't you with him?"

"I just didn't want to tonight," Stevi answered simply. She could tack on more. Something about Duncan. How she couldn't stop thinking about him. The way he kissed her, like he had all damned day and night to sample her lips and her tongue. The skin under her ear.

"Damn. That's like a kick in the teeth, Stevi. You have it at your fingertips, and you turn it down. Do you know how long it's been for me?"

"Well, there was that guy around Halloween."

"Yep. Pretty much that was the guy. The last time."

"Damn, Margs. Go meet someone."

"Hard to do."

"You say when. I'll watch Berkley."

"Love you."

"You, too."

She lowered the phone to rest on her belly and closed her eyes. What was he doing right now? Well, stupid question. The conversation buzz and the music over the phone line told Stevi the Queen was enjoying a busy night. Of course, Duncan was behind the bar, mixing drinks and serving them with that sexy smile.

She wondered again how often he hooked up with girls from the bar. Thought about his nineteen-year-old hookup. Remembered the way his warm breath had teased the skin under her ear.

She didn't do this often, but she was desperate. Duncan had twisted her into knots with that first kiss. And the few kisses since then had left her needy, and Grant would have obliged, but she didn't want Grant. Still early enough that Leah and Trace shouldn't be home for a while, Stevi slipped her hand inside the soft, faded shorts she wore to bed.

CHAPTER 13

STEVI SPENT SUNDAY WORKING IN THE YARD. LEAH TOLD HER A few times to let it go, that Trace would take care of it. But Stevi needed the distraction from all the thoughts in her head. She felt Leah's eyes on her several times while she mowed and trimmed, but she ignored the guilt. She couldn't look Leah in the eye right now, not after wondering out loud the other night if she was jealous of her. It hurt to think that, and it would hurt Leah's feelings, and the last thing Stevi wanted was an ongoing *thing* between herself and her sister.

When the yard was finished—Trace had come home from whatever errands he had been on and told her it looked great —Stevi had showered and gone to visit her parents for a while. She worked in the kitchen with her mom; they made cookies. Her mom had boxed some up and told her to take them to Trace and Duncan. Stevi had been careful not to look at her mom when she said that. She watched her parents interact, too, warmed by the constant touching between them. Never anything too over the top, though her dad had played with her mom's butt on occasion. She left their house after dinnertime, feeling alone and somewhat unimportant compared to their togetherness. But she painted on a big smile when she left them and offered Leah and Trace the same smile when she got home.

Leah talked her into going for a walk in the evening. Stevi managed to step around any question Leah dropped that had anything to do with Duncan. She talked her date up when Leah asked about Grant. Leah didn't ask why she had been home at midnight when she and Trace got in; Stevi didn't offer any details.

Two days of no conversation with Duncan made her a bee's nest of emotion and anxiety by Monday. She slipped in the back door of the Queen, part of her praying she wouldn't see him and the other part of her wishing she would run right into him. She didn't see him, though she had seen his car in the lot out back, so she knew he was here.

She went up to the office and settled in at the desktop. With the door closed and a bottle of water within reach, she searched the Internet for fun Octoberfest party ideas. They would feature German beers, of course, and Leah could order in some German wines, and Stevi thought maybe some sort of German appetizer. They hadn't done that last year, because none of them were familiar with German food. Might be something to look into.

The obvious draw for an event like that was sleeping with her sister. No question business had picked up since Trace Dixon had come to town. And yes, Stevi loved hearing him play. She loved watching Trace on the small stage he and Duncan had put together in the front of the Queen. But that seemed like a cop-out for someone who didn't want to do her job, and Stevi wanted to do her job.

In fact, she wanted to rock the job. And blow her coworkers away. Especially Duncan.

"What else?" she mumbled to herself. There was a sharp knock on the door. Stevi called out to come in and turned to see Duncan peek in at her. In a white t-shirt and worn jeans he was sexy and intriguing while still being the same old Duncan. "What's up?" she asked around her heart in her throat.

"Trace here yet?"

She opened her mouth to say something, but when she realized she didn't know, she could only shrug. Missing Duncan, though, she sat back in the chair, intending to ask him how his weekend was. But before she could, the door closed and he was gone.

Stung by the blow off, Stevi simply stared at the door for a moment, heart in her throat. She wondered if he had hooked up with someone from the bar. Gotten it out of his system.

Decided maybe it was for the best as she turned her attention back to the monitor. Maybe she didn't need Duncan, maybe she needed a big project to keep her busy. Something for the Queen, of course. What could she plan for the Octoberfest that would blow everyone away and keep people coming back for more?

She stayed busy the rest of the afternoon, and Duncan was either busy or determined to avoid her, because she didn't see him, much less talk to him until after they'd opened the doors. He was tightlipped, didn't say much to her other than passing drink orders back and forth and an occasional mildly flirtatious comment. Stevi was relieved the first time he winked at her and made a comment about the guys at the end of the bar trying to get her attention. But when nothing more came of it, when Duncan refused to stand next to her and talk to her, her heart sank with disappointment.

Maybe it would be better for them, better for the Queen, for everyone if they cooled things off. The flirting. The deep after-hours conversations. The kissing. God, yes, they needed to stop the kissing. More than once tonight, Stevi had found herself staring at Duncan's lips, wishing he would put them on her. And more than once, he had caught her staring at him. Might have been okay if he had looked as tortured as she felt. But he hadn't. He had simply looked away each time, as if the kisses they had shared weren't burned into his lips and his tongue like a brand.

Leah and Trace left the bar around nine, and Duncan chased Margo out by ten. Stevi might have hoped it was because he wanted to be alone with her, but after being treated the same distant, polite way he had treated Tania all evening, she doubted that was the case. Maybe he wanted to close in a hurry because he had a hot date waiting for him at his place.

The thought nearly made her drop the stack of glasses in her hands as she carried them back to the kitchen. Duncan glanced at her when she gasped out loud, but he didn't say anything. Didn't move to help her. Didn't even follow her into the kitchen when she loaded the glasses in the dishwasher. Stevi took a moment in the kitchen. Her hands trembled a bit, and her stomach quivered inside with fear that whatever had almost happened between her and Duncan was already over.

She cleared her throat, wiped her hands over the seat of her jeans, and considered going to get her keys and going home. She could let this go, let it die, and hopefully within a week or two, maybe, she and Duncan could be friends again and her whole body—heart and soul and all the girl parts, too— would stop wanting more.

Matchbox Twenty played in the bar when she walked back out. Duncan leaned on the bar, a glass of bourbon at his fingertips, his eyes on his phone. When he didn't look at her, she summoned the courage to talk to him—about whatever was going on—and sidled up to stand by him at the bar.

"So are you done with me now?"

Surprised that her voice was strong and confident when inside she was a quivering mess of nerves, she rested her elbows on the bar top and turned her head to look at him.

"What does that mean?" The tone of his voice gave nothing away.

"Bored with me?"

Apparently that sort of got him. He pushed his phone away; Stevi couldn't help glancing at it, wondering if he was texting someone. She felt a quick stab of relief when she saw that he was reading an article on a news app, but the relief was short lived. He stared at her with cool gray eyes. Lifted the glass to his lips and sipped the amber liquid.

"How was your date?"

Stevi blinked at him, wishing she could read his mind. But his face remained impassive, and the moment spun out to five seconds and then ten, and finally, Stevi raised her eyebrows and drew in a breath to answer him.

"Fine."

He nodded. "Good. Glad you had a good time."

"Duncan." She put her hand on his arm, squeezed gently when he didn't look at her. "Why are you doing this?"

"You didn't even tell me you had a date," he said quietly.

"Is that what—"

"Remember what happened last Friday night? In the kitchen? After we closed? Remember that I kissed you?"

Mouth dry, she could only nod in response.

"The way I kissed you in the cellar? My hands in your hair?"

"Yes."

"You didn't tell me you had a date," he repeated. "Kind of a big *fuck you, Duncan* if you ask me."

Her heart crashed to her feet at the same time her eyebrows kissed her hairline.

"Duncan, nothing happened."

"What?"

"We had a beer and burgers. I was back at home by ten. Alone."

Duncan stared at her for a moment before shoving the glass of bourbon away from him on the bar. Stevi watched a drop splash over the rim and just miss his phone screen.

"That's great." His voice dripped with sarcasm. Stevi steeled herself when he bumped into her and scooted her out of his way. She watched him move to the back wall to turn the lights off and then stalk back across the room to sit on the stairs. Was she supposed to follow him? Did he want her to go?

Her mind flashed Grant's words back at her. She owed it to herself to explore whatever this was, because for some dumb reason, her heart and her brain had decided maybe she felt something for this guy.

When she turned to move out from behind the bar, her eyes fell on the bar dice Duncan had brought in last week. Seemed like forever ago, now, and Stevi's cheeks blazed with flames. She'd wanted to do this for ages, to kiss Duncan, to see if there was something between them, and it had taken a bar dice game to prod her into action.

Feeling foolish and childish, and more than a little bit afraid that he would tell her to go to hell, she forced herself to move. The first step was so hard to take; her legs were weak and her throat was tight with emotion. But across the room on the grand staircase, Duncan sat with his face buried in his hands. His shoulders were hunched together. He looked as miserable as she felt.

"I'm sorry," she said quietly as she climbed the stairs to sit at his side. He didn't move, but she heard his sharp intake of breath.

"For what?"

"I don't know." She shrugged. "I should have told you I was going out. I should have cancelled the date. I don't know what the hell we're doing, Duncan. I don't know how I'm supposed to act."

"I spent the whole fucking night thinking about him with his hands on you."

Stevi groaned. The street out front was quiet, nothing to distract her from the conversation she was afraid to have.

"He didn't touch me," she finally answered.

"Then he's a stupid fucker who should have had his hands on you."

Stevi laughed softly. "Did you talk to Margo? About this?"

"About us?"

"Is there an us, Duncan? I don't know what we're doing."

"No."

"No?" Stevi heard the break in her voice. She tried to cover it with a cough, but Duncan turned his head to look at her. She closed her eyes and breathed deeply through her nose.

"No, I didn't talk to Margo. About us."

She nodded, but she didn't feel reassured about anything.

"Not really."

She rubbed her eyes and finally made herself look at him.

"I know I told you that Grant and I sleep together, and we have," she shrugged, "but nothing happened. I didn't want to be there with him, and he could tell."

"And by there with him, you mean…"

"We were at Jax." She tucked her hair behind her ears. "Watched part of the game. Had a couple of beers. And that was that."

"You weren't in his bed and not feeling it?"

"No, that would have been last time, which was before you kissed me."

"What was last time?"

"Not feeling it with him."

"You always tell me he's got moves."

"What else am I going to tell you, Duncan?" She rolled her eyes and shook her head. "That I've faked an orgasm with him the last several times we had sex just to get it done?"

"Have you? Done that?"

"Yes."

"And he can't tell the difference?"

"He said he knows."

"So you didn't have sex Saturday, but you talked about it."

She didn't answer him. She couldn't possibly tell him that she had confided in Grant, hoping to figure something out about her feelings for Duncan.

"You know that soft, breathy moan you do when I kiss you?"

"Well, I don't listen for it, no…."

"It makes me so hard, my dick hurts."

"Are we doing this?" she whispered. Up until now, Stevi couldn't be sure what they were doing. Messing around. Having fun. Breaking some rules. Kisses were one thing. Introducing the fact that her moaning made his dick so hard it hurt leveled them up, and Stevi's heart was a jackhammer in her chest.

Her heart nearly exploded out of her chest when he turned toward her and slipped his arm around her back.

"C'mere." He pulled her close and then continued to hold her until she moved and straddled his lap.

"Jesus, Duncan." She closed her eyes and rested her forehead on his.

"I must have wondered a hundred times if he did that to you. If he made you moan like that with just a kiss. Wondered what you sound like when you come."

"I was at home watching TV by ten."

"Why didn't you come in?"

Stevi, forehead still resting on his, shook her head slightly. "Thought some time to think might be a good thing."

"Was it?"

"I don't know."

"Stevi."

"What?"

"You know what I want."

He rocked his hips upward just enough to push his erection to the throbbing spot between her thighs. Stevi gasped, a little bit surprised and a whole lot turned on.

"I know."

"What about you?"

"I'm scared," she admitted.

"Of me?"

"What happens when the new wears off and you look for someone else?"

"We're not gonna lose what we have."

"How do you know? You hardly spoke to me today just because I had a beer with someone else."

"I don't share, Stevi." His breath was warm on her face. "I'm always gonna be right here at the Queen. Right with you and Margs and Leah. Whether we do this or not. But I don't share."

"You can turn it off? When we're done? You can just turn it off and walk away? No hard feelings?"

"I'm friends with ex-girlfriends. With women I've slept with. You told me you're friends with Grant."

Stevi's heart still pounded in her throat, but she couldn't deny the sinking feeling inside. Duncan was spelling it out to her that he was interested in sleeping with her, but he had no interest in anything permanent. Just as she had feared. He wanted to fuck her. End of story.

"So we're gonna be exclusive for…however long…we want to do this. And then what? You start ignoring me again?"

"I've never ignored you. I was…pissed…today. That's different."

"We're both gonna be exclusive, though? I'm not gonna find underage girls in your bed?"

"I knew I shouldn't have told you that." He dropped his head back and cut loose with a sigh of frustration.

"Yeah, probably never a good thing to share that sort of info with a woman you think you want to fuck."

"Stevi." He shifted, tried to reach for her as she backed off his lap and then stood over him.

"I need to go," she said quietly.

"Are you saying no?"

Her eyes burned with tears she didn't want to cry. At least it was dark enough in the bar that he couldn't see how upset she was.

"I don't know." She shrugged as she backed down the steps.

"So you have to think about it?"

"Yeah, I guess so."

"Stevi, are you upset?" He started to stand, so Stevi backed up a step.

"No. I'm fine," she lied. "I'll see you tomorrow."

CHAPTER 14

"What in the hell did you say to Stevi, anyway?" Margo asked him the next morning. Duncan hadn't slept much—again—damned, if Stevi Hague wasn't going to kill him one of these days, but Margo had asked him to come over to look at her dryer. Berkley shrieked at them from her bouncy seat. Duncan, on his knees in front of the dryer, glanced at his niece and then squinted up at his stepsister.

"I thought you promised me coffee."

"It's brewing," she answered. "Seriously, Duncan. Leah texted this morning. Said Stevi mentioned going to look at a house."

"What's wrong with Stevi going to look at a house?" He shrugged. "I think you need a new dryer."

"What's wrong with it?" Margo asked as he climbed to his feet. "And the house is somewhere in northern Iowa."

"Northern—" Duncan snapped his head around to stare at Margo in disbelief.

"Which is why I'm asking you what the hell you said to her."

"Dammit." He sighed. "I think the timer's bad. In the dryer."

"Which means what?"

"It's an expensive fix," he told her. "Isn't this the dryer that conveyed with the house when you got it?"

Margo nodded.

"Okay." He rubbed his eyes and looked up at her. "Then I think you'd be better off getting something new. Don't put more money into this one."

"Great." Margo pushed off the wall and headed toward the coffee pot. Duncan stepped away from the washer and dryer, and the little makeshift laundry line Margo had rigged up over the top of the machines. He had long since gotten used to finding her lingerie hanging there to dry, but that didn't mean he had to like it.

"Leah's upset, Duncan," she told him. "Do you want breakfast?"

"No. Thanks." He shook his head. "Just some scrambled eggs."

Margo snorted. "But no breakfast."

He grinned and shook his head. "No."

"She thinks she's done something to piss Stevi off."

"She hasn't."

"Yeah, I know, but I can't tell her what I know."

"You don't know."

"I know you said something to her to piss her off." Margo turned her back to him to get the eggs from the refrigerator.

"You told me to talk to her about what I was feeling."

"Yeah." Margo glanced at him and sighed. "I guess I expected more of you."

"What does that mean?"

"Well, she was at home Saturday night. Tapped out early on Grant. And you and I both know why. And the day after you have time alone with her, she's looking to move to Iowa?"

"Have you talked to her?"

"No. She won't take my calls."

"Margo, I told her I don't share."

"You said you weren't sleeping with her."

"I'm not." Duncan grabbed two coffee mugs when the machine beeped to signal that it was ready. "But there've been some things happening, and I let her know I'm not into sharing."

"And?"

"I told her if we reached a point where we needed to…see other people…then that was a good end date."

"You suggested getting involved in a relationship and addressed an end date to said relationship."

"I don't want a relationship, Margo. I just—"

Margo flinched and the egg in her hand cracked. Duncan broke the eye contact and looked at the mess, the gooey yellow egg dripping from her hand to the sink.

"Wait." She cleared her throat. "You told her you want to be fuck buddies? Are you kidding me, Duncan?"

Duncan lifted his gaze from the sink to meet Margo's eyes and then glanced at Berkley.

"I didn't say it like that."

"But you implied that it's all you want from her."

"Stevi's not interested in settling down with anyone. Sure as hell not me."

Margo sighed sadly and shook her head. "Maybe, maybe not. But no woman wants to be approached that way. Especially not by someone who claims to care about her." He watched her rinse her hand off and then turn the garbage disposal on to clean the egg out of the sink.

"You know I love you guys," Duncan mumbled. "All three of you."

"Yeah, well, I'm glad you can't hit on me like that. I thought you had more finesse than that. More feeling, Duncan."

"She kisses me back. When I kiss her. She kissed me the other night in the kitchen. She has this moan when I kiss the right spot—"

Margo shook her head enthusiastically. "I'm not saying she's not into you. I'm just saying you have no idea what she wants from a man. You have no idea what she's looking for, and if you go in all gangbusters like this, you're gonna hurt her. You probably already did."

"Isn't it better to be honest? So no one gets hurt by expecting more than the other person's willing to give?"

"Sure." Margo agreed. By now, she had cracked two more eggs in a bowl, added milk, and was mixing them to pour into a skillet. "As long as you're prepared to deal with the fallout and take her answer like a man."

"You think she told me no?"

"If I know Stevi," Margo said softly, "and I do, she'll think it over. And if she's into you, and she thinks this is what you want from her, she'll give you everything. Because that's who she is. Generous and giving. And then when you get bored with her and move on, she'll suck it up and go on working right by your side at the bar, fighting the heartache minute by minute."

"Margo."

"It's no way to live, Duncan," Margo whispered. "Hurting like that. Pretending that you're not."

"I don't see it." He squatted down beside the bouncy seat to make faces at Berkley. The baby offered him a grin and rattled off a long line of babble. Duncan laughed softly.

"You don't think she deserves more?"

"I don't think she's emotionally invested in anything between us. We're just having fun."

STEVI DIDN'T COME IN UNTIL FIVE MINUTES BEFORE DUNCAN opened the front door. She offered him a quick, impersonal smile as she carried her purse and her bag upstairs. Duncan watched her go, aware that Leah was watching him watch Stevi.

"Margo said her dryer is dead."

Duncan glanced at Leah and nodded. "Seems to be."

"That sucks." Leah slid onto a barstool. She rested her hand on the small curve of her belly. Duncan watched her for a second, and then he forced himself to look away. "She's been looking at preschools for Berk. They're all so expensive. Doubt she wants to spend the money now."

"Berkley's not even two," Duncan reminded Leah.

"She could start school at three," Leah answered, "and she should be on a waiting list."

"That's insane."

"Maybe." Leah shrugged. Duncan slipped behind the bar and eyed his stock closely. Everything appeared to be in order, so he finally met Leah's gaze.

"Can I ask you something?"

"Sure." He folded his arms over his chest and waited. Figured Leah was going to give him hell about Stevi.

"I was going to wait for Trace, but I can't." She laughed softly. "We want you to be a godparent to our baby."

Duncan blinked at her silently. "You want me to…what?"

"Be the baby's—"

"I heard you." He nodded. "Leah, I'm honored, but I don't… I'm not…I'm not the best role model for a kid."

"Right. You're a hard worker. And you're loyal. And you care about people." She raised her eyebrows. "Would you think about it?"

"I don't need to think about it," he said quietly. "Of course, I'll do it. I just…your kid's more likely to learn how to make the perfect mojito from me than how to be an upstanding citizen."

"Shut up. Besides, you never know when I might need the

perfect mojito." She climbed up to kneel on the barstool and leaned over the bar to hug him. "Love you."

"Love you, too." He gave her a quick squeeze.

"And Duncan, I don't know what's going on with you and Stevi, but—"

"Leah, it's—"

"Don't wanna know," she argued. "Not my business. Just don't hurt her. Please?"

He had expected Leah to give him hell, and though she hadn't, the whole conversation still left Duncan with a bad taste in his mouth. He was sincerely honored that Leah and Trace wanted him to be their baby's godfather. But he also didn't feel worthy.

He also wondered if Stevi was okay. She had been upset when she left the bar last night. Her eyes had shined with tears, but he hadn't called her out on it. He probably had been a dick about it, about how he handled the attraction—the mutual attraction—between them. He didn't want to hurt Stevi, but he wasn't ready to rush in and hand her his heart, either. She could stomp on it in those damned killer heels she favored and tear it up.

Stevi joined him behind the bar within the hour. She was friendly and warm, but he noticed she was careful to keep her distance from him, too. She had toned her usual makeup down, but it didn't matter. She had a natural beauty, and Duncan realized as he snuck peeks at her throughout the night, it was that natural beauty that he was drawn to. However, when she looked away from him, he could see the bruised skin under her eyes, and he wondered if she was sleeping okay at night.

She'd worn skinny jeans again tonight. Simple flat sandals and a soft white t-shirt. He wondered if she had chosen the outfit on purpose. No skin to tease him. No slender bare legs under a skirt. Tonight, she was pure and sweet Stevi. If she had hoped to kill his attraction to her, she had failed miserably. He wanted his arms around her. Tonight.

Forever.

Duncan gave himself a mental shake. He made his way down the bar several times through the night. He talked to friends, patrons who had become friends, new faces. All the while, he was painfully aware of Stevi, of her whereabouts and what she was doing at all times.

Later, close to ten, he lost her. They had cleared out; only one table near the back was taken, surrounded by seven people. Leah and Margo waited tables, and Trace had joined him at the bar, though they didn't both need to be there. Tuesday crowds had grown with Trace around, but it was still generally a quieter night.

Duncan cornered Margo at a table up front by the window. She stacked a couple of pint glasses and then snagged the lone wine glass on the table.

"Where's Stevi?"

"She's taking off early," Margo answered. "I'll stay."

"Why is she leaving early?"

"I think she's tired, Duncan," Margo said with a shrug. "I told you it's exhausting to deny what you feel and pretend everything's okay."

"Did she already—"

Duncan stopped talking when he looked up to see her coming down the stairs. She hadn't realized he was watching her yet. The strap of her purse was flung over her shoulder; she carried her keys in one hand. The other covered a big yawn.

"I'm gonna walk her out," he told Margo.

She shrugged and nodded. Stevi glanced at him as her foot hit the bottom step. She looked over his shoulder to Margo and said goodnight.

"Hey." She looked at him with a smile. "I'm beat. I'm going home."

"I'll walk you out," he said quietly. She wanted to argue; he could see it on her face. But she apparently thought better of it. She nodded and turned her back to him. He waited, hands tucked in the pockets of his jeans—which felt stupid, because he wasn't a hands-in-the-pockets kind of guy—while she hollered goodnight to Trace and then had a quick conversation with Leah.

August nights weren't so different from July, and Duncan followed Stevi outside into an oven. When she looked at him over her shoulder, her ponytail swung back and forth.

"I'm parked right there," she said softly. "You don't have to—"

"I'm sorry."

Still with her back to him, her shoulders lifted and expanded in a deep breath. "For what?"

"What I said last night."

"Which part?"

When she turned to him, she threw her hands up in question, but she was definitely upset about last night. He could see it in the sadness in her eyes and the downturn of her lips.

"Can we talk for a minute?" He took a step toward her, but he kept his hands to himself. "Or do you have somewhere you need to be?"

"I'm going home, Duncan," she answered warily.

"Is it because I told you that you make me so hard it hurts?"

Duncan moved closer to her. So close he could feel the warmth of her body on his. She had no choice but to look straight up to see him, but she refused. Instead, she ducked her head to avoid his eyes.

"Did I offend you?"

"You didn't offend me, Duncan," she said softly. "You know I'm attracted to you. You know what I want."

"Then what is it? What's wrong?"

"The way you kiss me." She finally lifted her face to look up at him. "So soft and so sweet. I'm not asking you to love me. To make promises you can't keep. But I want *that man* to want me. I want you to *make love* to me."

"Stevi." He groaned and lifted his hands to touch her. Tears welled in her eyes as she stared at him. He linked his fingers behind his neck and huffed out a deep breath.

"It's okay." She licked her lips. "This isn't a good idea, anyway. We shouldn't do this. Goodnight."

"Wait." He caught her arm and tugged her back to stand by him. "This isn't over."

"This didn't happen," she reminded him. "We want different things. And…what are you doing?"

He led her down the walk to her car.

"Can I come home with you?"

"What? No!" She looked around, paralyzed by his words. She watched him take her keys and unlock her door. When he opened her door and gently pushed her inside, she gaped up at him with big eyes. "We're not doing this."

"No. We're not," he agreed. "Not like this. But we're gonna talk."

"There's nothing to say."

"Stevi." He rested his hands on the car and leaned inside, over her.

"You kissed me. I kissed you. We can still walk away from this and—"

Maybe he wasn't ready to write her love letters and hand over his heart, but he sure as hell wasn't ready to walk away and pretend nothing had happened. Pretend there wasn't a potential explosion—forget about a spark—between them.

She stopped talking when he stroked his fingers over her lips and then over her face and under her chin. He felt her gasp in surprise, and then, when he settled his lips over hers, he felt her draw another quick little breath in before he felt the pressure of her lips against his.

"We're not kids, Duncan," she whispered against his mouth. "We can't do something impulsive and pretend it's not going to affect everyone around us."

"Nothing I feel about you is about being kids, Stevi Hague." He dropped a trail of kisses over her cheek and then rested his forehead against hers. "Be safe."

She nodded. Maybe she wanted to say more. Maybe she tried. He wouldn't know, because he turned and walked away without another word. He saw Margo glance at him from the front of the bar when he walked in, but he wasn't in the mood to talk to anyone. Nope. He'd rather punch something so he could get rid of the raging frustration inside.

CHAPTER 15

Stevi felt Leah's eyes on her, but she was slow to look away from her laptop toward the kitchen door to acknowledge her sister there. When she did, Leah stood propped in the doorframe, arms folded over her chest. She arched her eyebrows hopefully, but she didn't move until Stevi sighed and pushed her chair back from the table.

"Can I come in?" Leah asked softly.

"Really?" Stevi rolled her eyes. "It's the kitchen."

Leah shrugged.

"Yes." Stevi picked up her coffee mug and held it out to her. "If you get me more coffee. And by more coffee, I mean some coffee and a lot of creamer."

"Do you think I don't know that by now?" Leah asked with a small grin as she took the mug and carried it back to the counter.

"How ya feeling this morning?" Stevi watched Leah splash coffee into the mug and then add a healthy amount of creamer. Or depending on how you looked at it, not healthy amount, she supposed.

Leah shrugged. "It's better than it was, but not great."

Stevi thanked her when she brought her coffee back to her and sat down across the table.

"I am kind of jealous of you right now," Leah mumbled. Stevi, mug poised at her lips, stopped and stared blankly at her.

"Why would you be jealous of me?" Stevi hoped her face didn't give away the fact that she thought the idea was ridiculous.

"The coffee." Leah tossed her hand out at the mug and then rubbed her eyes and her forehead with the same hand.

"Oh yeah." Stevi sipped and nodded. She put the mug down on the table and clicked on a link for German appetizers. "Livin' the dream."

"Right." Leah nodded. "Which is why you want to go look at a house in Northern Iowa."

"I'm not gonna look at a house in Iowa," Stevi muttered. "God, Leah. You take everything so literally."

"You don't usually say stuff like that."

Stevi kept her eyes on the screen, not because she was enthralled by the ingredients in a chorizo mushroom tapa, but so she could avoid Leah's gaze.

"Yeah, well, it's been a while since I've fucked things up so badly." Stevi read over the list of ingredients twice, but she had no idea what she was reading. She hunched her shoulders to prepare for Leah's barrage of advice, the quiet disappointment in her voice. When minutes passed and

Leah didn't say a word, Stevi finally braved it and peeked at her.

"What?"

Stevi shrugged. "Nothing. Just figured you would have something to say about it."

"Doesn't matter what I say." Leah studied her fingernails now rather than look at Stevi. "You take everything wrong."

"I can't live here forever, Leah. Not now."

"I know." Leah shrugged and nodded.

"But?"

"I just." Leah sighed and stretched her arms over her head. "I feel like you're punishing me for being happy."

Done. Stevi clicked out of the recipe website. She would hit the shower, get to work, and shut herself up in the office to work. Leah's words hit too close to home for her. She didn't want to punish Leah for anything, and yet, Stevi's ridiculous, immature behavior seemed to say something else, didn't it?

"What're you doing?" Leah asked when Stevi closed the screen of her computer.

"I'm gonna shower. Get down to the Queen. I'm working on stuff for the Octoberfest."

Leah rolled her lips inward and nodded. "Is it him? Is it because I decided I wanted him for myself? Or is it just…me? Is it that—"

"No, Leah." Stevi reached for her hand and squeezed her fingers. "It's me. It's just me."

"You used to talk to me," Leah reminded her.

"I can't now."

"Because of Trace? Or because of Duncan?"

Stevi carried her mug back to the sink. She set it down and looked at Leah over her shoulder.

"Just me." Her voice was thick with tears she didn't want to cry.

DUNCAN GREETED HER WITH THAT GRIN THAT TURNED HER knees to jelly. Still uncertain where they were going and what she thought about it, Stevi wanted to be immune to him. To the grin. She had tried and failed a hundred times, but she had prayed the whole drive to the Queen that today would be the day Duncan was just Duncan and not the sexy, intriguing guy she had a massive, immature crush on.

At least she had a good game face. Sometimes, anyway. She had attempted a smile, the plain old smile she used to have when she saw her step cousin. But before her brain could tell the rest of her body to behave, parts further south were waking up to the memory of the way he kissed her, and instead of smiling, she grinned and she was pretty sure she wiggled her eyebrows, and her voice sounded funny even to her ears when she hollered at him on her way up the stairs.

Shaking with anticipation, with desire, Stevi put the laptop down on the desk and stood for a moment. She ducked her chin to her chest and breathed deeply. Made her brain leave Duncan alone and forced herself back through the ingredients for the chorizo mushroom tapas.

"Stevi."

She jumped and turned to look at Trace with her heart in her throat.

"Hey."

"Sorry." He chuckled. "Margo asked me to tell you there's a last-minute change to the schedule this week."

"Okay." She dropped to sit in the chair behind the desk and waited for him to say more.

"Late-notice book club coffee tomorrow morning."

"What?" She shook her head. "We don't do late notice anything, and we don't do coffee any mornings. We're not open until late afternoon."

"She said you would say that." Trace shrugged. "She said to write it down. She has some ideas she wants to discuss with you regarding morning coffees. Also, a retirement dinner booked for Friday night."

Stevi grabbed a pencil and jotted the two events down on the desk calendar. She was tired. The last thing she wanted to do was be in here tomorrow morning for coffee with a book club, but then again, maybe being flexible with times for bigger groups would help the business. If one of them needed to be here, why not her? Leah wasn't good with early morning anything these days, and Margo had Berkley to worry about. Stevi was free to be here whenever anyone needed her.

"Got it." She nodded.

"Stevi?"

Her stomach had finally settled, but now, at the sound of Duncan's voice calling her name, nerves fluttered to life again. She fiddled with the pencil in her hand and arched her eyebrows when Trace made way for Duncan to stand in the doorway with him.

"Hmm?"

"Joe." Duncan took a few steps into the office, hand outstretched to give her the cordless. Their eyes met; Stevi felt a flash of heat when his fingers touched hers, but he only smiled and slipped back out of the room. Happy that Joe had called, Stevi took a deep breath to push down the anxious feeling Duncan always seemed to wrestle to life inside her. She saw Trace tip his head at her, but he was gone before she could say anything else.

"Hey." She put the phone to her ear and tapped the power button on the laptop.

"Hey." Joe sounded good. "How's my favorite mama to be?"

"Well, fine, but you've got Stevi. Not Leah."

"I know that. I'm asking you how you think Leah's doing."

"Mm." She relaxed back in her chair while she waited for the computer to boot up. "I guess okay. I haven't talked to Leah much lately."

"How do you live with her and work with her and not talk to her much lately?"

"Busy," Stevi answered breezily. "How's Kenz?"

"Good days and bad days."

"And today?"

"Not sure yet. She's doing therapy right now. Addelyn's killing it on the swim team."

"Good. Liam?"

"Asked for a skateboard."

"Oh no. You didn't get him one, did you?"

"I didn't. Kenzi's dad did."

"Anything broken yet?"

"Not yet."

Stevi chuckled. She leaned forward and tapped the keys to pull up the recipe website she'd been on at the house.

"I talked to Leah, Stevi."

"Yeah? When?"

"Yesterday." Joe sounded sad. "What's going on with you?"

"Why? What did Leah say?"

"Stevi."

Stevi pursed her lips and closed her eyes. "Just…going through a thing, Joe. It's fine."

"You're going through a thing?"

"Yep."

"What thing?"

"Really? How detailed do you want me to be?"

"I'm not gonna cut you any slack, Stevi. Life's too short—"

"You know what, Joe? You can't do this. You can't throw Kenzi at us anytime something comes up. Life's short. Got it. But I don't know anyone who has all the answers all the time—"

"I don't, either. And I'm not claiming age-old wisdom. Leah said something's bothering you. She said you won't talk to her. She's so sure it's the baby and Trace that she's questioning whether she's doing the right thing with him."

"What?"

"I'm not judging you, Stevi. And I know you're happy for Leah. I just want you to know what she's thinking."

"Dammit." She sighed.

"You could just talk to her."

"I will." Stevi nodded, even though Joe couldn't see her.

"It's killing Kenz that Edison prefers me to her."

Stevi flinched. "He doesn't know any better."

"I know. He missed a lot of bonding time with her. Even now…she's not…"

Stevi swallowed a mouthful of guilt. Compared to Joe and Kenzi, she was living the dream as she had said to Leah this morning. So what if there was some drama? Of her own creation. Kenzi and Joe, their family, would never be the same.

"Do you think Kenzi would be up for a visit?"

"What?"

Stevi shrugged sheepishly and licked her lips. She missed them. Leah had taken a little spiritual trip earlier in the summer. Why couldn't Stevi hop in her car and drive away from this, from Duncan, and visit her friends?

"I don't know. Just. If I decided to come and see you guys."

"We'd love to see you, but don't run from that to visit us."

"Define that."

"If you're waiting for blessings, you have mine," he said quietly.

"Joe." She groaned. "What about—"

She stopped talking when she realized Joe had disconnected the call. Nice to have Joe's blessing, and she knew damned well he was referring to Duncan and whatever was going on there. Or whatever Joe thought was going on, but it didn't make her feel much better. She set the phone on the desk and left the office in search of Leah.

The break room was empty, but she heard Leah's voice on the main level of the bar. She stood for a moment at the ornate wooden railing on the staircase. Hard to believe this was their bar. That she and her sister and their cousin had pooled their resources and their dreams and created the Queen. Stevi wondered what their grandparents would think of the place, since they had invested family money into restoring Granddad's dream.

Leah and Duncan were behind the bar. Duncan was talking, Leah laughing, and Stevi was overwhelmed with happiness to see Leah cut loose this way. She was a little envious, too, because it seemed like forever since she had been so carefree and easy with Duncan. She wanted that back. She started down the stairs, still watching them talk.

But when Duncan lifted his eyes to look at her, the heat in his gaze was a slow, delicious burn from her heart to her toes. In that look, she remembered the taste of his soft lips and the feel of his fingers in her hair. The press of his erection to a spot that was begging for more. Right. Now.

She wanted to explore the possibilities. She dragged her gaze over his face, the dark scruff on his jaws, and down over his broad shoulders and admitted to herself she wanted to explore him. *Duncan.* She wanted to look her fill. She wanted to slide his shirt up over his belly and study his hard, solid abs. She wanted to push his jeans down and feast her eyes on the curve of his ass. His cock. Oh hell yes, she wanted to look and touch and taste Duncan Marks.

Leah cleared her throat and broke the spell. Stevi dropped her gaze for a moment and then turned to look out the front window at the summer sun and the park across the street. She counted to three, listened to Leah and Duncan continue their conversation about a road trip Duncan had taken years ago with college buddies. Stevi wanted to hear it; she wanted to be behind the bar with Duncan, listening to him talk and laughing at the crazy antics he and his friends had done. She also wanted to hop up on the bar, hook her ankles behind his back, and press his face to her breasts.

Not a good place to go, Stevi, she told herself. Get a frigging grip.

When she finally turned back to them, she found that Leah was watching her, and her big eyes, the wounded look she wore under the laughter, cut through her like a jagged-edged blade.

"Do you have a minute?" Stevi wanted to fold her arms over her chest, but it was a defensive gesture, and she didn't want Leah to read anything into it. "Can I talk to you?"

"Of course," Leah said softly. Both of them glanced at Duncan, who held up his hands, palms out and nodded.

"I know when I'm not wanted," he said, but he was smiling. When he slipped out from behind the bar, he trailed his fingers over Stevi's shoulders. The barely-there touch pulled a shiver from deep inside, and she knew Leah saw it. Still, she only smiled when Duncan looked back at her before he crossed the room to leave them alone.

"What's going on?" Leah asked her.

Stevi watched over Leah's shoulder until Duncan disappeared in the back, presumably heading down to the cellar.

"I just talked to Joe."

"Oh, God." Leah reached for the bar as the color leached from her face.

"No. No." Stevi shook her head. "It's not Kenzi. No change."

"Then what is it?"

Stevi climbed up on a barstool. Wished Leah would do the same. Her skin was ashen, and her big, sad eyes gave her the look of an orphan.

"If you ever...ever..." Stevi arched her eyebrows and jabbed a finger at Leah to drive her point and maybe her anger home. "Do something stupid...like changing any future plans with Trace Dixon because you think I'm thinking something, I will never forgive you."

Leah stared at her silently for a moment. She heaved a deep breath and stepped back to lean on the counter behind her.

"What does that mean?" she whispered.

Stevi watched her slide her hand over the tiny curve of her belly.

"It means I love you, and I'm in love with you and Trace, and I love that baby, and yes, I have a lot on my mind right now, but that doesn't change that I want you to be happy. I want you to have it all, Leah, and I love how that man loves you."

Leah gave her a curt nod, but she swept her gaze over Stevi's face and turned to look at the window. She didn't believe her. Stevi's heart squeezed so hard in her chest, that it took her breath away. She rubbed her hands over her face and then swallowed the emotion in her throat so she could continue. It wasn't fair that she had to vomit all of this emotion at Leah's feet, not when she wanted desperately to keep it to herself. But damned if she would let Leah do something stupid because she was worried about her.

"I want to move out, yes." Stevi felt Leah's eyes on her again. "It's time for me to move out. I love the house. I loved being there with you, but I can't be there when you're married and you have a child. I'm not a college kid who needs a place to crash. I'm an adult. I'll be fine."

"'kay." Leah sniffled.

"And dammit, Leah, yes, there's something going on with me and Duncan. The problem is I don't know what it is. I don't know what I want. I convince myself I need things to stay just as they are, because he's part of my heart, and I can't lose him. I can't just lose a piece of myself. And then I look at him, and I remember the feel of his face against mine, and the way he kisses me, and it just takes my breath away."

Stevi chanced a glance at Leah, but Leah only stared back, no comment, no expression on her face.

"It's like when he puts his mouth on mine, the oxygen in the room just burns up, and I need him to breathe."

"Okay." Leah nodded. She swiped at her eyes and turned away from Stevi. "Thanks for telling me."

"Leah."

"What?" Leah stood with her back to her now. Stevi watched her tuck her chin and breathe deeply.

"That's it?"

"I don't know what you want me to say. Because no matter what it is, I'll make you mad."

"If you could say something and know it wouldn't make me mad, what would you say?"

Leah looked at Stevi over her shoulder and laughed softly. "I'd probably ask you how long you've been sleeping with him. And I might remind you that you knew what was going on between me and Nashville the first night we were together."

Stevi shook her head. She dabbed at her eyes, blew out a long, sad sigh and left her lips puckered for a second.

"We're not sleeping together."

"So, it just happened once?"

"No." Stevi licked her lips. She smoothed her thumb over the smooth wood of the bar when Leah came back to stand by her.

"I don't understand."

"He kissed me last week," Stevi admitted. "We've been tiptoeing around the idea for a while. Flirting—"

"Don't I know that," Leah mumbled.

"I'm either so hot for him or so twisted in knots over what's not going on that I just…I'm not happy, Leah. I don't like feeling this way."

"Anything I can do?"

"Stop thinking this is about you. You know how happy I am that you have Trace. You know that." Stevi took Leah's hands in hers.

Leah nodded, but she pursed her lips and tipped her head. "Okay, but can I ask one thing?"

"What?"

"Why do you feel like you can't talk to me about this?"

"Because it's Duncan," Stevi said simply. "Because we've known him since we were kids, and it just feels…"

"Feels?"

"It scares the hell out of me, Leah. He and I could blow up everything around us. We could take down the Queen."

CHAPTER 16

DUNCAN SAW STEVI EMPTY THE BOTTLE OF DYKSTRA CAB INTO her glass, but he didn't comment. Today had been better; no sharp words exchanged, no snippy comments, no worrying about other guys with their hands on Stevi. But on the other hand, today had been too…polite. Too proper. She'd been friendly all day, and she had pretty much eye-fucked him earlier when she had come down to talk to Leah. That had sent the entire supply of blood in his body straight to his dick, and he'd gone down to the cellar to sit for a bit and chill the fuck out. He had moseyed around the shelving he and Trace were working on, all the while wishing his hard-on would stand down. Decided if they wanted to take a wall out down here, he could probably go at it with his dick. Felt like a battering ram in his jeans, and the memory of Stevi's eyes taking that slow hot slide over his face and his shoulders and as far south as they could go when he was behind the bar kept coming back to him.

After an hour downstairs, dick back to minding its own business and more wine stocked on the shelves according to how they had labeled them, he had come back up and pretended nothing had happened. Pretended Stevi hadn't lit him on fire as she had.

She worked the bar with him, waited tables, talked to men and women alike, and exchanged a long, intense-looking hug with Leah when Trace herded her out the door a couple of hours ago.

Now, alone, they had started the clean-up process, and Stevi was sipping wine, and Duncan couldn't read her mind. He wished he felt comfortable enough to slide down the bar to stand with her and talk, the way he and Leah had done earlier today. Stevi used to hang with him like that. Her laughter still touched him, stroked something deep and primal, but he didn't hear it as often as he used to.

"You and Leah okay?" he finally asked to break the silence between them. Trace's playlist had been on tap tonight, so Kenny Chesney currently serenaded them. Wasn't long ago that kind of music would have made his skin crawl. Country music always seemed too twangy, too sloppy. But something about it appealed to him now. The lyrics, the stories the lyrics told. The slow songs made him want to take a chance and put his arms around this woman and ask her to dance.

"Yeah." She looked up, apparently surprised either that he had spoken or by the question itself.

"It was a good night." He looked around the room to check the tables. They had cleared the drink ware. Duncan had wiped down the tables and the bar while Stevi loaded the dishwasher.

Her eyes grew wide with fear when he moved down the bar to stand by her. She watched without comment when he snagged her glass and took a drink.

"I should go." She cleared her throat when he put the glass down. Rather than answer her, he slipped by her and moved to the back wall to turn the lights off. He had always liked the Queen at night, tucked in for the quiet, restful hours. He loved the way the shadows played over the tables and the bar. Loved the silvery glow of the street through the front window.

Now, he loved sharing it with Stevi.

"What're you doing?" Her husky whisper had the same effect as her fingertip stroking his skin. He slid his arm around her waist and drew her closer.

"Dance with me."

His invitation caught her off guard, but she linked her arms loosely around his waist.

"I see what you're doing." She nodded, eyed him with suspicion.

"And what am I doing?" He grinned as he tightened his hold on her.

"Leah and Trace danced that night. That's all it took."

Duncan squeezed his eyes closed and shook his head. "Are you telling me that the night they were making out under the staircase, they had sex the first time?"

"Yes."

"While I like where you're going with that, I don't wanna think about Leah and Trace having sex."

"No?"

"He's not my type." Duncan shrugged. "And she's my cousin."

"Then what does that make me, Duncan?"

He lifted his hand to smooth his thumb over her full lower lip. Her lips were bare tonight—he noticed she'd toned everything down again—but Duncan loved the feel and taste of her soft, sensitive skin.

"It's different."

"It's not, though."

"I've never been attracted to Leah."

Stevi gave in and moved in his arms. He let go, assuming she was trying to wiggle away from him, but she only slid one hand up over his back. Drew the other around his side and rested it on his chest.

"I still don't think this is a good idea," she whispered, but when she lifted her chin to look at him, her eyes lingered on his mouth.

"Maybe we need to get the dice out again." He laughed softly when she rolled her eyes. "See if we can get to the next move."

"What about dice makes it any better?"

"Do you really wanna walk away?"

He held his breath, because if she said yes, he would let her go. She was right. They had the potential to hurt each other, and if they hurt each other, they would hurt everyone they loved. But they had the potential to be incredible, too, and Duncan wanted to explore that possibility with her.

"No."

The relief at her answer combined with his desire to touch her warmed his throat and his insides like a shot of expensive bourbon. And like a shot of his favorite bourbon, it only left him craving more of her. When he kissed her, she slid the hand that rested on his chest up and over his shoulder. Duncan sighed with pleasure when her soft fingers grazed the skin at the back of his neck. Stevi flicked her tongue over his lips and stroked it over his tongue.

He fisted his fingers around her shirt, dug them gently into her skin, and kissed her back. She was bold tonight, her tongue exploring his teeth and the roof of his mouth, and back over his tongue. Each stroke sparked the want in his gut, in his dick, until he was dizzy with need.

"Can anyone see us in here?" She breathed the words against his lips. Cupped his face in her hands and kissed him again.

"I don't know. I've never done this here." He laughed softly. She pulled back to look at him, her eyes glazed with lust. Duncan took advantage of the moment and licked a hot trail from her mouth to her ear. She rewarded him with that moan that made him crazy. Pressed her middle to his and did it again.

"Duncan," she whispered, drew his name out on a long, soft sigh as he eased her shirt up over her belly.

"You eye-fucked me today." He teased her with a peck on her lips and a feather light stroke up the middle of her back.

"What?"

"At the bar. Jesus, Stevi, five more seconds with your eyes on me like that, and I might have come just thinking about being buried inside you."

The words were out before he could close his mouth. Maybe, even though he had his dick pressed hard against her and she knew damned good and well what he wanted to do with her, maybe it was better to skip the dirty talk with her. She was *Stevi*, after all. But she didn't flinch.

"Me, too," she whispered.

"What?" He did it again. Traced a finger up her spine and felt like a goddamned warrior after a bloody victory when she shivered and moaned softly.

"I just…looked at you, and I wanted to see you. Everything. I wanted my hands on you. My mouth. I want everything you have, Duncan, but I don't wanna lose your heart. I can't lose your friendship for sex."

Duncan turned her so that her back was to the window. He eased her closer to the bar and slid her shirt up higher.

"Tell me to stop."

Rather than telling him to stop, Stevi covered his hand with hers and pushed her shirt up to reveal a skimpy lace bra.

"Don't stop."

Duncan splayed his hand over her warm skin. Her stomach quivered at his touch. Head tipped down, she watched him, but when he rubbed his thumb up over the white lace and traced the bottom curve of her breast, she flicked her gaze up to his.

He wanted to feast, to grab with both hands. Greedy for the feel of the lace under his fingers, for the warmth of her skin, the taste of her nipples on his tongue, he took a steadying breath. Ran through the list of wines he had shelved earlier today. Mentally recited the ingredients in a Long Island Ice Tea.

Knowing that he would stop, that he wouldn't undress her here and back her up against the bar or the brick wall—*I want you to make love to me, Duncan*—he rubbed the backs of his knuckles up over the lace on her breast until he touched her nipple. The sensitive skin already puckered and beaded with her arousal, he lifted his eyes to hers to find her watching him touch her again.

"Stevi." He gritted his teeth as he dropped his hand. Strummed his knuckles over her bare stomach and then used his other hand to lower the bright green material back to cover her completely. Eyes still glazed with heat and desire, she reached for his hand.

"You need to go."

She flinched.

"What?"

"I'll see you tomorrow." He leaned in to kiss her cheek, but she ducked her head away from him.

"Right." She nodded. "Tomorrow."

"Maybe we could—" He had planned to suggest they see each other outside of work. On Sunday, maybe, they could grab lunch or dinner together. She was right; he didn't want to *fuck* her. Maybe they would never make babies together like Leah and Trace, but that didn't mean they couldn't do this part right. While his dick was all in for ripping her clothes off her right here and now, while he wanted to bury his dick inside her and lick her body from head to toe and make her moan that sexy-as-hell moan, he would rather wait and let it happen naturally. At his place. Where he could take his time with her. He wanted her lying in his bed. In the lace. The heels she had suddenly stopped wearing. He wanted to sweep his tongue over her body, her flat belly and the hard muscle in her upper arms. He wanted to suck the skin of her inner thighs into his mouth, and he wanted to taste her desire for him.

Stevi was gone before he could get the words out. Before he could suggest dinner. A movie. A night out together. He blinked at the stairs, shocked that she had moved so quickly. Was she embarrassed? Angry?

"Stevi." He moved to the steps as she appeared at the top. But she took them quickly and shoved past him when she reached the bottom. "Stevi, wait."

"See ya tomorrow!" she called as she reached the back door. She pushed it open without hesitation and disappeared into the night. Duncan sighed and followed her to the door. He didn't step outside, because he worried she might shove the car in drive, instead of reverse, and run over him. But he watched from the door as she drove away.

CHAPTER 17

STEVI TOSSED AND TURNED ALL NIGHT. THE SCENE WITH
Duncan played out over and over in her head, and the desire
that built in her each time she remembered the feel of his
hand on her at war with the hurt when he had calmly pulled
her shirt down and told her to go home was torture. Her
conversation with Joe kept coming back to her, too—not the
part where she put her foot in her mouth and gave him hell
about playing the Kenzi card, but the thought of taking a trip
out east to see them. If she didn't move to Iowa—good grief,
she'd been on a real estate site looking at rental properties
here in Adam's Bay and clicked on the picture of a cute little
house that ended up being in Clear Lake, Iowa—she could
always pack up and take a long road trip. She would love to
see Joe and Kenzi, and even more than that, she would love
to get away from this ridiculous situation she had put herself
in here. Then again, hadn't Joe told her not to use a visit to
them as an excuse to run away from Duncan? Unable to lie
awake any longer, she climbed from her bed at six and went
for a run, which was a dumb move because she hadn't

exercised in ages, and she returned home with the ghost of Duncan still in her head and shin splints and sore feet.

When she stepped out of the bathroom after her shower, she sucked in a quick breath and a gulp of irritation. Trace and Leah were in the kitchen. Sounded like they were talking about baby names, and while there was nothing inappropriate about it, Stevi felt like she was intruding on a private conversation when she went to get a glass of juice.

"I made enough coffee for both of us," Trace told her. She poured the orange juice and took a healthy swallow before turning to look at him.

"Thanks." She moseyed over to stand behind Leah. Peeked over her shoulder into her teacup. "How many more days until you can have coffee?"

"Too many," Leah mumbled, "and I'm not even upset about the coffee anymore. I'm scared to death about delivering this baby."

"Yeah, kind of more fun to put the baby there in the first place, huh?" Stevi squeezed Leah's shoulder. Trace sputtered a drink of his coffee and then rolled his eyes.

"Warn a guy?"

"Sorry. I said something inappropriate." Stevi winked at him.

"Did you have a good night?" Leah looked up at her. Stevi had no idea if she was asking about closing the bar or if something happened between her and Duncan, but she only shook her head.

"No. I didn't." She shrugged. "The house in Iowa is looking more and more interesting." Kind of felt funny to joke about it—about Leah seeing her search history on the computer at the Queen and jumping to conclusions—when suddenly, the idea was at least a little bit appealing.

"You looked at a house in Iowa?" Trace cocked his head to study her like she had suddenly grown a unicorn horn in her forehead.

"I'm sorry," Leah said quietly.

Stevi nodded, but she shrugged at the same time. She finished her orange juice, put the bottle back in the fridge, and decided she should drink some coffee since Trace had made enough for her.

"I don't get him," she mumbled as she filled her mug.

"What happened?" Leah asked. When Stevi heard the chair squawking on the floor, she glanced back at Leah over her shoulder.

"I don't wanna talk about it." She added a generous amount of creamer to the coffee, stirred it, and then set the spoon in the sink. Leah had other ideas, though, and she followed her back to her bedroom. Stevi set her mug on the dresser and stood in front of the closet looking for something to wear. The last few days, she had gone with simple. She had decided she had been too bold, too flirty the past several months, only considering what Duncan would think of what she was wearing.

No more. No more giving a damn what Duncan Marks thought. She couldn't keep up with the guy. Either he wanted her, or he didn't. Maybe he had decided he wasn't that into her. Maybe he preferred them younger. Nineteen and twenty-year-olds were probably a hell of a lot more adventurous. Maybe a nineteen or twenty-year-old would have stripped down and leaned over the bar in invitation. Then again, Stevi might have done the same, but he had stopped her cold.

One slight touch and he was done.

Maybe he was disappointed with what he saw. She had average boobs; maybe he wanted big and bouncy. Whatever. She was done with the hot and cold. The lust she felt for Duncan rivaled anything she'd ever felt in her life. But the way he had hurt her the last few times they were together was far deeper than anything she'd ever felt. She'd go back to Grant Deavers. He rarely made her come anymore, but then again, he'd never made her cry, either.

"What happened, Stevi?" Leah leaned on the door at her back. "How did you get from mentally undressing him at the bar yesterday afternoon to…this…whatever this is?"

Stevi tossed a few blouses on the bed, their hangers clanging together. She glanced at Leah and then went back to her clothes.

"Maybe I should find a girlfriend," Stevi said quietly. "I'm so done with guys. I'm done with pretending it's all fun. I hate going out all the time. I hate being the fill in for cancelled dates, and I hate the damned mixed signals he's sending me."

"Mixed…" Leah closed her mouth when Stevi shot her an angry glare. "Duncan?"

Stevi sighed.

"Have you ever been with a woman?"

"No, but don't you think girls can hurt you just as badly?"

"I'm not hurt. I'm pissed."

Leah appeared to be on the verge of saying something, but again, when Stevi glared at her, she closed her mouth.

"Can I ask you something?" Stevi said softly.

"Yes."

Stevi nodded. She pulled her t-shirt over her head and tossed it on the bed. Leah blinked in surprise when Stevi turned to her and held her hands out at her sides.

"Is there something wrong with me?"

Leah pushed away from the open door and took a step closer to Stevi.

"What?"

"Me. The bra. Is there something unattractive about me?"

"No." Leah frowned. "I love the bra. I have it in pink lace. Why?"

Stevi tried to speak, but her throat filled with emotion. She shook her head.

"He walked away?"

"Yes."

"From this?"

"He had a peek. What if he's not interested now?"

"What's not to be interested in?"

"You're my sister. Of course you're gonna say that." Stevi rolled her eyes.

"Hang on." Leah reached out and laid her fingers on Stevi's arm. She leaned back toward the door and hollered for Trace.

"What are you doing?" Stevi hissed.

"Hang on." Leah held up the same hand she had just touched Stevi's arm with.

"Need me?"

Stevi tried to duck into her closet when she heard Trace's voice outside her bedroom.

"Would you tell my sister what you think of her bra?"

"What?" Trace laughed. Leah reached for Stevi again and tugged her arm to bring her back into the room so Trace could see her better.

"Do you like her bra?" Leah asked him.

Despite the heat flooding her cheeks, Stevi had to laugh at the look of horror on his face.

"Um." He glanced at Stevi, met her eyes, and then looked back at Leah, the look of panic ratcheted up a notch or ten.

"Seriously. Not gonna get mad. Look at her. Do you like it?"

"Leah." Stevi groaned.

"He's practically your brother-in-law, and it's no different than a bikini top."

Trace sighed, apparently accepting that he wasn't going to get out of the situation, and propped himself in the doorway. He looked at Stevi, eyes lingering on her face. When he grinned the lazy, southern grin he used on stage at the Queen, she laughed softly.

"Yes, I like the bra," he admitted. "The lace is pretty, and the cut is sexy."

"Thank you." Leah nodded.

"But."

Stevi nearly swallowed her tongue. She stared at him wide-eyed.

"But?" she repeated. "Not enough there?"

"Don't kid yourself, darlin'," he drawled. "I'm guessing this is about a guy thing. and you and me both know who that guy is. It doesn't matter if you've got the most gorgeous lace or silk on or if you're wearing spandex. Guys want to see you."

"So, it's me." She nodded. "He's just not that into me."

"Oh, he's into you." Trace shrugged. "I know that for a fact. And sorry, darlin'," he glanced at Leah. "You're a beautiful woman, and I can guarantee you he wants a good long look. If he got a peek at this much, he had a hell of a long night."

"Yeah?" Stevi arched an eyebrow. "Well, good, because did I."

"Still won't tell me?" Leah asked when Trace high-tailed it out of the room, claiming he needed to call Pearl Allen, his friend and former employer at a bar in Nashville, to check in.

"What do you think, Leah? We were messing around. He got a look. Pulled my shirt down and told me to go home."

"That doesn't mean—"

"Doesn't matter. It made me feel like I was fourteen, asking the star quarterback to feel me up. He's so hot and cold, I can't deal with it. I can't deal with this. I didn't ask him to love me. I didn't ask him to be gentle. I just don't want to be another girl he fucked and walked away from. I need him to care enough to see me, to see my face when he touches me."

"You're in love with him," Leah said softly.

Stevi nodded. "Maybe. Maybe not. He's not gonna know, though."

"He should know."

"Right." Stevi turned away from Leah and reached for the hangers on her bed. "If this is what love feels like, I don't want it. It hurts more than feeling nothing."

"You're not giving him a chance. He's tiptoeing around this the same way you are. Stevi, there's no question he's into you."

"What if…" Stevi glanced at Leah as she flung the hangers back down and yanked open the second drawer of her dresser. "What if he's not? What if he's bored? Hasn't had any action lately? And hey, Stevi's an easy lay. What if that's the attraction, Leah?"

"That's not what he's thinking."

"How the hell do you know? It's what you've thought about me all this time."

"It is not!" Leah snapped. "I have never thought that. I asked you about Duncan because we all see it. Me and Trace and Margo. We all see the thing you two are doing. You were with him that night when you were out of town—"

"Nothing happened."

"Okay!" Leah held her hands up in surrender. "Okay. I believe you. Stevi, I just wish you could step outside of this for just a second and look with my eyes."

"I can't, Leah. We're in this too deep now. No matter what happens, one of us is gonna get hurt."

Leah sighed in defeat. "Remember how you kept pushing me to tell Trace? About the baby?"

Stevi turned away from Leah. She tugged a t-shirt over her head and fluffed her hair. "So not the same thing."

CHAPTER 18

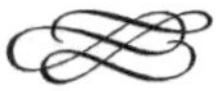

STEVI SPENT SOME QUALITY TIME IN THE OFFICE, RELIEVED TO have a nice list of menu suggestions for happy hour appetizers and dinner options for the Octoberfest. In addition to the chorizo mushroom tapas, she'd added fried brie in poached pears with lingonberries, a holiday strudel with mustard sauce, and of course, Bavarian pretzels for appetizers. For dinner options, she'd noted a recipe for a spring noodle soup, a red cabbage salad, Brathendl, or roast chicken, and possibly a tart with caramelized onions, apples, and red cabbage. Maybe Margo would do her own research and decide on completely different options, but since she was organizing the Queen's Octoberfest, she at least wanted to toss ideas out there.

Maybe she shouldn't, though. Maybe she shouldn't assume Margo would want her help. After all, Leah took care of wine orders and their wine selections and Duncan at least took care of their beer selections, if not the actual ordering. Maybe Stevi was wasting time obsessing over what to serve for appetizers and dinner. Probably because she was avoiding the issue of entertainment.

She snorted at herself and rolled her eyes. She was obsessing over this damned Octoberfest now for two reasons, the first being that after Duncan's comments the other day, it felt like the bar's less than spectacular showing at last year's Octoberfest—their sales should be through the roof as the festival was held in the town square, right across the street from the Queen, and being that they were the only bar on the square—was her fault. And also, it was a relief to think about something *other than Duncan* and the way he was dicking her around.

It surprised her. Duncan's games, the hot and cold, the sweet kisses and the cool, brusque way he'd laid out how they could be involved for a while and then walk away—that surprised her. True, Duncan had never been in a serious relationship, not one that lasted long, anyway. But Stevi had always thought he was a good guy. She'd believed him to be warm-hearted and fun-loving, and she'd assumed those qualities she admired in him as a friend were in Duncan the man, the lover, too.

The fact that he wasn't took her breath away.

She flinched and flopped backwards in the chair. Her eyes were bleary and tired from looking at the computer screen, and her hand was cramped from taking so many notes for the big festival. She supposed it wasn't fair to judge Duncan this way; just because he wasn't warm and attentive to her as a woman didn't mean he wouldn't be to the *right* woman. Honestly, she should be glad he'd spelled out exactly what he wanted from her. That he had told her what he wanted and promised her they could walk away as friends, because if they were honest up front, neither of them could expect more and be hurt when it wasn't delivered.

Except she already did want more, and because she loved Duncan so completely as a friend, because she trusted him so completely, she had expected him to feel…something… for her.

And after the other night when he'd started to undress her and then dismissed her, she wasn't sure he was even physically attracted to her.

Her head pounded with the damned circular thoughts. She'd obsessed over Duncan a hell of a lot more than she'd ever thought about any other man. Even after Leah had promised her she was attractive, even after all that stuff Trace had said, she was humiliated that Duncan had walked away from her, when she had been utterly willing to undress for him and give him absolutely everything she had.

"Stevi?"

She jumped when Trace tapped on the office door. Offered him a sheepish grin and laughed softly when he wagged his eyebrows and nodded toward her as if asking permission to come in.

"What's up?" She tossed her pen down on the legal pad covered in her small, neat hand writing for Margo.

"I was on my way up to the break room when Margo caught me. She asked me to suggest new posters with the city's Octoberfest logo on them…you know…to be displayed in the front window."

Stevi blinked at him, felt a frown draw her eyebrows down as he propped a hip on the desk.

"Um. Okay. Maybe Margo forgot that I know how to do that? That I know to do that at all? That it's only August?"

"She also suggested free Bavarian pretzels with a minimal beer purchase."

"Okay." She nodded and picked up her pen to jot that down. "Anything else? That Margo wanted me to know?"

Trace chuckled.

"I feel kind of weird talking to you now after checking you out."

Stevi snorted and then laughed out loud. "Know anybody looking for a date?"

"I do, actually." Trace gave her a pointed look.

"Um." She shook her head. "Nope. He doesn't count. Anyone else? Anyone in Nashville?"

"Lots of single guys in Nashville, but none of them are better than—"

"Any of them like you?"

Trace opened his mouth to speak, but apparently, he was at a loss for words, so he simply closed his mouth and looked at her in question.

"Relax, Nashville." She grinned. She sat up straight and leaned up over the desk, but she lowered her gaze to the legal pad rather than look at him. It hurt to beg for someone's attention; Duncan had taught her that. "I'm not hitting on you. I just…"

"What?"

She jerked her eyes up to his when she heard the note of concern in Trace's voice.

"Don't." She shook her head. "Don't feel sorry for me. I dug this hole. I'll figure it out."

"Stevi, he—"

"You know what I like about you, Trace?"

"Not my stunning good looks?"

Stevi couldn't help the laughter when he shot her that damned lazy smile.

"Nope. Not them."

"What?"

"You wanted my sister. You got my sister."

"It's different. Leah and I were strangers."

"Yeah, but you pursued her. You wanted to be with her, and you were patient, and you love her so perfectly."

Trace raised his eyebrows. Stevi saw a hint of the panic on his face that she'd seen when Leah asked him to look at her in her bra. She sighed. The last thing she wanted was pity; the next to last thing was to make Trace uncomfortable.

"Can I ask you something?" She cleared her throat. The thought had occurred to her somewhere in the small, dark hours when she lay awake thinking about Duncan. Thinking about how she had finally gone and done it. Fallen in love with the wrong guy and made a fool of herself. He was clearly playing, having a good time. Stevi had been the one to screw things up between them.

"What?"

"You still have your house? In Nashville?"

"Ah, Stevi—"

"Do you?"

"Yeah, but—"

"Would Pearl and Sampson hire me?"

"They would love you, but don't do this. You belong here You belong with Leah and Margo. You belong with—"

"No, I don't. Belong with him. He made it clear that he wants a good time, and I. .can't do it. I can't do it, Trace. And if one of us needs to leave, it should be me. Duncan's the face of the bar."

Trace scrubbed his hands over his face.

"I'm not selling you my damned house, Stevi."

"Okay." She shrugged. Trace's shoulders sagged in relief at her lack of argument. "Let me live there for a while. I'll pay you rent."

"Dammit."

"I just need a break," she said quietly. "Leah needed a break. She spent a few days alone on the beach and came home with you in her life. I'm not gonna find someone like you, but let me just get away and breathe."

"For how long?" he asked with a long, guttural groan.

"Six months?" She arched her eyebrows hopefully.

"Six—? Stevi, you're gonna break Leah's heart."

Stevi swallowed hard. "Lucky she has you to fix it."

Trace stood and paced the room. He stopped in front of the window Leah hated, shoved his hands in his pockets, and turned to look at her over his shoulder.

"I have no problem with you using my house, and no, I wouldn't take a dime for it. But dammit, Stevi, don't make any rash decisions. Please?"

"How would you feel? If you were me?"

"Why don't you just talk to him?"

"We did talk, and he told me exactly what he wanted." She drew in a deep breath and looked away, a little embarrassed to admit to Trace that Duncan was all in for a fling (was he still?) but had no intention of committing to more than that. "I'm the one who wants…more."

She swung her gaze back to him, saw the wince on his face before he looked back to the window.

"Only if you talk to Stevi and Margo first."

She wanted to argue. Kind of felt like the best course of action was to pack a bag and leave and then call from Nashville to tell them where she was. But Trace had turned to stare at her now, and the hard look on his face left little room for argument.

"Okay."

She nodded, watched him cross back through the room. Hands on his hips, head ducked low, she could sense his frustration with her.

"But Stevi?"

"Hmm?" She rested her cheek on her folded hands and stared at him in the doorway.

"You're wrong about him."

"No, I'm not," she said quietly. "He's a great guy, Trace. But he's not mine."

Trace heaved a deep sigh and turned his attention to the woodwork around the door. He slid his fingers up the wood and smoothed his thumb over it, eyes fixed there rather than on Stevi. She wondered if he and Duncan had talked about this, about her. And what Duncan might have said. A tiny little feather of hope unfurled in her belly. That wouldn't do. No sense in romanticizing anything about her friend, Duncan. She squashed the hope and looked back at the legal pad.

"Would you do me a favor?" She cleared her throat.

"What?" Trace sounded hesitant, as if he knew just what she was going to say.

"Would you keep this conversation between the two of us?"

She didn't give a damn if he mentioned it to Leah or Margo, but she didn't want him to say anything to Duncan. They had shared a few intimate kisses, but they hadn't crossed the line. If Trace mentioned to Duncan that she was looking to pack up and head south, Duncan might get a wild hair and decide it would be best for the Queen if he left, and then they would be tearing down the business they had all worked so hard to build. Wouldn't it be ironic if Stevi backed away from a physical affair with Duncan to salvage the Queen and ended up damaging their working relationship anyway by walking away?

Still turned sideways in the doorway, his hand still caressing the woodwork reverently, Trace gave her a curt nod. Before she could say more, he was gone. Stevi stared after him for a moment, but she spurred herself into action quickly. Maybe nothing would come of the discussion. Maybe she'd move to Nashville and love it so much, she would never come back home. Whatever the case, mooning over Duncan had to stop now.

She picked up her pen and then flipped the page in the legal pad. Smoothed her hand over the fresh yellow page and with a sad, weary sigh, she put the pen to the top of the paper.

Dear Duncan—

We were wrong to do this, to get started on something we can't finish. As much as I wish things were different, I know I will never regret anything so much as what we've shared, because while it was too much, it can never be enough. I've loved you so much as a friend, and because you love the Queen and our clientele loves you, I'm going to walk away.

Take care

Stevi

Everything about the words hurt. Stevi tapped her pen on the paper for several quiet seconds, lost in the memory of that first kiss. The safety she felt with Duncan with a tiny little kick of danger and excitement, like driving a hundred miles per hour down the freeway with a safety harness tucking you into your seat. The surprise in the softness of his lips and the firm pressure of those lips on hers. The electric thrill that tingled through her body when he stroked her tongue with his. The need he'd awakened inside her that would now never be fulfilled.

She stirred when she heard Leah's voice out in the hall, but when she heard Duncan respond to Leah, she quickly closed the letter in a trifold and stuck it under the desktop calendar to worry about later.

"Was Trace just in here?"

Stevi nodded as she glanced at Leah, now leaning into the office. But Duncan hovered right behind her, and their eyes met and held. Stevi ordered herself to be bold, to stare him down. But the sadness, maybe it was regret, on his face hurt too much, so she looked away and made a show of studying the computer screen again.

CHAPTER 19

"WHAT ABOUT A DANCE OFF?" MARGO SUGGESTED WITHOUT lifting her eyes from her laptop. Leah laughed softly, but Stevi wasn't sure if she was laughing at Margo or Berkley, who was belted into a highchair by the bar, lapping up the baby food lunch Leah fed her.

"Yeah, we'll sign Nashville up for that one." Leah nodded as Berkley smacked her lips together around the spoon of baby bananas. "I'd like to see him do the Macarena."

Stevi couldn't help the chuckle, but she was exhausted and while technically she had time to pull this together, the days were sliding by with alarming speed and Octoberfest would be here before they knew it. She felt better after squaring away some menu ideas, and knowing Duncan would handle the beer selections and any German wines Leah ordered. Might not ever handle her, but she trusted him with the details of the bar and the business. She just wanted to come up with some kind of entertainment that would bring down the house.

"I'd kind of like to see Duncan do the Macarena," Margo mumbled. Stevi flicked her eyes at Margo over the top of her own laptop, but Margo still wasn't looking at her. Three days had passed since Duncan had stolen a glance at her, given her a quick stroke—to humor her, maybe—and then tucked her away and told her to run home, another since she had talked to Trace about his house in Nashville. While every bone in her body told her to rail at him or pack up and go look at the house in Iowa, or better yet, head south and learn to appreciate country music and not just her sister's boyfriend, Stevi had taken the mature route and shown up for work every day since, plastered a cheap, fake smile on her face, and dodged his attempts to get her alone. What was the point of being alone with him if they were going to continue playing games? Games that left her strung out and hurt at best.

"Hey."

Stevi groped for her water bottle. She uncapped it and took a long drink, set it back on the bar, and finally looked at Leah.

"Hmm?"

"Anything happening?"

"Nope." Stevi turned her attention back to the laptop. "What about a Euchre tournament?"

"Seems sort of stodgy, and yet, it has some possibilities." Leah tipped her head to consider it and then roared with laughter when Berkley did the same. "Is it a German game?"

"Wait." Margo's hand hovered over the top of her screen. "What did you just say?"

"I asked her if Euchre is a German game." Leah spooned the last of the bananas from the jar and offered them to Berkley.

"Yeah. This website I'm on says it was brought here by early German settlers in the—"

"No." Margo shook her head. She closed her laptop and looked from Leah to Stevi. "What did you just ask her?"

Leah glanced at Stevi and arched her eyebrows.

"Margo, I asked Stevi if Euchre—"

"You said *anything happening?*" Margo tipped her head and stared at Leah. "And Stevi said *nope.*"

When Margo looked back at Stevi, she nodded. "Yeah, that's what we said. Can we move on?"

"What's that about?"

Stevi groaned. She looked at Leah, but her sister was busy wiping Berkley's chin with her bib.

"Duncan," she admitted, but she dropped her gaze back to her computer and tried to read more on the origins of the card game. She agreed with Leah. Sort of sounded stodgy and lame, but on the other hand, somewhat appealing. She just wasn't sure it was for their crowd.

"Duncan," Margo repeated.

Stevi licked her lips, her cheeks on fire under Margo's direct stare.

"Yeah." She shrugged, hoped she sounded nonchalant, but she knew before Margo spoke again that she had failed. Her voice shook a bit, and the furious blush only burned a little hotter. She ducked her head and rubbed her cheeks. Margo opened the cooler in front of her and grabbed a chilled longneck. She twisted off the cap and then scooted it over the bar to Stevi.

"Welcome to the broken hearts club."

"Wait. What?" Leah finally looked up. "No. You can't have a club that I can't be a member of. That's not fair."

"You want a broken heart?" Margo asked in disbelief. "You got the guy. And *what a guy*. And a baby on the way."

"I don't want a broken heart, but you can't just exclude me from this conversation."

"I don't have a broken heart," Stevi interrupted them. "Nothing happened."

"Stevi."

Stevi groaned and flopped backwards in her seat.

"Something happened?" Margo jumped on the awkward silence. She leaned over the bar and stared at Stevi expectantly.

"We were messing around." Stevi waved her hand as if to brush the subject away. "And he just stopped. Told me to go home."

"Where were you?"

"What?"

"Where were you?" Margo asked again.

"Here."

"When was this?"

"A few nights ago." Stevi cleared her throat. "Look, whatever. I'm not doing this. We're adults. He's either interested, or he's not. I'm not playing games. I'm not—"

"Maybe he didn't want to do it here."

"What?"

"It's a bar, Stevi," Margo reminded her. "Yes, it's a gorgeous place, and yes, it can be sexy to mess around or sneak around in a place like this. But this is Duncan. And you. Maybe he wanted something better for you."

"And maybe he decided he wasn't interested." Stevi shrugged. "It's okay. I don't love the Euchre idea, either, Leah. But I'm gonna make a note of it."

"You know you can ask Trace, don't you?" Leah made a show of not looking at Stevi. "I mean, he's connected. He's not a big deal here anymore—"

"Right." Margo rolled her eyes. "I saw three girls nearly fall off their stools last Saturday when he was playing his guitar up there on the stage."

"You're right." Stevi laughed softly. "I think I heard one say he made her ovaries weep."

Leah sighed and pinched the bridge of her nose.

"Well, he makes mine sing." She maneuvered Berkley out of the high chair and held her on her lap.

"Who makes your what sing?" Duncan asked as he appeared through the door from the kitchen. Leah blinked and pursed her lips.

"I'm not sure you want her to answer that question," Margo said with a laugh.

"Hey." He dropped his hands on Stevi's shoulders and gave her a gentle squeeze. "A beer? At noon?"

"Apparently Margo thought I needed one."

"What's wrong?" He leaned over to rest his chin on the top of her head. Stevi's stomach flip-flopped; she hadn't been this close to him since the night he had sort of touched her and then sent her away.

"Just trying to put something together for the Octoberfest."

"Euchre, huh?"

Stevi closed her eyes when he leaned even closer. He moved, pressed his face to hers as he studied her computer screen. She breathed deeply and slowly, Duncan's spicy cologne more intoxicating than all of the liquor behind the bar. She lowered her hands to her lap and counted to ten, wishing he would leave her alone.

"Not really our vibe, though, is it?" Leah asked.

"No, but I do like it."

"How about a battle of the bartenders?" Margo suggested.

"Sure. Duncan and who else?" Leah stood and grabbed Berkley's highchair to scooch it out of the way.

"Stevi," he answered as he lifted his arms to rest his hands on her keyboard. She laughed softly and pushed at his arm to let her move.

"Right. I can make two drinks, pour wine, and twist the tops off beer bottles." She slipped off the stool and moved away from him.

"But you're pretty." He glanced at her, but he was quick to look back at the computer. "You'd win, hands down."

"Yeah," Stevi rolled her eyes as she stepped behind the bar with Margo. Her heart still raced from how close he had been, but she felt somewhat safer now with the massive bar between them. "I'll talk to Trace, Leah."

"For what?" Duncan finally straightened. He looked from Stevi to Leah and back to Stevi.

"Entertainment," Margo told him. "For the Octoberfest."

"I'd rather figure this out on my own," Stevi mumbled. She walked back down the bar until she was even with Duncan. Their eyes met as she pushed her laptop closed and picked it up. "I may not be a bartender, but I'm absolutely capable of doing my job." She hooked a finger around the bottle and then turned her back to him.

"No one doubts that, Stevi," Leah called as she crossed the floor and headed to the stairs. "But maybe part of your job is knowing when to ask for favors."

"Yeah, I've had my fill of favors, thanks." She didn't look down as she moved at a steady pace up the steps. Flustered, she hurried into the office, closed the door, and set the beer and the laptop on the desk. Rather than sit there, she went to the window and stood for a moment.

When she and Leah and Margo had been kids, they had started a club. Well, Margo and Leah had started a club for girls in the sixth grade and up, but only Margo and Leah were in the club so Stevi had known that they had done it just to exclude her. Fortunately for her, their mothers had known it, too, and they had put an end to that after the longest day and a half of Stevi's life.

Funny that she and Margo were now exclusive members of a broken heart club, and she would rather be Leah: the only one of them on the outside.

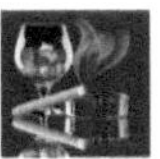

SOMETHING ABOUT A WEEKEND ALWAYS BROUGHT PEOPLE IN. Stevi always wondered if it was the stress of the work week that drove people to drink or the celebration that there would be a couple of days off that pulled them in. Whichever was the case, Stevi usually loved it. There was nothing better than having a hand in a place where people gathered in good cheer to have a drink and listen to live music.

Except she didn't love it here lately. As much as she wished she and Duncan could have been a thing, that they could have found what Leah and Trace have together—obviously her work week had stressed her out if she was thinking she and Duncan would ever have been a permanent thing—she regretted that anything at all had happened. She supposed she had to give him credit for trying. He had talked her ear off tonight, anytime she had found herself standing with him behind the bar. He had even made her laugh with shared stories and conversation with patrons sitting at the bar. But she missed him. Yes, she missed the flirting, the innuendo. She missed the warmth of his body when he pressed her up against him to kiss her. The soft, sweet pressure of his mouth on hers.

But she missed the easy friendship they used to have, and because of those sweet, soft kisses and all of the innuendo, everything they'd said to each other, they could never go back to that same friendship. Leah believed Stevi was in love with him, and though Stevi didn't know a damned thing about this kind of love, she trusted Leah to see something in herself that she couldn't see. Margo recognized her as walking wounded.

Stevi wondered exactly what Duncan saw when he looked at her now. A missed opportunity? Too easy? Should she have played harder to get? Or should she have ridden him that night on the stairs, when he'd told her in black and white terms that he wanted her but only for a while?

As closing time drew near, the butterflies in her belly spread their wings. Not anticipation. Not anymore. For a while, those late-night hours when just she and Duncan were here —even those before the kissing started—had been some of the best of her life. Before they had started swapping stories about dates and flings gone way right or wrong, before Duncan had introduced his carved-up version of bar dice, before she tasted bourbon on his tongue, they had tried to continue the karaoke game. When it fell flat after losing both Margo and Leah most nights, they had started with riddles and top five lists. They had danced while they cleaned, but never that slow, sexy sway that had led them to trouble the other night.

Now she dreaded the possibility of being alone with him. Because she was sure he wasn't into her, that maybe he had considered it—out of boredom or curiosity—and decided against it. And she was also sure that if he lapsed back into boredom or if he saw her flirt with someone else and needed to beat his fists on his chest and flex his muscles and be possessive of her, she would let him. She wanted everything about Duncan Marks, and she hated that she was willing to give him everything and get so little in return.

She finished in the ladies' room and then stood at the sink for a moment. Kind of silly to hide out in here trying to come up with an excuse to duck out early. She hated to do that to Margo, although she was sure her aunt had Berkley tonight, so technically Margo could stay here. Leah and Trace had already gone home. Stevi studied her reflection in the small rectangular mirror over the sink, but she didn't like what she saw. Not the bags under her eyes or the lines around her mouth. But what they represented.

Never one to wallow for long, she was down and she didn't know how to pick herself up this time. With a deep breath, she flipped the light switch and stepped back out into the main bar area. She heard a giggle to her right, near the back door, and turned to see who was stumbling inside. Her heart slammed, and her stomach twisted in knots when she saw Duncan, back against the wall, with a redhead leaning into him. The giggle must have come from the redhead—because Duncan sure as hell had never made that sound—but Stevi wondered how she'd made a noise, since her mouth was fastened on Duncan's neck.

Duncan's head rested on the wall, and his hands hung at his sides, but there was a trace of a smile on his face. The shock had made her freeze, but now the rush of pain made her move. Just get out of here, she told herself. Get away from Duncan before he sees you.

She turned the other way, intent on finding Margo and smacked into Tania, on her way to the restroom.

"Oh, damn!" Tania cupped Stevi's upper arms in her hands. "I'm sorry. Are you okay?"

"I'm fine." Stevi nodded. She flashed a quick smile at Tania and prayed that the girl—Stevi had grown to consider her a friend, but not one she wanted to cry to about what was going on in the hall behind her—would let her go.

"Hey. Someone was in here earlier looking for you."

Stevi swallowed down a groan, afraid that Tania was going to say it was Grant.

"Yeah? Who was it?"

"I don't know. She didn't give me a name."

"Hmm." Relief coursed through her at the word *she*. "Okay. Seen Margo?"

"She's at the bar."

Stevi flinched when she heard Duncan answer from behind her. Tania ducked by them now, intent on getting to the restroom.

"Mm." She nodded when she saw Margo at the far end of the bar, head tilted as she listened to a woman talking to her. "Okay. I'm gonna go."

"What?" Duncan stepped in front of her to cut off her escape route. She fisted her hands at her sides, frustrated that her purse and keys were upstairs. They needed a locked cabinet down here to keep their bags in so running away could be easier.

"I'm leaving. Margs can lock up with you."

"Why?"

"Duncan." She smoothed her fingertips over her forehead. "Just don't."

"You've been avoiding me since that night—"

"Since the night you took one look and turned me down?" Her voice had an edge to it, one she didn't feel. Inside, she wanted to cry. She dropped her hands to her sides again.

"Is that what you think?" His turn to reach for something, but when she stepped back he raised his hands in the air and then linked his fingers behind his neck. "Stevi—"

"Doesn't matter now, does it?" she shrugged.

"What does that mean?"

"Wasn't that the end game?" She jerked her head back to indicate what she had just seen in the back hall. "Didn't we have that discussion not long ago?"

"Stevi."

Afraid she was going to break down in front of him, she lifted her chin and met his gaze.

"Let me go. Please?"

Duncan bit off a string of words that broke her heart, but he stepped aside to let her pass. She didn't hurry, though she wanted to. Instead, she took her time as she made her way through the dwindling crowd, stopping to talk as she walked. Her legs trembled a bit, and her stomach railed at her, ready to toss her burger and beer back up. She promised herself a good cry and a shot of tequila or a bottle of wine or whatever the hell she wanted once she got home. But for now, she was a business owner, not a woman rejected by someone she was stupid enough to want.

CHAPTER 20

S̲HE BROKE HER PROMISES TO HERSELF. H̲ER EYES BURNED WITH tears on the drive home, but damned if she would cry them yet. It was late, but it was possible that she would run into Leah and Trace when she got home. Wouldn't happen if she lived alone, but she wasn't in the mood to wallow over her shared living space. Not now.

The living room window glowed with welcoming light, but Stevi crossed her fingers that Leah and Trace were already upstairs for the night. She parked her car in the drive and then tiptoed inside as quietly as she could. The house was still; no guitar sounds coming from the basement, no murmured conversation or anything more intimate from the attic stairs that led to the bedroom Leah now shared with Trace.

Stevi turned the lamp off in the living room and then ducked into the bathroom to wash her face and brush her teeth. She didn't want ice cream or tequila or wine. And the tears could wait a few more minutes. When she finished there—she avoided the mirror this time, because the last forty-five minutes had probably carved the sadness deeper into the skin around her eyes and her mouth—she hurried to her room, slipped inside, and closed the door.

In the dark, she stripped off the sleeveless purple blouse and white capris she had worn at the Queen and groped around her unmade bed for her pajamas. When she found them, she tugged on the soft knit shorts, took her bra off and tossed it to the floor, and then pulled the worn, soft pajama shirt on and crawled into bed. She lay on her stomach; her arms up under her pillow.

Eyes open, the darkness suffocated her. She wasn't afraid just hot and uncomfortable. Eyes closed, she had the perfect backdrop for the vision of Duncan and the redhead. Stevi had seen the girl in the bar before, always at the bar, always with her eyes on Duncan. To be fair, Stevi would admit she had never seen Duncan hit on her. He talked to her, but Duncan was friendly, and he was a bartender, so he talked to everyone. Still. The girl had looked ready to climb him like a tree and wrap her legs around him, and while Duncan hadn't appeared to be participating much in the make out session, he hadn't been intent on pushing her away, either.

Funny that her eyes had burned with tears she wouldn't allow herself to cry, but now that she was home and tucked up in her bed, alone, she couldn't summon the tears. Emptiness swallowed her whole, and Stevi lay for hours, wide-awake, wondering what to do with the mess she had made of her life.

She heard her phone buzz, but she waited a while after the second buzz before she picked it up. She pushed herself up on her elbows and pressed the home screen button. Even before she saw his name, she told herself nothing good happens at 3:00 in the morning. Not for her, anyway.

Are you awake?

The text had come in nearly fifteen minutes ago. She dropped her face to her pillow, not surprised that the tears would come now. Why wouldn't he just leave her alone? The phone buzzed again. Stevi turned over to lie on her back and looked at the screen.

Stevi?

I'm awake.

Will you talk to me?

I'd rather not.

Come outside.

Why?

I'm at your house. Come outside.

Stevi sat up in bed and turned her face toward the window. The curtain was closed, but it wasn't like she would see anything in the dark, anyway.

Stevi? Please?

With a weary sigh, she scrubbed her hands over her face and slipped out of bed, careful to be quiet. Assuming she would step out on the porch for a few minutes, she tiptoed to the front door in her pajamas and pulled the door open just far enough to step outside. The air was still thick and muggy, and Stevi had a flash of summer nights from years ago when she had been a teen, sneaking out to meet her friends.

Duncan's car was in the driveway. She crossed her arms over her chest and watched from the porch as the driver's door opened and he climbed out.

"Done with her already?" She spoke quietly, but in the still night, her voice carried. He rested his elbows on the top of the car and stared at her. When several minutes of silence passed, she shook her head and turned back to the door.

"Come with me."

"Where?"

She reached for the door handle, but suddenly Duncan was behind her, reaching around her to stop her.

"Come with me."

She expected him to touch her neck. To kiss her. Something that he knew would get to her. Instead, he rested his head on her shoulder.

"Please come with me, Stevi."

She swallowed hard and winced at the ache in her throat. She could ignore him. Go inside and go back to bed. Or she could follow him to his car and go wherever he wanted her to go and do whatever he asked of her, take what she wanted from him. Either way, it didn't matter. Because no matter what happened now, there was no going back to the way things were before.

Why drop a match when she could throw a torch on the bridge and make it burn bigger and brighter and faster? She pressed her lips together and pulled the screen door open. Duncan grunted his disapproval, but Stevi only reached in to pull the storm door closed before she turned to follow him to his car.

"Nothing happened," he told her once they were buckled in and he had backed out of the driveway.

"Okay." She nodded, but she was careful to keep her face turned away from him. A little bit chilled, she drew her legs up to rest her feet on her seat and wrap her arms around her knees.

"Stevi, I don't…there were no plans. I don't even know her name."

"It doesn't matter, Duncan." She shook her head.

She knew from the turns he made and the streets he drove that he was taking her to his house. She also knew that once they stepped inside and he shut the door on the rest of the world, there would be no talking. As much as she wanted him, the thought hurt almost more than it excited her.

When he pulled his car into his own driveway, she eyed his house warily. Duncan eased into the one-car garage and then killed the motor and pulled the key from the ignition. The ticking of the engine as it cooled was the only sound.

Curiosity won the battle inside her, so she rolled her head on the seat to look at him. He stared straight ahead; his hands folded together at the top of the steering wheel.

She opened her mouth, ready to tell him to take her back home. But he looked at her then, and rather than a smug face or that same look of dismissal he'd given her that last time he had kissed her, he looked tortured.

"Will you come in?" His voice was gruff and quiet. Stevi shoved her own hurt down a little deeper, ready to soothe his. She licked her lips and nodded. Still, neither of them moved for a moment, eyes locked in a look of desperation.

When he moved, she did. Without a word, they climbed from the car, and Stevi followed him inside through the back door. He tossed his keys to the counter. Stevi set her phone next to them and stood for a moment, eyes on the floor at her feet, afraid to look at him.

"I didn't want this to happen." His voice was still gruff, though this time, his words were so quiet she wasn't sure she heard him right.

"What to happen, Duncan?" she whispered. Finally, frustration making her bold, she lifted her gaze to look at his face. Enough moonlight shone through the kitchen window that she could see the planes of his face in shadow. "Why would you bring me here and then say that to me? This—"

His arm shot out like a snake striking to bite. But his fingers around her arm were gentle. Stevi's heart lurched, but not in fear. The silence in the room pounded in her ears as he tugged her closer and lowered his mouth to hers. This kiss wasn't sweet or soft, but she welcomed his power, his aggression, and answered with her own.

He let go of her arm, but he cupped her head in his hands and plundered her mouth with a hunger that unleashed her own.

"Duncan." She stretched and turned her head to offer him better access to her neck when he pressed his open mouth over the spot under her ear. His warm breath on her wet skin sent shivers down her back and made her legs tremble with desire. She fisted her hand in his shirt, holding on when the floor seemed to tilt and the room tried to spin. Her other hand found skin, hot and sticky, and she splayed her fingers over his back, the hem of his shirt covering her.

He came back to her lips, and she was ready to kiss him again. Her breath caught when he bit her lip, and she moaned softly when he stroked his tongue over her to take away the sting. Hands sliding down over her sides, he slipped his hands inside her shorts and curled his fingers around her hips.

"Do you moan like that when you come?"

"Make me come, Duncan." She molded her hand up over his back and licked her lips when he drew back to look at her. "Please?"

He moved his hands, and Stevi mewled in protest, but then his fingers were pushing her shorts, her panties down over her hips and her legs. Eyes locked, he watched her step out of them, her fingers letting loose of his shirt and trailing down to the button of his jeans.

"I want my cock inside you, Stevi. I gotta get inside you."

Her stomach tightened, and she worked the button of his jeans with fumbling fingers. Duncan rested his hands on the counter behind her and lowered his mouth to hers again as she eased his zipper down and parted the fly of his jeans.

"Duncan, put your hands on me." She nibbled on his lip this time. With fire in her hand, she stroked the length of his cock through the black cotton briefs. "Touch me. Please."

He moved with that same quick motion that he had started with. Stroked his hand down over her back and cupped her bare ass in his palm. Stevi closed her eyes, felt his touch everywhere on her body. Duncan turned her around and settled his hands on her hips again.

"Jesus, Stevi, you have the sweetest ass," he groaned.

He squeezed her cheeks firmly and then one finger stroked down the curve of her ass, and he moved the other to the ache between her thighs.

"You're wet." He snuggled up close behind her and licked the back of her neck. She whimpered as he slid his finger over her throbbing center. "Damn, Stevi, babe, you're so hot, I'm gonna come before I ever get inside you."

"Please don't stop." She dropped her head back to rest on his shoulder and covered his hand with hers.

"Show me." He pressed his open lips to her neck. "Show me how you like it. I wanna make you feel good, Stevi. I wanna make you feel like a fucking queen."

She guided his hand over her swollen, sensitive skin and let him take her weight as the first wave of heat washed over her. His lips and his tongue moved over her neck, licking and sucking as she rode his hand and bucked against him. The orgasm—the first true orgasm she'd had in what felt like forever—lapped at her slowly, rolling over her body like warm ocean waves. The heat spread from her core to her fingertips and her toes, and still, he moved his fingers over her in big, slow circles, drawing it out as long as he could.

"Did you hear that moan, Stevi?" He nipped at her earlobe. "I dream about that sound coming from your lips. I dream about you, naked, in my bed. Your legs wrapped around my waist, and your pussy hot and tight like a glove on my dick."

She looked at him over her shoulder when he drew his hands away from her. Watched him pull his wallet from his back pocket and dig a condom out. She looked up to meet his eyes when he dropped the wallet to the floor and stuck the package between his teeth.

Hungry to see him, she watched him shove his jeans and his briefs down over his hips, freeing his erection. Again, she looked up to meet his eyes as he took the condom and tore it open with his teeth.

When he had rolled the rubber over his long, thick cock, he reached for her again. Stevi braced herself with her hands on the counter and sighed with pleasure as he eased into her from behind. He was still for a moment, his hands on her hips and his cock deep inside her. Stevi's thighs still tingled with the aftershocks of the orgasm. She wanted him to move again; she wanted to feel his cock sliding and pressing inside her.

"Are you okay?" His voice was quiet and tight, and Stevi knew he was hanging onto the little thread of control he still had.

"Gimme more." She tilted her hips just a tiny bit, and he rewarded her with a low, guttural growl. Fingers still molded around her hips, Duncan slowly drew back and then eased into her again. Stevi's heartbeat felt powerful and erotic in her throat as Duncan moved inside her. She rocked on her feet to move with him, moaning softly each time he filled her, and gasping in relief when his fingers clutched her harder and he moved faster, the tension inside her begging for release again.

She held onto the counter with one hand, but as Duncan's breathing grew rougher and faster, when she felt him ready to explode inside her, she let go of the counter with her right hand and stroked the sensitive skin of her core again. Duncan gave her one last deep thrust, and then he held her still as his body convulsed inside, against hers. His whispers traced chills over the skin of her neck; his words of pleasure and praise were a hot, tingling thrill down to her toes.

"You okay?" he asked again after several long moments of heavy breathing and soft, sexy murmurs.

"Yes."

Was she? Was she sorry they'd finally had sex? No. Was it as incredible as she thought it would be? Yes. But she wanted more. She needed more. The feel of his clothing—the occasional rub of denim against her bare legs and the feel of his shirt touching her where her pajama top had inched up over her back—was a little bit sexy, a little bit intriguing, but she wanted skin. She wanted to be naked, and she wanted to press her mouth to every inch of Duncan's body, to his skin.

"I'm sorry."

Sorry. Why was he sorry? Stevi bit her lower lip and tucked her chin to her chest.

"Sorry?" she whispered. "What does that mean? You're still inside me, and you say you're sorry? How am I supposed to take that?"

He loosened his grip on her hips. Stevi sighed softly when he stroked the palm of his hand over her stomach.

"It means I didn't mean for this to happen this way." He kissed her hair and nuzzled his lips to her neck again. "I didn't bring you over here to do this—"

"You didn't come to my house and ask me to come with you with this in mind?" She was hurt, but she was pleased that her words had a sharp, sarcastic edge to them. If they were still stuck in this play together and walk away mode, damned if she would let him see her heart.

"I didn't mean to do you up against the kitchen counter," he said quietly. "I wanted to talk. To take you to bed."

"Duncan, I'm not a china doll." She closed her eyes. "I don't break. I've had sex against walls and on the floor and in cars."

"Not with me." He kissed a trail of soft, sweet touches down her neck. "We can walk away now and pretend we got it out of our systems."

Stevi swallowed hard and tried to pull in a deep, calming breath. But her shoulders jerked against his chest, and he probably knew she was fighting not to cry. For a moment, she considered it. Grabbing her clothes and running. Pretending this hadn't happened, pretending, at least, that it meant nothing to her.

"You can do that?" Her voice was gruff with emotion when she finally spoke.

"I don't want to." His words wrung another shiver from her. Palm still flat on her stomach, he eased his fingers down lower. "But I can if that's what you want me to do."

"You know what I want you to do, Duncan?"

"I wish you would tell me, Stevi, because I can't read you. I don't know what the hell you're thinking, what you're feeling—"

"I want you to take my clothes off me. I want you to take your clothes off. And I want you to take me to your bed. I want you to touch me."

"Are you sure?"

"The only thing I am absolutely sure of right now is how badly I need your hands on me. Everywhere."

She waited for him to say something, to move. When he didn't, her eyes burned with tears.

"Do you not want me? You don't want the whole package?" She cleared her throat.

"What? How can you possibly ask me that?"

"I'm asking you to take me to bed. I'm asking you to touch me, and you're frozen there behind me. Like you don't want to have to look at me. Is that so it'll be easier tomorrow to face me, or is it because you already got what you needed?"

"Jesus, Stevi." He groaned. She looked over her shoulder as he finally eased away from her. She watched him move through the gray darkness, one hand holding his jeans up and the other he used to dispose of the condom in the garbage can under the sink. She faced him when he turned back to her.

"Which is it?" she whispered. "Because I never in a million years thought it would be like this between us. I thought you—"

"Be like what between us?"

Frustrated, hurt again by Duncan's apparent lack of desire Stevi threw her hands out to her sides.

"You are an awesome guy." She squeezed her eyes closed. "You're one of my favorite people in the world. I thought this would mean more to you than it does. I'm not asking you to give me the rest of your life, but I thought you would be different."

"Stevi, you're not—"

She dropped her hands and gathered her shirt in her fingers. Whipped it off and dropped it to the floor.

"Touch me." She took a step toward him. "Touch me, Duncan. Trace promised me if you had a peek the other night, you would want—"

She stopped talking when he moved. He kicked out of his jeans and strode across the room with a glint of anger in his eyes. Stevi gasped in shock, outrage, when he picked her up to haul her out of the room.

"What are you doing?"

"Taking you to my bed, Stevi Hague," he growled. "Don't say you didn't ask for it."

CHAPTER 21

STEVI'S SKIN WAS WARM AND SOFT UNDER HIS HANDS, AND damned if he didn't want to stop in the hallway and press her to the wall and take her again. He wanted to smooth his hands over her flat, hard belly and sculpt her breasts in his palms. Touch her nipples and watch them bead with pleasure. But he refused to stop walking, refused to lower his eyes to look at her until they were in the bedroom. He was done with being careful. They were in way too damned deep now to rewind and recover their same, easy friendship, and he intended to lay her down and make love to her as if she weren't one of his—hell, what was she? A best friend? Family? One of his favorite people in the world, that almost covered it.

Which was no one. Duncan didn't even flinch at the thought. Nope, he'd never been so damned blinded by love and lust that he was thinking about things like grocery shopping together to fix dinner together and sitting on the porch together only until night fell and they could go to bed together and make love and wake in the morning and do the same delicious things all over again. Every day.

Until now.

Goddamn Stevi Hague. Duncan Marks wanted her. *Life* with her. He wanted to hold hands with her. He wanted to take her to movies and dinner and concerts. He wanted her to lean on him when she was tired or sad. He wanted her voice to be the last he heard every night, not the goodnight at the back door of the Queen. But lying beside him in bed, his arm around her waist and her back to his chest, he wanted a softly spoken goodnight as she drifted off to sleep.

Once down the hall and in his bedroom, he put her on her feet. The lighting in here was no better than the kitchen; just enough gray over black to see the outline of her nude body, the tiny curves of her hips and the proud thrust of her perfectly sized breasts. Her nipples were already small and tight, and her chest heaved—probably in indignation at the way he'd just manhandled her and carried her in here.

His dick throbbed, wanting more of that same slick heat.

"What the hell does Trace Dixon have to do with you and me and your naked body?"

She stared at him silently, chin tilted up in defiance.

"Fuck it." He shrugged. He'd worry about Trace and whatever the hell Stevi meant by what she had said later. Right now, he needed Stevi. Eyes locked with hers, he unbuttoned his shirt in record time and shrugged out of it. She fought the urge to look at him; he saw her chin tip a fraction of an inch, but when he hooked his fingers in his shorts, she lost the battle and looked.

He wouldn't have thought it possible, but her hungry gaze, the flare of her nostrils as she breathed deeply, and the uneven hitch of her chest when she gasped with arousal turned up his own heat. Duncan wasn't sure he'd ever wanted a woman as badly as he wanted to consume Stevi Hague.

Touch her. Taste her. Own her.

Pleasure her.

Oh hell yes, he wanted his hands on her breasts. That little slice of skin he'd been watching for the past several months had been the subject of far too many dreams, and now he would put his hands, his mouth on her there. Suck the puckered scar into his mouth. Drag his teeth over her taut nipples and then close his lips on her and suck her there until she cried out for more. He planned to kiss his way down her stomach and push her thighs open and bury his face there. He wanted to taste her arousal, wanted to hear her break in his bed, with his tongue on her clit, and his fingers inside her.

She lifted her head and caught her breath when he stepped closer to her. He leaned around her and then tugged the quilt and top sheet back on the bed, his arm brushing hers. For all he knew, sparks flew from the skin-to-skin contact.

"Last chance to change your mind." He sounded brusque, but Stevi only stared at him, her eyes glazed with the same need that consumed him.

"I'm still waiting for you to touch me." Her voice was quiet but firm. Duncan watched her wet her lips with the tongue he tasted every night in his dreams since that first night he had kissed her.

He let his eyes roam over her lean, luscious body again and felt like a damned kid in a candy shop. Hungry, greedy, he wanted to touch her everywhere at once. He wanted his hands and mouth all over her, but when he lifted his gaze to look at her again, her brows were arched and her face almost frozen in a look of pain.

She honestly believed he didn't want her.

He would just have to prove her wrong. And if it killed him, he would do it inch by inch from her head to her toes. After fucking up the grand plan earlier, he would make the rest of his night about Stevi. Maybe he wasn't ready to tell her he was in love with her, but he would worship her all night, and he would love every second with her.

He wanted to start with her face. She was beautiful, and her smile was like an arrow in his heart. He wanted to kiss her smile. But first he had to find it. He had hurt her far too often the past several days; the fact that it was unintentional didn't change that.

"Every day at the bar," his voice was a little sideways, so he cleared his throat as he reached to cup her breasts in his hands, "I want this. Every goddamned time you lean over, you better fucking believe I look, Stevi. The little v of your skin. I know when you've been in the sun. Sometimes, you move just right, and I can see the curve of your breasts under the lace. And I spend the next half hour talking my dick down. I'm a bartender, not a male dancer. Not cool to walk around with my dick so hard, my pants look two sizes too small."

He lifted his eyes from her breasts long enough to meet her eyes. Saw that the skin around her eyes had smoothed as her frown eased, but she still watched him uncertainly. The curves of her breasts rested in his hands, but still with his eyes on hers, he thumbed her nipples. When she sighed with pleasure, he did it again.

"I'm not sure what Trace has to do with you and your breasts and your nipples," he tipped his head as he rubbed his thumbs over her now in circles, "but I told you I don't share. I want this body—all of this body—to myself."

"It wasn't like that," she whispered.

He knew it wasn't like that, because Trace was in love with Leah, and because Trace was his friend. But there was something to the comment, and he intended to get to the bottom of it. Later.

"What's this scar from?" He traced his fingertips over her left breast and touched the scar at the base of her neck.

She flicked her tongue over her lips causing Duncan's dick to twitch.

"Curling iron."

"How?"

She shrugged and shook her head. "Dropped it."

"Every day I see your scar, I want to kiss it."

"And now?"

"I'm gonna kiss you everywhere, Stevi Hague." He nodded. "Starting right now."

"Duncan." She breathed his name, but she dropped her head back when he leaned in to press his lips to the scar. He dragged his fingers back over her breasts, pausing to tweak her nipples. "That feels good."

"You feel good," he whispered. "That first night I kissed you?"

"Mmm." She lifted her hands, brushed her fingers up the backs of his arms.

"I came home and went to bed and thought about you."

"Me, too."

"I jacked off, Stevi. Thinking about you."

He waited for her to slap him. Push him away. She only curled her fingers around his arms.

"Have you ever done that?"

"Mmm."

"Touched yourself? And wished it was me?" He flicked his tongue over her collar bone and moved his hands again. One he stroked lower over her stomach and around to her back. The other, he used to play with her breasts.

"Yes."

"When?"

"The night I was out with Grant."

Duncan drew back in surprise and met her gaze. He couldn't help the grin that tugged at his lips.

"You cut a date short? To come home and touch yourself and think about me?"

"Yes."

"Why didn't you tell me that?"

"You didn't want to talk to me much the next time I saw you," she reminded him.

"Did you come?"

"Yes."

Duncan lifted his hand and cupped her chin. She stared at him expectantly, but he was done talking.

"Let me make you come." He licked her lips and took her hand in his. Her eyes went wide with wonder when he pulled her hand to his groin. He drew back to look down their bodies when she closed her fingers around his hard shaft.

"You have an incredible body, Duncan."

He sucked in a sharp breath and rolled up to his tiptoes when she smoothed the pad of her thumb over the tip of his dick.

"That feels incredible." Gently, he pulled her hand away and backed her closer to the bed. "But you first. I want you on your back, and I want my mouth on you."

"Duncan." The soft whimper and the flash of desire in her eyes almost did him in.

"Can I make you come? With my mouth?"

Eyes locked with his, a look of desperation on her face, she answered with a slow nod.

"Are you sure you don't wanna—"

"Stevi." He leaned in to rest his forehead on hers. "Look."

"What?"

"Look at my dick." He cupped his hands around the back of her neck. "I'm so fucking hard right now just thinking about the things I want to do to your body, I'm gonna blow. I'm not gonna take more from you until I make you see how sexy you are. I'm gonna lick you until I hear that moan I love so much."

Rather than answer him, Stevi reached for him. They fell to his bed together, and Duncan rolled her over to lie flat on her back. He scooted down her body, desperate to taste her. Stevi arched her back and sighed when he flicked her nipple with his tongue. He played at her breasts, wondering if this was a one-night thing, if he would ever sleep with her again. Because as much as he wanted to keep going, as badly as he wanted to put his mouth between her thighs and slide his fingers inside her, he would stay here and love her breasts and her nipples forever, if this was their only time together.

Her hands roamed over his shoulders and his neck. They were warm and soft over his head. The more he licked her sensitive skin, the harder she pressed his head to her chest. Finally, he closed his lips around her and tugged her nipples —one at a time—into his mouth. Stevi murmured her pleasure, but when she closed her legs around his back and arched into him, pressing her wet heat to his chest, he nipped at her and then eased down her body.

She was pliant, and when he pushed her thighs apart, she lifted her head from the bed to watch him. He smoothed his hands over her inner thighs, dragged one hand back over her leg, and flicked his fingertips over the back of her knee.

"Duncan!" she hissed when he opened his mouth on her inner thigh and sunk his teeth gently into her skin. He was quick to follow with his tongue, the scruff on his jaw marking her tender skin.

Instead of moving to her core, he turned his attention to her other leg and played with her knee and rather than bite her, he fastened his lips on her thigh and sucked her skin gently into his mouth.

"Please." She propped herself up on her elbows and watched him again. When he lifted his head to look at her, she arched her eyebrows and offered him a pretty little pout.

"What do you want?" He lowered his mouth and blew over her. Watched her writhe a bit on his sheets.

"Please, Duncan?"

"What do you want, Stevi?"

"Make me come. Please."

Because she expected his kiss first, he pushed her legs apart again and stroked his thumb over her center. When he found her hot and wet, he slid his finger inside her. She swallowed hard when he flicked his gaze up to meet hers again.

"More?"

She nodded quickly.

Duncan eased another finger inside her and then stroked her slowly and deliberately, eyes on her as he moved his fingers.

"Tell me." He pressed his lips high on her thigh, where her panty line would be if she were wearing any.

"What?"

"When it feels good."

"Duncan, everything about tonight feels good."

"Good." He kissed a trail over her mound and looked up at her again. "But I mean when I hit the spot here. Tell me."

She nodded.

Her face was flushed with desire, and her nipples were so small and tight, Duncan thought they probably hurt. She shifted slightly on the bed, and Duncan moved his fingers over the same spot inside her. She dropped her head back for a moment, and Duncan focused on her breasts.

"Is that it?" he asked softly. "That spot right there?"

"Mmm. Yes." She sighed. He slid his fingers around again and again, watching the tension build in her body. She moaned softly, body twisting and turning with pleasure and pain.

"Stevi?"

"Hmm?"

"Do you like that? Right there?"

"God, yes."

"You're beautiful, babe." He ducked his head as she lifted hers to look at him. He slicked his tongue over her, felt his dick throb when her eyes glazed over and her eyelids closed. She moaned again, and her breathing grew heavier as he tasted her desire. He added his thumb to the pressure on her core and groaned in appreciation when she crashed back to the bed and lifted her hands to stroke her breasts.

"Let go," he whispered when he felt her tighten a bit around him. She reached for him, stroked her fingers over his head, and Duncan lifted his face to kiss her hand. Finally, she wrapped her legs around him and broke with a long, low moan of sheer pleasure. "I got you, Stevi. Let go. Still feel it? I've got you. It's okay."

Her body quivered under him, and still he stroked her, kissed her, the sound of his name on her lips so arousing, he worried that he would come before he got inside her again.

"That was …" She rolled her head on his bed and shrugged as he moved up her body. "Jesus, Duncan, I'm so incredibly jealous of every woman you've ever been with."

"It's you, Stevi," he promised her. "I need you."

"Yes, please." She reached for him as he leaned to the right to open the drawer of the nightstand. He grabbed a condom, but she took it from him and opened it.

"Let me, or we're not gonna need this," he said with a shaky laugh as he took the condom from her and rolled it on.

"Don't," she whispered as he eased the tip of his cock inside her.

"Don't what?" He clenched his teeth and squeezed his eyes closed.

"Don't be gentle, Duncan." She threw her arms around him. "You're not gonna hurt me."

CHAPTER 22

STEVI STRETCHED AND SLID HER HAND OVER THE COOL SHEETS to touch Duncan. After making love with him here in his bed, they'd curled together—her head on his chest, his arm around her waist, and her leg over his—and slept. Through the remaining hours of darkness, she had felt his presence there with her, whether his hand stoked her back or his arm held her possessively or just the heat of his body lying so close to hers. The cool sheet set off alarms in her head. She blinked her eyes open, sad to see that daylight lit the room through the filmy curtains on his window.

So, he was gone. She sighed and buried her face in his pillow. Half of her wanted to revel in the memories of what they'd done together the night before, and half of her wanted to cry because it was over. And apparently, Duncan had skipped out of his own house to avoid waking up with her. She turned to her side, away from the side of the bed where Duncan had slept, and reached to the nightstand for her phone. When her fingers came up empty, she remembered she had left it on the kitchen counter. Not like she'd had any choice when Duncan had picked her up and carried her in here.

She wondered what work would be like now. If the past few weeks had been hell, how would they find their way back to friendship now?

"Hey."

She looked over her shoulder as the mattress gave. Duncan, still gloriously nude and incredibly beautiful in daylight, slid into bed behind her. He scooted close enough to her to press his chest to her back and drape his arm around her waist.

"I thought you left," she whispered. Facing away from him, she rolled her eyes at herself for the confession.

"Why would I leave with you here in my bed?" The light drag of his fingers over her belly tickled.

"It's daylight." She shrugged. "Lots of things change in the light of day."

"Is that your way of telling me you want me to take you home?" He stilled his hand. "Because I don't want to. I want you right here in my bed, in my arms."

Stevi swallowed hard and took a deep breath. "I don't wanna go anywhere, Duncan."

"Would you promise me one thing?" He kissed her shoulder, kept his lips pressed there while he waited for her to answer.

"What?"

"Don't ever fake it with me."

Stevi stared at the wall for several long moments. What the hell did that mean?

"Stevi?"

"I promise," she said softly.

"Remember when I told you that making a woman come is my biggest turn on?"

"Mmm." She remembered a lot more than that about that conversation, but she didn't want to talk about his affinity for nineteen-year-old girls, so she kept her mouth closed.

"I meant it." He dragged his fingertips over her stomach again. "I wish you could have seen yourself when I had my fingers inside you."

Stevi couldn't help the smile that played at her lips.

"I wish you could have felt how good that felt to me."

"Don't fake it. I wanna make you feel like that every time we're together."

She took a deep breath, considered questioning him, and decided against it.

"What?" He kissed her shoulder again. "Talk to me. Please?"

Stevi leaned into him and settled on her back when he eased back to give her room.

"Hi." He smiled when their eyes met. Soft, sweet smile. Stevi could almost swear his eyes were twinkling. "You're beautiful in the morning."

She snorted and rolled her eyes. "Yeah. You made me cry last night, so my eyes are probably puffy and gross."

He dropped a kiss on the tip of her nose. Stevi felt it like an arrow in the heart. She tried to hide her flinch, but she saw from the look of interest on his face that she failed.

"What's wrong?"

"Faking it…" She pressed her lips together.

"If you tell me you faked that last night, I'm gonna tell you to get a job in the sex industry—"

She cut loose with a loud, sharp laugh. "I promise I didn't fake a thing, Duncan."

"Then what're you thinking about?"

"Are we doing this? Is this a thing? A relationship?"

"Do you want it to be?"

Stevi's stomach clenched with fear at the thought of being honest with him. But if she lied, if she let him believe making love hadn't meant anything to her, she could lose him.

"I do." She lifted her hand and brushed her fingers over his lips. "But I'm scared."

He nodded and took her hand in his. Kissed her fingers and then opened them to press his lips to the palm of her hand.

"What are you scared of?"

"Well, we haven't done a great job at this so far," she reminded him. "I don't wanna hurt you. I don't want you to hurt me. I don't wanna hurt the Queen."

"Last night was perfect, Stevi."

She stared at him silently. "The sex was perfect," she agreed finally. "But what about what happened before?"

"I didn't come on to her—"

"But you let her do it to you. Because you wanted me to see it."

She expected him to deny it, so she was surprised when he ducked his chin and turned his slight frown away from her.

"Not my proudest moment," he said quietly. "I didn't mean to hurt you. I wanted your attention."

"You've had my attention for a long time now," she reminded him.

"You stormed out of the Queen that one night, and it was like you were just done."

"That one night." She arched her eyebrows. "Do you mean the night you got a look and turned me down?"

"What?"

"Do you know what that did to me?" Her voice broke, so she rolled her head on his pillow to avoid his intense stare.

"You think—?" He grunted with frustration. "You think I didn't want you?"

"You looked at me. You touched me. And you told me to go home."

Duncan bit off a string of muttered curse words and leaned closer to press his forehead to hers.

"Stevi, we were at the Queen." His voice was tight with emotion. "Do I have fantasies of sitting you on the bar and doing what I did to you last night? Fuck yes, you bet I do. But I wanted *this* for the first time. I wanted to lay you down and blow your mind here. In my bed."

"Why didn't you just say that?"

"I tried." He rubbed his lips over her forehead and then kissed a trail over her cheek to her lips. "I was going to suggest we go out. Take a Sunday and go out."

"Out." She arched her eyebrows.

"On a date." He shrugged. "I thought we could go out on a date. And then I could bring you here, and we could take things slow and make love. Instead, I pissed you off, and then when I did bring you here, I was so hot for you, I took you in the kitchen against the counter."

"I'm not complaining." She smoothed her hand over the scruff on his chin.

"I know I handled it wrong that night I told you I wanted to be with you." He pulled back from her. "I'm sorry for that."

"The night you put an end date on whatever it is we're doing?" she asked him. "Because I get it. If you still need to have that…deadline…but yeah. Kind of hurt when you said it like you did."

"So." Duncan's eyes were stormy gray now. "Where do we stand? I mean…I gotta be honest with you, Stevi."

She flinched and closed her eyes. "Okay, but you have a harsh brand of honesty."

"I don't wanna play for a while and walk away." His whisper was gruff. Stevi opened her eyes and lifted her head from the pillow. She kissed him and scooted closer to him.

"What do you want?"

He took a deep breath. "I think we deserve a shot at this. At what we're doing."

"And what if we screw things up?" Her voice thick with emotion, she met his eyes boldly when he looked at her again.

"I don't know, but I can't just walk away from this. From you."

"I can't, either, Duncan." She nodded.

"There's one other thing I need to ask you about."

"What?"

"Trace."

"What about Trace?"

She pushed gently at his shoulder until he moved to lie on his back. Duncan's eyes grew wide with surprise and pleasure when she moved to straddle him.

"Do you have more condoms?" She grinned as she leaned over him to brush her breasts over his face.

"Yes."

"Good."

"I made coffee," he told her.

"Okay." She smiled and reached way over the bed to the drawer he had opened last night. "In here? Condoms?"

"Yeah, but don't you want me to—"

"Nope. My turn to do you." She smiled sweetly as she grabbed a condom and then shifted back over to straddle his waist. He stacked his hands under his head and watched with delight as she tore the condom wrapper with her teeth and then moved to put the condom over his straining cock.

"Wait." He caught her wrist and tugged until she looked up at him.

"What?"

"Tell me."

"Leah." She shook her head. "I was upset. After you turned me down. She asked Trace if he found me attractive."

"She asked Trace if he found you—?" Duncan frowned. "Were you parading around like this for him?"

"No." She rolled her eyes. "No, Duncan. I'm not that person. I hope you don't think that. I don't sleep with every guy I date."

"I don't think that, but I don't get this thing with Trace."

"I was getting dressed. She invited him into my bedroom Asked him if he liked my bra. And he said yes. And he said you would, too."

"The one you were wearing that night?"

She nodded.

"Dammit."

"It's a bra, Duncan," she said softly. "No different than a bikini top."

"It is, though," he muttered. "Bras...all that lace...they're intimate. And I could see your nipples through the lace."

"Yeah, well, I'm sure Trace didn't look that hard—"

"I'm sure he did," Duncan corrected her.

"Duncan? Trace has Leah." She shrugged. "He's not interested in me."

"I'm still pissed," Duncan said with a small laugh. "At myself. I drove you to that."

"Oh my God. No." She sighed. "Nothing happened. He's in love with Leah. I'm in love with the idea of them. I would never—"

"I know." He nodded. "I just…I don't ever want to share you." He moved, lowered his arms and reached to stroke her breast with his fingers. "Like, I *never* want another man to look at you and touch you like this."

Stevi arched her eyebrows. "Okay."

"You don't have to make that promise, Stevi." He tweaked her nipple. "Just let me have you to myself while we're together."

"I don't want another man, Duncan," she whispered. Before the word *ever* could slip out, she bit her lip and covered his hand on her breast.

She leaned back. Felt him watching her when she rolled the condom over him and then she moved forward to her knees and sank back to take him inside her body.

CHAPTER 23

Duncan worried that Stevi still might run, but they spent all morning in his bed together. They played and slept, stroked and kissed, always skin-to-skin. When she slipped from his bed to use the restroom, he went to the kitchen to grab their coffee. He brought her phone to her, too, because he worried that if she made her way to the kitchen for it, she might decide she needed to go home. Back in his bed, she sipped the coffee and announced that she hated that she couldn't brush her teeth. They laughed, set their cups aside and shared coffee-flavored kisses.

She texted Leah to tell her the front door was unlocked. Duncan had a key, so Stevi would just use it to get inside later to shower and get ready for work. But Leah texted her and said she'd noticed that the door was unlocked and had left it that way for her. Pressed to his side, Stevi glanced at Duncan and looked back at her phone. Leah and Trace had already left the house; Leah had an appointment with her ob-gyn, and Trace went with her. Leah said she assumed Stevi hadn't been kidnapped, but she hoped she wasn't with Grant.

Duncan noticed a bit of color in Stevi's cheeks when Leah's next text dropped on her screen. Leah hoped Stevi was with Duncan, and if she was, she would forgive her for that tiny little stick of worry she had felt earlier when she had finally gone to check on Stevi when she hadn't come out of her room for coffee.

"Do we need to talk about Grant?" Duncan brushed his lips over Stevi's hair and then settled his chin on her head.

"Not unless you wanna talk about your hookups, and I gotta tell you, I don't wanna know about any more of your girls."

"I promise you it was one time, and it was several years ago."

"Women my age can't compete with—"

"There's no competition, Stevi." He smoothed his fingers up her arm. "Lots of pretty women out there, but you own a room when you're in it."

Stevi tilted her head to look at him with wide eyes.

"Every guy that walks into the Queen wants to get near you. And I get to stand behind the bar night after night watching every damned one of them put their eyes all over you."

She cleared her throat and jerked her head in a quick no.

"Duncan, they've never mattered to me. None of them matter to me."

"Except Grant."

"He's just a friend."

"A friend you sleep with."

"There's no competition, Duncan." She lifted her hand and pressed her thumb to his lower lip. "I promise you that."

"Okay." He nodded. "So. Next maybe we need to talk about Leah and Margo."

She stared at him boldly, her eyes still wide with something that bordered on fear. He wondered if she was afraid that he would want to hide what they were doing or if she was afraid he wanted to tell everyone. It was hell trying to read her; it had been much easier before, when they were just friends.

But it mattered more now.

"They know," she finally admitted. "At least they know how I feel."

"About me."

He couldn't help the grin when she nodded.

"How do you feel about me, Stevi?"

Her laughter was soft and sweet, but he noticed she didn't offer him a direct answer.

"They know that you've kissed me, and that I wanted…more."

"Margo knows." He rested his head on the pillow propped against the head of the bed. "In fact, Margo ripped me apart for how I handled the approach."

Stevi relaxed against him again and rested her cheek on his chest. She stroked her fingers down his bare chest and flattened her hand on his stomach. Duncan stared at her hand there, her bright strawberry pink nails pointing down toward his dick.

"I can't go to work and pretend this didn't happen." He pushed the words out quickly, praying she wouldn't argue with him. "I can't sneak around and kiss you in the cellar when no one's around. I don't want to stand behind the bar and watch you work the tables and wonder if some guy with big guns and fast hands turns you on."

"I don't want to hide it, either." She turned her face slightly to kiss his chest. Duncan ate up the delicious feeling of her warm hand sliding lower and her fingers wrapping around his dick. The sight of her pretty hand on him was enough to make him hard again. "Women watch you, too, Duncan. That redhead is in the Queen all the time."

"So, if we go in tonight and I grab you around the waist and turn you around and lay one on you, you're gonna be okay with that?"

He felt her smile against his chest.

"Yes. Just don't throw me up on the bar during open hours. That could get messy."

"Seriously. You're okay with this? You're okay with me touching you? Putting my arm around you in front of Leah and Margo?"

"You think they don't know what we've been doing all day?"

"But them knowing what we're doing and us being open about our feelings…two different things, Stevi. Is that okay with you?"

"Yes."

Duncan studied her face when she lifted her chin again and tilted her head to look at him. Their eyes met and held. The air throbbed with other things he wanted to say, with all the things he needed to hear her say. Duncan's heart pounded frantically in his chest; Stevi noticed, because she flattened her hand there over his heart. But neither of them said more, neither of them acknowledged that there might be something more going on. For Duncan, and maybe Stevi, too, it was too soon.

"Are you going to text Leah?"

A hint of a smile touched Stevi's lips.

"What? To promise her I'm not with—"

Stevi had promised him that Grant wasn't competition, but that didn't mean he wanted to talk about the guy anymore. Not when he and Stevi were naked and lying together, and he was hard and ready to take her again. He didn't even want to hear the guy's name again.

"To tell her you're with me."

Stevi blinked at him. His eyes were drawn to her mouth, where she nibbled uncertainly on her lip.

"Do you want me to?"

"Kind of. Then again, I kind of want you to put your phone down. So we can play."

"Again?" She laughed softly, but she arched her eyebrows. "I do have to walk in tonight. You know that, right?"

"Are you sore?" he asked quickly.

"No, but you've totally blown any records you might think I hold or want you to break."

"Not about breaking records, Stevi." He brushed her hair from her face. "It's just how much I want to touch you. Make you feel good."

He watched her when she broke the eye contact. When she looked at her phone, he held his breath, wondering what she would say. Technically, he was late to work. They didn't open the doors for customers until four, but Duncan was always in the building by noon, busy doing some kind of upkeep or stocking the bar or even working on the continual organizational project in the cellar.

She texted *I'm with Duncan. We'll be in soon* and then twisted around to set her phone on the nightstand. Duncan relished the feeling of her warm, soft skin sliding over his as she moved in his arms. Funny that it was time to get moving, time to get ready for work—past time to get ready—and he didn't want to leave his bed. Well, more to the point, he didn't want to leave Stevi.

They worked together. He reminded himself that as she turned back to him. They could get ready together, and he could drive them both back to the Queen and they would spend the whole evening side by side behind the bar. But Duncan worried about how things would go once they were outside his bedroom, once they were back at the Queen and surrounded with real life and people and family. Would Stevi change her mind? About telling people they were involved? About being involved with him?

He used to be the guy who did a woman—usually okay with lingering until both he and his partner achieved orgasm—and walked away, no looking back. No regrets. He didn't treat those women badly after they were together, but Duncan had never promised a woman anything more than sex. He'd never wanted anything more than sex. Now here he was, afraid to press play with Stevi, afraid to move forward in case Stevi decided one night with him was all she needed.

CHAPTER 24

STEVI CRANKED THE IPOD UP IN HER BATHROOM AND MOVED through her shower, hair, and makeup routine with ridiculous pent up energy. Which was crazy, considering she and Duncan had gotten little rest during the hours they were together. They had showered together, too, but Stevi showered again to start from scratch with her hair. Her phone beeped with a text when she put her hair dryer away. She figured it was Leah, ready to ask for details.

Duncan's name on the screen made her a little warm and gooey inside. She picked up the phone to read his text.

You could wear those strappy sandals.

Stevi laughed softly. Did he want her to wear the strappy sandals, or was the text an excuse to reach out to her and make sure they were...what? Okay? Just okay? Stevi leaned a shoulder on the bathroom wall and stared at her phone. Butterflies raced a circuit in her belly as she relived the last ten hours. She and Duncan had stripped away each other's clothes and spent priceless hours getting to know each other's bodies. Even now, the thought of Duncan moving inside her, moving over her, one hand at the back of her neck and the other holding on to his headboard for leverage, took her breath away and made her weak in the knees.

You like the strappy sandals?

They hadn't stripped away everything, though, because even though she had said she wanted to give this…thing…a shot, she hadn't come clean about what she was feeling. Okay, that was partly due to the fact that she didn't know for sure what she was feeling, but more than that, she was afraid to admit to Duncan Marks that maybe she was in love with him. Because Duncan Marks—the Duncan she had known forever—scoffed at true love and said it was for other people.

I think they'd go well with your nails and my sheets.

Stevi hissed out loud when she read his text. She felt a zap of heat straight from her belly to the girl stuff, and it took her a moment to make her brain work so she could answer him. He beat her to it and texted again before she could respond.

Actually, you could come to work in a garbage sack and you would turn me on.

Stevi laughed softly.

If you don't stop, I'm not gonna make it to the Queen.

She had hesitated earlier when Duncan brought her home. Invite him to wait for her? She had the feeling Duncan had wanted her to ride with him to the bar, but she needed a few minutes. Not to nurse any regrets, but to revel in thoughts of what they had done together. She thought Duncan was disappointed that she didn't want him to wait around for her, even though he had laughed when she reminded him the likelihood of them getting sidetracked if he came inside to wait for her while she showered and dressed for work.

Was he insecure? Stevi didn't want a clingy relationship, but on the other hand, this was new and she and Duncan had some weird dynamics to deal with, so she was sort of... relieved...that he was uncertain about the hour—two, tops —separation.

Now, though, with that text, she wondered if he was just flirting with her. Sexting, maybe. Or if that was his way of being sure she hadn't stomped inside and changed her mind the second he was out of sight.

I'll stop, because you are the best part of being at the Queen.

Stevi blinked at her phone and set it back on the sink again. She left it there when she went to her room in search of something to wear. For months now, she had been planning her wardrobe based on what she thought might turn Duncan on, and then completely fed up with him and the games, she had done a one eighty on him and dressed for comfort. What the hell did she wear now?

Nerves tingled in her fingertips as she slid the hangers right to left in her closet, searching for something that Duncan would like. She stared long and hard at a tight, skimpy skirt that she hadn't worn in at least a year. When her mind automatically offered her the visual of Duncan sliding the skirt the rest of the way up her thighs and sliding his hand between her legs, a rush of heat climbed her neck. She rolled her eyes and fanned her cheeks and passed on the skirt.

She considered a simple black t-shirt dress, but again, the thought of Duncan with his hands under the dress and between her legs made her blush and laugh. As intrigued as she was at the thought, it seemed a little too obvious. Finally settling on a pair of skinnies and a white sleeveless blouse, Stevi took a few minutes back in the bathroom, making sure just the right amount of cleavage would be visible to Duncan.

Had he sent that last text? Because that was the one that really touched her. She checked her look one last time in the mirror and decided she was ready. Considered texting him back, because she loved being with Duncan every night at the Queen, but she hesitated. Because what if he hadn't sent that text? What if Leah or Margo had snatched his phone away and sent it to mess with him? Kind of ornery, but Stevi could see her sister or her cousin doing it for fun.

Doors opened at the Queen at four, and Stevi rolled out of the driveway and crossed town to arrive at the Queen a minute after. Her stomach was all jumpy again as she climbed out of her car and made her way up to the back door. She knew no one in the bar was going to judge her for sleeping with Duncan. But that didn't mean she wasn't a little anxious about how they would feel about watching… something…going on between her and Duncan. It was one thing to talk about Duncan kissing her. Admitting that she was attracted to him. It was something totally different to be affectionate—like lovers and not longtime friends—in front of the people she loved most in the world.

She was also anxious about seeing him. She couldn't wait to get inside and get her eyes on him. To see his shirt—he had pulled a gray tee on after their shower—molded over his chest and shoulders. The same shoulders she had smoothed her hands over, the shoulders she had explored with her lips and her tongue, the shoulders she had slid her legs over when he had buried his face—

"Hey, darlin'."

Stevi looked up as she neared the back door. Trace, on his way out—probably making sure the patio tables and chairs were ready for patrons—held the door open for her. Nerves jumped to her throat, but the smile on Trace's face warmed her. She swallowed the fear and answered with one of her own.

"Hey."

"Leah's been watching for you."

"Oh, I'm sure," Stevi mumbled. Trace reached out and tugged gently on her hair, making her second guess her decision to leave it down.

He chuckled. "Well, that, too. But she's excited about her appointment today."

"Oh! Everything went okay?"

"Yep." Trace nodded. Stevi was torn between throwing her arms around him because she was excited for him and Leah —and because she was still high on the time spent with Duncan—and hurrying by him to avoid any awkward moments when they made eye contact and tried to decide if they were going to acknowledge that Stevi had spent part of the night somewhere else. With Duncan.

"You…okay?" He took another step outside as Stevi slid by him. She turned in the doorway and opened her mouth to let a breezy *yep* out. But their eyes met, and Stevi flashed back to the day in the office, when she had asked if he would rent his house in Nashville to her. He had said yes, but he hadn't wanted to. Not because he didn't want her to live there, but because he thought there was something between her and Duncan.

Trace Dixon was one of them now, and she couldn't blow him off just because the thought of talking to him about the things she did with Duncan lit her cheeks on fire.

"I am." She nodded. She heard a tiny note of uncertainty in her voice, and apparently Trace did, too. Stevi nodded again. "Yes."

"Good." Trace let go of the door, but instead of walking away, he stepped closer to her and dropped a hand on her shoulder. Stevi felt a rush of warmth when he leaned in and dropped a kiss on the top of her head. "Be happy, Stevi."

She squeezed her eyes closed and lifted her hand to touch his chest. Maybe way back when Trace Dixon was just an award-winning songwriter from Nashville, she thought he was smoking hot. Now, Trace Dixon was soon to be her brother-in-law, and she was pretty sure Duncan Marks was the hottest guy she'd ever laid eyes on.

Stevi stood on her tiptoes and pressed a kiss to Trace's cheek.

"Thanks, Nashville."

"Leah was in the office when I came down," he told her as she backed away from him. With a small smile and a nod, Stevi mumbled a thank you and went inside. She heard the quiet swish of the glass door closing behind her, but she swept her gaze around the bar in front of her. Her heart rate had been a bit jacked up earlier—well, making love with Duncan had made her breathless with desire and anticipation and ecstasy —but even on the drive here, she had been aware of her skittish heart beat pounding fast and hard in her throat and her chest. Now, though, she felt like someone was line dancing on her chest, and then when she finally saw him at the opposite end of the bar, her heart skidded and pounded extra hard and then there was a calmness inside that made her wonder if she had just died inside. Maybe it didn't matter after the last ten hours. She felt her lips tug up at the corners. Oh yeah, if she died now, she'd die happy.

But if she was still standing here in her favorite place watching Duncan's back and shoulder muscles bunch and ripple under his t-shirt as he talked to a couple of guys at the bar, that meant there could be more of what she'd been doing earlier. More kissing. Kissing Duncan was…incredibly… erotic. Lying naked in his arms, his warm skin pressed to hers, she'd been surprised at the time he had spent just kissing her. Sweet and soft. Deep and wet and slow.

Stevi shivered, aware of the tingling in her thighs and her nipples. She imagined that whole skirt scenario again—the one where Duncan pushed the material up over her hips and slipped his hand between her legs—and wobbled a little on her feet. In the strappy sandals.

The strappy sandals Duncan thought would go well with her nail polish and his sheets.

She strangled a small cry of need and slipped her phone from her pocket to check the time. She'd been here a whopping seven minutes.

"Great, Stevi." She blew out a frustrated sigh. She was wet thinking things about her skirt and Duncan's hands, and she only had at least seven hours to go before they could see how well her sandals worked with his sheets.

If she didn't move now, Trace would come back inside and run over her. She groaned, dug deep for another cleansing, calming breath, and started walking. The steady tap of her heels on the hardwood floor finally drew Duncan's attention. Still standing with the two guys at the end of the bar, he turned to look at her and stopped talking.

Stevi fought the urge to make a run for the bar and climb up over it to kiss him. She had to put her purse away in the office. She should probably check in with Leah, because she most definitely wanted to hear about Leah's appointment with her ob-gyn. And because she wanted…well, she kind of wanted to tell Leah that Duncan had blown her mind and that she was so wrapped up in love with him, there would be no peeling her off of him. But…maybe that part could wait. Maybe it would better to play things a little closer to the vest for a while. Enjoy—check that—love the hell out of what he did to her body, the way he responded to her touch, and all that fun stuff here, too, now that they were hopefully back to that level of ease together and not worry about the future.

Duncan made no attempt to be coy as his eyes took a trip south over her body. He took a step away from the guys and braced his hands on the bar. Stevi felt a flicker of heat between her thighs when he leaned further to look at her feet and then dragged his eyes back over her body to meet her eyes.

His lips quirked up in a slow, lazy, sexy-as-fuck smile.

"Hey."

She wondered if him just staring at her like that could make her come. Maybe if she wiggled a bit right there on her feet. On the strappy sandals that Duncan apparently liked.

He arched an eyebrow, and Stevi felt another rush of heat. She grinned, forced herself to look him in the eye, and tipped her head in reply.

"Leah still upstairs?" She cleared her throat and patted her purse as if to remind him she needed to run up there to put her things away.

"Yep."

She nodded. The guys Duncan stood near were involved in their own conversation, so neither of them paid attention to the two of them as they eye-fucked each other in the main room of the Queen.

A little uncomfortable, a lot twitchy and bothered under Duncan's intense gaze—the same way he'd watched her face the first time he'd spread her legs and slipped his fingers inside her, patiently stroking until he found the spot that made her eyes roll back with pleasure—Stevi licked her lips and started to speak. Duncan's gaze moved from her eyes to her mouth, and she suddenly thought maybe she should have worn a dress after all.

"I'm…" She cleared her throat again. Wrapped the fingers of one hand around the purse strap thrown over her shoulder and pointed upstairs with the other hand. "Gonna…"

He nodded, but he didn't move. How the hell was she going to get through the next six hours and forty-five minutes when every look he gave her stoked the slow-burning fire he had started last night? She ducked her head as her cheeks flushed again and turned to go upstairs.

Those same tingles of anticipation—the ones she felt that first night he leaned in close and kissed her, the ones she felt in the middle of the night when he slipped his hands inside her shorts and panties and pushed them down, the ones she had felt just moments ago when he had unapologetically looked his fill at her body—danced over her skin. Her nipples were hard beneath the skimpy silk bra she wore, and she resisted the urge to rub her arms or hands over them to ease the tightness. Who the hell could work for hours with her nipples painfully aroused?

"Hey!" Leah greeted her with a grin when she stepped into the office. "I'm so excited, but I wanna know what's going on with you first."

"Nope." Stevi leaned over and tugged the bottom drawer of the desk open. She dropped her purse in but snagged her phone from the outside pocket before closing the drawer. "You go first."

Leah rolled the office chair back a bit and flopped backwards. Stevi studied her sister, relieved to see the flush of happiness in her cheeks. Her sparkling eyes flashed with something—eagerness to share but curiosity, too, maybe— and she sank her teeth into her bottom lip.

"You sure?"

"Yes."

"Okay, well, first, I talked to Joe earlier. And I talked to Kenzi for a few minutes."

"Yeah?" Stevi rested her butt against the corner of the desk. "How is she?"

Stevi noticed the slight frown cross Leah's face. She wondered again how Leah was dealing with her anxiety over giving birth. But Leah's smile came back quickly, a bit smaller, a little bit sad, but it was there.

"Kind of the same." She winced and shrugged. "But…Stevi… maybe this is the new…normal. For them."

Stevi nodded. She absolutely thought this was the new normal for Kenzi and Joe. And it was the saddest and happiest thing in the world, as far as she was concerned. Kenzi could have died in the birthing room. Joe could be raising his kids without his wife, without the love of his life. So, things had changed; in Stevi's mind, change was doable. Death wasn't. She couldn't imagine the grief of losing someone you loved so intimately.

When her eyes filled, she looked away and prayed Leah hadn't noticed. Sure, she wished, she prayed for Kenzi to continue to make progress in therapy. And she prayed for Joe and the kids and Kenzi's family that they could accept and adapt when maybe Kenzi didn't improve.

The thought of losing Duncan—

Where the hell had that come from? Okay, yes, she had known Duncan for years. Loved him as…a friend or family… for years. But now…

"Um." Leah nudged Stevi's leg with the toe of her flat brown sandal. "We heard the baby's heartbeat."

"You—?" Stevi jumped away from the desk as if an errant pencil had goosed her. "You heard the baby's heartbeat?"

Leah nodded. "Nashville and I both heard it."

"Oh my God, Leah." Stevi squatted in front of her sister, surprised at the pull of sore muscles in her legs and her back. Duncan had given her more of a workout than she had had in a damned long time. She bit back the smirk on her face and pressed her hands to Leah's still small belly. "That's so…incredible."

She lifted her chin to look at Leah, not surprised to see tears —happy tears, she knew—sliding over her face.

"We want you to be the baby's godmother," Leah told her.

"You know I am honored to do anything and everything in the world for your baby."

Leah nodded. "Something else."

"Okay." Stevi arched her eyebrows and waited for Leah to continue.

"I want you to be there. When the baby's born."

"Of course." Stevi shrugged. "Wild horses won't keep me away, Leah."

"With me. In the birthing room."

Stevi nodded. "Promise."

"Because I'm still scared to death, but I can do it. I can do it. With you and Nashville."

Stevi squeezed her eyes closed and swallowed around the knife in her throat.

"There's nothing wrong with being afraid," Stevi whispered. "I would be scared, too. But you can do it. You can do anything, Leah. I know that about you."

Leah dabbed at her eyes and nodded. She let out a quiet sob that turned into a sharp laugh. "Well. I have to. At some point, this kid's gonna demand to come out."

"I can't wait." Stevi nodded. Overcome with emotion, she leaned into Leah and kissed her high on the belly. Rested her head there for a moment. "I gotta tell you I never thought I wanted this, Leah. I didn't think I wanted love and marriage and babies." She swallowed again and took a deep breath. "And now I do, and that's kind of hard to deal with."

"Why? You would be such a good mommy." Leah stroked her fingers through Stevi's hair.

"Because I'm almost thirty, and I haven't settled down, and I don't—"

"I thought when you said you were with Duncan that…you guys…"

"We did." Stevi nodded. She shifted her weight a bit and twisted around to sit on her butt on the floor in front of Leah.

"And it wasn't…what you wanted?"

Stevi met Leah's eyes.

"Oh, Stevi, baby, you love him." Leah smiled, but she ducked her head and dabbed at her eyes again. "Don't you?"

"So much," Stevi whispered. "So much, Leah."

"And he doesn't feel the same?" Leah asked, her face drawn with concern.

"I don't know." Stevi shrugged. "We didn't—"

"Wait." Leah took a deep breath. "Tell me. Everything….Well. Not everything. But…"

Stevi glanced at the open office door.

"He's at the bar. He can't just come up here," Leah reminded her.

"It was…I left here last night pissed off at him. Hurt—"

Leah nodded. "I heard."

"What?"

"Margo and Tania."

"Tania knows?"

Leah chewed on her lip. "Stevi, you guys have been mooning over each other for months. Probably the majority of our customers know what you're both thinking and feeling."

Stevi groaned and dropped her head back to rest on the desk drawer.

"He showed up at the house and texted me. It was rough, Leah. I mean, the kissing…the flirting has been fun, but we made a mess of things, too. And even when we started messing around at his house…"

"It doesn't have to be perfect to be perfect."

"What?" Stevi rubbed her forehead and looked up at Leah with a frown.

"It doesn't have to be romance novel perfect. To be Stevi and Duncan perfect."

Stevi shrugged. "It got perfect," she said quietly. "It was… every kind of perfect."

"Then what's…"

"I'm just…scared."

"You didn't say the L word."

"No."

"But…"

"We both decided we want to…be together. See what happens."

"Why are you scared? You should be on top of the world."

"I am." Stevi nodded. "Leah, he kisses me like I'm oxygen and he needs me to breathe. I've never…I've never been kissed so…intimately. Ever."

"But?"

"We want to do this, and we agreed that when we're done, we would walk away and be friends. For the Queen. For you guys. For us."

Leah winced.

"I can't do that. If he decides he's ready to move on, I can't stay here and watch him live and kiss someone else that way."

"Maybe you should tell him you're in love with him?"

"Duncan Marks?" Stevi rolled her head on the desk and shrugged hopelessly. "He doesn't believe in love. Remember?"

"And then there was you. Pretty sure Duncan's had a lot of women—" Stevi flinched at Leah's words. "Sorry, but we've watched him go through women quicker than he empties whiskey bottles downstairs. Sounds like he spent more time kissing you in one night than he takes to have a fling with other women."

Stevi laughed softly.

Leah coughed and cleared her throat. "You know I have to ask."

"I told you it was perfect."

"So. He's…good?"

Stevi snorted. "He's so fucking good, Leah. He's so giving. So tender."

"Duncan?"

"Right?" Stevi nodded.

"Honey, he's in love with you." Leah tossed her hands up as if to say what can you do? "Get your butt down there with him.

He's probably in knots worried about what we're talking about."

Stevi grinned, but Leah was probably right. If she were up here alone, and Duncan was down at the bar talking to Trace or even Margo, she would be climbing the walls, wondering what was being said and if he was just avoiding her after what they had done.

"He asked me to wear the strappy sandals."

Leah laughed. "Yeah, well, Nashville wears his boots to bed sometimes."

"Well, thank you for that mental image."

"Good traction."

"Duncan's got a great headboard. For gripping. For leverage."

"Go."

CHAPTER 25

WHAT THE HELL WAS STEVI DOING UPSTAIRS? DUNCAN KNEW for a fact that Leah's appointment with her doctor went well. She and Trace had both walked in earlier with big, cheesy smiles—so bright, Duncan had wished for his shades—and they had plopped right down at the bar and gushed all about the baby and the heartbeat, like he wanted to hear it. He did, though. Maybe a year ago—hell, maybe a few short months ago—he would've rolled his eyes and reminded them that they were bringing yet another mouth into the world to feed and that babies were a financial burden, and they took up too much of your time.

But today, he had slumped on the back bar, crossed his arms over his chest, and listened eagerly as the happy couple spoke about the heartbeat and wondered if they were having a boy or a girl or if they wanted to know for sure. Leah had gotten a little teary-eyed again over the baby they had lost, but Trace had simply linked his fingers with hers, and they had shared some sort of kumbaya moment there together and left Duncan yearning for…more.

For Stevi.

For more with Stevi.

He didn't dislike babies. He loved Berkley, loved his favorite uncle status. He had just never thought fatherhood was for him. But maybe that was because he hadn't believed in loving a woman enough to want to share that bond with her, a bond that should last a lifetime. He wasn't jaded, either. He didn't hate that his dad had married Margo's mom and that they were happy. He didn't hate that his mom had moved to Chicago in search of a new life; he talked to her often enough. No hard feelings.

And also he didn't hate the idea of being with Stevi. Long term. He wasn't sure he was ready to dive in head first with baby stuff—it would probably be best to take plenty of time to practice making babies first. But he couldn't deny that warm feeling that kind of spread through his chest and his gut at the thought of always having Stevi in his life. The possibility of hearing her laugh every day for the rest of their lives. Watching her sleep. The way she turned to him to snuggle against him and rest her head on his chest. Kissing her a hundred times a day. Every day. For the rest of their lives. The way she used to belt out lines from Elvis songs back when it was just the four of them playing around while they cleaned up once the Queen was closed.

Knowing Leah was okay—happy—really made him wonder what the hell Stevi and Leah were talking about up there in the office. Duncan sighed as he mopped up a clean spot on the bar for the fourth time—no one had even sat at that spot yet, since it was early and there were currently only a handful of people here. He supposed they could be talking business, but that didn't explain that nagging feeling in his gut. The twitchiness he had been feeling since leaving Stevi at her house to get ready for work.

He hadn't wanted to leave her. And he wouldn't admit it to anyone else—Duncan didn't do clingy, yet here he was the new poster child—but he wondered if she had been champing at the bit to get away from him. Had she needed time alone because she had regrets? Doubts? Was she upstairs right now with Leah spilling about how she had made a huge mistake with him?

Duncan whooshed out a quick breath as the memory of their goodbye came back to him. He had hinted that he wouldn't mind waiting for her, and she had licked her lips and grinned suggestively and said they both knew they would be late for work if he came in to wait for her.

But she hadn't answered that last text, either. He'd taken that leap earlier—where the hell that courage or stupidity had come from, he wasn't sure—but he'd sent that text about her being the best part of being at the Queen, and she never had answered him.

Or was she simply sharing details?

Simply?

He blinked and tossed the bar rag down. With another long-suffering sigh, he swept his gaze over the five guys currently in the bar, ready to sweep in and pour refills. No one needed him, though. Not even Stevi. He would never for one second believe Stevi Hague needed him for anything. Other than sex. They had been hot together. No question. If she had faked those orgasms, he would eat the next liquor bottle he emptied.

Was she telling Leah that? Was she telling Leah about how he had leaned her up against the kitchen counter and taken her from behind? Had she liked that? Sure, she had come apart in his hands before he slid his pants down, but had she really wanted it like that? Should he have been gentle? Okay, so they had taken things to his bedroom and slowed everything down and taken long, tender moments to explore each other—

Duncan turned his back to the room at large and squeezed his eyes closed. His dick was awake and ready for more.

"Duncan, do you know where Margo is?"

He groaned and huffed out a quiet breath. Glanced at Trace over his shoulder and shook his head.

"Try the kitchen?"

"Yep."

Trace slipped back through the door to the kitchen, and Duncan reminded himself he had a hell of a long night to get through before...well, maybe even before he could talk to Stevi. Really talk to her. Make sure she wasn't having doubts.

He smoothed his fingers over his lips, pushed thoughts of Stevi's soft hands on his lips and his neck away, and reached for his bottle of water. He took a swig and then nearly choked on the swallow when he heard the telltale sound of Stevi's heels on the stairs.

He turned slowly to watch her. Felt all of his blood head south as a smile crossed his face. Hair down around her face, falling over her shoulders, the pensive look on her face and the sandals—the strappy sandals—kicked his pulse up by about a thousand beats per minute.

She looked up suddenly, as if she felt his stare. The water bottle slipped in his hand a bit when their eyes met, and her lips tipped up in a soft, sweet smile.

A soft, sweet smile that did nothing to ease his nerves. In fact, Duncan had to lean forward and rest his forearms on the bar, because Stevi's smile sucked the air from the room, and he felt a little overwhelmed. Guys didn't swoon. Jesus Criminy, how did he even know the word? Guys got turned on. Guys had to adjust their dicks and keep it cool.

She hit the bottom step and turned toward the bar. Duncan watched her when she stopped at the one occupied table near the front window to talk to the customers there. Three middle-aged guys. All with wedding rings—yep, he had looked. Stevi beamed that dazzling smile at them. Duncan looked away. Yeah, no way he was going to be able to stand this now. Not after being with her and knowing from experience how hot she was. How sweet. Giving.

He stalked down the bar and slipped back through the door to the kitchen. Margo was up to her elbows in diced vegetables, prepping for happy hour appetizers. She glanced up at him with arched eyebrows.

"Need something?" she asked.

"No." He propped his hands on his hips and turned a tight circle in the small room.

"Maybe a drink," she suggested. Duncan thought he heard Tony—their chef—snicker. He eyed the back of Tony's head suspiciously, but when Margo stepped away from the prep counter and toward him, he snapped his gaze back to her. "You okay?"

He nodded.

"Duncan—"

"Did Trace find you?" He cut her off with a severe frown.

"Um." She nodded once and stared at him with concern.

"Okay." He turned and marched back to the bar, surprised to find Stevi there pulling a beer for someone who had slipped in while he was in the kitchen. He started to protest, to tell her he would do it, but she only offered him a smile—it was different than the one she had flashed at the table of guys a few minutes ago—bumped the tap and set the glass on the bar top.

This guy—old enough to be Stevi's dad, at least—nodded and mumbled his thanks and turned his eyes to the folded-up newspaper in his hand. Stevi turned sideways and watched with big eyes as Duncan joined her at the bar.

"Hey." Her grin was a bit uncertain, and if he didn't know her well enough to know that, the way she nipped at her bottom lip and raised her eyebrows in anticipation was a dead giveaway.

"Hey." His gut was almost rolling with nerves, and his blood pressure was probably somewhere between heart attack and stroke, but he couldn't help the smile he gave her in return. She had worn a touch of makeup—something that made her eyes pop—and her lips were natural pink and shiny, and he wanted to kiss her. Lick that gloss away and see what it tasted like. What she tasted like underneath it. Feel her soft skin against his lips.

"I missed you."

Her whispered words flipped a switch in his gut, and in true domino effect, a rush of warmth flooded through him. He couldn't answer her, not just yet, because his throat was a little tight.

"Duncan?"

The note of uncertainty in her voice was a direct hit in the heart. Still a little choked up—and damned if he knew how to fix that, because he didn't remember a time when he had felt that way before, unless maybe after Berkley was born— Duncan reached toward her and linked his fingers with hers.

He nodded.

"Would you say it?" Her voice was gruff, and he realized she was a little overcome with emotion, too. She coughed quietly and looked away, as if she believed he hadn't missed her during the short time they had been separated.

"I missed you, too, Stevi." He spoke so low that he knew only Stevi could hear him. She nodded, eyes still on his chest, and finally lifted her chin to look him in the eye again. He wondered if she wanted to kiss him then as much as he wanted to kiss her. Slide his arms around her and draw her in and hold her.

"Hmm." Margo cleared her throat behind him. She stepped around them and picked up her iPad that she had left by the register just before they opened. "And so it begins."

Duncan felt Stevi flinch, but when they turned to look at Margo, she was grinning. She winked at them, tucked her iPad under arm, and moved back around them without another word.

This was it. Give her fingers a squeeze and pretend like they were going to control themselves and have a fling and no one was going to comment on it. Or give in to what he wanted and mark her as his in front of everyone—the bar wasn't busy, but the people who mattered most were here. Might have seemed a little weird to Duncan the first time he'd seen Trace kiss Leah here in the bar. In their place of business. But then again, Trace hadn't thrown Leah back over his arm for an old-fashioned dip and laid one on her. Not when the bar was open, anyway. Just a soft, sweet kiss that left no doubt about what was going on between them.

Duncan wanted the people who mattered to him to know what he felt for the woman standing with him behind the bar. It was new to him—this thrilling mix of happiness and possessiveness—but he thought he kind of liked it.

Stevi watched him with wide eyes as he stepped close enough that he could feel the heat from her body. Her breath hitched and shot a jolt of *hell yeah!* through him when he leaned in and brushed his lips over hers.

Sweet and soft, Duncan kept his tongue in his mouth, even as badly as he wanted to taste her lip gloss and her skin. But her breath was warm over his face, and she kissed him back, with the same soft, intimate pressure of her lips on his. Duncan's heartbeat was through the roof, the way it had been last night when he'd slid his hand between her legs and touched her in the most physically intimate way a man could touch a woman.

"You didn't answer that last text." He drew back and forced himself to meet her eyes. Her eyebrows jumped in response, and this time, she squeezed his fingers and then rubbed her thumb over the back of his hand.

"I thought maybe Margo or Leah sent it," she shrugged apologetically, her smile a little sad, "to be ornery."

"I sent it, Stevi." He let go of her hand, but only to settle his on her hip. "I love every minute I spend here with you."

That sweet blush that he had seen on her cheeks several times earlier today flushed her face again. Her smile turned shy, and then she nodded, and that *hell yeah!* he had ridden earlier turned into *I'm fucked.*

He was head over heels in love with Stevi Hague, and Duncan knew how to do a lot of things. But being a man in love wasn't one of them.

"Me, too." She stood on her tiptoes and kissed his cheek and then before he could read anything into that, she turned her face, still close enough to feel her heat, and kissed him again on his mouth.

Business picked up as the evening crawled by. Definitely a good thing, Stevi knew, because they needed thirsty customers to keep the Queen open. But she was dying for the clock to hit eleven, so Duncan could lock the doors, and they could shoo everyone else away and relive the passion they had shared earlier. Good to be busy, too, just because it made time go faster.

But not tonight. Of course. Being busy meant Stevi was away from the bar more often, waiting tables. And Duncan was at the bar, deep in discussion with anyone and everyone up there, including the damned redhead. Apparently, she thought she had finally hooked him and she was back to reel him.

Stevi wasn't worried.

Well. Okay. She was sort of on edge as she moved from table to table, taking orders, bringing refills. Duncan wasn't rude to the woman—and Stevi wouldn't want him to be—but he wasn't tugging on her line, playing along, either. The Duncan she had known forever might tease and flirt with her, even if he had a little something going on with someone else. Not exactly cheating, but he never committed to anyone, as far as Stevi knew.

Hard to reconcile that with the man who had made love to her through the early morning hours and then held her close and told her he wanted to explore whatever it was they had going on. Had he ever said those words to another woman? Didn't matter how long or how well she had known him, that was something she would never know with certainty.

She trusted him, though.

Right?

Well. Yeah, she did, but then, Stevi had never felt this fluttery, tingly, warm feeling over any guy in her life, and she had never lain in a man's arms and said she wanted to see where things went, either. She trusted her friend Duncan not to hurt her, but she was a little bit afraid to cut loose and love Duncan Marks.

Which pretty much sucked, because she did. Even before Leah spelled it out for her, even before Leah hinted at it— back when Leah had hurt her feelings for asking if she had slept with Duncan—Stevi knew that the way Duncan made her feel safe and scared all at the same time was something different. And because it was something different, she suspected she was in love with him.

Just hadn't known what to do with it.

Still didn't.

"Breathe, Stevi." Leah's voice at her ear made her jump. She blinked and realized she'd stopped to watch Duncan. The redhead was still vying for his attention; she wore a cold shoulder blouse tonight that Stevi thought was pretty. Her hair fell in luscious waves down her back, and Stevi realized she was wondering if Duncan preferred red to her dark blond.

She turned slowly toward her sister and stared at her silently for a moment.

"Can I ask you something?"

"Yeah." Leah lifted a shoulder casually. Stevi followed her when she backed away from the tables to stand a few feet from everyone. Stevi refused to look at the bar again, but her skin tingled with awareness. He was looking at her. They'd laughed together, after that sweet moment earlier. It was almost like all the tension had simply drained out of both of them, and then they were Stevi and Duncan, forever friends and now lovers, and Duncan had even caught her in the kitchen for a quick kiss with a little bit of tongue.

"How do you do it?"

Leah arched her eyebrows and pressed her lips together. Stevi rolled her eyes and shook her head.

"Well." Leah shrugged and tossed her hands up helplessly. "Remember when you were twelve, and you came to me and asked me how to kiss boys?"

"I wouldn't have asked if I hadn't seen you kissing Evan Newman."

Leah smiled. "Yeah. And since I wouldn't tell you how to kiss boys, you told Mom you caught us."

Stevi narrowed her eyes at Leah. "I always thought it was

gross. The whole tongue thing. I mean, do I really wanna know what the guy I'm gonna kiss just put in his mouth?"

"When did that change?"

"I'm not sure when that changed, but I can tell you when I fell in love with kissing."

Leah's smile turned soft, so Stevi rushed to continue talking. There was no time to get gooey and sentimental right now. She needed to grab a beer and hit two more tables. And if the tingling sensation in her nipples and along her inner arms was any indication, Duncan was still watching her.

"How can you watch Trace talk to other women? And not… want to kill them? Every last one of them?"

Leah threw her head back and laughed.

"I'm not kidding, Leah. I mean, Trace is gorgeous. You know every woman in here is undressing him with her eyes."

"Okay, first," Leah reached for her and rested her hand on Stevi's arm. "If you're worried about the redhead, she's got nothing on you—"

"Well, great, Leah, but you weren't the one making out with her—"

"Neither was he." Leah shook her head. "She was hanging on him. He was letting it happen. Wrong? Sure. But not the same as if he had actively participated."

"And so, if you found someone munching on Nashville's neck, you'd—"

"And also, I trust him. Completely."

The words were a knife in Stevi's heart. If she didn't trust

Duncan, there was no way they would ever be a couple. A real couple, like Leah and Trace.

"So, this relationship is never gonna—"

"Hang on." Leah squeezed her arm. "You get the beer you need for that table. Let me get the ladies up front. Meet me back here in five."

Choked on frustration—over the interrupted conversation and the worry that she and Duncan weren't equipped to go the distance—Stevi simply nodded. Still, she hesitated. Watched Leah move to a tall table up front and greet the four ladies there. Finally, she gave herself a mental shake and moved toward the bar.

"You look upset." Duncan eyed her for a moment before he grabbed a pint glass to fill for her.

Still distracted by the conversation, she only shook her head.

"But you do," he told her when he set the beer on the bar. "What were you and Leah talking about?"

"Actually," Leah breezed up beside him and winked at Stevi. "I was telling Stevi that my boobs have been really sore. Since I've been pregnant."

Duncan didn't flinch. "Yeah? So have the guitar picker rub them."

"Oh, he does," Leah said with a grin. "I need two glasses of Dykstra cab, a chocolate martini, and a water."

Stevi took advantage of the distraction and picked up the beer to deliver it. She checked on another table as she waited for Leah to deliver her drink order and meet her near the back of the bar, nearly under the stairs.

"Okay." Leah fiddled with the ring Trace had put on her finger a while ago. It wasn't an engagement ring, exactly, but pretty much everyone Stevi knew looked at it that way. Including Trace and Leah. "You guys are different. You walked into this whole relationship in a totally different way."

"I don't know many women who get a fairytale love affair like you did." Stevi tipped her head, but she and Leah shared a grin.

"I had a fairytale," Leah agreed, "but you do, too. It's just a different story."

"Trace followed you across the country."

"Duncan has loved you from afar for years."

"Right." Stevi nodded. "Because, what? He was in love with me when we were kids?"

"He loved you then." Leah shrugged. "Didn't he? Didn't you? Love him? All this time, haven't you loved him?"

"Well, yeah, but not...I didn't..."

"But it's love. And now, after all these years, he started pursuing you. Sweetie, if you wanna pretend like you didn't see it, okay, I'll go with that. But we did. Margo and I noticed stuff. He walks you out every night—"

"He walks all of us out when we leave alone."

"He fixes you special drinks."

"I'm the only one who'll taste test for him."

"He teaches you drink recipes."

"Maybe because he's the only bartender here, and he'd like a night off."

"Maybe. Maybe it's because he likes to be around you."

"Leah, I trust the Duncan I've always known not to hurt me." Stevi held her hands up to put a stop to Leah's longwinded argument. "But this is so new. With Duncan. And just new for me, because I've never felt like this before."

"I know." Leah nodded. "I get it."

"You didn't? Feel this way?"

"You know how I insisted forever that Nashville and I were just friends?"

Stevi nodded. Noticed Duncan watching them again, but she saw Margo join him behind the bar.

"The first time we made love, I just…He laid me down, and I told him how much I loved him. It was just…the most natural thing. To say it. You guys haven't said the L word yet. It's okay, Stevi. This is new."

Stevi sucked in a deep breath. She gave Leah a reluctant nod.

"So, are you saying I should tell him how I feel?"

"I am," Leah nodded, "but I get that you're scared, and I want you to guard your heart, too."

"Wow, that's pretty helpful."

Leah grinned. "Sorry. I love you, Stevi. And I love him. But if he hurts you, I'm gonna kick his ass."

"It's nice that you have my back."

"Always."

LATER, WHEN DUNCAN FINALLY FLIPPED THE LOCK ON THE door, Stevi looked around, frustrated that everyone was still here. Margo had told her earlier that her mom had taken Berkley for the night, and Stevi had encouraged Margo to head out early for a little time to herself. Obviously, that hadn't worked. Leah seemed tired, but sitting on the end barstool with her chin propped on her arms folded on the bar, she didn't appear to be in any hurry to leave.

"Okay, I'll admit one thing," she said quietly. Stevi was the only one close enough to hear her, but still, she moved to stand closer to her. Margo's laugh rang out through the bar from the kitchen. Stevi assumed she was talking to Trace. Unless she was on the phone. Would she laugh like that with Jess? She used to, but Stevi doubted Jess could make her feel that carefree and happy anymore.

"Spill." Stevi leaned against the end of the bar to listen to Leah, but she kept her eyes on Duncan as he gathered empties from the front tables.

"When Nashville left...on Tanner's tour," Leah sighed. "And I was here and pregnant and feeling old and unattractive—"

"What. The. Fuck. Ever." Stevi rolled her eyes. "You are so beautiful, and he knows it—"

"Thank you." Leah met Stevi's eyes and then nodded at her. "For making my point. Hello, beautiful Stevi."

At a loss for words, Stevi rolled her eyes again. Still. Leah's words sent a warm feeling through her chest.

"I hated that he was gone. I hated that he had women all over the country looking at him and thinking about the things he does with me."

Stevi licked her lips and answered her with a slow nod.

"Yeah. I get it." Stevi dragged her fingers back through her hair. "I want…"

"What?" Leah coaxed her. "What do you want, Stevi? Because you have to know before you move forward."

"I want to be the last woman he's with, because I want him."

"Ladies." Duncan winked at them as he hustled by them, two big stacks of empty pint glasses in hand.

"Why doesn't he use a tub?"

"He will," Stevi answered absently. "But he always carries as much as he can on the way back to get one."

Leah yawned.

"Are you going home with him tonight?"

"I hope so." Stevi shrugged. She caught the *wow!* look on Leah's face and laughter bubbled up inside her. "I'm sorry. Is this weird? I guess it probably is for you, but Leah, it feels so right."

"As long as I don't think about you being a stick thin fifteen-year-old with a braid and Duncan being an eighteen-year-old who was always partying and drinking. That makes it kind of…weird."

Duncan reappeared from the kitchen, his hands empty. Stevi glanced at him over her shoulder, but before she could say anything, he cupped her upper arms in his hands and spun her around to face him.

"Sorry, Leah, but I have waited a thousand years to do this."

Stevi gasped in surprise when he dipped his head and kissed her. A real, slow, wet kiss that lit little sparks down her body. Her nipples tingled so hard they ached, and knees suddenly a little weak, Stevi reached for him. Eyes closed, she pressed one hand against his chest, but just in case he thought she was pushing him away, she gathered his soft t-shirt in her fingers and held on. The other hand, she slid up the back of his arm. She didn't know if Leah heard him, but when she sank her fingers into his shoulder and curled her tongue around his, Duncan growled low in his throat.

"Yep, that's a little weird," Leah said softly.

Stevi opened her eyes to look at him when he drew away from her.

"Too weird?" Duncan looked at Leah, but he smoothed his hands down Stevi's back. He cupped her butt in his hands and gave her a playful squeeze. Stevi laughed softly and ducked her head to rest on his shoulder.

"No." Leah sounded sincere. "It's cool. Just…"

Stevi lifted her head to look at Leah when she hesitated.

"Well, actually, it's a little bit fascinating."

"Fascinating." Duncan nodded, but Stevi could see the slight frown on his face.

"I figured you couldn't keep a woman, not that you didn't want to," Leah teased. "I guess I have to admit I was wrong."

"Wow." Duncan rubbed his chin over Stevi's head and then looked down at her to kiss her cheek. "Nice to know you believed in me all this time, Leah."

She laughed softly.

"I'm hearing you're the man." Leah tossed her hands up in defeat, making Stevi blush a furious red.

"I've never seen her blush like that," Margo announced as she made her way through the back doorway to the bar.

"Oh my God." Stevi buried her face in Duncan's shoulder again. "You guys, stop."

"Why don't you guys go on home?" Leah suggested. "Let us stay and clean up tonight."

"No." Duncan rubbed his fingers low over Stevi's butt again. He hauled her in close, close enough that she felt his erection against her middle. "You have to be tired, Leah. You go home. Stevi and I have closing down to an art."

"You guys deserve some time off," Leah argued. "Besides, I'm gonna sit here and supervise, while Margo and Trace do the dirty work."

"Seriously, it's okay." Stevi stepped away from Duncan. "You go—"

"Oh my God. Margs?"

"You guys have eye-fucked each other no less than seven times tonight." Margo rolled her eyes. "And don't deny it, because not one of us is blind. Go home. Get naked. Have fun."

Duncan glanced at Stevi and arched his eyebrows in question. She shrugged.

"I'll get your stuff," he told her as he headed back down to the other end of the bar. Stevi watched him go, her heartbeat pounding in her throat at the thought of what they would do once they were finally alone.

"Stevi."

She jerked out of her thoughts and looked at Leah.

"He's hot." Leah grinned. "For you."

"Yeah, sure," Stevi nodded, "but does he love me?"

CHAPTER 27

Stevi found that planning—or searching frantically for something to wow everyone for Octoberfest was probably more accurate—for the Octoberfest was more fun when there was a possibility of a random sweet kiss or tender touch. She and Duncan had always had a strong work ethic, and they stayed true to that, but suddenly, he was more affectionate—publicly, romantically affectionate—and he would appear in the office for a kiss or sneak her down to the cellar for a quick, impromptu make out session. He tended to touch her more in the bar, too. Nothing inappropriate, but definitely in ways that left nothing in question about their relationship.

Never having been a part of something like this—of a relationship—Stevi found it both thrilling and comforting, and never mind the fact that maybe her sister and Trace did the same things. God only knew what kind of action the couch in the office had seen lately. Stevi and Duncan had shared some pretty heavy kisses there, though both of them had drawn the line there.

She went ahead and penciled a Euchre tournament in for the restaurant side of their place. Definitely German, definitely different from anything they had done since they were open, and as far as she could tell, something no other bars in the area had done in recent years. Still wasn't enough, though. She wanted something more. Something fun, a little bit rowdy, maybe, on the bar side.

When she mentioned it to Leah and Margo again—they were at Margo's house, taking a morning break from the Queen—they both reminded her they loved the idea of a battle of the bartenders. Stevi, on her knees on the floor playing with Berkley, sat back on her heels and looked from Margo to Leah.

"You really think so?"

"Yes."

"You guys, I don't make drinks like Duncan. None of us can make drinks like Duncan."

She turned her head away, suddenly consumed with thoughts of late night drinks with Duncan. He'd asked her recently, after a particularly slow, hot round of making love if she'd like to taste Sex With Duncan. She hadn't recognized the sexy rumble of laughter that came from deep inside her chest. When she agreed, said she wanted to try it, he had climbed naked from his bed, and curious, she had followed him through the dimly lit hall to the kitchen, eyes on his deliciously tight bare ass the whole way.

He had poured a splash of bourbon over an ice cube and handed her the tumbler. Rather than drink it, Stevi only stared at him over the rim of the glass.

"Isn't this just bourbon?"

"After making love with Duncan."

She had grinned, completely at ease standing naked with him in his kitchen, and finally, she sipped the whiskey and relished the burn as she swallowed.

"Like it?" He arched an eyebrow as she lowered the glass to sit it on the counter.

"Mmm." She stepped closer to him and settled her hands on his hips. "I might need to taste it again."

"Yeah?"

"Yep. Pretty sure."

Duncan lifted his hands to cup her face and then sank his fingers in her hair. Stevi let him draw her in closer for a kiss, but she had moved quickly and kissed her way down his neck and then his chest.

"That's a different drink," he had said when she went to her knees in front of him.

"You got a whole line of drinks?" she had asked as she pressed her mouth to his hip.

"I do."

"I hope I'm the only one tasting them."

"Always."

Stevi jumped when something soft hit her side. She squeezed her eyes closed and gave herself a mental shake, remembering that she was at Margo's, with Leah, and she was on the floor playing with Berkley. Definitely not the time or place to indulge those thoughts.

"Hey." She glanced at the wadded up pink fleece blanket on the floor and then lifted her eyes to Leah.

"I don't wanna know what you were thinking about." Leah winked. "But let's get back to business."

"Sorry."

"Can Duncan teach you some drinks?"

"Well, sure. But is he gonna wanna teach me drinks just to be his competition? Besides, just because he teaches me something or shares a drink recipe, that doesn't mean I can make the same drink he does. Kind of like Mom trying to teach us how to do her cinnamon rolls or apple salad."

Margo shrugged. "But you have time? To pick a few things up? Between now and then?"

"Well." Stevi scooched around to sit on her butt. She watched Berkley climb into her lap and reach for the blanket Leah had thrown at her. "Yeah. I think so. But again—"

"Okay, first?" Margo held her hand up to stop Stevi. "It's all in fun, so it's not like you guys are in a cutthroat competition. And second, you put your gorgeous face behind the bar with Duncan and call it a battle, and you're gonna win hands down."

Stevi chuckled softly. "Thanks, Margo."

"Okay. So you'll talk to Duncan?" Leah arched her eyebrows. She stretched her legs out in front of her and rubbed her hands over her sweet, little belly.

Stevi ducked her head as her mind raced back to Duncan's line of specialty drinks. She wasn't sure she could pick a favorite. Not when even Kissing Duncan—which consisted of lots of slow, wet kisses and ice-cold beer—was delicious.

"Never mind." Leah snorted. "I'll talk to him. And we'll get that ball rolling. I know it feels like we have a lot of time, but we're gonna blink and it'll be October."

She was right. Time had a way of sliding into warp speed. Especially when you were happy and determined to slow things down and hold onto that happiness.

"Okay." She laughed as Berkley twisted in her lap and used her red t-shirt to climb to a standing position. Berkley flashed Stevi a beautiful baby grin and plopped her hands on Stevi's lips. She wanted this. For herself. That didn't mean she was selfish, did it? Of course she wanted Leah and Trace to have a beautiful, healthy baby and a long, happy life together and maybe more babies and a house in the suburbs and cookouts and a soccer mom van. But wasn't it okay to want that for herself, too?

With Duncan.

She swallowed down the panic and took Berkley's hands in hers. A thrill shot through her when she kissed the baby's palm and Berkley cut loose with a loud, happy shriek.

What if Duncan didn't want that? What if he didn't even want her in his life permanently?

"How are we gonna do it, though? Like measure who wins?"

"We'll count tip money." Margo's answer was simple.

"We could donate the tip money," Stevi suggested. She lifted her eyes from Berkley and looked at Margo over the baby's black ringlet curls. "To the community. Or something. I mean, it's not like it'd be a ton of money, but—"

"We could do that." Leah dropped her head back on the sofa

cushion and closed her eyes, hands still roaming over her belly. "And the bar could match whatever you get."

Stevi looked from Leah to Margo and lifted her eyebrows in question. They could do that. That might actually bring more people in. She didn't believe for a minute that anyone was going to get too excited about seeing her behind the bar, and no way was she going to bring in big tip money. Not compared to Duncan.

"You okay?" Margo leaned from her end of the couch and touched Leah's wrist.

"Just tired."

"You sure?"

Leah opened her eyes and looked from Margo to Stevi.

"I'm sure."

"You're not having contractions, are you?"

"No." Leah sat up. "No, guys, I'm fine. I'm just tired." She grinned sheepishly. "Trace…rubs my belly…at night. Before we go to sleep."

Stevi felt a sudden rush of affection for the stud from Tennessee, but she groaned out loud. "God. Toothache. You guys are just so damned cutesy and sweet, I could barf."

"Hey." Margo curled her fingers around Leah's wrist, but she shot Stevi a look. "Who are you to complain? You're practically living with Duncan. Getting steady sex. Steady good sex, apparently, and I'm…not. I haven't had sex since January…maybe. Or maybe it was December. October."

Stevi narrowed her eyes at Margo. "Um. First. It's not good sex." She shook her head.

"Oh, here we go," Leah groaned and closed her eyes again. "Good job, Margo."

"He's smokin' hot, and it's phenomenal sex," Stevi corrected Margo.

"Damn." Margo sighed. "Pushed the go button, didn't I? Rub it in, Stevi."

Stevi laughed softly.

"And stop already. God, I don't wanna know how hot my brother is—"

"Don't say it like that." Stevi scooped Berkley up in her arm and buried her nose in the baby's neck. Her heart nearly swelled to bursting when Berkley wrapped her little arms around her. "We're not related—"

"I know. But still. Don't wanna think about that."

"Does it bother you?" Stevi asked softly.

"Not at all, but I still don't want details." Margo picked up her coffee cup and stared at it for a second. Stevi figured it was either empty, or anything left in it was cold. "Well, I do, kind of. Is that weird?"

Stevi's grin grew wider as she rocked Berkley in a big, exaggerated arc.

"Mom and Dad were cool with it," Leah reminded Stevi. "Surprised, maybe, but Mom's ready to plan a double wedding shower."

"Yeah, let's not push that," Stevi mumbled. "We haven't said the L word. Duncan might have a heart attack if you said the W word in front of him."

"Say the L word, Stevi," Leah whispered. "It felt so good when I said it and I saw his face light up."

"I think if I said the L word, all I would see is him hauling ass to get away from me."

"Stevi."

Stevi turned to look at Margo. "And you are…having phone sex, though? Right? With Jess?"

Margo snorted. "Nope."

"No. He quit calling?"

"He calls," Margo said quietly, "but no. We're not doing that. At all."

"So, you were lying?"

"That's harsh." Margo watched when Stevi plopped Berkley back on the floor and the baby squirmed around to all fours and then crawled toward her. "I was being brazen and bold and putting up a good front and maybe hoping it would happen."

"What's he calling about then?" Leah asked with a frown. Eyes still closed, her hands rested on her belly now.

Margo shrugged and shook her head. "I don't know. We just…sort of talk. About his life. My life. He asks me about Berkley. He's never hinted that…he wishes…things were different."

Stevi sighed.

"But, he's calling you."

Margo picked Berkley up and climbed to her feet. "I think we need to get to work."

"We haven't figured out the rest of Octoberfest," Stevi argued. "Have we? Are we done with that?" She watched Margo cross the living room with Berkley in her arms and then looked at Leah. "Really? Just the battle of the bartenders?"

"I think it's a great idea." Leah scooted forward on the couch.

"Guys, last year sucked. I don't wanna fail at this again."

"What?" Leah drew back as if Stevi had slapped her.

"I let you guys down. I didn't do enough."

"What're you talking about? We did okay."

"We didn't do enough. We should have had big numbers that month. And we didn't. Because I didn't plan big enough."

"Stevi," Margo said from across the room. The hallway was dark behind her, and from Stevi's vantage point on the floor, she looked much taller and a little bit scary with that big scowl on her face. "It wasn't you. We're all in this together. Every one of us. I mean, the only thing you could have done differently is offer lap dances or put in a pole. We're a bar. We serve dinner. We all plan it. We have an awesome chef to create those dishes. We sell liquor and wine and beer. We do it. We sink or swim. Together."

Stevi licked her lips and took a deep breath. Okay, so she had needed to hear that. She hadn't even known how badly she needed to hear that. Throat too tight to speak, she simply nodded.

"And again." Leah tipped her head as she stood up. "Use what we have available, Stevi. He loves being part of the Queen, and he loves to get his hands on Loretta."

Stevi grinned. Trace had named his favorite acoustic guitar Loretta, and she was pretty sure there was a close second named Lucille that he kept upstairs in the bedroom he shared with Leah.

"Okay."

"And." Leah held her hand out to Stevi, but Stevi shook her hand and climbed gracefully to her feet without help. "Don't forget he's connected."

"I don't want Tanner here," Stevi mumbled. "He makes me think of…" She shook her head, thoughts of Leah's miscarriage and Trace being on the road with Tanner threatening to overwhelm her.

"I know," Leah agreed.

"Hey." Margo patted Berkley's back and rubbed her cheek over her soft curls. "Joe's calling." She held her phone up as if they could see the screen from where they were and needed proof that Joe was, indeed, calling.

"Speakerphone?" Stevi suggested.

"We're gonna be late," Leah complained.

"It's noon." Stevi cast an *are you kidding me?* look at Leah. When Leah only grinned, Stevi felt her mouth drop open in shock. "Really? Nooners at the Queen? Leah, I'm shocked!"

"Like you and Duncan don't sneak down to the cellar for more than whiskey and wine."

"That's…I'm scarred." Stevi shivered.

"Once." Leah shrugged. Stevi shivered again, and Leah grabbed her by the upper arms.

"Guys!" Margo silenced them with a shout. "Joe? Remember?"

CHAPTER 28

THEY MIXED DRINKS. THEY TASTE TESTED. AT THE QUEEN. AT Duncan's place, though those tastings were a lot more involved. They played with different recipes at Stevi's, too, but Leah couldn't taste, and Trace maintained that he didn't drink much hard liquor. Still, they had fun. Stevi supposed she was learning; she thought anyone could follow a recipe. But as she had told Leah a few weeks ago at Margo's when they had made the final decision on the battle, that didn't mean she could make the same drink as Duncan and guarantee it would taste as good.

Still, they were having fun. And the whole battle of the bartenders was all in fun, anyway. The five of them had bellied up to the bar on a late Monday night after closing and decided that the Queen would, indeed, match any tips Stevi and Duncan were given the night of the Octoberfest. Together, they decided to donate the money to the American Stroke Association. Because if things had gone differently, if Kenzi had delivered Edison in a normal birth, Joe and Kenzi would still be around. But Nashville wouldn't be. Leah had shed a few tears over that thought, but she promised she wasn't wallowing in guilt. Just thankful Kenzi had survived and was fighting for every inch of recovery and progress she could make and that Leah had found the love of her life while searching for herself and her own truth in the aftermath of the stroke.

Stevi still hadn't talked to Trace about entertainment for the big night. Sure, she knew he would play. Some nights he spent a couple of hours playing and singing, and yes, even though Stevi had Duncan now, the way Trace kept his eyes glued to Leah when he sang love songs almost gave her a stomachache. Hard to mesh the happiness for her sister and the wistfulness she still felt about her own future.

So, while she planned on Trace playing at least some of the night, she had to decide if she wanted him to call in a favor or invite some hotshot country music person here to headline the entertainment. Seemed like a no-brainer when she considered profit margins and what it would mean to the Queen to pack the house. On the other hand, they—the Queen—had never been about brash, over-the-top anything, and a hotshot music person of any genre felt...too impersonal.

So, she struggled with that decision. In the daytime hours, before the door opened downstairs, she spent a lot of time up in the office, working on the marketing stuff for the Octoberfest. Yes, the community economic foundation had their own logo and their own banners and posters around town, and the Queen was a proud sponsor of the event, so their name was, indeed, on said banners and posters.

But Stevi wanted more. She wanted posters in their big plate-glass windows announcing the Euchre tournament and their dinner and drink specials. And yes, she needed something about the entertainment on anything she printed or posted online. Having a big question mark on the entertainment portion of the evening made this part just as hard to do as anything else.

Maybe it was stressful, but she loved life right now. Margo was right; she was spending several nights a week at Duncan's. Often, they were too wired to go right to bed when they got home from the Queen, so they curled up on the couch to watch movies. And sometimes, they watched movies. Sometimes, they were more interested in each other's skin and sighs and moans.

And the kisses. God, she loved the way he kissed her. There were nights when they lay together and Duncan simply kissed her. There were nights when they were so exhausted from a busy run at the Queen that they went straight to bed just to sleep in each other's arms. There were nights after closing when it was just the two of them at the Queen when they danced—or barely swayed in each other's arms to music that ranged from Van Halen to Tanner Dixon and the Lightnin' Congregation. Sometimes, they played Bar Dice, and that always led to messing around and that line of drinks Duncan had that he only shared with her. They still turned the lights off and sat together on the stairs. Sometimes they sipped wine or bourbon and told stories from days gone by. Sometimes they didn't talk, just took in the street and the park in the silvery moonlight and marveled that they were together.

Three things could make life better right now, and those three things were completely out of her hands. She wished with all of her heart that Kenzi was one hundred percent Kenzi and that she and Joe and the kids were still living here, still a part of their daily lives. And Stevi knew it would never happen, and she knew she should be grateful for what Joe and Kenzi had been given. She wished that Leah's pregnancy had been easier for her. Leah had been selfless to the point of ruin, pushing Trace to go and help his brother and then his mom, and thank God something had changed her mind and she had climbed out of her bed, out of her grief, and she had stopped Trace from leaving again. If he had left, if Leah had pushed him away again, Stevi thought they might have both lost the love of their lives because of the rest of their lives getting in the way. Last, she wished Margo was happy. Whether that meant with Jess or that Margo would find someone new, she wasn't sure. Margo loved her baby girl, and she was happy...enough, but Stevi wished some great guy would come along and recognize that Margo was an incredible woman and then stick around to prove that to her every day.

The computer screen in front of her had started to blur. Stevi rubbed her eyes and rolled her head on her neck. She had to nail this down. Figure out what to do about the entertainment so she could finalize the posters and banner with the printer.

"Stevi?"

She jumped when she heard Trace's voice. A sheepish grin mixed with a yawn, and she covered her mouth, but a laugh escaped as she turned to watch him slip inside the office.

"You got a minute?"

"Yep." She nodded. The tired, contented happiness inside—she carried it now, always tucked somewhere near her heart—crept a little deeper inside when Trace closed the door. "What's wrong?"

Closed door discussions didn't happen often. And when they did, they made her worry. Hadn't she just sat here and catalogued her wishes for the people she loved and then reminded herself that they were all blessed, and maybe wishing for more was greedy?

"Nothing." He grinned as he perched on the corner of the desk.

"Yeah?" She glanced at the door again and then swung her gaze back to him. "Gonna tell me some great idea you have to surprise Leah?"

"No." He frowned. "I think surprises should be mild right now."

"Why?" She straightened in her chair. "Is she okay? Is she having contractions?"

"No. NO." Trace held his hands up defensively. "No. This just…it's not about Leah."

She swallowed hard. Tried to ignore the buzz of anticipation in her belly. Was it something about Duncan? But weren't they too old for that kind of talk? It was one thing for Stevi to share her feelings, her happiness and her fears with Leah and Margo. She would never send them to Duncan to ask him if he loved her. Nor would Duncan send Trace to her for the same reason.

"Okay." She arched her eyebrows. "What gives? You're killing me."

Trace took a deep breath. Okay, Trace was her sister's guy, and Stevi was committed to Duncan—even though he didn't know it—but that didn't mean she couldn't appreciate a damned good-looking man perched on her desk. She let her eyes roam up over his wide chest, his broad shoulders—the faded blue t-shirt hugged the muscles she knew her sister loved to hang onto—and finally met his gaze.

"Pass inspection?" he asked with a smirk.

She chuckled. "Yeah. I'm not blind, Nashville. Just appreciating the view."

His lips pulled up in a bigger grin, and he shook his head.

"So. Leah mentioned that you were kind of…struggling…for some…new entertainment angle. For the Octoberfest."

"She did, did she?" Stevi sighed.

Trace winced and studied her for a moment.

"You don't want my input."

Struck with a zap of guilt, Stevi sucked in a quick breath. "It's just…"

"It's okay. You're not gonna hurt my feelings if you don't want me to—"

"No, no, I do." She leaned forward and nudged his denim-clad leg with her fist. "I do. I just…You're one of us now, Trace. And while I love it when you play…every woman loves it when you're singing…I also want you to be with us. Having fun. Yeah, we're working, but we're doing it together. And that makes it fun. I'm hoping you'll do an hour or so…"

"And then you need another act."

She met his eyes again and nodded.

"Okay. What about—"

"I don't want him up here. He makes me think about—"

Trace shook his head to make her stop talking. "Not Tanner. I don't want him around Leah, either."

"Oh." Stevi flopped back in her chair. "Then what're you thinking?"

"Are you dead set against country? Or do you definitely want country?"

"I…" She started without thinking and then let her words trail off. "I don't know. I really don't know…"

"Well. This is just a thought." He shrugged. "And it's not gonna make me mad if you're not interested."

"What?" She waved her hand in a circle to tell him to get on with it.

"There's a girl in Nashville. She's at Left Fork. Just…kind of getting started on the stage. Pearl wasn't gung-ho on her performing yet. Sampson and I wanted to give her a shot… She's young. She's a super sweet kid. And she's got a beautiful voice."

"Really." Stevi blinked at him. Okay, this had possibilities.

"Her name's Kadie. I've played for her. With her. I've heard her play guitar, and yes, she's damned good. She actually plays a twelve-string."

Stevi shook her head. "I don't know what that means."

"It means she kicks ass."

"Okay, I'm impressed."

"She sings a little country. She does some singer songwriter stuff. Sort of folksy. And she has a couple of original songs, too."

Stevi nodded. "Would she come up here? If she's that young?"

"Well, her parents might join her. Sampson. Angie. Hell, I don't know. But yeah. I think she would. I think she'd be comfortable with me. And I think she would love you girls."

Stevi nibbled on her lip.

"Do you have a recording of her performing?" As if she was a good judge of talent. Good grief, she was talking to *Trace Dixon*. The guy had lived in Nashville his whole life, until a few months ago, and he wrote chart-topping hits for some damned big names. He knew the business, and he knew talent.

And he knew people.

"I don't, but I could get one."

"No." She shook her head. "I don't need that. I love it."

Trace snuck a peek at her, but his double take made her laugh out loud.

"Really?"

"Yep."

"Huh." He nodded. "Okay."

"What's that mean?" She toed his leg this time with her shoe —a different heeled sandal that Duncan decided he liked nearly as much as the other pair.

"I didn't think you'd go for it," he admitted.

"What? Because she's just getting started? You think I'm a snob?"

"No." Trace tipped his head and treated her to that slow grin. "Leah just said you were determined to figure this out alone."

Stevi sighed and finally shrugged. "I was. Because I felt like the Queen kind of…floundered last year at this event. And I thought they blamed me. I was determined to do better this year."

"I've never seen anyone here point the blame at anyone else about anything."

"My mistake," she agreed. "I guess I got a little inside my head and stopped listening to everyone else."

"Happens." He clapped his hands on his thighs and lifted his butt from the desk. "I'm glad things worked out for you and Duncan."

She answered him with a smile, heart full with love for Duncan Marks. And crossed her fingers—her hand was draped over her lap, and Trace wouldn't notice—that maybe someday Duncan would feel the same way about her.

CHAPTER 29

DUNCAN DRUMMED HIS FINGERS ON THE BAR AND WATCHED Stevi tip the vodka bottle over the cocktail shaker. She splashed in just the right amount and glanced at him when she set the bottle down.

"What?" Eyes wide with panic, she looked around. Duncan watched her check the bottle, the shaker, the muddler that she had just used on the lime and brown sugar, and then slowly lift her eyes back to meet his gaze.

"Nothing." He shook his head.

"You're looking at me."

"You're practicing. I'm your teacher."

The way her eyes grew wide with ideas was a turn on, but then everything about this woman turned him on. Even finding her on his couch late in the mornings, hair piled on top of her head, and her legs clad in long, fleece, owl-covered pj pants.

"But…" She cleared her throat and finally turned her attention back to the drink she was making him.

"You've got three days left to be as good as me." He winked when she lifted only her eyes to look at him.

"Um, yeah. It's never gonna happen. I'm totally going for a sexy look so I have a chance in hell of beating you."

"Sexy, like how?" He leaned forward on the stool. Because as far as he was concerned, she was sexy every damned night she was here. And all the male eyes in the room watched her every step. Hell, plenty of women watched her with hungry eyes. If she got any sexier, Duncan might die of a heart attack or go to jail for beating some dumbass who couldn't keep his eyes or hands off his woman.

"Not tellin'." She shook her head. "You'll just have to wait and see."

"But. Skin? Are you showing skin?"

"Not. Telling. Means I'm not telling you."

"Topless?"

"I'd do that for you," she answered simply. "But no, not for anyone else."

"Really?" He dropped his gaze from her face to her breasts, imagined them tucked away safely inside her black blouse and deep purple bra. He knew for a fact that it was purple, because she'd gotten dressed for work at his place earlier. His dick throbbed to life at the thought of Stevi parading around behind the bar in heels and maybe some lace panties—she refused to wear thongs, told him she'd go commando for him before she wore a thong—and nothing else. Definitely a topic he would like to revisit later.

"I'd do anything for you." She shook the drink and poured it into a glass tumbler. Heaped some crushed ice over the top and scooted the glass at him over the bar. "Don't you know that by now?"

Duncan adjusted himself when she licked the tip of her finger.

"Brown sugar and lime," she announced.

"And would anything include letting me lick brown sugar and lime juice off your nipples?"

"Yep."

"Fuck, Stevi. I've gotta raging hard on and nowhere to go with it for hours."

"That what we're gonna call that drink? When you lick it off me?" She dazzled him with a smile. "A raging hard on."

"Already a raging hard on cocktail out there, but sure, just between you and me, it works."

"How about raging hard on for Stevi?"

"Yeah?" He raised his eyebrows when she leaned into the bar and stared at him boldly. "You make that drink for anyone else?"

"Nope."

"I like it," he announced. And then he picked up the drink she'd mixed and tasted it. In all honesty, probably not exactly the same as he made it, but still very good. "That's good."

"Yeah?"

"Yep."

"You wouldn't just tell me that?"

"Why would I do that?"

"So you can beat me at the battle of the bartenders."

He grinned. "Most people are gonna order beer or wine. And it's more like a popularity contest than any true taste contest."

"Wanna make a little side bet?"

He took another drink. "Like what?"

"Well, like if I win, I'll take you home and make you a raging hard on for Stevi."

"And if I win, we could stay right here at the Queen, and you can make me a raging hard on for Stevi."

"Well, if we've got sex on the table both ways, I think we're both gonna win," she pointed out.

"Okay. How about this? In addition to that…if you win, I'll make you come right here at the bar. With my tongue."

She dropped her head forward and hissed out a desperate sigh.

"Okay."

"And if I win…"

"So, the winner gets extra oral attention." She lifted her head and grinned at him. "Okay, but…Duncan?"

"What?" He reached over the bar to link his fingers with hers.

"I think we should probably practice those moves, too. Before the big night."

"I think we can do that."

She stared at their hands, suddenly fascinated by the movement of her thumb over the back of his hand.

"So. Why were you drumming your fingers?"

"What?"

"When I was mixing this for you, you were drumming your fingers."

He had been. Because he had been thinking. Not about making Stevi come with his tongue or about licking lime juice and brown sugar from her nipples.

"Finger drumming is a sign of boredom," she told him. She spoke so softly, Duncan wasn't sure he heard her correctly. She tilted her head just a bit to give him a shy look. "Are you getting bored with me?"

"What?" He squeezed her fingers.

"Don't drag it out, okay? If you're done, just be done."

He watched her struggle to control herself, admired her fight.

"Babe, I'm not bored." He shook his head. "At all."

She lifted her chin again and stared at him straight on.

"Because you'll hurt me more if you pretend after the feelings are gone."

"Stevi." He sighed. He wasn't bored. What the fuck had given her the idea that he was bored with her? He had been studying room sizes and closet space in his house. Watching for sale signs going up around town, eyeballing those houses. Trying to decide if he should ask her to move into his current home, or if it would be a better start for the two of them to look at houses together.

Yes, he had been drumming his fingers, but that was because he had seen Trace slip upstairs to the office one day a few weeks ago. And he had seen that office door close, and Trace had been in there awhile—and Duncan knew for a fact Stevi was up there working—and then Trace had come back out with a smile on his face, and he had whistled a happy little tune all the damned afternoon.

And neither of them had mentioned the private little powwow to anyone else.

Did Duncan really think Trace had gone upstairs to service his girlfriend's sister? No. But he was a guy, and Stevi was his, and fuck yes, that closed door had done a number on his head.

"Wow." She straightened. Duncan watched her draw in a big breath and then let it out in a big whoosh.

"What?"

"You're drumming your fingers, and you're sighing at me." She licked her lips.

"I'm not bored," he said softly. "I don't think I could ever be bored with you, Stevi Hague. I'm enthralled by everything you do."

She gasped. "Enthralled?"

"Yeah." He nodded. "I am." He scooted the barstool back and climbed up on it.

"What're you doing?" she asked with a little giggle.

"I'm gonna put my arms around you," he said as he climbed up on the bar. Stevi backed away and stared at his black boots on the bar. She laughed out loud as her gaze climbed up over his legs and his waist and she finally met his eyes. "Watch out."

Stevi moved as he walked a few steps away from her, squatted, and jumped from the bar to stand with her. He held his arms out to her. When she moved without hesitation to snuggle against his chest, Duncan felt something warm spread through his chest. He wrapped his arms around her and held on, buried his face in her hair and breathed deeply.

"I don't plan on letting you go," he told her as he pushed her hair back from her face and nipped at her neck. "Don't you know that?"

"Keep talking," she whispered, breathless already.

"I've been thinking a lot about us." He nibbled his way up her neck and then pressed a kiss to the corner of her mouth.

"Like the drinks? What we can do with them after hours?"

"Like how you spend every night with me, and you keep saying you need to move out of—"

"Hey, Stevi!"

She groaned, kissed Duncan quickly, and stepped away from him. He watched her lift her eyes to the mezzanine floor where Margo stood, fingers curled around the railing.

"What?"

"Are we doing dinner music?"

"What?" Stevi took a step closer to the west end of the bar, although she wasn't technically closer to Margo, since she was upstairs. "Trace and his friend are performing. I've got that on posters all over town."

"Yeah, but before that." Margo folded her arms over her chest. "I was just thinking about that. On the other side during the dinner hours, before Trace and that Kadie girl play."

"Well." Stevi shrugged. "I guess so. I mean…we usually have something instrumental over there."

"Do we have German instrumental music?"

Stevi sighed. "I don't even know what German instrumental music is."

"Isn't Wagner German?"

"Um." Stevi ducked her head and rubbed the back of her neck. "I don't…know? Do you mean the "Here Comes the Bride" guy?"

"Beethoven's German," Duncan mumbled. Stevi, head still ducked, pivoted on her heel and looked at him.

"Seriously?"

"Yep." He nodded.

"Damn." She sighed. "Okay. I'll take care of it, Margs."

"Great. And also, Leah's already having some pregnancy brain, so she didn't get the cards, either."

"Leah's got what?" Stevi yelped.

"Chill." Margo laughed. "She's getting forgetful. She was supposed to get ten decks of cards, right? Isn't that what you guys figured out from the reservations that have come in?'

"Yes."

"Okay. She forgot."

"Great. Anything else you guys need to tell me? Bandits stole the posters around town, and no one's coming in for drink specials? We ran out of wine last night?"

"Nope, that's it." Margo tossed her a wave.

"I will be so glad when this is over," she said with a soft groan. Duncan watched her as she covered a yawn with her hand.

"Me, too. Because then one of us is going to have some seriously big fun right here behind this bar."

"We're gonna do that bet thing right here? Did you forget there're windows? Big windows?"

"It'll be dark in here. No one will be out there at that time, anyway. And if anyone is out there, they're not going to know to look in our window to watch some incredible real-life porn action."

Stevi's eyes glazed over. She cleared her throat. "But we are going to practice that, right? To make sure we get everything right?"

"We are." Duncan stepped toward her and snagged his fingers around the back of her neck. "For now, I'm gonna go get some cards for you. And I'll look for some mix CDs, too."

"How'd you know Beethoven was German?"

"Smart like that," he told her.

"Well, I mean, I know he's a composer, and I've heard some of his…symphonies. But I don't know. I thought maybe he could be from Austria or something."

"Germany." Duncan gave her a quick peck on the lips and backed away. "Need anything else while I'm out?"

"No, but don't be gone long. It's almost time to open."

"I won't be gone long," he promised. "But don't panic if I get caught in traffic."

Stevi snorted. "Duncan, this is Adam's Bay. Traffic gets backed up when school gets out and the buses are out."

"You're a bartender now," he said with a shrug. "You can handle anything. Only one of the things about you that I think is enthralling."

He waited for that smile—the one that lit up the room, before he backed away from her to leave. She said something, but she said it so low, he didn't hear her. But if he read her lips, he was pretty sure she said *enthralling*.

CHAPTER 30

STEVI FOLDED HER CHECKLIST OVER AND TUCKED IT BACK IN her pocket. Everything on the list had been checked off. And now here they were, somehow in the middle of October, in the midst of an Octoberfest celebration. She and Duncan had strolled the park across the street for a bit before the Queen opened. Hand in hand, walking among the people of Adam's Bay—some of them regular customers, and others Stevi hoped would end up stopping in before the night was over and deciding they liked the place well enough to come back again—she had felt like she was right where she belonged. Adam's Bay was her hometown, the Queen was her home, and Duncan was her king. She wasn't sure she'd ever been happier, and though she still eyed the future wistfully and tucked thoughts of love and babies away, she reminded herself to be in the moment with him.

She was especially glad now that she had taken a little time to live in the moment, because the bar was hopping, the Euchre tournament on the restaurant side was well under way, and it was almost time to exchange her planning role for her new bartender role. Trace was singing about his pickup truck, which made Stevi snort and roll her eyes—good thing she loved him, because that song felt stereotypical of country music, and she wasn't normally a big fan—and his friend, Kadie, was singing backup. The girl had arrived last night—with her parents, as Trace had suggested would happen—they had all spent the evening together, getting to know each other. Stevi thought the girl was a sweetheart, and that the sweetheart had a little case of hero worship going on for Trace.

"Be right back," Stevi told Leah as she stepped away from the bar.

"What? Where are you going?"

Stevi checked the time on her phone and then lifted her eyes to see Leah watching her with a look of panic on her face.

"Why? Just gonna run upstairs for a second," she said with a quick shrug. "Touch up my lipstick."

Because she had known Duncan was a little concerned about what she had meant the other day when she said she was dressing sexy tonight, she had gotten ready at home. She had dressed in short denim shorts and a sleeveless green blouse over a crème-colored cami. She'd pulled her hair up and worn simple flip-flops for the walk through the Octoberfest celebration at the park with Duncan.

Time to run upstairs and step it up if she had a snowball's chance in hell at winning this battle. And if Duncan was going to stand behind that bar and go down on her later for winning, she most definitely planned to win. The practice round the other night had blown her mind and left her a quivering mess of tears.

"But." Leah shook her head. "You—it's just about time—"

"I know. I think everything's good. Gonna run upstairs for a sec. I'll be right back."

"Do you think…" Leah started, but when Stevi arched her eyebrows expectantly, Leah simply nodded. "Go. Just hurry! I want you to win."

Stevi cut loose with a wicked laugh and then laughed harder at the look on Leah's face.

"Oh, I wanna win, too." Stevi nodded. "Trust me."

As she climbed the steps to the office, she swept her gaze over the room below. Patrons were lined up at the bar, and most of the tables were taken. She'd seen the place busier, but it was early, and she had a good feeling about tonight. She had hung several posters all over town in the previous month, and she had overhead a lot of their regulars over at the park earlier talking up the drink specials and the battle between her and Duncan.

He had loved the denim shorts. Stevi knew he assumed that was what she had chosen for the night, but as she hustled into the office, she wondered what he would say when she came back downstairs.

She stepped out of the flip-flops and then unbuttoned her shorts.

The German dinner had been a hit. Stevi had nibbled on a pretzel earlier, but she was too jittery to eat much. Forget about adding beer to pretzel and the jitters. Maybe later. For now, she had to focus. Not just to make sure she beat Duncan later, but to make sure the rest of the night went as well as it had started. She had poured her heart and soul into planning for tonight, so she would really take it personally this time if they didn't hit her projected sales mark.

Earlier, when she had first come in, she had brought a duffel bag upstairs with her purse. She had dropped the bag to the floor at the end of the couch, knowing Duncan wouldn't think a thing about it, if he even noticed it. She closed the office door now and then went to retrieve the bag. Stevi set it on the couch and unzipped it with one hand and used the other to slide her shorts over her hips.

Duncan seemed to have an obsession with thongs. Stevi had always called them butt floss and told him she would rather just not wear underwear. Because she planned to win tonight —beg, borrow, or cheat—she had visited a trendy lingerie boutique on the square and purchased a scrap of black lace complete with the floss just for him. She had debated earlier on whether to wear it all day or change into it. She had put it on under the shorts, and mostly, she hated it. But the thought of Duncan finding it later, the thought of his eyes glazing over with lust and the way he would suck in a quick breath of surprise and then touch the lace with his fingers and his teeth, his tongue, had kind of made it more bearable.

She kicked the shorts off and pulled a pair of dark skinny jeans from the bag. Stepped into them and tugged them up over her hips. She zipped them and then immediately went to work on the buttons of her blouse. She had set her phone on the couch before she took her shorts off, and now the screen lit up. Stevi shrugged out of the blouse, whipped the cami off, and dropped both to her bag. She glanced at the closed door and said a silent prayer that Trace didn't choose his moment to stroll through. And then she reached back and unhooked her bra. With another glance at the door, she leaned over and tucked the lace in her bag and pulled out the clingy red shirt—with a dramatic dip in the back that cut nearly to her waistline, therefore no bra would work—she had found just for tonight.

The office was cold, and her nipples tightened. She laughed softly as she pulled the top over her head and settled it over her upper body. She paid careful attention to how it fit her breasts, pleased that it really did look sexy. Not one to go braless in public, the rub of the material over her nipples was a new feeling. Not necessarily bad, but definitely different.

Knowing she was running out of time, she leaned back over the bag to find her heels. Her feet would hate her by the end of the night, but she pulled the red fuck-me heels from the bag and slid the first one on. They weren't new, but she didn't wear them often. She took a second to wiggle her toes, before hopping around to slip the other one on.

The door opened as she stood up.

"What're you doing up here?" she yelped when Duncan walked in. He looked distracted, but when he got a look at Stevi, he froze, a look of adoration on his face. "Who's got the bar?"

She reached up to pull the elastic out of her hair and then ran her fingers up through the waves to fluff it.

"Fuck me." He shook his head. "What the hell are you wearing? That is…" His eyes roamed over her face and her shoulders and stopped on her breasts, where her nipples were suddenly very turned on by his attention.

"Like it?"

"Um." He laughed and coughed. "This is gonna be fucking torture. Waiting all night to get my hands on you."

She sighed, a little bit relieved by his reaction.

"Turn." He twirled his finger in a circle, and Stevi obeyed and turned for him. "You're not wearing a bra. Are you?"

"Nope."

"'Kay. I'm gonna go turn the heat up to ninety. I don't want you to be cold downstairs, because no one needs to see those sweet nipples but me."

"Oh, but they do, Duncan." She stepped closer to him and settled her arms on his shoulders. "Because I plan to win tonight."

"Yeah?"

"Oh yeah. I want to stand behind that bar later in my heels and nothing else and watch you go down on your knees in front of me."

Duncan answered with a sexy smile. He kissed her, but she suddenly remembered that he was supposed to be down at the bar. The taste of bourbon on his lips stirred a familiar longing low in her belly, but she groaned and slid her hands down to his chest to push him away.

"Why are you up here? Who's at the bar?"

"Leah and Margo," he answered. "Tania called in sick."

"Tania what?" Stevi shrieked. "Are you kidding me? Sick? Tonight? She better be terminal to pull this shit—"

"Her son's in the ER. Fell on playground equipment. Broken arm. Gash in his forehead."

"Oh damn." Stevi winced. She felt a flash of guilt mix with the panic. "What—what're we gonna do? We're gonna need someone else. It's last minute. Leah and Margo can't do it all—"

"Relax. I came up to find the schedule. I was gonna call a few of the girls and see if I can find someone."

"You were?"

"Leah was on her way up." He shrugged. "I wanted to do this. To help you out. Leah and Margo are having a good time down there. You go…" He swallowed hard as his eyes took another trip over her body. "Finish…whatever it is you need to do. Not sure what you can add to the look to make you any sexier, but whatever…"

"You like it?"

"I do." He nodded.

He scooped her butt cheeks in his hands and hauled her against his middle again, and Stevi's eyes drifted closed at the feel of his erection against her.

"I might have a surprise for you later," she whispered.

"Can't wait," he answered. He leaned in closer. Stevi sighed with pleasure when he rubbed his jaw against hers, the feel of his whiskers on her cheek reminding her of his very intimate kisses when they were alone in the bedroom. "Stevi."

"Hmm?"

"I um…" He shrugged. "I know this isn't the best time to ask you this, but…"

"What?" She stepped back and flattened her hands on his chest again. When he squeezed her butt, she giggled and shook her head. "Stop. We're gonna end up against the wall with our pants around our ankles in two minutes."

"God, I hope so." Duncan nodded.

"Ask me."

He huffed out a deep breath and then stared at her for a long moment.

"Move in with me."

"What?"

They were in the middle of the biggest night of Stevi's work year—so far—and in a bit of a crisis since Tania wasn't going to make it in. Stevi wasn't sure if they had a future beyond the sex—and yes, it was admittedly, the best sex she had ever had and she suspected no other man would ever make her feel like Duncan did—and he had never said he loved her.

Was it wrong that she wanted to hear him say he loved her? What if she moved in and it didn't work out? What if Duncan woke up one day bored with the same woman in his bed? He had never stuck with anyone as long as he had been with Stevi. She supposed she could assume she meant something special to him. Either that, or she could wonder if that meant her time was up at any second and Duncan would kiss her goodbye, put her away, and find someone new.

Younger.

Like Trace's friend, Kadie. Why hadn't she thought of that? What if Duncan was attracted to her? What if—?

"Stevi."

She heard his voice, though in her head she was a million miles away. Hopefully being stupid. Worrying about Duncan with other women. With that sweet little blonde downstairs with the breathy voice and the southern twang. And the maxi dress and cowgirl boots. Did Duncan like that look?

Leah liked Trace's boots. She had said they gave him extra traction in bed.

"Stevi."

"What?" She licked her lips. The jitters she had felt earlier were nothing to the way her stomach was rolling now. She dropped her hands from his chest and rubbed them on her jeans. "Who are you gonna call? We should…" She shrugged and shook her head.

"I just asked you to move in with me."

"Yeah, I know, but you just hit me out of the blue, Duncan. I…I mean…"

"You said you're ready to move out of the house. To give Leah and Trace some room."

She nodded. "I am." But did that mean she should move in with Duncan?

He sighed and looked away. With a shrug, he tossed his hands up in defeat and stepped back from her.

"I'm not saying no," she said softly. "But. Can we…can we talk about it when tonight's over?"

"Sure." He shrugged and nodded.

"Duncan." She stepped closer to him and pressed into him again, needing to assure him…well, that she loved him. Except she was afraid to say it. She'd never said those words to a guy in her life, which gave them a hell of a lot more meaning than a lot of people assigned to them. "I'm sorry. I didn't mean to—"

"It's okay," he said softly. He dropped a kiss on her forehead.

"Tonight. Tomorrow. We'll talk about it. I shouldn't have asked you like this."

"Maybe it was the nipples?"

"Definitely could have been the nipples on my mind. I'd like them in my mouth right about now."

She laughed softly.

"Go on. I'll find the schedule and get someone in here to help Leah and Margo."

CHAPTER 31

DUNCAN WATCHED HER WALK OUT THE DOOR, HIS DICK AT attention and his heart...what? Broken? Not exactly, but definitely a stress fracture or something. Okay, so he hadn't meant to spring it on her like that. Throwing it out there about her moving in with him. He could have handled it differently. He had been thinking about a romantic dinner once this whole Octoberfest thing was over with. Duncan had no doubt that tonight was going to be a hit, especially after seeing the way Stevi was dressed to battle him behind the bar. In fact, he wouldn't mind losing to her, because he wanted nothing more than to strip her jeans down her luscious legs and go down on his knees in front of her in those fuck-me heels and that clingy red shirt that hugged her nipples just so and put his mouth on her.

He could taste her now. Thoughts of the other night weren't exactly welcome right now; Stevi was right. They didn't have time for this right now. But he couldn't shake the image of her spread out on his bed, her fingers rubbing that delicious mixture of brown sugar and lime juice on her nipples and then trailing low over her belly, beckoning him to taste her.

With a groan, he adjusted his dick and moved around to stand behind the desk.

Yeah, Tania's phone call had kind of thrown them for a loop, but Duncan had no doubt tonight was going to be a hit. Stevi had worked her sweet little ass off on this project, and so far, everything had been smooth sailing. So he would find a replacement for Tania—hell, if they were desperate, he knew Margo's mom or Stevi and Leah's mom would come in and help wait tables, though probably Stevi would see that as a personal failure—and the rest of the night would fly by. He was looking forward to working side by side with Stevi—most nights she waited tables and pulled an occasional beer. But tonight, he and Stevi would be behind the bar together for three solid hours, and no matter who won the damned contest, he was going to be on his knees worshipping her before the night was over.

He sank into the chair and pulled the desk drawers open one by one. Maybe he should have thought to ask Stevi where the schedule and phone numbers were. Sure, he probably had the numbers in his phone—some of them anyway—but some of their wait staff already had a max on hours this week, and he knew one for sure was on vacation in Florida.

Dammit. He should have waited. Once this whole festival was over, things would settle a bit. At least until Halloween. That was a big night here. Not something Stevi usually planned for, not in the way she had planned for tonight. But they would have a party, and it would be more fun, Duncan thought, because Stevi would be more relaxed.

He admired that she was determined to make the Octoberfest a hit. He admired that she fussed over details. And he was proud of her; she was sharp and witty and fun, and she was his.

Right? Wasn't she? He could have waited to ask her to move in. When things were quiet here, Leah and Margo would have covered for him and Stevi so he could take Stevi out. He wasn't ready to pop the question, yet, but he could have made a night of it. They could have done a nice little scavenger hunt and driven by all of the houses he'd been looking at. He could probably have set up some tours of those houses. That would have been fun; he and Stevi looking at floorplans and backyards and trying to decide what would fit them and their life together best.

She hadn't been excited, though, when he asked. Sure, his timing sucked, blah blah blah. But wouldn't she have sort of been just a little bit excited about it if she wanted to live with him? She still could have asked if they could talk about it later or tomorrow, but would it have hurt her to wear a smile on her face with the question?

Did that mean she just wasn't interested? She wanted to get out of the house with Leah and Trace for them, but she had no interest in living with Duncan? No interest in a future with him? They were good together. Duncan had never been with a woman who kept him hungry for more even when he had his dick buried deep inside her. And he'd never been with a woman that turned him on like that and delivered in the bedroom that he loved hanging out with doing things like washing dishes and grocery shopping and playing twenty questions and tending bar. He wasn't a TV person, and yet, he had willingly let Stevi suck him into that damned Bloodline show on Netflix.

And they watched it, too. Always together on the couch. Her back pressed to his chest or him on his back and Stevi draped over his chest. Always some sort of skin touching, whether it was the slide of her foot over his leg as she got comfortable or her soft cheek on his bare chest. It was comfortable. And intimate.

Duncan straightened in the chair, struck by that thought.

He had never had that sort of intimacy with a woman. He had put his dick inside a lot of women through the years, but he had never been intimately involved with a one of them the way he was with Stevi.

Because he was in love with her.

His stupid mouth—the one that had blurted out that question, because as much as he was in love with her, he wondered now if she was just enjoying the newer benefits of their friendship—tipped up in a stupid grin. Definitely new to him. Feeling giddy about a woman. No alcohol involved.

Okay, Romeo, get back in the game. Find the schedule. Make a few calls. Fix it and get back downstairs to the party.

To Stevi.

Not finding any sort of schedule or phone directory in the drawers—he ransacked all of them, trying not to make a big mess—he dug through a small pile of papers on the desktop. Some invoices. A list of local musicians. Christmas party dates. Nothing that would help him with what he needed.

He pushed the pile away and studied the desk calendar. Lots of notes, written in all different hands, including his own. Still not what he was looking for.

Desperate, because no way in hell was he going to tell Stevi he couldn't find a schedule or a list of available employees or numbers, he picked up the calendar. One folded sheet of paper. He shrugged and pulled it out. It was a Hail Mary, for sure, but he wanted to handle this so Stevi wouldn't have to worry.

His gut clenched when he saw the note. At a glance, he could see that it was Stevi's handwriting, and it was addressed to him. No date.

He didn't need to read it to know what it said. His body told him all that he needed to know: his chest was so tight, he couldn't draw a fucking breath, and there was a fucking hammer pounding right between his eyes.

Dear Duncan—

His stomach in knots, the bourbon he had swallowed just before coming up to do this favor for Stevi, before finding her in that fuck-me red blouse and those heels, soured now on the back of his tongue. No wonder she had put him off about moving in with him. He was in love with her, and she was ready to call their fling done and walk away.

Pretty fucking ironic, considering she had asked him if he was bored with her the other day. He wasn't. Wasn't sure he could ever be bored with her. But maybe the thrill was gone for her. Maybe she wasn't interested in any sort of romantic relationship. Maybe she was using him for sex. God knows, he had done the same with a number of women. She had told him more than once that she was bored with all of her dates, and she had hinted that she hadn't had good sex in a long time.

She had even admitted to him that she faked orgasms with her friend Grant.

So who was to say she didn't fake it with him? Duncan thought he would be able to tell, but who the hell knew? Either she liked his dick and what he could do with it or she was a hell of an actress and was suddenly over it and trying to figure out how to walk away and save the Queen and their family.

One thing was certain.

Stevi Hague wasn't in love with him. Never had been. Didn't seem likely to happen anytime soon.

She was working the crowd when he finally went back downstairs. He had found the goddamned schedule and a complete list of their employees and phone numbers, with notes about who was always willing to pick up a shift. All he'd had to do was pound his fucking fists on the desk. The mouse had jumped, and the computer monitor had come to life, and right there in front of his fucking face—on the home screen—was a file folder titled Employee Numbers.

Duncan watched her as he descended the stairs. She had swept her hair up again, but in a loose, sexy knot at the back of her head. The hair that had slid loose of the knot curled slightly at her face, accentuating her cheekbones. Small gold hoop earrings caught the light when she turned her head. Her lips were fire engine red, and for a moment, he imagined kissing them. Imagined them around the head of his dick. Reminded himself that was done. If she was ready to move on, by God, they would move on. He wasn't going to beg for her attention.

Still. The thought of what he had planned to do to her tonight made him hard again. Stevi was talking to someone at the bar, and yes, technically, he was now late to his own damned battle to defend his bar. As his foot hit the bottom step, he wondered how the hell this was going to work now that they were going to officially be done.

He had told her he could do it. Sleep with her. And then walk away and consider her a friend. He was friends with a lot of women he'd slept with. At the moment, he kind of hated Stevi Hague, though, which didn't bode well for the future of their friendship. And if their friendship dwindled down to the two of them regarding each other as exes or someone they used to sleep with, he wasn't sure how that would work with the Queen. Probably, he would have to go.

He sure as fuck couldn't stand around now and watch her sashay across the room and flirt with every fucking guy who put his eyes on her.

But he loved the Queen. Leah and Margo. The bar.

The bar was his.

She tipped her head, and her eyes lit up when she saw him step behind the other end of the bar. How the hell did she do that? And why? Hadn't they decided to be honest with each other when they were ready to move on?

He took a deep breath. Pushed the anger, the hurt—fuck yes, she had hurt him, but no way he was going to let her know that—down and looked around. The bar—the actual wood bar right here in front of him—was his. He had built the fucking bar for the girls. With his own two hands. This was his comfort zone. No way he would go down without a fight.

He heard Stevi ask if he had found a replacement for Tania. Rather than move toward her to talk, he simply nodded and turned to look at the patrons at the bar. There were twice as many people here now as there had been when he had gone upstairs just a few minutes ago. Back before he realized he was just a fuck buddy for Stevi.

He tamped down the surge of hurt again and made eye contact with the redhead that Stevi most definitely didn t like. The girl offered him a slow, sultry smile.

Game. On.

CHAPTER 32

STEVI FELT A FLICKER OF UNEASE WHEN DUNCAN TURNED AWAY from her. She had expected him to answer her when she asked if he found someone to take Tania's shift. Instead, he had nodded and turned away. And yippy skippy, found the damned redhead right across the bar from him.

She ignored the catcalls coming from both ends of the bar now and watched Duncan look at the girl. The redhead was giving him some serious sex vibes, with that slow smile and the way she dragged the tip of her tongue around to wet her lips. Jealousy ripped through her, but she reminded herself that the first night he had made love to her, he had told her there was no competition. Still, when she looked from the girl to Duncan, the look of interest, intrigue on his face was a knife in her heart.

What the absolute hell? He just asked her to move in with him and now this? This wasn't the battle of the bartenders flirting for tips. Stevi had been doing that for the past ten minutes waiting on Duncan to come downstairs. She had been flirting, scoring tips, talking to the girls like a best girlfriend would. Because she had been aroused by the way he'd looked at her upstairs, and she was bound and determined to win this battle. She couldn't wait for Duncan to flip the lights and the lock and then slide her jeans down her legs to find the thong.

Now she wasn't sure about that. If he considered this fair play, she'd let him win. But she sure as hell wasn't going to get on her knees and blow him if he was going to flirt like this. Stevi wouldn't put it past the girl to slip him her phone number.

"What's wrong?"

Stevi jumped when she heard her sister's voice in her ear. Leah moved up behind her and cupped her upper arms. Stevi shrugged and shook her head.

"Nothing. I'm fine."

"You sure?"

"Yeah." She nodded and patted Leah's left hand with her right. "Let's get this party started."

"Hey, I'd ask Trace to play that one, but it's...not his style." Leah gave her a gentle squeeze and moved back to the end of the bar. Stevi grinned, though it felt fake and it felt like everyone in the Queen could probably see that it was fake. She took a deep breath, because her long night of anticipation had just become a long night of anxiety, and she wanted to take her heels off and walk away.

Go home.

Alone.

Why had he asked her to move in with him? Is that what this was about? Was he pissed because she hadn't jumped on the idea? Really? Because if that was the case, if Duncan intended to use other women to hurt her anytime they had a fight, there was no hope for anything to last between them. She wasn't going to do this. It hurt just to watch him look at the redhead, but Stevi wasn't going to play along.

She would do her job. And go home. And figure out what to do from there.

"What can I get you?" She turned her attention to a tall, stick thin guy, flashed him a smile because she was friendly not hoping to make Duncan jealous, and reached to grab him a longneck when he asked for one.

One down.

Trace and Kadie were playing together now, which hadn't been the exact plan, but it was working. They sounded good; and they appeared to be having fun. Everyone appeared to be having fun. Except Stevi.

She served more beer than anything, but she was thrilled to see the dollar bills tucked into her tip jar. Now and then she saw a high denomination, but she didn't attempt to add the numbers in her head. Rather, she concentrated on the patrons who bellied up to her end of the bar, requesting drinks. She mixed two margaritas and noticed from the corner of her eye when Duncan uncapped the bottle of bourbon that the two of them often drank.

Thoughts of their after-hours time—the quiet conversation on the stairs when the lights were off—warmed her heart, but when Stevi lifted her eyes to meet his gaze, he stared at her coldly and turned back to the bar. Something had changed, and as far as Stevi knew, it could only be that she had hesitated when he asked her to move in.

She swallowed the hurt that stuck in her throat. Reminded herself to keep moving. Get through the actual contest and then she could leave. No one would say a word if she ducked out, even if they were busy. Duncan had called someone in to replace Tania, and Duncan could have his damned bar back.

She didn't want it.

Or him.

Except that she did. Already, there was a gaping hole in her belly, her heart, and it was Duncan's shape, and she needed him back there, back with her to make things feel right again.

Time flew by, and other than that whole heartbreak thing, she sort of had fun. She made a few of the crazy drinks Duncan had taught her, including a raging hard on, which had made her sad. She bit her lip when she handed the drink over the bar and took the next request like a pro.

Trace took a break, and Kadie's sound evolved into something a little bit harder, with a little more edge. Stevi looked up and searched Trace out when she covered a Joan Jett song. He grinned and shrugged as if to suggest he didn't know what all she could or would do. The crowd stayed with her, singing along, a few people dancing toward the back of the bar. Out front, through the window, darkness had fallen, but the park across the street was still lit up and it appeared that plenty of people were still celebrating October there, too.

Someone with callouses on his hands got close enough to slide his hand over her bare back when he leaned in to order. Stevi had stiffened and moved away from him, all the while scolding him in a light tone. But when she handed the guy his draft beer—she was pleased to note their German selections were selling well—he leaned in to whisper in her ear that her competition was giving away kisses.

Shocked, she had turned, ignored the feel of the guy's hand on her back again, and found that Duncan was indeed leaned over the bar in a lip lock with some girl. Not even the redhead, though she was still there, and appeared to be champing at the bit for her turn. Stevi stared at him as he pulled back and flashed the girl—this one was a blonde, and she didn't look legal to be in the bar—a grin. And then started on a drink for someone else.

Stevi felt her stomach clench when she saw him reach for a slice of lime. He glanced at her, almost as if he wanted her to see him. He was mixing the drink they had been playing with the other day. She served another beer and then talked to two girls she had seen in the Queen before as she poured two glasses of Chardonnay for them.

When she looked back at Duncan, he was pushing the drink over the bar to the redhead. Stevi's eyes burned when the girl picked up the drink to sip it. She stared in disbelief when he leaned over the bar and kissed her.

Before she could move or say a word, Leah appeared at her side. She ignored her sister for a second, but Leah tugged insistently on her arm.

"What?" she snapped and finally turned her back to Duncan. She swallowed hard, but the knife of emotion was still jammed sideways in her throat.

"What's going on?" Leah whispered.

"I don't know." Stevi shrugged. "I don't…"

"Do you need a minute?"

Stevi ducked her chin and breathed deeply. Hell yes, she needed a minute. All of the memories with Duncan had just faded to that one moment way back at the very beginning, when he had told her he could sleep with her and walk away when he was done. And still be friends.

She had saved her heart for someone special, and she had fallen so hard, so much in love with Duncan that she couldn't imagine laughing and loving with another man again. And he was done.

"No." She cleared her throat.

"You sure?"

"Yeah." She nodded. "I'm fine."

"I can step in."

Stevi lifted her eyes to meet Leah's gaze. "I won't give in."

"Okay." Leah nodded. She wanted to say more, but Stevi was relieved when her sister reluctantly backed away. Curious as to how much longer she had to stand here with him, she pulled her phone from her pocket and took a peek at the home screen. Less than an hour to go, thankfully.

She served more drinks, noticing that Duncan had been right. Most people were asking for beer or wine. She had envisioned something crazy like you might see in the movies, dueling bottles of vodka or tequila. Then again, what Duncan was doing on his end of the bar was crazy, and there were more than a few guys pestering her for a kiss. She managed to summon a smile each time, but she refused to kiss anyone. She wasn't interested in games, and after tonight, she wasn't interested in kissing, either.

When their time was almost up, she felt a hand on her back again, and turned to find Duncan watching her with a cool smirk on his face. But he wasn't teasing, as he sometimes did when he looked at her like that. His eyes were hard and cold.

"I think it's we time we count our votes," he suggested. He stepped close to her and slid his arms around her. As if he intended to kiss her.

She pushed him away when his lips hovered over hers.

"No?" He arched an eyebrow. "Done with that, are you?"

"I don't really want your tongue down my throat, after all the other mouths it's been in tonight." She spoke quietly so that no one would hear her over the music and the buzz of conversation.

"Yeah, I get it. How many hands were on your back tonight, Stevi? How many guys do you think were fantasizing about your bare tits under that shirt?"

She drew back from him, his words stinging like a slap in her face.

"Well." She cleared her throat. "I know you aren't. Looks like you'll have plenty to keep you busy later."

She glanced around, looking for rescue. Relieved to see Leah slipping through the crowd toward her.

"Hey. Time's up!" Leah sounded cheerful, but Stevi knew Leah was worried about her.

"Great. I'm going home."

"You're what?" Duncan shook his head. "Don't you wanna see who won?"

"Actually, no." She shrugged. "I don't."

"And what about that side bet?" He folded his arms over his chest, though the rest of his body was arranged in an aggressive pose, legs spread wide in a stance that invited attack.

"We didn't shake on that," she reminded him.

"I put your purse and your bag in the kitchen." Leah leaned in close and spoke directly to her. Stevi's knees buckled under the relief of knowing she didn't have to traipse across the room, up the steps to get her things, and then back down again to escape.

"Thank you." She nodded. "I'll see you later?"

"Do you want me to come home with you?"

"No. I…" She swallowed again, but the tightness in her throat didn't ease. "I need…"

Leah nodded. "Call me. If you need me."

Stevi sniffled and offered her a smile. Duncan was watching them, but she ignored him as she slipped out from behind the bar and headed back to the kitchen to grab her things.

"Hey." Margo met her half way there. "What the hell?"

"I dunno." Stevi shook her head. "I don't know. I don't wanna talk."

"Okay." Margo dropped a kiss on her cheek and moved past her. Stevi stalked the rest of the way to the kitchen. Finally alone, she gave in. Just an inch. Just enough to blink and let the tears go. Her stomach was sore, stiff from clenching it all evening, and her head hurt because she had wanted to cut loose and cry three hours ago. Nothing she could do about either of those things, except go home and cry. And she would.

But her feet hurt, and she could damned sure take care of that. She lifted her left foot and yanked the heel off as Duncan appeared in the doorway.

"What the hell was that about?" she asked, not caring when her voice broke. "What the hell, Duncan? Why—"

"Like it matters to you."

"What?" She dropped her shoe and then lifted her other foot to yank that shoe off. "What does that mean? You asked me to move in with you, and ten minutes later, you're slobbering all over that girl again."

"You don't wanna live with me."

"I didn't say that. I didn't say no!" She swiped at her nose. "But, no, I don't if this is how you're gonna treat me when you're mad at me."

"Maybe I realized my mistake!" he yelled. "Maybe it hit me that I was doing something stupid. Shacking up. Making a commitment to you."

"I'm that bad? Committing to me is that bad? That you had to come down here and fuck around with half the women in the bar?"

"It's not you." He shrugged and tossed his hands up. Stevi stared at him in horror. In all the years she had known him, she had never seen this side of Duncan Marks. "I guess you saying no, oh, sorry, saying let's talk about it later—of course that means no, Stevi, if you're gonna blow me off, then own it, for fuck's sake—made me realize it's not what I want. It was fun. We had some good times. I'm ready for a change. Those young girls with expensive tits who like to suck dick. That sounds like fun to me."

"Fuck. You."

"Maybe you should look for a sugar daddy," he suggested. "Look for someone with some years, with some gray in his hair. You'd be a prize for a guy like that."

Stevi lifted her arm and took aim. Her heel flew across the room before she realized she intended to throw it. It hit the wall several feet from him. She smoothed her hands over her face as he watched the shoe fall to the floor.

"I thought we talked about this." Duncan, unaffected by the shoe thing, lifted his steely gaze back to hers. "About walking away as friends."

"Leave me alone." She sniffled.

"I told you I don't fuck 'em and forget 'em. We can still—"

"Get the fuck away from me!" She shouted. "Leave me alone. Go fuck that girl on the bar. Maybe she'll give you what I apparently lack."

They stood for a long moment, eyes locked. Stevi's chest heaved with her frustration, with the need to scream more and cry harder. Duncan could have been made of stone, he stood so still as he watched her. She saw him swallow and lifted her eyes to his face again, curious if that was regret she had seen on his face. If it was, it was long gone now. He turned without a word and walked out of the room.

Stevi took a step back and pressed up against the industrial-sized refrigerator behind her.

"C'mere." Margo appeared, and Stevi's instinct was to push her away. She wanted Leah. She needed Leah. Margo was Duncan's sister—in this case, the step didn't seem to matter

—and so Stevi needed Leah. But Margo grabbed her by the arms and hauled her in close.

"I gotta get outta here." Stevi buried her face in Margo's neck. She couldn't talk around the knot in her throat, and her voice came out hoarse and thick. The stupid red shirt she had wanted to dazzle Duncan with was uncomfortable now on her nipples, and she was almost cold. Tears streaked her face, so she imagined her mascara and eyeliner mapped out her broken heart on her face.

"I know." Margo smoothed her hand over Stevi's back. "I know. Go to my house."

"Why?" Stevi lifted her head. "Why your house?"

"Because if he gets a wild hair to go back at this for round two, he won't know you're there."

Stevi considered it for a moment. She wanted her own bed. She wanted to bury her face in her pillow. If she couldn't have Duncan, she at least wanted her own bed for comfort.

"As soon as things calm down out there, I'll come," Margo promised.

Stevi sniffled again. "You don't blame me for this?"

Margo shook her head. "I'm not gonna do that whole stupid team thing. I have no idea what the hell is going on, but this right here and that show at the bar, is all Duncan."

"He just asked me to move in with him," Stevi whispered. Her hands shook when she lifted them to dab at her eyes again. "And then this happens."

"What did you tell him?"

"I just asked if we could talk about it later." Stevi shrugged. "I mean…I just wish…that he would have said he loved me. First. Guess now I know why he never said it."

Margo winced, but she didn't argue. She didn't defend Duncan.

"You have my key."

Stevi nodded.

"You're more than welcome to go there."

"Thank you." Stevi picked her bag up from the floor and reached for her purse on the counter.

"Here's a shoe," Margo said as she scooped it up from the floor.

"I don't want them." Stevi shook her head. She would drive home barefoot. If she got a ticket, she didn't care.

"Stevi." Margo caught her as she slipped by her to leave. Stevi sucked in another deep breath and looked at Margo. "I love you."

The sigh of relief whooshed out before she could stop it. This had been her nightmare all along. What if things didn't work out? She loved Margo like another sister, and she knew damned well Leah loved Duncan like family. She didn't want anyone to hate Duncan—well, okay, at the moment, she kind of did—but she needed Margo to still love her.

"Me, too." She nodded.

CHAPTER 33

MARGO HAD HEARD THE WHOLE SHOWDOWN. DUNCAN DIDN'T know if she had said anything to Leah or not. Not that he cared if the whole damned bar knew the things he said to Stevi in the kitchen. None of it mattered. No one mattered right now.

Well, Stevi kind of did.

But not enough. Or maybe it was that *they* didn't matter enough for Stevi.

He spent the rest of the evening stewing over the letter he had found. Wondering when she had written it. When she had planned to spring it on him. Maybe later tonight? After he had knelt before her and put his mouth on her and made her come one last time? Was that the surprise she had mentioned? *Hey, thanks for the orgasms, let's go back to being friends?*

Even now, thinking about her back here behind the bar with him, in that slinky red top, the way it had clung to her breasts and accentuated her nipples, he was hard as steel.

Kind of sucked to be so pissed off and still want to fuck her like he did.

The redhead was still here, too. Hell, three of the women he had kissed earlier—he regretted it now, after the way Stevi had looked at him as if was kicking puppies—were lingering at the bar, as if they thought he might be open for after-hours business. He wasn't. He didn't want a damned thing to do with any of them.

He wanted Stevi.

Okay, yeah, right now he wanted to argue with Stevi. To fight. Throw those horrible words at her and make her say horrible things back to him. It would feel better to get it out. Because nothing could feel as bad as walking around with this feeling inside. This...gaping...nothingness. All of the questions about when she had decided it wasn't working out. *Why?* Yep, that was definitely a big question. Why had she suddenly changed her mind? Hadn't things been good? Really good? They had more than sex, didn't they?

Duncan swept his arm out over the bar to wipe it down and then threw the towel down and counted to three. He'd rather throw a glass or two. Maybe a bottle of whiskey. He needed the satisfaction of throwing something and hearing it shatter. He thought of Stevi throwing her shoe at him—sort of—and almost laughed. If she would have hit him, he might be en route to the emergency room right now with a gouged-out eye.

Kadie was still singing, and on a good night, Duncan would admit she was good. But right now, he either needed something loud and hard or nothing at all. He threw back another swallow of bourbon and saw from the corner of his eye that Trace was watching him. Spoiling for a fight, he set his tumbler down and looked around the bar for Leah and Margo.

The night had dragged. Even the three ridiculous hours of the battle of the bartenders—that was supposed to be fun—had crawled by. Because they weren't even speaking to each other. He guessed that was his fault, but what was he supposed to think after finding that letter?

And another thing. A letter? Really? After all that they had shared, she couldn't even just say it to his face?

He realized not long before closing that Trace was waiting tables. And he looked pretty at ease about doing it, too. Not like he was seething about having been stuck with the job. Duncan saw Natalie—Tania's replacement—hovering at a table near the back, but he still didn't see Leah and Margo. Which meant that they had probably both left to be with Stevi. Which meant they were going to get her side of the story and think he was a total ass for the things he had said.

The skin on the back of his neck crawled. He shivered and tried to shake the feeling off. The headache that had hammered at him all fucking night. He hadn't eaten much over at the park, only a brat and a few french fries. Now he was half hungry, but on the other hand, his stomach was so fucking twisted up in knots, he wouldn't be able to eat anything, anyway.

What was Stevi's side of the story? What was she saying right now?

"Gimme the keys." Trace's voice stirred Duncan from his thoughts.

"What?" He shifted his face into a scowl and tugged the keys from his front pocket.

"Either give me the keys or go lock up." Trace stood with his hands braced on the other side of the bar, watching Duncan with narrowed eyes.

"I got it," Duncan mumbled, not willing to admit that he had lost track of that last half hour, if not longer. He spotted the redhead lingering at one of the front tables as he stalked over to the door to flip the lock. She met his eyes and raised her eyebrows suggestively.

"I could wait for you," she purred.

"Time to go," he said quietly. Embarrassed that he had been such a dick earlier—he had hurt Stevi, and apparently, he had given this girl the wrong impression, which was a dick move —he flicked his eyes away from the girl and offered her a small, apologetic smile.

"You sure you don't want me to wait?" She slid off the stool and moved to stand in front of him. Duncan decided she might be pretty under all of the makeup painted over her face. He might have found that sort of pretty a whole lot of interesting several months ago. But now he looked at other women and thought of Stevi.

"You seemed kind of interested earlier tonight."

"It's been a long night," he answered. "You okay to drive?"

"If I say no, will you drive me?"

"No." He pulled the door open and leaned on it. "But I'll call you a cab."

"Can I leave you my number?"

"I'm involved with someone," he answered simply. Because even if Stevi was done with him, he was much too wrapped up in her to take anyone up on any offers like this one.

"Really." The redhead nodded. "And what did your girlfriend think about you kissing all of us girls earlier?"

"I'm pretty sure she didn't like it." He shrugged. "Goodnight."

The girl opened her mouth as if to say more, but when Duncan nodded his head toward the open door, she slipped by him. He started to step back so he could close the door and lock it, but she pressed her hand to his chest.

"My number," she told him when he peeled her fingers from his chest. She pushed a small yellow sticky note into his hands. "For when your girlfriend dumps you for all the kisses you gave away tonight."

His mind flashed that picture back at him. His hands flipping the desk calendar up to find that folded letter. The stab of pain when he saw *Dear Duncan*. Stevi's writing. He heard Trace moving around behind him, so he curled his fingers around the number and pushed gently at the door. The girl gave him one, last smoldering look before she whirled around and left the building.

Duncan leaned into the door when he heard it click closed. Flipped the lock.

God, what a night.

He turned back to the bar, completely drained. Mentally and physically exhausted. He had been involved in more than one bar brawl through the years, and he had been on the receiving end as often as he had thrown the first punch. But he had never had a screaming match with a woman he was in love with before. That hard rush of rage now long gone, he was beat. And he still had to clean the damned bar up and get home. Home to sheets that still smelled of Stevi's flowery perfume.

He met Trace's eyes as he shoved the sticky note in his pocket.

"What in the hell are you doing?" Trace asked before Duncan could say a word. Not that he planned on it. Saying a word. Nope. He would just do his job and take his ass home. Hit the bottle there and maybe sleep it off on the couch. Tomorrow sure as shit wasn't going to be any better. Not with Stevi gone. But if he slept a bit, maybe he would feel...fuck if he knew. Nothing was going to feel right now that he and Stevi were over.

Especially not after the way they had just...imploded. He had never in his wildest dreams—and he had some damned good wild dreams about Stevi Hague—would he have believed the two of them could fuck things up so badly. He had just stupidly assumed they could add some great benefits to a great friendship and then be okay when they decided it was time to cool it. Okay, so he had known for a long time now that it wouldn't be that simple. That didn't mean he thought they would tear each other apart like they had tonight.

"I'm gonna clean up and go home." He pushed off the door, but Trace was in his face before he could pick one foot up to take a step.

"You just took that girl's number."

"I didn't take it. She gave it to me."

Trace nodded and threw his arms up in disgust. "And you put it in your pocket."

"Well, I'm not gonna throw it on the floor." Duncan moved at Trace, led with his shoulder, and felt a flash of disappointment when Trace grudgingly stepped back out of his way. He started stacking glasses, still tempted to pitch a handful of them at the wall.

"What the hell happened?" Trace turned where he stood. His eyes were heavy but heated with emotion. "You guys were all gooey and sweet over at the park and a few hours later, you can't help yourself but climb over the damned bar for a bunch of girls made up like they had stopped in for a drink before hitting their corners for work?"

Duncan shot Trace a look of fury as he carried the stacks of glasses back behind the bar, through the door, and to the kitchen. Unfortunately, Trace followed him a few minutes later. Duncan, busy loading the glasses in the dishwasher, ignored him when he carried in two more big stacks of glasses.

"Where are the girls?"

"They went home. Leah was a wreck."

Duncan felt a flash of panic. "Is she okay?"

"She's fine, but she's pissed, and she was worried about Stevi."

Duncan groaned out loud. He wrapped his hands around the rounded edge of the counter and leaned forward. Hung his head and tried to breathe through a wave of intense pain. His throat was tight with emotion when he finally lifted his head and straightened to look at Trace.

"You wanna talk about it?" Trace hitched a hip against the counter across the small room and folded his arms over his chest.

"Where's Kadie?" Duncan asked, his voice gruff with pent up emotion.

"Left with her parents. Natalie's gone. It's you and me."

Duncan leaned back on the counter, braced himself with his hands on the counter at his sides, and stared at Trace sullenly.

"She was gonna leave me anyway."

Trace didn't flinch. Didn't frown. Didn't move. Didn't appear to breathe.

"Come again?"

"She was done—"

"What the hell gives you that idea? She's crazy about you." Trace pushed off the counter and started across the room. He stopped near the door and turned as if he expected Duncan to follow him. Duncan had no desire for a lecture; the fact that it would be Trace rather than Leah or Margo to chew his ass out made no difference.

"She left her shoes?" Trace mumbled as he used his booted foot to scoot Stevi's sexy red heels out of the way.

"She threw one at me."

Duncan thought he saw Trace's shoulders hitch a bit, like maybe he shrugged.

"Did you deserve it?"

Duncan followed Trace out to the bar and climbed up on a barstool. Fuck yes, he deserved Stevi throwing her shoe at him. Even if Stevi wanted to move on and walk away from what Duncan had believed to be something that would last forever, they had agreed to part as friends.

Stevi had broken him just because she was ready to walk away. Duncan had broken her because misery loves company. Which pretty much made him a first-class asshole.

"Yeah. I guess I did."

Trace mulled that over. Duncan watched him reach into the cooler and pull out a couple of longneck bottles. He twisted the top off one and handed it to Duncan.

"So, what happened?" Trace asked, quieter this time. "I thought from what Leah said you guys were…" He waved his hand in a circle and shrugged, clearly at a loss for words.

"Stevi and I have been friends for years—"

Duncan stopped talking when he realized Trace was shaking his head.

"Can I tell you something?"

Duncan took a long pull from his beer and waited.

"I was in love with Leah Hague the first time I laid eyes on her. God, I was in the back corner of the bar. Dark little stage, playing to paltry applause most nights. So damned mad at my little brother. Done with the woman that came between us, but so angry with him. And then there she was. I talked to her—"

"She said you hit on her," Duncan interrupted him.

"I didn't. Because I knew even then that she was different. I texted her. I called her. I hounded her, because by God, I wanted her attention. I wanted to be her everything, but I was ready to settle to just be part of her world. When I came up here, Leah thought she was being smart, holding me at a distance, and locking me into permanent friend status."

"Your point?" Duncan narrowed his eyes at Trace.

"Maybe we were friends, but that whole time, we were falling in love. She said it first, but I told you that I felt it the first damned time I laid eyes on her. When I left here to do those show dates with Tanner?"

Duncan nodded. He took another pull on the beer and kept his eyes on the bottle Trace held.

"I didn't think I would be back. Leah's too damned strong. Too stubborn. I think she loved me enough that she was willing to sacrifice her own happiness so I could get things right with my mom and my brother."

"Well. Stevi—"

"When you called me," Trace shook his head and kept talking, "from the hospital to tell me she had miscarried…" He stopped talking when his voice got high and tight. "I died inside, Duncan. I died a hundred times before I could get back here to her. Before I could hold her again. And then her damned pride almost forced me out the door again."

"Stevi and I don't love each other," Duncan argued. But maybe he had died a hundred times tonight, back here with her behind the bar, thinking that she was bored and ready to move on and wouldn't even have the courage to say that to his face. Maybe he had died a hundred more knowing that his one shot at love was gone. And one of his best friends was gone right along with it.

"Don't you?" Trace asked quietly.

"It's never come up."

"Well, I'm sleeping with her sister, so I hear things. I don't know what burr you got up your ass earlier, but Stevi's crazy about you."

Duncan drained his bottle. He rubbed his hand over his face and groaned out loud.

"I was looking for something upstairs in the office. And I found…something she had written to me. About what we were doing not being worth the effort. That she was ready to move on. Thinking of leaving town again."

"Again." Trace frowned. "Wait. Was it dated?"

"What?"

"The note. Was it dated?"

"Hell if I know," Duncan snapped. But he reached back to pull the folded up note from his pocket and passed it to Trace.

Trace winced when he read it. Put it on the bar and met Duncan's eyes.

"I get it. That had to hurt—"

"It pissed me off," Duncan argued. When Trace only stared at him, he finally shrugged and gave him a curt nod. "Yeah. It hurt. I asked her to move in with me. She didn't give me an answer, and then I found that note."

"It's possible it's an old note," Trace suggested.

"What?"

"Well, I know you guys sort of had a bumpy start."

"So, Leah…and therefore you…know everything that went on between us?"

"Pretty sure I don't, because I learned really fast how to not listen when the girls talk to each other."

"She's different."

"Yep." Trace nodded. "She is."

"She was talking about the house in Iowa." Duncan sighed.

"Well, one day when she and I were upstairs talking, she asked me about renting my house in Nashville. Putting in a good word for her with Pearl at Left Fork."

Duncan felt a stab of a pain again. Sharp and cold like lightning, it ripped through him and left him dazed. Guess he had his answer now. Trace hadn't gone up to the office for a quickie with his girlfriend's sister. He had gone up there to arrange Stevi's escape.

"That's great." Duncan shook his head. Not only was she ready to move on from what they had been doing, she was going to up and leave town to get away from him. He had driven Stevi away from the one thing she loved the most.

"So. You find the letter, and rather than talk to her, you start handing out kisses to better your tips? Make her jealous?"

Stevi had won the bartending contest, as Duncan had known she would. She was beautiful. Men and women alike had flocked to her all night, and underneath that hard knot of anger and betrayal, Duncan had felt a streak of pride in her.

"No time to talk. She had already blown me off about moving in with me."

"Kind of a dick move, though, wasn't it? Kissing that girl when Stevi was standing right there?"

Duncan rested his elbows on the bar and covered his face with his hands. He rubbed his eyes and then dropped his hands to the bar.

"Yeah. It was. I was so pissed. So hurt."

"Because you're in love with her."

"Yeah. I guess if being fucking miserable right now because she wants to break it off and feeling even worse for being an asshole to her when before any of this started, we were friends…I guess I am in love with her."

"Why didn't you ever tell her?"

Duncan shrugged. "Never said it before. Never needed to. Never felt it. I guess it kind of snuck up on me."

"You were scared."

Duncan opened his mouth to argue, but he changed his mind when he saw the look of commiseration on Trace's face.

"You know that Dante guy?" Trace finally drained his beer. "That Leah dated?"

"Yep."

"I fucking hated that guy."

"She never got serious with him," Duncan reassured him.

"Yeah. But still. She's up here in Adam's Bay with that guy. I'm in Nashville, in the friend zone. And she's texting me about going to dinner with him. And Stevi telling her she needed to get laid. That's why I showed up when I did. Pearl and Kadie and Angie kicked me out of the Fork."

"You were scared?"

"Hell yes, I was scared she would sleep with that guy. Fall for him. She was adamant that she wasn't interested in that kind of relationship with me. I've never had a problem getting a woman to sleep with me in my life, but the one woman I wanted more than anything? Said no. No thanks. You're damned right I was jealous as hell of any man up here when I was there. And yeah, I wanted to tell her ten times or more when I was here that I was in love with her, but I didn't. And then the night…"

"The dancing." Duncan rolled his eyes.

"See? You know things, too. She said it. That night. Before."

"Stevi hasn't said it."

"So get your head out of your ass and knock it off with the other girl. That's got nowhere to go but down. Grow some balls and go apologize to Stevi."

"It's not gonna fix it." Duncan shook his head. "Yeah, I know. I was a dick, and I owe her an apology. But those two words can't erase the ones I said to her in the kitchen."

"Nope. But the other three might."

Duncan hated to admit it, but he knew Trace was right. Well, not that he had any words in his vocabulary that could make up for what he had said to her earlier. But he did owe her that much, and no matter that it was too damned late, and that she was moving on, he could tell her he loved her. Maybe that he loved her too much to let her go. The Queen was her baby; she and Leah and Margo had put their hearts and souls into the business. He loved it, too. He had put his heart, his soul, his back into all of the work here when they had first pooled their money and dared to dream. But he loved Stevi a hell of a lot more than he loved the bar, and if one of them had to go—and one of them did, because he obviously couldn't deal with her deciding that she was ready to end that part of their relationship—it should be him.

"Give her tonight with Leah and Margo," Trace suggested. "Let her lick her wounds, because it sounds like you did a number, man. Give her some space. Tomorrow give her flowers."

"Trace." Duncan blew out a harsh sigh.

"'Hmm?"

"If she's planning to go to Nashville," Duncan met Trace's eyes, "put her off a bit. Please? Don't talk to Pearl yet."

Trace answered with a solemn nod.

Duncan felt guilt for that deceit layer over the other crappy things in his gut. Trace probably thought Duncan was asking him to stall so he could talk Stevi into staying with him. Duncan knew that was impossible, so he was simply going to talk Stevi into staying.

And then he would leave.

CHAPTER 34

Stevi stayed at Margo's all day Sunday and Monday, too. She had stripped off the stupid clingy red shirt and thrown it on the floor of Margo's bedroom. Dug the cami she wore earlier Saturday at the park with Duncan out of her bag and put it on, scrambled out of the blue jeans that she had looked so forward to Duncan sliding over her hips to find the thong, and climbed into Margo's bed. The tears had been falling since she'd driven away from the Queen, so not quite an hour later when Leah and Margo both crawled into bed with her, she closed her swollen eyes and slept.

She talked to Leah and Margo, both, Sunday. She even talked to Trace. But she refused to talk to Duncan. Or she would have, if he would have come around and tried to talk to her. No sign of him anywhere near Margo's place. No phone calls. Not even a text message.

Not that she wanted to hear from him. If he had more hateful, hurtful things to say besides the awful things he had said to her in the kitchen, she didn't want to hear them.

She went home on Monday, stayed away from the Queen. Leah didn't know it yet, but she had asked Trace again about his house. Not forever. Not yet. Just as a safe place to hide out and think about what had happened, what the hell might have gone wrong, and figure out what she would do with her future. Trace had pressed the key in her hand, curled her fingers around it, and made her promise to tell Leah before she left.

He also suggested that maybe she talk to Duncan. If she had had any energy, she would have laughed in his face. Instead, she reminded Trace of the show Duncan had put on at the bar, and when Trace had the nerve to open his mouth—as if there was an excuse for that kind of behavior—she had simply stared at him, wide-eyed and silent.

For a quick trip to Nashville, she wouldn't need much besides clothes. She threw her hair care products, skin and body care, and her makeup in a bag, too. Not that she gave a damn what she looked like right now. But if Nashville felt good, and she decided it would be a good fit, she supposed looking presentable would be a plus on a job hunt.

Trace told her he would talk to Pearl, but only after she had been down there for a few days and had had time to think through her decision. When he hugged her goodbye Monday morning before he left for the Queen, he spoke quietly so that no one else would hear—no one else being Leah, since it was just the three of them there—and told her maybe Duncan loved her and maybe she owed it to herself to stick around and find out.

Stevi surveyed her room now. She had changed the sheets and made her bed, so Trace and Leah could use it if they needed to when she was gone. They wouldn't. Leah had a comfy bed upstairs, but Stevi's room would be a good spare room for now, and maybe once the baby came, they would want to move their bedroom downstairs. Stevi would already be well out of their way.

When he said that—when Trace said that maybe Duncan loved her—her heart had done this stupid little fluttery thing like hope had given it wings, and then she had tamped that ridiculous runaway feeling down. She'd been living with that hope for months now, the hope that Duncan loved her, that they were something more than fuck buddies. And he had crushed her the other night when he had not only let her know he was bored and ready to move on, but with the horrible, cold way he spoke to her and threw her biggest fears back in her face. Stevi had told Trace that if Duncan loved her, she might be more suited to a Nashville kind of man. Stevi couldn't imagine Trace Dixon saying to Leah the things that Duncan had said to her.

The room was clean. She had left her framed photos of herself and Leah and Margo on the dresser—all but one, anyway. She had to have something along with her for comfort, after all. But this way, it didn't look like she had packed up and moved out. If she decided to stay or if she decided to roam somewhere else, she could always come back and get what she needed. She and Leah had furnished the house together, but again, Stevi wasn't worried about it now.

She had dusted and vacuumed. Pulled the drapes to let the sunshine in. Nothing left to do now but go. As much as she wanted to hit the road, she hesitated. Not because she wasn't ready for a long stretch of highway with nothing to do but think. But because she had to go to the Queen and say goodbye to her sister. Hard enough right there. She had to tell Margo goodbye. She had smooched all over Berkley yesterday, because this plan that she had shaped so long ago had come back to her in the wee hours Sunday morning, with her sister and her cousin sleeping on opposite sides of her.

She would have to say goodbye to the Queen, and that hurt nearly as much as the thought of leaving her family.

And worst of all, she might run into Duncan when she was there. And Stevi was certain her heart couldn't take one more run in with the man she was so in love with who had thrown their relationship, even their friendship, in her face two nights ago.

Resolved just to do it, to get this part over with, she turned her back to her bedroom and wandered through the house one more time. This part, at least, felt right. The house needed to belong to Leah and Trace now. And maybe—if she moved out of town—maybe when she came back, she would get to meet her new niece or nephew.

Guilt tugged at her heart. Leah needed her. She was being selfish, after all, walking away to lick her wounds, when her sister was living her biggest fear with a smile on her face. She forced the guilt down, reminded herself there were all kinds of ways to talk to someone instantly now, and picked up her bags from the kitchen floor. She swung the straps over her shoulder, patted her pockets down to find her phone, and then dug her keys from her purse. She pulled her house key off the ring and set it on the table, her throat and chest so tight, she couldn't breathe.

The weather had turned decidedly chilly in the past two days. Stevi thought it was fitting. She shivered as she pulled the back door open, glad she had put a sweater on with her jeans and her boots. With a deep, shaky breath, she locked the door and pulled it closed behind her.

She stood for a moment on the back stoop. Tears burned and since she was alone, she gave in. Let them fall. She had officially locked herself out of Leah and Trace's house. Nowhere to go now but forward. She sniffled as she jogged down the three cement steps and crossed catty-cornered over the dead brown grass to get to her car quicker. The temperature was in the fifties, but the wind was sharp and cold.

Without looking around—she didn't need to see the patio where she, Leah, Margo, and Duncan used to hang out, back before Trace had become part of their lives, and before she had fallen in love with a friend—she yanked her car door open and tossed both bags inside. She pulled the driver's door open even as she swung the other door closed. Forgetting that it would hurt, she took one last peek at the house and squeezed her eyes closed to ward off the memories and more tears and dropped to the driver's seat. She ducked her head for a second and breathed deeply, in and out, until she was somewhat under control. She had to get a grip, because her sister would probably go lay down in front of her car in the parking lot before she would let her drive off like this.

Stevi set her purse on the passenger seat, pulled her phone from her pocket, and tossed it—without looking at it—to the seat beside her purse. Nothing left to do, she stuck her key in the ignition and started the car. She put it in reverse, but again, she hesitated. She didn't immediately recognize the song playing, but it was slow and soft, and she couldn't possibly listen to any sad songs while she drove. She jabbed the power knob and then breathed in the silence.

Finally, she eased off the brake and looked in her rearview mirror. There was a car behind her. She groaned and dropped her head forward to gently bang it on the steering wheel. Probably someone in the wrong damned driveway, but if she got out to point that out, she would have to go through the whole getting in the car to drive away process again.

She jumped when someone knocked on her window.

"Why today?" she whispered as she lifted her head. But when she turned to look at the person, she froze, stunned to see Duncan standing there. She had already put the car in reverse, so the door was locked. He couldn't pull it open. Preferring to keep this conversation short—preferably *get out of my way*, with maybe a please and thank you—she put the window down not quite half way and stared up at him.

"What?"

"Where are you going?"

She blinked, eyes roaming the hard angles of his face, taking in the dark circles under his eyes. Maybe he at least felt guilty for being such a dick to her and that guilt had kept him up the last two nights. That thought almost brought a smile.

But then she remembered the redhead. Maybe other things had kept him up all night.

Jerk.

She dragged her eyes away from his and wondered if she had accidentally on purpose said that out loud.

"I'm going to the Queen for a second to talk to Leah and Margo." She spoke so softly—her chest and throat were still so tight, she couldn't draw a deep breath—that he had to lean over closer to the window to hear her.

"Can we talk for a minute?"

"No."

"Stevi, please?"

"What do you possibly have to say to me? After Saturday night?"

She dropped back to rest on the seat and stared up at him. Her eyes filled again, but she would rather shove a box knife under her fingernails than cry in front of him again.

"Can we…" He shook his head. Rested his forearm along the top of her open window and leaned down again. "Can we go inside? Please? Just for a minute?"

"Actually, no, we can't."

It was probably wrong to feel a flash of satisfaction. She wouldn't have done this to Leah or Margo, but she had a sudden impetuous desire to hurt him. To make him feel just half as bad as he had made her feel at the Queen.

"Why?" He pinched the bridge of his nose with his other hand and squeezed his eyes closed. She wondered if he was cold standing out there in jeans and a lightweight t-shirt with three-quarter length sleeves. She kind of hoped he was.

"Because I just locked the door."

"So, unlock it."

"I don't have a key anymore, Duncan."

"You don't—?" He backed up a step and propped both hands on top of her car. Hung his head low for a second and then finally, he lifted only his head to look at her with bloodshot eyes. "You're mov—? You're moving out?"

"Yep."

"Where? Where are you going?"

"Please don't do this." She forgot that just a minute ago she would rather practice self-torture than cry in front of him. Tears streaked her face. "Duncan, please. I trusted you. I trusted what we always had, the friendship we've always had, and I believed that whatever we did, whatever we played at… that you wouldn't hurt me…like this."

Her voice was small and an octave higher, and Duncan had nearly plastered himself to her window to hear her.

"Stevi."

"I just…" She covered her mouth when she sobbed. "You broke my heart. And I don't even know why. Please just let me go."

"I can't."

She licked her lips, not surprised at the taste of salt.

"Can I at least get in your car for a minute? Are you really just gonna leave us like this? With that being the last things we said to each other?"

"There's no more us." She sniffled and shook her head. "You broke us."

"Please. Just give me five minutes."

Stevi drew a ragged breath. Her hand shook as she reached to unlock the door, Duncan already halfway around the car when she hit the button. He yanked the door open and fell in, as if he was afraid she would change her mind and drive off.

Stevi stared straight ahead, her elbow propped on her door, her chin propped in her hand.

"I'm sorry."

"Great." She nodded.

"I mean it."

She turned her face slightly to look at him and saw that he was sitting sideways so he could watch her. He had scooped her purse and her phone up and was holding them, and his shoulders were tense, and he sort of looked….miserable.

"Okay." She sighed. "Thanks for the apology."

He waited, but she looked away.

"That's it?" he asked in disbelief.

"You might be sorry, and you might mean it, but it doesn't make me feel better. It's not even the women, Duncan. I don't get that. I don't get how you went from asking me to move in with you to deciding to wave the white flag. Red flag." She shrugged. "Whatever. The things you said to me…' She shook her head. "I'm sorry doesn't make that all go away."

"I know." He scooted around in the seat and set her purse and phone down on the floorboards. "I know. I was awful. And I hate myself for hurting you."

"Yeah, well, we shouldn't have done this. We knew we were playing with fire—"

"I love you."

Her heart pounded and fluttered again, and Stevi squeezed her eyes closed. She pressed her knuckles to her chest and shook her head.

"No, you don't. You don't say that—"

"I was hurt. I lashed out."

"Because I hesitated? When you asked me to move in?"

"No." He rubbed his eyes and then smoothed his hands over his head and turned a desperate look on her.

"Then what? What did I do?" Her whisper was thick with tears.

He pulled a piece of paper from his pocket and handed it to her. Stevi stared at it for a moment and then finally lifted her eyes to his.

"What is this?"

Her eyes dropped to his throat, hungry for signs of his struggle to control himself. His Adam's apple bobbed, and he groaned impatiently. Finally, he reached out and unfolded the paper.

"Found it just after I asked you to move in with me and you said no—"

"I didn't say no."

"You didn't say yes." He shrugged. "I know I asked at a bad time. But it wasn't just a random thought. I've been looking at room dimensions at my house and looking at closet space, and I was trying to decide if we would be better off looking for a new place together. And then I find out you have no intention of committing yourself to me. And I was pissed. And I was wrong to handle it like I did. And I'm sorry."

Her heart hurt. She looked at the paper, and the pain in her heart nearly ripped her in two.

"Duncan," she whispered. "Oh, God."

"I'm sorry. Above all else, I've always loved you as a friend, and I treated you badly, and I have never regretted anything so much in my life."

"I wrote this before we made love. When you laid it out for me how you planned to fuck me for a while and then move on and still be friends…and then when you touched me at the Queen and changed your mind and sent me home. I guess I forgot about it."

Duncan dropped his head back to rest on the seat and closed his eyes.

"Fuck."

"If you had just asked me…" She shook her head.

"Stevi, babe, please. Don't leave."

"You know why I hesitated, Duncan?" She turned to face him again.

"Why?"

"Because I needed to hear you say you love me. I needed that before I was ready to live with you. Because I've loved you for so long, and I feel like I've been doing that all alone. And I need you to love me back."

"I do love you back," he promised. "So much."

"Then why would you say those things to me?"

"Because I was pissed. And I was hurt."

"You used my insecurities against me."

"I know." His eyes glassy, he nodded and then wet his lips. "I know. I wish I could take it back, because I didn't mean any of it. I said it just because I knew it would hurt you."

"What a mess." She covered her face with her hands and rubbed her eyes.

"People fight. This is a fight. It was big and nasty and horrible, but it's a fight."

"Not helping." She shook her head.

"I should have told you a long time ago how I felt about you."

"When did you know?" She cleared her throat.

"What?"

"When did you know you loved me?"

"Before I kissed you. I didn't recognize the feeling, but I was desperate to get close to you. Closer than what we had. When you went out with Grant, and I was ready to rip apart the wine shelving in the cellar, I knew I loved you. I didn't know how to say it."

"Do you now?"

He nodded when she looked at him.

"You made it so clear what you wanted from me. From what we were doing. I was afraid to say it."

"Are you now?"

Stevi considered what he was asking. Was she afraid to say she loved him? To admit to him how she felt?

"No."

"C'mere." He held his hand out to her. Stevi put her hand in his, but she didn't move. He closed his fingers around hers and squeezed. He tugged gently until she climbed from her seat to straddle his lap.

"You broke my heart," she reminded him as she rested her forehead against his.

Duncan cupped her face in his hands and smoothed her tears away with his thumbs.

"I love you, Stevi."

She laughed and sobbed and pressed a kiss to his eyebrow.

"I love you, too."

"You're technically homeless."

"I can just get my key back."

"Move in with me," he whispered as he slid his hands down over her back. "I can't sleep without you in my bed."

She leaned back to look him in the eye and nodded. "Me, too."

** THE END **

Thank you for reading Forever, Duncan. Please consider leaving a review on your favorite bookish site.

Keep reading for Chapter 1 of Always, Jess.

ALWAYS, JESS

Chapter 1

He cut his hair.

Margo lowered her gaze to the pint glass in her hand and watched the amber liquid fill it, careful to limit the foam at the top. She hadn't given anyone good head in a damned long time, but a Mississippi Queen customer wasn't a good place to get back in the game. She snorted and rolled her eyes and then realized Jess Covey had just walked into the bar.

Hadn't he? God, was she hallucinating now?

Scared to look up—what if she was imagining things? Was she so desperate for Jess to come back that she was dreaming him up and seeing his face on every guy in the bar now?—she pushed the tap back and set the pint glass on the bar to nudge it toward Leah's friend, Dante.

"Thanks." Dante's voice drifted to her over the bar. Rather than look around, rather than scope out the guy who had walked in wearing the black leather jacket and Jess' face

Margo offered Dante a smile. Glass at his lips, Dante's brown eyes warmed, and he arched his eyebrows in response. His olive-colored skin was smooth, and his thick dark hair was slicked back neatly. He wore a beige dress shirt, open at the collar, with a brown sport coat over it.

She wondered if Leah had ever slept with him.

Probably not. Dante had asked Leah out not long before their friend Kenzi had a stroke. Leah happened to be with her and her husband, Joe, at the time, and the experience had been traumatic for her. Maybe she had been attracted to Dante, but the timing hadn't worked out, and then along came Nashville.

Margo realized she was still staring at Dante. Afraid that she might have given him the wrong impression—he was much too pretty for her taste—she blinked and laughed and prayed that he didn't notice the heat rush her face. She wasn't interested in sleeping with him, but he was easy on the eyes.

Suddenly aware of someone standing a few feet down the bar, she stepped back and looked away from Dante.

When Jess left last year, he'd worn his black hair long. When he made love to her, it would fall around her face, like a curtain affording them privacy. She wondered now if he had left it loose with the other women. How many of them had run their fingers through the long, dark silk while he pumped his hips over theirs?

He wore it short now, cut in a quiff style. Margo might have decided again that she was projecting, thinking too much about Jess and seeing him in men she thought attractive, but Jess turned then to look at her. His golden-brown eyes flipped a switch inside her, and suddenly, her belly and her lungs and her heart seized and flared with electricity.

"Hey."

The irony of standing behind a fully stocked bar where she could have any drink at her fingertips while her mouth was suddenly dry wasn't lost on her. She tried to swallow and worked to calm her racing heart, to breathe around the clenched fist that held her stomach in a tight grip. A shock of thick black hair fell over his forehead and dipped over his left eyebrow, almost giving him the same rakish appeal the longer hair had.

Back when they were lovers.

She wasn't ready for this.

He had been gone for over a year, and though they spoke on the phone sometimes, she wasn't prepared for *this*. He wasn't supposed to just show up like this and catch her off-guard. She might have spent the last year lying to herself that she was over him, immune to his charm, but still, a heads–up would have been nice.

"What're you doing here?"

She wanted to sound tough, at least, if not mean. Unfortunately, the words came out on a rugged, breathless whisper. Margo was glad for the ornate wooden bar she stood behind, because it hid her legs, which trembled a bit now under his stare.

"Hey."

Trace Dixon—her cousin Leah's unofficial fiancé—appeared at the end of the bar. God, where was her army? Where were Leah and Stevi? She needed them now; just their silent support would go a long way toward getting her through the next few minutes.

Jess narrowed his eyes as Trace sidled up next to her and dropped his arm around her shoulders. Margo leaned into him and snuck a deep breath, comforted by his familiar scent.

"You okay?" Trace tightened his fingers around her upper arm in a gentle squeeze.

"Mmm."

"Duncan and Stevi are digging out Halloween decorations," he told her. Jess was still watching them, his eyebrows slanted in a harsh frown. Stomach still churning under that intense stare, Margo had to snort at Trace's words. Duncan hated the Halloween tree. Stevi loved it. They had been bickering about it for over a week now. Apparently, Stevi had won the battle. Margo wondered what she had surrendered to get her way.

Not wanting to go too far down that rabbit hole, she straightened and patted Trace's chest. Jess wasn't going to go away, no matter how badly she wished he would. She wanted him to leave, right? Didn't that uneasy feeling in the pit of her stomach mean she wanted him to leave? Or did she want him to stay? To talk to her?

The phone calls had been about Berkley, mostly. Jess called now and then to update her on his sobriety. To promise her he had a steady job. To ask her about their daughter.

But maybe showing up here unannounced was something else. Was he jealous? Of Trace? Could the scowl on his face be anything other than jealousy?

"Trace." She cleared her throat and lifted her hand to tuck her hair behind her ear. In case either of them was looking closely, Margo tucked that same hand into her hip pocket so they wouldn't notice the slight tremble. "This is Jess Covey."

It hurt to say his name, to toss it out there casually in an introduction. Because she had to add those other things. Other words. My *ex*. *Berkley's father*. She didn't have to say them for Trace's benefit. But maybe for Jess. Maybe for herself. Maybe she needed to be reminded of the way Jess had hurt her. "Jess is Berkley's father," she mumbled, and Trace moved again to offer support. His hand stroked her back, much the same as Leah's would if she were standing here right now.

"Jess." Trace was contained, his face impassive.

Not Duncan. If Duncan were standing here right now his hand might be fisted and swinging for Jess' face.

"Good to meet you." Trace offered his hand to Jess now, and Margo noticed that he said *good* to meet you and not *nice* to meet you. Because maybe it was good that he now knew what face to protect Margo from.

"And you are?" Jess tipped his head a bit, the dark look softened just a bit by the hint of a smile.

"Trace Dixon."

Margo knew Jess wouldn't recognize Trace's name. He wouldn't know Tanner Dixon, either—Trace's younger, country-music-star brother. Jess' musical taste leaned toward classic rock with a bit of metal. He wouldn't know country from polka.

"We agreed that it would be weekly."

Duncan's voice carried from the back of the bar and wound through Margo's shoulders and neck. She loved her stepbrother to the moon and back, and she loved his protective side, but the last damned thing they needed was a brawl here in their bar. It was early yet, but Dante wasn't the only patron here, and a standoff between Jess and Duncan would be enthralling entertainment.

"You have five freebies," Stevi reminded him. "I don't care how or when you use them. But the number doesn't change."

Margo pressed her lips together as she considered what sort of freebies they were talking about. Also something that didn't need to be done in front of their patrons, a conversation about sexual favors in any form.

"You'll have to handcuff me, Stevi," Duncan told her. Margo glanced at Trace, amused by the smirk on his face, and then looked past him toward the back of the bar. Duncan led with his back; he and Stevi carried the boxed Halloween tree between them. "I can't keep my hands off you."

"Duncan and Stevi?" Jess' eyes popped open and made Margo think of a cartoon character. She trilled an honest laugh and then covered her mouth with her hand when Duncan shot her a look over his shoulder. She breathed easier when he looked back at Stevi, not noticing or not recognizing Jess at first. Jess glanced at her and arched his eyebrows in question. She gave him a quick nod and a shrug and realized there was someone standing by him. The woman stood to his right, her head bent over a smart phone.

Without bothering to explain to Jess who Trace Dixon was, Margo slipped in front of him and braced her hands on the bar.

"Can I get you something?"

A cute ponytail flipped as the woman lifted her head to look at Margo. Big green eyes, thick long lashes, and creamy skin dotted with a smattering of freckles, the girl—not a woman; she looked younger than Stevi—tipped her lips up in a sweet smile.

"Oh. Can I—"

"She's with me," Jess said distractedly. He glanced at the girl with a warm smile and then looked back at Margo. "Since when?"

Margo felt a wave of nausea sweep her from her head to the soles of her black boots. This kid was with Jess? She was cute; not a lick of makeup on, but Margo thought she was adorable. Glowing with natural beauty or health. Or sexual satisfaction. Margo knew Jess Covey knew how to please a woman. She supposed he had the same finesse for girls.

She felt a stab of guilt for the rush of hate she felt for the girl on the opposite side of the bar. She didn't hate easily, but she had found that where Jess was concerned, it had become doable.

Jess moved his mouth again, but Margo didn't hear him. She wasn't listening. How could she listen? Two minutes ago, she had considered the possibility that Jess had gambled and shown up here to sweep her off her feet. That maybe he hadn't been calling just about Berkley but that he had wanted to be part of her life again.

The joke was clearly on her. Jess didn't need her if he had that sweet little body warming his bed now.

"What're you doing here?"

Margo processed the words. Duncan's voice. The sound of the box hitting the floor as if it was dropped from knee-high.

A hand smoothed over her back, but this time, that same hand curled possessively around the curve of her waist. She smelled Stevi's perfume as her cousin pressed into her side.

"Hey." Stevi squeezed her waist. "You okay?"

"Yeah." Margo stirred. "Yeah. I'm fine." She wasn't fine, but she sure as hell wouldn't let on to Jess that something was wrong. That once again, he'd yanked her heart out. After all, this one was on her. He had no idea she had this ridiculous fantasy that he would come back for both her and Berkley.

She turned to look at Stevi, careful not to meet her eyes, and let her gaze skate over to Trace.

"You and Duncan?" Jess asked with a laugh.

"Yep," Stevi answered without hesitation. "This guy is the love of my life."

Margo hoped her words were enough to calm the angry beast. As tempting as it was to sic her stepbrother on Jess, it really wasn't the time or place.

Or Jess' fault.

"How are you, Stevi?" Jess' voice dropped to that low, sexy tone that used to drive Margo crazy in bed.

"She's good." Duncan suddenly appeared at Margo's other shoulder. "Why are you here?"

"Duncan," Stevi chided him softly. "Maybe he's here to see Berkley."

"She's not here," Margo mumbled. She brought Berkley to the Queen with her now and then before their business hours, but most of the time, her mom watched her.

Margo appreciated the show of support—the very same one she had wished for a few minutes ago—but now, she felt smothered. She stepped away from Stevi and cut a glance at Duncan. He stood like a brick wall, legs spread wide and his hands braced on the bar now. Hulking and aggressive, like he was considering climbing over the bar and knocking Jess' face in.

She wanted to tell him to stand down, but then again, that would only draw attention to her and Jess and what was already a tense, awkward situation. Instead, she looked back at Jess, surprised to find him ignoring Duncan, eyes on her.

"Do you want something? Water? Soda?"

Was he still sober? Should she offer him a beer? Would she give him one if he asked for it?

"I'm fine." Jess shook his head slightly, but he glanced at the girl at his side and arched his eyebrows in askance. Margo couldn't hide the surprise when the girl asked for a beer Seemed kind of rude if she was sleeping with Jess to order alcohol when he was a recovering alcoholic.

Rather than comment, Margo simply nodded and leaned into the cooler to grab a longneck for her.

Jess started to speak, but Margo held her hand up to stop him.

"Excuse me? For a second?"

He nodded. She stared at him a moment longer. Catalogued his intense golden eyes. The thick, dark eyebrows she used to brush her lips over. The dark stubble on his cheeks and his chin. His soft, generous lips that used to glide over her skin.

She turned and slipped away in one move, aware as she hurried on impossibly steady legs to the ladies' room that she was leaving Jess to Duncan and his anger. She knew from the click of the heels behind her that Stevi was following her. Needing to be alone, she pushed the door open and let it close. But Stevi caught it and stepped into the room behind her.

Margo stood with her back to her, but she heard the door click closed. Heard Stevi flip the lock.

"I'm…" Margo stopped talking and tried to draw a deep breath and push the emotion back down her throat. "I'm so stupid."

"Margs."

"So fucking stupid, Stevi," she whispered.

"Margo, no." Stevi's fingers gripped her arm just above the elbow and turned her around. Margo ducked her head, embarrassed by the tears that welled in her eyes. "No, you aren't."

Stevi still held her elbow. She reached with her other hand to tip Margo's chin up, but Margo tossed her head the other way to escape her. There was a harsh knock on the door, quickly followed by Leah's voice.

"Let me in, guys."

Margo didn't want an audience. She didn't want to cry in front of Stevi or Leah. She didn't want to talk about how naïve she was. She couldn't admit that she had secretly hoped that Jess would eventually come back for her.

But she didn't want to be alone, either.

Stevi loosened her hold on her—wasn't like Margo could escape—and reached back to unlock the door. Margo watched the gold doorknob turn, and then the door cracked open, and Leah slipped inside. She pushed the door closed and leaned back on it, reaching back to twist the lock.

If either of them was going to lecture her about wasting time and letting an ass like Jess hurt her—again—it would be Leah. Margo drew herself up to full height and drew in a deep breath, ready for Leah to rip into her. And let it roll off her shoulders. Because she couldn't help the way she felt about him, could she? God, she'd kicked him out over a year ago, and her heart was still in love with him.

"You okay?" Leah asked softly.

Her kindness was Margo's undoing. She covered her face with her hands and sobbed quietly.

"Hey. Hey." Stevi moved in close again. "Not here. Don't do this here."

"I can't help it." Margo sniffled and dabbed at her eyes. "Who the hell is she? She looks like she's fifteen."

"Sweetie, you have to go back out there." Stevi's voice was gentle but firm. "You have to go back out there and face him."

"Give her a minute, Stevi." Leah pushed off the door and reached out to touch Margo's arm.

"I thought…"

"I know." Leah nodded. Margo swiped at her nose and swallowed hard.

"I can't believe he brought her here."

"You need to get back out there with Duncan." Leah cut her eyes to Stevi. "He looked ready to whale on Jess."

"Trace is out there." Stevi shook her head.

"Trace is tending bar, because Duncan is standing there staring Jess down like a junkyard dog."

Margo groaned out loud and wished she were at home. It was early, and even if her cousins suggested she go on home, she wouldn't. No way in hell would she let Jess or his new woman think they had run her out of her own territory. She blew her nose on a paper towel and then checked her eyes in the mirror over the sink.

"I look like shit," she decided. "But then, whatever I was before wasn't enough—"

"Stop it!" Stevi grabbed her by the wrist this time and swung her around to face them again. "This is on Jess."

"Nope." Margo shook her head. "Not this time. That other stuff was on Jess. This is me." She swallowed hard and shrugged. "I never could learn a lesson."

**

If you would like to read the rest of Margo & Jess' story, click here:

Always, Jess

ALSO BY TRACY BROEMMER

Women's Fiction Novels:
Luther's Cross 10th Anniversary Edition
Just Like Them
Small Hours
Picket Fences
Two Story Home
Say Everything
Sketching Litchfield Lake
Damsel
The Valentine Suite
Fairytale (Writing as Therese Kinkaide)
Green-Eyed Girl
Come Home For Christmas
Ever, Again
Safe as Houses

Every Little Thing, Lorelei Bluffs, Book 1
Two A.M., Lorelei Bluffs, Book 2
Blind, Lorelei Bluffs, Book 3
Leaving July, Lorelei Bluffs, Book 4
Hesitation Marks, Lorelei Bluffs, Book 5
Four Letter Words, Lorelei Bluffs, Book 6
See Kate, Lorelei Bluffs, Book 7
Loved You More, Lorelei Bluffs, Book 8
A Lorelei Ending, Lorelei Bluffs, Book 9

I Do, Lorelei Bluffs, Book 10

Truth Is, The Williams Legacy, Book 1

Other People's Ugly, The Williams Legacy, Book 2

Omissions, The Williams Legacy, Book 3

Contemporary Romance Novels:

Destiny's Calling: Your Future Is Waiting

Wedding Day Shenanigans

Holiday Fling

The Kiss Off

Something Like Love

Plus One

Hold Onto the Stars, Book #5 in Blue Collar Romance series

The Jane Thing, Book #2 in Meet Cute Book Club series

Shameless Santa, Book #7 in Welcome to Kissing Springs series

Sunshine & Soulmates, Welcome to Kissing Springs, Sunshine Season

Bourbon & Bedposts, Book #7 in Welcome to Kissing Springs, Bourbon Season

Doctor Divine, Doctors of Eastport General, Season 2

Beach Daze, Flamingo Island

Moonlight in Montreal, The Vagabond Series

Christmas and Other Inconveniences, Betting on Christmas Collection

Eggnog in Amesbury, Christmas in Amesbury Series (Sweet Romance)

A December Wish, Wishing for Love Series (Sweet Romance)

A Naughty Lesson

The Santorini Sack, The Vagabond Series

Love, Nashville, The Mississippi Queen Trilogy, Book 1
Forever, Duncan, The Mississippi Queen Trilogy, Book 2
Always, Jess. The Mississippi Queen Trilogy, Book 3

Gettin' Hitched, The H Books, Book 1
Hookin' Up, The H Books, Book 2
Holdin' On, The H Books, Book 2.5

Intoxicate Me, 515 Whiskey, Book .5
Taste Me, 515 Whiskey, Book 1
Scrooge Me, 515 Whiskey, Bonus Short Story in Let's Get Naughty
V 3

Contemporary Romance Novellas:
Indian Summer
Dear Jaclyn Perris
French Stuff
Holdin' On (The H Books)
End in Flames
Mistletoe Mishaps
Toasted: A New Year's Eve Novella
Endless Summer (Timberton Hounds)
Homeless Holiday (Timberton Hounds)
Restless Hearts (Timberton Hounds)
Timberton Hounds Novellas Boxset
Boone's Girl

Intoxicate Me (515 Whiskey)

Seducing You (Welcome to Kissing Springs and Lockland Distilling: Keys to Love)

Kissing You (Welcome to Kissing Springs and Lockland Distilling: Keys to Love)

Swipe for Fangs

Swipe for Ghouls

Feels on Wheels (Love in Motion Duet, Book 1) (Sweet Romance)

Rings on Wings (Love in Motion Duet, Book 2) (Sweet Romance)

Love in Motion Boxset

Other Novellas:

The Devy Man, A Horror Novella

Today, Again (Sweet Love Story)

Women's Fiction Short Stories:

India Falls

Luther's Cross: 87,600

The Candy Cane Tree of Willow Lane

Delays

Same Time Next Year

Contemporary Romance Short Stories:

Perfect Pictures, The Wine Tasting Series, Traminette (Sweet)

Coming Home, The Wine Tasting Series, Edelweiss (Sweet)

Save Me Every Dance, The Wine Tasting Series, Rosé (Sweet)

Marry Me, The Wine Tasting Series, Shiraz (Sweet)

Birthday Wishes, The Wine Tasting Series, Muscat (Sweet)

Dad Jeans, The Wine Tasting Series, Vignoles (Sweet)

The Wine Tasting Series Boxset (Sweet)

Peppermint Lane

Priceless Memory (Timberton Hounds)

Truly Dante, A Mississippi Queen Trilogy Short Story

Strawberry Wine

Love Letter

Leaving You, A Lockland Distilling: Keys to Love Short Story

Sambuca Santa

Deadman's Hollow

ABOUT THE AUTHOR

Tracy Broemmer is the author of several contemporary romance novels including the 515 Whiskey Series, the Welcome to Kissing Springs: Bourbon Fever Collection, and the Mississippi Queen Trilogy. Tracy also writes women's fiction and is the author of the Williams Legacy series as well as several stand-alone titles.

Tracy's books have been called gripping, emotional, and timely, and readers describe her characters as real and relatable.

Tracy lives in Midwestern Illinois with her husband of 31 years. Visit her on the web and sign up for her newsletter at www.broemmerbooks.com